# THE PUPPETMASTERS

K.D. LAMB

Author Disclaimer
This is a work of fiction. The characters, names, and events in this novel are the product of the author's imagination.

Published by
Applet Island Publishing
P.O. Box 50585
Bellevue, Washington 98015-0585
appletisland@hotmail.com

Edited by Lynette Smith

Interior and Cover Design by Monkey C Media
Cover Image Credits: U.S. Army, Vetman, ISAF Headquarters Public Affairs Office, Cncplayer, W. Rebel

Printed in the United States

ISBN: 978-0-9850167-6-0

Library of Congress Control Number: 2013915019

www.kristilamb.com

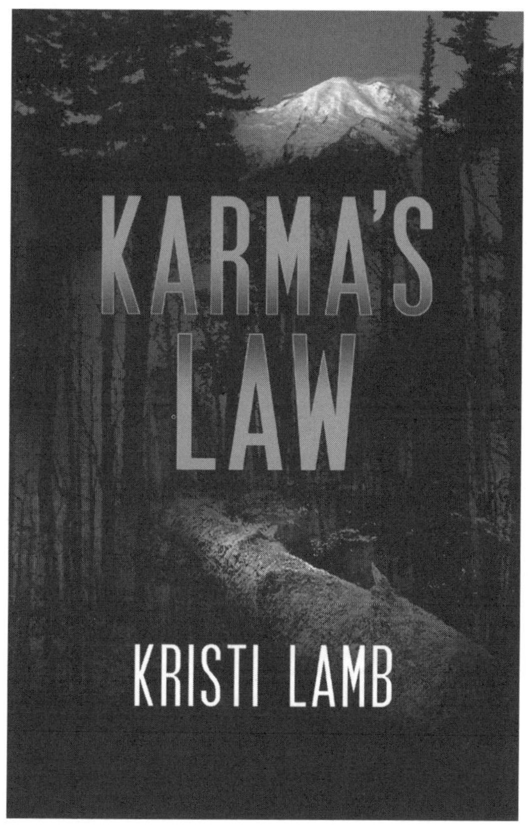


## ALSO BY K.D. LAMB

**KARMA'S LAW – A Tangled Tale of Murder, Malice, and Revenge**

Charming Tate Sawyer, a serial Casanova, is found murdered off a popular hiking trail. As the investigation unfolds, Lieutenant Greg Kennedy and his team discover that Sawyer left behind an embittered string of wealthy women, each harboring her own motive for ending his life.

Family secrets and sibling rivalry further complicate this dark mystery.

Who was this man? Is he destined to a bitter, deceitful legacy, or is there more than meets the eye? *Karma's Law* is a tale so tangled it resembles the twisted cypress of its Pacific Northwest and Alaskan settings.

ACKNOWLEDGMENTS

I WOULD LIKE TO THANK my friends Pauline, Cindy, Joe, Rick, my sisters Sandra and Susan, and daughter Erika. I really appreciate their candor and well-meaning critique. It's made me a better writer and helped me grow in my new passion. The confidence they expressed in my abilities pushed me along to do my best and keep moving forward.

I would also like to thank Jeniffer and team at Monkey C Media for their amazing expertise and creative input. You guys are the best!

Finally, to my editor, Lynette at All My Best Business. Thank you for the painstaking review work. Your wonderful sense of humor helped more than once during that frustrating part of the publication.

When cunning hares have all been hunted,
fleeing hounds will be cooked as food.

Chinese proverb
—Fan Li

# CHARACTERS

**Abdul Bashar Alam**
Pilot

**Ahmad Akeem**
Second son of Mujtaba Shazeb

**Alex**
NSA

**Anthony Zanders**
Special-agent-in-charge, FBI

**Benjamin Zimmerman**
Director Mossad

**Caitlin McDougall**
Mickey's sister

**Candace Lawrence**
CIA

**Daniel Blumfeld**
Site and IT manager at Orion Premier datacenter

**Eric "Mickey" McDougall**
Orion Premier head of security

**Faisal Omar**
General, Afghanistan military

**Frank Reynolds**
NSA

**Glenn Carson**
Orion Premier CFO; childhood friend of Paul Fields

**Gwen Albertson**
Orion Premier senior vice president, legal department; friend of Kendall's

**Heather Jacobs**
Kendall's neighbor

**Imran**
Security officer at the Afghanistan government offices

**Jangi Khan**
Bamiyan farmer and guide

**Jeremy Levy**
Kendall's boyfriend

**Kendall Radcliffe**
Director of operations at Orion Premier

**Lutfi Jabar**
Afghanistan captain

**Maysah Siddra**
Female Afghanistan doctor

**Mushtaba Shazeb**
President, Afghanistan

**Paul Fields**
Orion Premier CEO; childhood friend of Glenn Carson

**Ping**
NSA

**Poya**
Stable boy

**Qadi**
Afghanistan Captain

**Quinn Pendleton**
U.S. secretary of defense

**Rashid Sharif**
Childhood friend of Ahmad and Saaqib

**Saaqib Waqas**
First son of Mujtaba Shazeb

**Shane Menard**
Mossad

**Taheem**
Palace head chef

**Tzuk Reichenfeld**
Israeli commander

**Waleed**
Palace head of security

**Yuhannis**
Kabul butcher

# CHAPTER ONE

Kendall Radcliffe hummed to herself as she showered and got ready for her date with her boyfriend of over two years, Jeremy Levy. She was a little surprised that he had taken such pains to schedule a dinner date mid-week, given their hectic schedules. Her stomach was queasy, and she was doing her best to push those feelings aside. What really didn't make sense was that Jeremy, who wasn't particularly known for his spontaneity, reserved a table at her favorite restaurant, Canlis, on lower Queen Anne just north of Seattle.

There was no specific occasion for celebration, and her birthday was over a month away. None of it made sense, but Kendall, ever the optimist, decided that something special was going to happen. So she set her mind to viewing the evening as some sort of a surprise celebration. She began to glow at the thought that he was going to formally propose ... turning the event into a joyful, auspicious occasion.

After all, Jeremy had been making comments lately about needing to put down roots and getting serious about his responsibilities. He even transferred his membership in the exclusive Columbia Tower Club to his law firm, saying he had other priorities.

She chose her dress carefully, deciding on a *Nicole Miller* emerald green strapless twist bodice dress. She knew the color would set off the green of her eyes, the low-scooped neckline draw attention to her full breasts, and the above-the-knee hem length highlight what she regarded as her best feature ... her incredibly long, slim legs. Since it was late spring, and the weather was still quite cool, she would wear the *chic* three-tier, fox-fur stole that Jeremy had given her for Christmas.

Even though he was Jewish, he had no problem celebrating Christmas with her. In fact, he enjoyed his law firm's Christmas party and the family gatherings at her mother's on Christmas Eve. His large extended family was in Palm Beach, Florida.

She was pleased that he was so caught up in the Christmas festivities last year, and decided that converting him was going to be a lot easier than she thought. Besides, as long as she had known him, he had never attended a prayer service, observed the Jewish holy days of Rosh Hashanah, Yom Kippur, and Passover, or even seemed interested in defending his religion when the subject came up. He always dismissed it with ambivalence and mocked his family's strict adherence to traditional Jewish laws and customs. In fact, it was Kendall herself who bought a *mezuzah* for his front doorpost. Personally, she viewed it as mystical-like. But if it brought him spiritual luck and protection, then she was all for it. Plus it looked cool on the front door frame, and she got a thrill every time she saw it.

As she swept up her chestnut-colored, shoulder-length hair into an elegant French twist and applied her makeup, she again got that uneasy feeling in the pit of her stomach. *What is wrong with me?* She tried to convince herself that it wasn't so much of an anxious feeling as it was the anticipation of a romantic evening capped off with perhaps a marriage proposal and the presentation of a stunning ring.

Her intuition had always been frighteningly accurate, and she knew that something was definitely up for the evening. She just couldn't imagine how right she was about an evening to remember, yet so off on how the events would actually play out.

# CHAPTER TWO

THE GREEK RESTAURANT, CANLIS, WAS known for its great stone fireplace, angled windows, and copper charcoal broiler in the center of the dining room. Kendall and Jeremy dined there several times a year. As she was escorted into the dining room, she spotted Jeremy first. He was lost in thought, gazing intently out the window. He was just finishing a bourbon whiskey as the waiter placed a second round on the table. *Wow, he started without me. He's obviously been here awhile.* Now, Kendall was even more intrigued. *He must be nervous too.*

Jeremy's fixed stare was broken when the waiter set his drink before him. Over the waiter's shoulder, he caught a glimpse of Kendall making her way to their table. She looked even more stunning than usual and walked with purpose and confidence. He didn't meet her eyes as she reached the table, and he made no remark about her appearance. Instead, he got up, gave her shoulders a squeeze, and kissed the side of her mouth, while the hostess patiently waited to assist Kendall into her chair.

*Oh, that's Jeremy,* she thought, *not wanting to make a public display of affection before this kind of upscale, staid crowd.* He was from the East Coast, after all.

Kendall's stomach leapt at the thought that she could be engaged by the end of the evening. When Jeremy leaned in to kiss her, she could tell he'd had at least two drinks. He swayed ever so slightly. In fact, if she didn't know any better, he was acting extremely nervous.

Jeremy was never fearful. He was a person always in control and master of his senses. Nothing could upset him. Even when he had reason to be anxious, he was able to present a calm, commanding demeanor.

She didn't know quite where to begin. Her eyebrows rose, and she deliberately said in a teasing voice, "No fair! You started without me!"

Jeremy's smile was forced as he responded somewhat defensively, "Oh, I had an errand to run and finished early. So I thought I would relax a spell."

Kendall smiled to herself as she pictured Jeremy shopping for a ring. But she felt nervous and fidgety. *Stop it! Relax! Take a deep breath!*

She decided she was way too anxious to drink; she wanted to keep her wits about her. She declined the offering from the waiter and listened to the nightly specials. The waiter left them to discuss their choices, and Kendall realized she hadn't heard a word he'd said. She sighed and opened the menu.

She glanced up to find Jeremy staring at her. *Oh, he's nervous. No, he looks uncertain, as if he doesn't know where to start. Well, I can't stand it. I'm going to help him.*

She grabbed his hand, saying, "Jeremy, what is it? You look like you have some news! I don't know whether to start celebrating or crying."

His eyebrows lifted, and he seemed to hold his breath. Kendall suddenly felt sick to her stomach. She quickly knew she didn't want to hear what was coming.

He patted her hand, gave her a huge grin, nodded his head in affirmation, and said, "As a matter of fact, I have some pretty serious news. I think you'll be excited for me."

That was an odd statement. It sounded so one-sided and final, like the news related only to him. The smile on her face slowly faded. She grabbed the side of the table and steadied herself. Again, with the artificial perky voice, "Well, what is it? Did you get a new client, or maybe a big case?"

"Sort of."

He sat back in his chair and took a large swallow from his glass.

"My mother has decided that I need to relocate to Florida to run the family business."

There, it was out. Now he only needed to explain the rest of it.

The family owned a chain of savings and loan associations throughout Florida. While it had not been forced to receive any federal bailout money to keep afloat after the 2008 financial crisis, the profits were way down. The banks clearly needed careful management.

Jeremy was not only a respected business attorney, but he had a Master's in Economics from Harvard and was generally considered an expert in financial management. He was, in fact, the perfect person—and the only one, in his mother's eyes—to turn around the financial outlook of the banks. Given the current economic climate, the banks could limp along for a few more years, but there would be no growth. As his mother saw it, if Jeremy took over as president and director, he would be able to show solid growth and a tidy profit within a year.

Kendall gave a dismissive wave of her hand. "Is that all? You told them no, of course. You love your life in Seattle."

Jeremy put up both of his hands to stop the nervous babble and shook his head.

"No, Kendall, I am moving to Florida. It's been decided."

She was stunned into silence at the finality of his tone and couldn't believe what she was hearing. She couldn't begin to process the information, because he seemed so unconcerned with the implication on her life. She wasn't in any position to move to Florida.

She had worked her way up the corporate ladder at Orion Premier Net Services for the past ten years and had recently been promoted to director of operations. She was serving as the primary liaison between divisions and was often asked to be a corporate witness for various high-level lawsuits and governmental inquiries. No, there was no way she would up give all of that up. Something didn't make sense.

It suddenly occurred to her that she hadn't actually received any vibes that she was even part of his relocation plans. She contemplated that thought when the waiter came back to take their dinner order. By now, Kendall had completely lost her appetite and simply ordered the soup special. She was again taken aback when Jeremy ordered an appetizer and the seafood special. He looked as if he had a new lease on life. It dawned on her that he was relieved.

She tried to keep the accusatory, hurt tone out of her voice as she inquired in measured tones, "And where do I fit in this plan?"

He had the decency to squirm a bit in his chair and look away.

"Kendall, I'm moving to Palm Beach, Florida, by myself. It's time I got on with my life and put down roots. You know that I love you, but we just don't have a future together."

*Yeah, yeah, the Jewish roots thing again! I refuse to buy it.*

"How can you just make this kind of decision? How can you give up on us just like that?"

She was nearly in tears, but was not about to let him see her distress. She grabbed on to her anger when he responded with, "In truth, there's more to it than you can possibly understand. There's the cultural differences and financial consideration."

"I have no idea what you are talking about! What cultural differences and what financial consideration? We've always gotten along so well. I thought we had a future together!" *Careful, there, girl! You don't want to sound pathetic.*

Jeremy meticulously brushed a speck of lint from the sleeve of his tailored suit.

"I have an image and reputation to uphold in the Jewish community. There are certain expectations of one in my position. I thought you knew that."

She shook her head as if to shake the nightmare free. "No, we never had any discussions about there being no future for us. In fact, you brought up the subject of our living together a few weeks ago. Something changed. What was it?"

She angrily brushed some errant strands of hair out of her eyes.

"You know how close I am to my mother. I respect her business acumen and the decisions she makes."

*Oh, here we go!* Kendall steeled herself for more of the onslaught.

"Go on."

"My mother sacrificed a lot for me. She carefully planned my future and sent me to the best boarding school in Switzerland."

Obviously, there was more. "And?"

"She tolerated my moving to Seattle, so that I could learn about other businesses and cultures, work my way up the partnership ladder, and hone my financial expertise. But she always expected me to someday repay her by moving back to Florida to run the family business."

How *nebbish* of him, she uncharitably allowed herself to think. Kendall was puzzled. She was missing something. "I still don't get it. Why now?"

"We've been having this discussion for some time now. Frankly, this morning, my mother sweetened the deal."

*I knew there was a carrot in there somewhere.* "What did she do?"

"She released my trust fund in its entirety."

Jeremy's tone was way too formal. He sounded like he was negotiating a deal rather than delicately and sensitively letting her down easy. But his love for money and all the power that it brought had unfortunately colored his feelings. He had simply discarded the emotional and embraced the practical and logical. The result was an insensitive, hurried explanation.

He realized he had just screwed up the whole revelation. He told himself that it wasn't like he was practiced at this type of speech, so it was probably better that she heard it in plain-speak, anyway.

Kendall was not about to ask for the details of his trust fund. That was none of her business. She certainly had nothing to offer him that would sway his apparent resolve to alter his life in such a drastic way.

She raised her chin and asked when he planned to pick up and move. He responded that he had already informed his partners and had begun transitioning his clients.

"I will be in Seattle for another three weeks. There's no reason why we can't still see each other until my last day. I have no hard feelings, and I certainly hope you would want the best for me. I want the best for you."

*Manipulative, self-centered, insensitive bastard!* With tears in her eyes, she rose from the table. "Actually, Jeremy, it would be best if we just ended it now. Since there is no future for us, there is no reason to prolong this. I'm disappointed that you let your mother—and her money—choose your life and affect your happiness. That you could push me out of your life just like that says a lot about your ability and capacity for love and commitment ... and more importantly, your honor and integrity. You've lost my respect."

She paused and then concluded with, "I wish you the best."

With all the dignity she could muster and with eyes swimming in tears, Kendall turned toward the exit. Her hip bumped the table as she stumbled away. She missed the last scene, as Jeremy's water goblet, from which he had just nervously taken a sip, teetered furiously and then fell over, spilling its contents in his lap. The commotion turned more than few heads towards Jeremy's table. He smiled grimly, figuring he had that coming.

Kendall managed to get home before the dam broke. She got undressed, wrapped herself in her favorite fluffy fleece throw, and poured herself a generous glass of brandy. She sat on the couch staring out the window of her condominium in tony Belltown, which overlooked Puget Sound, and let the tears stream down her face. She was a pragmatist, and not one given to a lot of emotional outbursts ... certainly never in public. She told herself that she would allow these few minutes of unchecked grief and then would pull herself together. After all, she had weathered disappointment and heartache before and knew that the trick was to keep busy.

*Just push it down, and it'll go away. It always does.*

Soon, events would pull her into a whirlwind of drama that would leave her broken heart far behind.

# CHAPTER THREE

THE RARE SPRING SUN MADE an appearance through Kendall's bedroom window when she awoke. She didn't even notice. Her heart was heavy, and her body didn't want to move. She went through her morning routine in a fog but managed to maintain her usual schedule. She had to check twice to make sure she had matching shoes on.

*Get going, girl! Move it! Shake it off!* She stopped for her usual morning light mocha and a multi-grain bagel and forced herself to assume a cheerful exterior. She had an important position, overseeing general operation of the company, and could not get bogged down with a lot of emotion. Because she was a woman, she also had to take care not to be seen as emotionally unstable or falling apart in any way.

She pulled into the company parking garage, taking care to wave at the security guard as she passed by. Kendall had no idea how she got into the building, but found herself walking into her spacious office.

She sat in front of her terminal and zoned out. After thirty minutes, she finally realized she hadn't even turned on her computer. She hit the power button and gave a big sigh. *Keep going! You're doing great!* She sat there staring at the unopened emails. The phone rang, startling her. *God, what if it's Jeremy? Damn! It's not.*

"Kendall Radcliffe," she said in a clipped, businesslike tone.

"Whoa! You sound intense."

"Oh, hi, Gwen. Just in the middle of my morning emails."

It was Kendall's friend and the senior vice president of the legal department, Gwen Albertson. She was a feisty red-headed corporate executive who specialized in intellectual property litigation. Since the company was constantly being sued for some perceived trademark, copyright, or patent infringement, she was very much in demand. The law was her passion, and she was loyal to a fault. She defended the company with all the vigor and enthusiasm of a pit bull. After hours, though, she was the life of the party.

This morning she had received some particularly bad news. The company was being investigated by the Federal Trade Commission for possible violations of the Consumer Protection Act.

"Kendall, I need you to go to DC as soon as possible. Today, if you can. You need to meet with outside counsel to review the anticipated charges and start formulating our defense."

Kendall's wheels were already turning. There was nothing like a good legal fight to take her mind off personal matters.

"What's the issue?"

"I don't have all the details. But it sounds like claims of unfair business practices. From what I understand, this is only an investigation at this juncture. We've agreed to meet with the FTC in an effort to assuage their concerns. If anyone can halt the investigation, you can. I need you to work your magic and talk the FTC through our business strategy."

*Perfect! Get me out of the fucking office!*

Kendall was psyched. "Let me finish my emails and make a few calls. I have an 11:00 a.m. conference that will take about an hour. I can probably catch an early evening flight and commit to a morning meeting."

They exchanged the DC meeting details, and Kendall finished her work to go home and pack. Her admin was able to secure a reservation on a non-stop flight leaving at 7:15 p.m. She would not arrive in DC until the wee hours of the morning. She fervently hoped she would be able to sleep on the plane.

She wove through the congested Seattle traffic on her way to the airport and made excellent time. As her seat in the first class section was called for boarding, her cell phone rang. Caller ID flashed Jeremy's name. She stabbed the power button shutting it down. *Wow, that felt good! Now who's in control?* Or so she thought.

# CHAPTER FOUR

KENDALL AWOKE WITH A START. She blinked as the dazzling east coast morning rays lit up her river-view hotel room. Her brain was momentarily confused and foggy from the lack of sleep, cross-country travel, and the overly soft mattress of the king-sized bed she had slept in.

She groaned, sat up, and then caught the time on the bedside clock. "Oh, shit!"

She flew out of bed, took a quick shower, dressed in a slightly rumpled suit, and dashed into the luxury hotel coffee shop for a muffin and coffee to go.

Kendall sweet-talked her way into the front of the hotel's taxi line and settled in for the fifteen minute ride to the office of the company's outside counsel and follow-up meetings with the FTC. As she nibbled on her muffin, she enjoyed the gentle swaying of the cherry blossoms that lined the streets as they made their way into the heart of the city. Springtime was Kendall's favorite time of year to visit DC, and today put a rubber stamp on it.

As a burst of anger and flood of tears simmered just below the surface, threatening to make an appearance, Kendall acknowledged them and then boot-kicked the emotions right out of her mind. She wasn't about to give into a sudden display of sorrow and ruin a most spectacular ride. She concentrated on the thought that she was so fortunate to be able to enjoy the sight of the city's more than 3,000 cherry blossom trees in full bloom. She chose, instead, to view the sweet landscape as a personal gift to her. *I accept.* She smiled as the taxi pulled up to her destination.

Kendall had two very busy days of meetings, including with the FTC, video conferences, and rushed, late dinners. At the end of each day, she arrived back at her hotel only to make a couple phone calls back to the office on the West Coast, check her emails, maybe catch a headline or two of the evening news, and then flop into bed for a restless night of sleep. Even though she traveled quite a bit, she never got used to a new bed until about the third night.

Kendall checked out of her hotel on the third morning and left her luggage with the hotel porter for the day. She had an evening flight back to Seattle and hoped she would make that flight.

Early that evening, she consulted her watch as she stepped out of the taxi in front of the hotel. She was startled by the commotion of luggage and boxes being loaded into a black stretch limo, blocking her path. Absentmindedly, she walked around the bags and cortege of uniformed bellhops scurrying to and fro, appearing competent and helpful—obviously hoping for a generous tip.

As Kendall approached the bell captain's desk to retrieve her stored luggage, a well-dressed man hurried over and gave a slight bow. He was nothing if not the epitome of efficiency. One could see that no mistakes were to be tolerated under his watch.

"Good evening, Ms. Radcliffe. I'm the hotel's evening manager, at your service. Your bag has already been loaded."

Perplexed, Kendall snapped to attention, and her brows furrowed. "What? Where?"

"With the others."

"What others? I'm not traveling with anyone else. I only have one bag."

The manager frowned and started wringing his hands, as if that would help. "Oh dear, what could have happened? Oh, I know."

*Good grief, the man is talking to himself. I don't know whether to laugh or slap him.* She awaited his explanation with barely contained patience. Her eyebrows rose, hoping to prompt him for a more speedy response. He caught her probing stare and jumped as if he'd been goosed.

"Oh, yes, Miss—er—Radcliffe. Well, you see, your bag has the same company luggage tag as some other bags that were stored, and they were all pulled for the livery service vehicle outside."

He looked like he was going to cry. He couldn't believe he was part of this mix-up. As he figured it, if she complained, he would receive another poor report in his personnel records. He had only been the night manager for a few months and had already amassed quite a few negative reports. She could see that he was flustered beyond reason.

"Oh, for God's sake. I'll do it myself."

She turned and ran out the door, waving wildly to the single remaining valet who had just closed the door of the stretch limo. As it started to roll forward, she yelled, "Stop, you've got my bag!" She realized that she sounded like a crazy woman and willed herself to calm down as the limo slowed to a stop. Because of the tinted windows, she could just barely make out two heads in the backseat turning around to see what the problem was.

Her personal possessions meant more to her than the embarrassment of causing a scene. She ran to the back of the vehicle and pounded on the trunk. The two gentlemen occupying the backseat looked at her as if she'd lost her mind. Then, one of them said something to the other, leaned forward, and opened the door on his side of the limo. The surprised valet ran to assist in opening the door. As the odd-looking businessman exited the limo, he squinted at Kendall, and she recognized him.

*Oh, Lordy, this is not happening,* she thought with a panic. It was Paul Fields, the CEO and brainchild of the company she worked for, Orion Premier Net Services. She'd recognize that wild-maned, unkempt man anywhere and had sat in on more than a few meetings with him at the company headquarters in Seattle. Apparently, he recognized her as well. Fortunately, she stumbled across him on one of his better-mannered days. He was known to be quite rude and dismissive of those he felt were eminently beneath him intellectually, starting and ending with employees at his own company.

He pointed his finger at her, saying, "It's Kendall Radcliffe in Operations, right?"

"Uh, yes, Mr. Fields. I'm so sorry."

She gave a nervous laugh and continued. "You see, my luggage was accidentally put in your vehicle."

His eyebrows raised in surprise. "Really? Are you headed back to Seattle?"

She peered at her watch anxiously and nodded. "Yes. My flight leaves from Dulles in a little over an hour."

Paul Fields appeared to be weighing his options, consulted his watch, frowned, and then blurted out, "I've got a charter at Dulles, if you'd like to ride with us back to Seattle."

Kendall felt a crimson blush spread across her face, started to sputter a polite decline, and then, realizing he was somewhat amused, suddenly threw caution to the wind and responded, "That would be perfect." *Geez, what have I gotten myself into?*

Upon locating her luggage in the trunk and depositing her laptop bag there as well, she climbed into the limo. She soon saw that the second gentleman was the company CFO and childhood friend of Fields, Glenn Carson. He was as affable as Fields was mercurial and arrogant. He seemed to take the altered plans in stride and patiently awaited the explanation as Fields re-took his seat at the back of the limo. Fields wasted no time in the explanation.

"It would seem, Paul, that we are going to have company back to Seattle. Do you know Kendall Radcliffe from Operations?"

He did not wait for a response but continued in a dry voice, "We almost absconded with Kendall's luggage, and have certainly caused her to miss her flight. So the least we can do is offer her a ride back to Seattle."

Carson nodded, smiled, and proffered his hand to Kendall. "No, I don't believe we've met. You are very fortunate, Kendall. We had a successful day on the Hill today, and therefore nothing could alter our run of luck." He would soon be taking back those words.

As the limo headed to Dulles International Airport, Kendall vaguely recalled hearing about Fields needing to testify before some House Committee. She was not interested in making small talk with the two men and was more than intimidated, but determined to hold her own. She just smiled and looked out the window.

The sedan sped to the waiting Bombardier Challenger 850 aircraft parked at one of the private backside hangars at Dulles. Feeling the smooth glide of the sleek limo, Kendall felt a surge of excitement that she was given this opportunity. She was also a bit nervous about flying on a smaller aircraft than the usual crowded commercial jet filled with noisy passengers.

As they approached the shiny executive plane and one by one made their way up the retractable stairway and into the plane, she could see that it was luxurious. Certainly a higher class of jet than she had ever seen. A smartly uniformed flight attendant met them at the top of the stairway and took their coats as they continued into the seating area of the cabin. There was a heavy smell of leather and the look of finely polished wood throughout the interior.

Kendall hung back, waiting for direction on where to sit. The two men continued to engage in deep discussion and ignored her as they chose seats in the middle of the plane. The flight attendant raised her eyebrows, unsure where Kendall fit into the picture and not knowing how to assist her. She deliberately chose a seat several rows behind the men to give them privacy and planned to basically make herself invisible for the duration of the flight.

Kendall was overwhelmed by the luxury all around her. She chose a seat in a cluster of four, with two seats facing her. Her seat was better than the average first class seat on a commercial jet. As she looked around in wonder, the observant flight attendant realized this was a novel experience for her and came over to point out several useful devices nearby. Kendall soon saw that her seat rotated 180 degrees, and that she had a personal LCD video screen that was larger than her window. *Wow! Super cool! I may never fly commercial again. Yeah, in your dreams, sister!*

The attendant distributed their drinks, and the three passengers began to visibly settle in and relax for their cross-country trip. Carson suddenly remembered the unexpected guest and turned around to see what became of Kendall. He smiled when he caught sight of her several rows behind them and nodded.

"Making yourself comfortable, Ms. Radcliffe?"

She was instantly nervous again and almost dumped her drink on her lap.

"Yes, Mr. Carson. And please call me Kendall."

"Okay, Kendall. And you may call me Glenn."

This all appeared to be a grand adventure to Kendall, and she was thrilled at her fortuitous encounter as a result of the mix-up at the hotel. She frowned when she realized that a disquieted sensation filled her body. Her stomach felt knotted and tight. *What the hell's wrong with me? I sure hope I don't throw up!*

# CHAPTER FIVE

Kendall turned when she heard the sound of several sets of footsteps coming towards her. She realized this must be the crew when she saw their matching uniforms and caps. They nodded at her as they strode past and stopped at the executives' row. The captain, leading the way, stepped forward, introduced himself and his officers, and shook their hands.

"Good evening, gentlemen. We've got a fierce headwind tonight, so relax and try to get some sleep. We'll be off the ground in a few minutes."

He inclined his head toward the man furthest back and continued, "We've got an extra man tonight."

Fields frowned. He was not good with changes to his schedule and was already pissed that he had extended the offer to have Kendall accompany them. He was a man who was always reining in his temper. The picture of him taking a deep breath and trying to hold back the irritation was quite frightening to those around him, particularly the recipient of his ire. His face turned red and blotchy, and he looked like he would explode. He simply stared at the captain and raised his eyebrows. The captain gave a slight cough and croaked, "Officer Alam is training. There will be no charge for the extra personnel, Sir."

Fields pursed his lips and said in an even tone, "I would hope not. Let's get going."

To make matters worse, the company jet was undergoing maintenance, and they had been forced to charter this jet and were unfamiliar with this plane or any of the pilots. Fields liked and trusted his regular crew and was put out that he had to suffer through these unknown quantities.

The airplane crew made their way to the cockpit and busied themselves with the pre-flight checklist. Finally, the exit door was closed, everything loose stowed away or locked into place, and all passengers and crew belted into their respective seats.

The plane was backed out of the hangar and began to taxi toward the runway. Looking out her window, Kendall was struck by how small they were compared to the jumbo jet that just rumbled past them. It felt like a small earthquake when the giant engines roared by. She realized that she had to look way up to glimpse the passenger windows. She grinned at the thought that she might feel tiny in this much smaller aircraft, but it more than made up for its size in quality and personal space. She re-adjusted her headrest for the hundredth time and closed her eyes. Again, the nagging feeling and foreboding threatened to send her into a panic attack. She grabbed the armrests and willed herself to calm down. *I've really lost it this time!*

She was so frantic to calm herself down, that she allowed herself to focus on Jeremy. *The jerk!* Now her emotions changed to anger, since she wouldn't allow herself to be maudlin when she was having such a wonderful—if not downright scary—adventure.

When the aircraft reached its cruising altitude of thirty-five thousand feet, the flight attendant was already moving about serving drinks and preparing dinner.

As Kendall finished her lemon oregano chicken, rice, and asparagus, she sat back with a sigh and waited to see what lovely dessert would be presented. She contemplated requesting another glass of Chateau Ste. Michelle Chardonnay. She frowned as she heard a muffled but distinctly loud sound from behind her. She couldn't process it, and chalked it up to weird airplane in-flight sounds. The plane gave a jerk and a slight, but distinct roll.

Fields began to look around and peered at his watch. All of a sudden, seeming completely out of control, he jumped up, peered out the window, threw his cloth napkin on his seat, and shouted, "What's going on? I want to talk to the captain. We're headed east instead of west." He strode up to the cockpit door and banged loudly. Kendall watched in horror at the scene, not understanding what was happening. The flight attendant's eyes grew wide, and she shrank back against the wall of the plane.

The cockpit door opened slowly, and the barrel of a Sig Sauer P-226 nine millimeter handgun was slowly pushed through the opening. Officer Alam sneered at Fields and commanded, "Go sit down, or I'll shoot everyone on the plane—NOW!"

For once, Fields was stunned into silence. He was a man who took control at meetings, and was usually the most knowledgeable guy in the room. But he was clearly out of his element in this instance. He knew nothing about guns other than to recognize a handgun when he saw it. As his mind attempted to grasp the reality of the situation, he could do nothing more than back away from the door. It closed with a hard slam. In stunned silence, he stumbled back to his seat, wobbling ever so slightly as he went.

As Fields stood in the aisle, both Kendall and Carson looked at their CEO with gaping mouths and stunned expressions. Fields ran his hand through his unkempt hair and willed himself to calm down and assess the situation. He looked back at the flight attendant. She was shaking uncontrollably. He nodded his head and hissed at her, "Come here!"

She didn't move, but began rocking.

He raised his voice, "Here! Now!"

She got up, and on unsteady legs, stumbled her way to their row. Fields put his hands on her shoulders and practically shoved her into a seat facing him and Carson. He began firing questions at her as he pointed at the cockpit door, his finger stabbing the air for extra emphasis.

"Who is that third man? Do you know him? Have you worked with him before?"

The flight attendant shook her head and in a very shaky voice said, "N-N-N-No—never seen him before. D-d-d-didn't know he was going to be p-p-p-part of the crew."

Fields was irate. Shaking his head, he exploded at her.

"How can that be? You all work for the same charter company! You would have been copied on the paperwork, wouldn't you? Or at least been notified of the change?"

She just shook her head and shrugged her shoulders.

Carson, having gotten his bearings, quietly inserted wryly, "Paul, it really doesn't matter at this point. If we live to investigate it, we can ask these questions. Let's figure out what we can do right now."

With barely a second to inhale, and his mind racing through their options, he continued, "Let's try our cell phones."

He removed his phone from his pants pocket and turned it on.

Fields was nodding his head, "Who are you going to call—security? Mickey?" Damn! He was furious that he had let his regular security team stay behind to attend a high-level FBI-sponsored tactical weapons seminar in DC the next day. Yes, they had done it on the last DC trip, and it had worked out fine. After all, they'd never really had any serious threats to their safety in the past. It just seemed prudent to use security with company assets over several billion dollars ... not to mention that the company insurance required it. He felt sick when he recalled the strenuous objections of Mickey to even a five minute gap with no security detail, and how he had overruled him.

"Yeah, I'm calling Mickey at the security patch-through."

He dialed, listened, frowned, and then slowly looked at each of them in dawning horror. In an even voice, he enunciated each word slowly, "The cell phone service is blocked. They must be using some sort of jammer."

Carson whispered, "They?"

Fields just glared at him. He was alternately furious that this was happening to him, and that someone had the audacity to think they could outsmart him. Well, they had, and he was just going to have to deal with it.

Carson got up and grabbed one of the courtesy phones on the sidewall near their seats. Shit! It was dead too. He asked the flight attendant if there were any other phones in the interior of the plane or the galley that might have a different line. She was only too happy to help, just so she could take her mind off of the possible gruesome outcome.

"There is one other in the galley. I'll check it."

She got up and ran up the aisle to the galley.

Kendall had been quiet during the initial upheaval, taking it all in. She was no longer nervous or intimidated. This was a matter of life and death. Her regular duties involved problem solving and handling would-be crises on a regular basis. She jumped in, saying, "This appears to be a well-planned attack. My guess is that the galley phone has been disengaged as well." Both men frowned at the logic.

All three were thinking, *But why? What is the plan? Where are we being taken?*

The flight attendant ran back, shaking her head, "None of the communications work."

They stared at each with a mixture of fear and terror.

# CHAPTER SIX

Just then, a voice could be heard over the intercom. "This is your captain speaking, Abdul Bashar Alam. Please do not be disturbed. I do not wish you any harm. We are en route to my native country—Afghanistan! You are invited guests of our beloved President Mujtaba Shazeb. He has urgent state business needs that require your personal and professional attention. Please sit back and enjoy the trip. In order to ensure your cooperation, I disconnected all communication devices. In these turbulent times with terrorists among us, I did not want to worry the authorities that anything was wrong with this flight. You may wonder if our flight deviation will be noticed by air traffic control. I am a very smart man, and I have successfully overridden the transponder code so this flight appears to be headed to Seattle. Our real course is basically cloaked on radar, and for that reason I must watch out for approaching traffic. Therefore, do not cause any trouble, or we will not safely reach our destination."

The passengers looked at each other in astonishment. The plane was being hijacked! But for what purpose? If it weren't so implausible, it might be humorous that the "pilot" referred to terrorists—of which he most certainly was one—in derisive tones. He apparently viewed his mission as nothing less than honorable.

Alam continued, "Uh, unfortunately, in order to persuade the captain and co-pilot to hand over control of this wonderful plane, I was forced to incapacitate them. They do not pose a threat now. I am, however, quite concerned about the rest of you. I have rigged a small explosive to the inside of the cockpit door. If you attempt to open the door, you will be severely injured. Since you Americans seem to always need proof in the face of threats, I will be showing you, in the very near future, that I mean business. I am sorry to have to do this, but these things cannot be helped. It is for the greater good."

Kendall felt her stomach hit the ground. This was clearly a veiled threat that was intended to be acted upon. What is this deranged man going to do? Something told her to get out of her seat and crouch against the inner wall of the plane—basically making herself invisible to anyone at the front or back of the plane.

All of a sudden the cockpit door flew open, and Alam, having put the plane on autopilot, stepped out. He took several steps towards the passengers, aimed, and shot the flight attendant right between the eyes. She fell forward at the men's feet.

Alam turned, and with a satisfied and determined look, went back into the cockpit, attached the explosive device to the inside door, and resumed his seat at the controls.

The interior of the plane was deadly silent, its passengers in shock at the sudden, violent act whose consequence now lay at their feet.

Kendall did not see the shooting but concluded that the flight attendant had been murdered. She soon realized that had she been sitting in the attendant's seat, it could've just as easily been she the pilot shot. She knew that the men were most likely safe, since they were the major "assets" of Orion Premier Net Services. That meant that from this point forward she was *excess baggage;* if she wasn't careful, she could become *collateral damage.* The men reached that same conclusion as they gaped at the lifeless body.

In a low tone, Carson spoke first. "We've got to protect Kendall. I think we're safe in the air, so long as we don't do anything to piss him off."

Fields nodded grimly with lips pressed together. "I agree. He's on a mission, and it doesn't appear to involve crashing the plane. Therefore, let's ride this out. Once we're on the ground, Kendall should be okay."

They looked back at Kendall and were surprised not to see her. She popped her head up above the seat, scrambled to her feet, and stared open-mouthed at the slumped body of the flight attendant. "Why?" she whispered.

The two men looked at each other, and with uneasy but knowing glances, said nothing. They had a pretty good idea what all of this was about.

Kendall saw the look pass between them and wondered what they knew.

# CHAPTER SEVEN

The remainder of the flight was uneventful. The three passengers regrouped, and Kendall was placed in a row in front of the men, so they could keep an eye on her. She was instructed to recline all the way back to escape visual detection should Alam reappear.

Each person was lost to his own thoughts. Kendall purposely shifted her thoughts to Jeremy. *Will I ever see him again? Would he even care?* That line of thinking just made her angry again, so she pushed it into the recesses of her mind. She began to think about the history of Afghanistan and how it was now impacting her life.

She had only a sketchy knowledge of the Middle East and Asia from her undergrad classes. She thought it was a shame that a few years after the U.S. pulled its troops out of Afghanistan, the country had soon dissolved into anarchy as the tribal warlords took over and fought for power. Eventually, the U.S. closed its local embassy for security reasons. Mujtaba Shazeb, the current leader, was nothing but a ruthless warlord who ended up being the "last man standing." No *loya jirga* elected him. He soon became a dictator who pillaged Afghanistan's western-financed modernized oil fields and terrorized the citizens into silent submission. He even engineered the deaths of his own two brothers and a brother-in-law. He trusted no one and imagined that everyone was out to get him.

Shazeb gained power by uniting the Afghan citizens against the reappearance of the Taliban and Al Qaeda in the early days after the Americans and the West had left Afghanistan. He made a power grab in a single-minded purpose, abolishing the two legislative bodies: the *Wolesi Jirga,* the House of the People; and the *Meshrano Jirga,* the House of Elders. He was astute enough to see the usefulness of allowing the western business interests to share its resources, in the form of massive financial contribution, in an effort to modernize and stabilize Afghanistan and ultimately propel the fledgling democratic country out of the dark ages. That was never to be. The western world soon found out that their fragile partnerships were rife with dishonesty and corruption that began and ended at the top rung of the Afghanistan leadership.

Because of the financial turmoil in the western world in 2008 and continued market upheaval through the next decade, each country had its own unique domestic issues to contend with. The West had simply lost interest in the constant struggles within Afghanistan. The desire to continue the fight had long since been abandoned.

Since the U.S. had experienced no national security issues with Afghanistan under Shazeb's rule, the West largely ignored and tolerated the despot. The West was relieved that he had thoroughly modernized, organized, and built the vast oil fields so that money had, for some time now, been flowing in.

Most importantly, there were no requests for international assistance of any kind—troops, money, or counsel. Afghanistan appeared to be quiet and self-sufficient, and desirous of being left alone. The Americans and the rest of the West were only too happy to oblige and overlook reports of Shazeb's overzealous handling of his citizens.

In reality, Afghanistan was a ticking time bomb. Lately, the wealthy nations realized that once again there was a huge heroin problem. For years it was known to be coming from either Columbia or Burma, but the word on the street now was that the current product was purer and more deadly. A new source was suspected. The West was beginning to take a look at Afghanistan.

Kendall focused her razor sharp instincts and pondered Shazeb's intentions. She replayed the events of the last couple of hours and realized that with Alam's command of the English language and customs, he had most certainly been educated in the West. He must have resided in the West for a long time. He was likely nothing more than Shazeb's lackey. But why would a man such as Alam, so clearly educated in the West, turn against it in single-minded devotion to his leader? One had only to review the events of September 11 to understand that mindset.

She stopped, realizing she was making some possibly erroneous assumptions. Perhaps there was more to the story. Maybe Alam wasn't an enemy of the West. *An enemy of Orion Premier Net Services?* That thought gave her pause. Yes, Orion was a powerful high-tech company that had been in business now for fifteen years and was a leader in net services, including web design, installation, maintenance, and repair.

Additionally, Orion Premier owned the most popular and stable web browser. It was the most secure browser in the market and had never been compromised. The technical code was so proprietary and sought after, that no single employee of Orion had access to the original master source code.

In the last year, Orion Premier had introduced an impressive USB thumb drive that could be switched off and de-activated, rendering it useless to an unknown party should they come across a lost device. The thumb drive basically operated as a micro-computer and could perform tasks that were unknown to the ordinary user, not to mention most of the Orion employees. In fact, much of Orion's layered technology was known only to a few in the R & D department.

# CHAPTER EIGHT

The plane landed without incident in Kabul after making a quick refueling stopover on some unknown island. Since the refueling had been without incident, with no one—not even the pilot—leaving their seats, Kendall figured the brief touchdown had been pre-arranged with a "friendly" nation. She looked out the window and saw a few flickering lights on what appeared to be a private landing strip. She had lost track of time, but it was dark and obviously evening.

The plane pulled up to a banged-up, rusted warehouse-like structure that served as a hangar, and it was immediately surrounded by twenty-five grim-faced uniformed guards carrying bayoneted military rifles. A middle-aged, portly soldier, who scowled as if he had been interrupted during dinner, broke away from the group and approached the plane, his hand on his weapon.

The cockpit door flew open, and Alam quickly stepped out, yelling, "Do not move!" He strode to the exit door, opened it, and pushed the stairway down into position. His pistol was trained on the passengers, and they remained frozen in their seats.

The annoyed-looking military man rushed up the stairs, stepped into the plane, marched down the aisle, nodded his head at the passengers, and spoke in a clipped, no-nonsense, loud voice.

"Good evening, my name is General Faisal Omar, at your service. You will stand up ... now!"

The three weary Orion Premier employees struggled to their feet, dumbstruck with fear. They noted the general also spoke English, albeit with a distinct accent.

Paul Fields' mind was racing. It dawned on him that the country of Afghanistan had certainly made more progress than he realized. That Orion should make a concerted effort to establish a local sales team, particularly given the English that seemed to be spoken by a lot of Afghans, from what he had seen so far. He even thought that maybe he could help get the three of them out of this unfortunate ordeal by turning the whole event into a sales pitch. He began to breathe normally, and realized that he needed to gain control—get the upper hand—and maybe use a little charm later, which did not come naturally to him.

Assuming an affable demeanor and in complete control, the general continued, "Ah, I see you are surprised I know your native language. I primarily speak *Dari* and *Pashto.* I prefer *Dari,* so I can communicate better with my Iranian relatives. You will find that our military is the mightiest in the world. Our little country is now well educated and can compete with the western world on many levels. We are a rich country, and our citizens enjoy the best!"

*Hardly,* Paul Fields thought. He had heard enough of this bullshit. He was not known to be a patient person, and at the moment was beyond tired, hungry, and wrestling with his temper. He was ready to explode, sales be damned! He was furious that his travel plans had been usurped, and that he had to listen to this bombastic oaf.

He leaned forward. "I demand to know why we are here. This is unconscionable; people have been killed here! Do you know who we are? This is going to cause an international incident!"

The general roared, stabbing his index finger into the air, "Silence! Empty your pockets now!" He turned his head and barked an order for his captain to enter and gather the discarded items. Two soldiers—*sans* weapons—entered with a large plastic bag.

Fields and Carson emptied their pockets and looked on helplessly as the soldiers gathered up all their personal belongings. Kendall felt sick when she saw her purse going into the bag and wondered if she'd ever see it again. Fields could barely hand over the keys to his brand new Bugatti Veyron Super Sport. Carson was shaking as he handed over his cell phone ... his last link to the outside world.

The general, observing their defeated expressions, threw back his head and laughed derisively. "No one knows where you are, and they won't until our issues have been dealt with." Fields and Carson exchanged glances, thinking, *Oh, that little matter!*

Carson mumbled in a pleading, somewhat whiny tone, "What issues? There has been a mistake. We don't know what you're talking about. If you'll let us go, we'll get a pilot here. We promise not to notify the United Nations of what you've done."

With a red face, the general poked his finger into Carson's chest. "No talking! You will all follow me. I will take you to your rooms for the night, and you will be meeting with President Mujtaba Shazeb tomorrow."

The general was not without a sense of humor. With a grand gesture he proclaimed, "I hope you enjoy your stay here."

In a proud and haughty manner, the general then raised his head and turned around. The three employees were marched to a waiting panel van and taken to a nearby military compound. They were separated and each assigned small, comfortably sparse rooms—locked from the outside. The windowless rooms had dingy, whitewashed walls. Unknown to the trio, their rooms were adjacent to each other. The three were relieved to find they had a tiny but fairly clean bathroom in their room. It consisted of a toilet, pedestal sink, and shower stall, with one large whitish-gray-colored towel hanging on the stall door. While the water pressure was practically non-existent, they were grateful they had not been thrown into a prison, considering the way they had been treated so far. Kendall was thrilled with the meager amenities. *Thank God! Indoor plumbing ... a real toilet, and not a hole in the ground!*

They were each brought a set of poorly made clothes to change into that consisted of ill-fitting jeans, undergarments, and a gauzy shirt, with a *hijab* for Kendall to wear on her head when she left her room. While Afghanistan had long since moved away from the strict requirement of a *chador* or *burka* in the cities, it still adhered to a modest dress code for its citizens, primarily the women.

A weak bowl of Afghan soup, or *Shorma,* and thick fresh bread called *obi naan* were brought to the "guests." They were given an orange for dessert and *Chai* tea to drink. The Orion people, sitting on the one chair at the little table next to their rock-hard single beds, ate in silence ... each bone-weary and lost in thought.

Later, as the trio lay in their respective beds, their minds circled back to the last twenty-four hours. Kendall thought of Jeremy, who didn't even know what was happening to her. For that matter, no one knew that her travel arrangements had been changed and that she was now on an Orion Premier chartered flight. Tears slid down her face. For the first time in her life, she felt alone and vulnerable. Fields and Carson were thinking the same thing. However, they also wondered how much the Afghans knew, and how the hell they had found out. All three fell into an exhausted, fitful sleep. Tomorrow would bring some answers but also up the ante.

# CHAPTER NINE

The security team at Orion Premier was frantic. Eric "Mickey" McDougall received a call from the FBI that the Orion chartered plane had mysteriously disappeared off radar approximately thirty minutes after taking off from Dulles. The Special Agent in Charge, Anthony Zanders, explained that the FAA was fairly certain the plane had not crashed. Evidence of mechanical or catastrophic failure would have shown up on radar or via radio transmission. The last transmission prior to disappearing off radar indicated it was flying at thirty-five thousand feet. Furthermore, the radio communication and plane transponder were purposely de-activated. Zanders could only conclude that something was certainly afoot.

The FBI was the first agency notified. After being apprised of the details, sketchy as they were, the FBI notified the National Security Agency, or NSA. Within the secret world of cryptology and electronic intelligence, it was generally believed that a new and very dangerous technology had recently been perfected allowing a plane to "go dark" or disappear off radar completely. The unsubstantiated rumor was that during a transponder's frequency converter process, the codes being transmitted through the standard sequence of pulses was interrupted and altered so as to cancel out the simultaneous receipt and transmission signals. The plane's flight path could not then be tracked or traced to a destination, not even to a general area. The plane's heading couldn't even be determined.

The NSA was familiar enough with the scuttlebutt within the worldwide intelligence community that it realized the stories it had been hearing were true and that this had to be the first known instance of its use. They now needed to know everything about the occupants of the plane in order to figure out the why and, hopefully, the where.

Mickey was no fool. He knew something was up. Agent Zanders was not telling him everything. In fact, what exactly was the FBI's involvement? They had spoken for a few minutes, and Zanders was asking very probing questions.

He didn't seem to have a personal concern about the Orion Premier employees onboard the flight. Mickey caught the hint of a bigger concern.

"May I call you Mickey?"

"Certainly. Why is the FBI involved?"

Agent Zanders knew he had to give some information to gain Mickey's trust but wasn't about to reveal the NSA's involvement. The goal of the phone call was to disclose the event and find out who the passengers were. Knowing full well the worldwide scope of Orion Premier's products and business in general, Zanders was trying not to think about how high the level of executive was on board that flight. His gut was warning to prepare for the worst. The higher and more well known the executive, the more this looked to be an international incident. It would most certainly then require the involvement of the highest levels of government.

"Mickey, the FAA informed us shortly after the plane disappeared from radar. Apparently, it is standard protocol when planes chartered by executives go missing. All I know is that a plane chartered by Orion Premier Net Services had disappeared from radar. I imagine that a chartered plane would normally be used for an executive. Therefore, I need to know immediately who was on board. That might help us determine whether this is some sort of kidnapping or extortion attempt."

Zanders felt as if he was babbling. In reality, he sounded reasonable, strong, very much in charge, and quite competent. Mickey was straining for signs of stress or indications that he wasn't getting the full story. He proceeded cautiously.

"There were two executives on board: the CEO, Paul Fields; and the CFO, Glenn Carson."

"What was the nature of their business in DC?"

Mickey hesitated only because he detested giving away information. He also realized he had to be completely up front given the situation and players involved. He took a deep breath. "They were testifying at a House committee hearing. Unfortunately, I do not know the exact nature of the testimony. Do you think that might have had something to do with the plane going missing? He felt that if he kept them talking, he wouldn't have to reveal so much about the Orion executives' itinerary.

"I have no idea, Mickey." Again with the low-key, straightforward questions to put Mickey at ease. In a soothing voice, Zanders continued, "I'm just gathering all the facts. You know the drill."

Mickey detected a hint of a patronizing tone. His investigation radar signaled a blip. He wondered what was really going on, and realized that he had to keep Zanders talking in order to learn as much as he could.

"Were the men accompanied by security? If so, how many? And were they your own people?"

"Shit," Mickey blurted, and ran his hands through his hair. Zanders waited patiently for him to continue, his senses heightened. He leaned forward in anticipation.

"Uh, there was no security on the plane trip home. The regular Orion security team stayed behind to attend a training seminar. We've never had security issues beyond the usual nutcase emails, letters, and tweets. An Orion security team was set to meet the plane at Boeing field."

Zanders frowned, thinking they wouldn't be making that mistake again. In a clipped tone he said, "I'll need the names and contact information of the security detail that stayed behind in DC, plus those planning to meet the plane at Boeing field." He decided to go for broke. "In fact, give me the info on every Orion security team member ..." He paused and took a breath, "And make it past and present employees and contractors."

Mickey went as red as his thick Scottish mane. "Don't you think we're getting a little ahead of ourselves? We don't even know that a criminal act has occurred, let alone something untoward." His temper was building. "Do you realize what a violation of privacy it would be to give you that kind of personal info based on the facts you've given me so far?"

Zanders quickly weighed his options whether to tip his hand at this point. He figured that if a kidnapping or extortion event was unfolding, which was what his gut was telling him, that the Orion executives would be safe for the time being. So, it wasn't crucial this very minute to obtain the personnel data, but he decided to push one last time for the info.

"Mickey, how about I make you a personal promise that if you'll give me the info and it turns out that the plane developed mechanical difficulties, I will immediately shred everything you've given me."

There was no answer as Mickey contemplated the consequences.

"You know, Mickey, we're both on the same side. Look at me as an extension of your team. I have better resources than you, and I can get faster answers. Let me help you ... Orion! It's my job—I want to help!" His voice rose to an urgent level, leaving no doubt that he would not take no for an answer.

Mickey sighed. "Maybe."

*What the hell?* Zanders thought. "I don't understand. Are you going to give me the info or not?" His frustration showed through quite clearly as he squeezed the phone with one hand, and threw his pen across the room with the other.

"I will gather the info and decide whether to give it to you tomorrow. It's going to take me the better part of a day to get it anyway. I will most likely give it to you. Just let me think about it. Maybe this whole thing will resolve by then."

Zanders stood up at that point and waved his arm. "Fine. I'll be in touch with you as things are known. Just for tonight, I'm going to lay low as far as communicating with the families. Would you please inform the two families that the plane has gone missing? Don't speculate. It'll only alarm them. Make sure you have them notify you immediately if they are contacted in any way ... by email, letter, phone call, tweet, etc. And I'm talking about both home and business communications."

"Fields' and Carson's professional emails, letters, tweets, and phone calls are all accessed, reviewed, and, for the most part, responded to by their executive admins."

"I'll need those names and contact info too. We should know what's going in the next day. If this develops into something major, I'll be flying out there and will want to speak to the families immediately. But you should know the FBI is taking point on this investigation. I want and expect your full cooperation."

"One other thing, Agent Zanders. I don't think you understand the global ramifications if this becomes public. Orion Premier Net Services is a Fortune 500 publicly traded company. If this info gets out, the stock is going to take a nosedive."

That only mildly concerned Zanders, and he hadn't really given it much thought. But he needed to at least act like he cared. "Well, then let's keep this quiet until tomorrow when we have a better handle on the matter. If anyone calls asking for info about the plane going missing, just say that you don't have any info on it. You know, stall! The DC Air Traffic Control, the FAA, and Boeing Field have been instructed they are not to publicize or even speak about this yet. We also talked to the charter company that owned the plane. That was a little trickier, because it involves huge assets for the company. We, shall we say, persuaded them to remain silent for the time being. Once they were made to see that one of their charter planes going missing wouldn't be good for business, they were only too willing to stall for a day or two. They have also agreed to provide all of the personnel records for the crew, as well as maintenance records for the plane. So let's keep in touch."

Mickey felt a huge weight on his shoulders. He could only stall for so long. "By close of business tomorrow, the board of directors will need to know what's going on. I'm not stalling any longer than tomorrow at 5:00 p.m."

Zanders was really getting irritated. "Fine! I don't think we could keep it quiet beyond that anyway. There are already too many people in the loop. Later!"

They rang off, and Mickey steeled himself for battle. This was not what he had signed on for. This had all the hallmark of an international element. There was definitely something cloak-and-dagger going on. Just how far reaching was it? Or had they let their imaginations run wild when it was nothing more than a simple mechanical failure? That too, could be a catastrophic event for the company.

He sighed, grabbed his leather jacket and keys, and strode out the door toward the elevator that would take him to his oversized black SUV. He stopped at security and advised them in as nonchalant a tone as possible that the executives' travel plans had changed. The security team could stand down, and no one needed to meet the plane at Boeing Field. Mickey had never lied like this before, and he felt slightly sick as he began to realize the enormity of the situation.

He drove out of the company building on Lake Union and merged onto Interstate 5, heading north. After less than a mile, he merged onto 520 eastbound. Fortunately, both executives lived within two miles of each other in the exclusive waterfront community of Hunts Point. He arrived at the Fields estate and parked in the garage off to the side of the main house. He headed to the elegant Mediterranean-style house and stepped up to the colonnade leading to the ornately carved double entry doors. He stared at the elaborate carving that spanned the matching mahogany doors and with a heavy heart finally lifted his arm and pushed the doorbell, which was offset to the side.

For a moment he got a perverse sense of pleasure from hearing the custom chimes of the doorbell. That was the only feature he had ever liked about this monstrosity of a house. When the chimes stopped playing, and the sound of approaching footsteps brought him out of his reverie, Mickey prepared himself for the coming scene.

# CHAPTER TEN

KENDALL AWOKE WITH A START when her door was abruptly and violently flung open. It banged against the wall in a crash. She looked around in the dim light—startled and unable to grasp her surroundings. *I must be dreaming. Good Lord, please make this a dream!* A man accompanied by two soldiers set a tray of food on the small table near her bed and told her—in broken English—that she had thirty minutes to eat, shower, and get dressed to leave. She perked up when she saw a toothbrush and some unknown brand of toothpaste on the tray. *Thank God ... they are civilized!* She couldn't tell if it was new and wouldn't allow herself to go there.

She flew into action and choked down the round sweet flatbread or *Roht ...* the local breakfast fare. It came with a small bowl of thick plain yogurt, apricots, and more *Chai* tea. *I hope I don't get sick!* She was in and out of the shower in five minutes, pausing a bit longer to smell the fragrant shampoo. *Hmm ... smells like pomegranate.* The bar soap in the shower looked old and dirty. Kendall was thoroughly grossed out but used it anyway, desperately scraping off the outer layer of dirt and sweat with her fingernails. When half an hour had passed, Kendall was pacing the floor while running her fingers through her hair, trying to both dry and comb it. She had put on the ill-fitting clothes and looked quite lost in the oversized garments. At least the jeans fit her just enough so as not to fall off.

Precisely at thirty minutes, the door was pushed open, and the same man who brought the tray walked in a few feet, looking at the empty plate and then to Kendall. He appraised her wet hair and pointed to the *hijab.* "You will wear *hijab* like all Afghanistan women when you go out. Put it on now! Hurry!"

She quickly picked it up and pulled it over her head and shoulders. The fit was snug and completely masked her wet hair. In fact, it covered every inch of her shoulder-length hair.

Kendall was led to a large room that looked to be a conference room of sorts. Fields and Carson were already there, trying not to look anxious.

Fields frowned when he saw her, and Carson looked guilty. She caught both expressions, and had the distinct impression they knew what all of this was about. Carson wondered if he should ask that she be set free. But he was afraid they would use her as a bargaining chip or, worse, dispose of her altogether. To be safe, for the time being he decided to say nothing.

The three were escorted by General Faisal Omar to an awaiting, much-used military transport truck. As they climbed into the large, jeep-like truck, Kendall quickly looked around at the compound they were at. She saw they had stayed in a building that was surrounded on all sides by identical long rectangular barracks constructed of concrete and rebar. The whole look was that of a utilitarian environment. No attempt was made to adorn or even soften the surroundings. Strangely, the place was quiet. She had no idea that the presence of the three Americans was known only to a handful of people at the base. Most of the ordinary soldiers had been dispatched to the training areas outside the base.

The Afghan people didn't dislike Americans. But they didn't embrace or welcome them either. They were relieved when the American military finally exited the country years ago. The western world contractors and their big business plans followed a short while later, after some strategic localized bombings that helped incentivize them. Hope for their billion-dollar enterprises was long forgotten in the rush to save their collective asses.

The group drove for about five miles under a cloudless, blue sky ringed in the distance with rugged mountains devoid of trees. They entered a stone archway. An impressive twelve-foot-high security gate gave the feeling of a place of great import. All three Americans were nervous.

Kendall was in awe of the strange and foreboding complex they'd just entered. It was clear that someone important lived here. After a short drive down an olive-tree-lined road, their vehicle rounded a bend. All three Americans gave a collective gasp. An enormous building that could only be described as a palace stood on a hill directly in front of them. The austere, stone monolith-like structure seemed to radiate an intense stare, as if to glean every last hidden thought from them.

As they pulled up to the front of the huge formation, Paul Fields turned his head, pretending to look around. When his mouth was inches from Glenn Carson's ear, he quietly whispered, "You know nothing." Carson was relieved that he could deny everything, but that meant the whole burden was on Fields' shoulders. As loyal as he was to his childhood buddy, Carson wasn't going down for this. He didn't have the technical know-how and had never been part of the research and development process. The remarkable but evil contrivance was not his brainchild.

# CHAPTER ELEVEN

The vehicle came to a stop, and General Omar disembarked. His driver came around the back of the truck and opened the backdoor. General Omar looked at the three seated "guests" and commanded, "You will get out now and follow me!" The three passengers scrambled out of the truck and reluctantly followed the general up the stairs and into the building. Columned marble lined the walls, and twinkling chandeliers hung throughout the interior.

The assemblage made their way up a side stairwell, down a hallway, and into a large oval room. Fields found the attempt to replicate the Oval Office in the White House quite amusing. He suppressed a smile by looking down and pressing his lips together.

The room was very large. Suddenly, a door at the back opened, and a tall male in *Kabuli* attire, complete with *qaraqul* hat made from the fur of an aborted Persian lamb fetus, strode into the room. His piercing brown eyes were unfriendly and flashed with anger.

Behind him at a careful distance came two dark-haired, mustachioed young men, obviously brothers. One was of average height with a bulky physique. The other was slightly taller and more muscular. The shorter man's face held a sneer, and there was a decided cruelness about his mouth.

Kendall was surprised that the young men wore western blue jeans. Both men were conversant in English, while the older man's English was only passable. She figured the young men were in their early thirties. From the fearful looks they cast at the older man, she concluded they were his sons.

In deference, or perhaps sheer terror, General Omar stepped to the side of the "guests" and away from the older man, who now directed his gaze at the military officer.

"I am pleased, General Omar. You have done what I ordered."

The general looked relieved that he would be keeping his head for the time being and bowed. "President Shazeb, may I present our guests. Paul Fields, CEO of Orion Premier Net Services, Glenn Carson, CFO of Orion, and Kendall Radcliffe, director of operations at Orion."

At the mention of Kendall's name, the president walked slowly and determinedly to Kendall with his arms behind his back. "I must say, I was not expecting three Orion employees. And a female at that." He clasped his hands together in the front. "This is going to work nicely into my plans. I shall have better control of all of you, and I am sure your company will work extra hard to search for you and bring you back." His eyes roamed Kendall's body and gave her a decidedly creepy feeling. She almost wished she was wearing the full floor-length *burka.* He then walked a short distance in front of the trio, turned, and addressed them as a group.

Throwing his head back and in a haughty manner, he declared, "Let me introduce myself. I am Mujtaba Shazeb, President of Afghanistan. You are all here as my guests. My people will be speaking with each of you separately to determine who is the most knowledgeable about our issue. You see, we are having technical concerns regarding private matters of Afghanistan. Since we are using several of your services and devices, our technical experts have concluded that the issue is with your products. It is so serious that it is affecting the operation and the very well being of our beloved country. We will talk about this more a little later."

He looked over to the younger men and inclined his head. "These are my sons, Saaqib Waqas and Ahmad Akeem. You will see them every day during your visit. Saaqib is my oldest and is very smart with computers. He is in charge of the technology division in my administration and has designed and configured all of our computers and networks."

Saaqib glared at the trio, nodded his head, and directed a pointed stare at Kendall. She gulped. Shazeb continued. "You will not fool Saaqib, so don't even start with the lies."

With a twinkle in his eyes, he said, "Saaqib Waqas means star warrior in Arabic. He is a mighty soldier and knows how to get to the truth. Don't push him."

He pointed to his younger son, the taller of the two, and with warm affection, stated, "Ahmad Akeem is in charge of my security forces. He is a strong and athletic soldier. Most importantly, he is wise. Do not underestimate him." The younger son did not move or acknowledge them.

***********

Paul Fields was prevaricating on how far he could push the Afghans. He decided on one small attempt and cleared his throat. "President Shazeb, we do not understand why we are here. Mr. Carson and I merely run Orion. We do not do any of the day-to-day technical work. Ms. Radcliffe simply administers the business practices by the most efficient means. We are business people, not technology wizards."

President Shazeb stalked over to Fields, wagged his finger, and roared, "Enough! Do not treat me like an idiot! I have seen your impressive résumé, and I know what you are capable of. Now, if you lie to me again, it will not be without consequence. I may decide to remove one of your fingers or have you flogged."

He then turned to his son, Saaqib. "You will take Paul Fields to your department and show him what is happening to Afghanistan's property. Persuade him to work with you to determine the source of the technical issues. Do not inflict bodily harm on him just yet. You must check with me first. We should treat them as our guests for the moment."

The president caught Kendall's thoughtful look and said, "Ah, you do not understand why the more physical of my two sons is not in charge of my security forces? That is very observant of you. You see, I found that while Saaqib is the stricter disciplinarian, he often loses his head and orders immediate punishment, usually severe. With Saaqib in charge, the military was always in need of replacements. He's a bit too enthusiastic, shall we say." He gave a disgustingly loud laugh at his own joke.

"Besides, Saaqib's true strength is in computer science. For some reason, it calms him."

The back door suddenly opened, and a tall, rugged-looking man with a careful gaze stepped in, followed by a woman wearing a full *hijab.* The woman quickly looked around, spotted Kendall, and moved to her side, quietly awaiting further orders.

The president looked delighted at the interruption and exclaimed, "Ah, Rashid, my son. Come in." He turned to his "guests." "This is my sons' childhood friend, Rashid Sharif. He is practically a member of the family. I think of him as my own son. He is a trusted advisor to all of us, and a gentle and loyal servant of the people. He keeps my sons in line and, most importantly, away from each other's throats. They do like to fight ... especially Saaqib. Rashid can beat them both, so he keeps the peace."

Rashid gave an ever-so-slight bow and raised his eyes. In a flash of a second, Kendall could see that Rashid had coolly appraised all of them. She was intrigued. For some reason, he kept his thoughts and actions hidden. She realized there was far more to this man than his extreme good looks, flashing brown eyes, and unmanageable, thick, wavy hair. She felt a fluttering within her that took her breath away. She quickly looked down and hoped the attraction signals translated only as curiosity to the others. She was furious at the mutinous feelings coming from her body, but welcomed the distraction from thoughts of Jeremy Levy.

President Shazeb crossed over to Kendall again. In the traditional Afghanistan term when addressing a female, he began, "Kendalljan, this young woman is Doctor Maysah Siddrajan. She will check on you every day to see to your medical and female needs. Afghanistan has progressed quite far in the last fifteen years. Half of the country speaks some English, and we now have many female doctors."

Glenn Carson had been trying to suppress a cough, and it now devolved into a major coughing fit. Carson's color was pale, and he looked as if he might faint. The president stepped back and looked aghast at him. Addressing him in formal tones, he said, "Carson *Khan,* you look quite ill. This is not good. I will not have you sick while you are my guest." Never mind that three people had been murdered so far under his orders.

Carson croaked, "I'm fine." Everyone could see that he was anything but. The president gave a dismissive wave to the doctor. "Go, Doctor Siddrajan, and take Carson *Khan* with you. Please have him checked out. He should remain at the Base's clinic until he is thoroughly well. Be sure to post a trustworthy guard, someone who already knows of his presence. I do not need to remind you that the existence of our guests is to be kept secret for now." He looked over at his younger son. "Ahmad, please escort the doctor and Carson *Khan* back to the base." Ahmad's eyes flashed in anger. He did not want this babysitting duty, but he was too afraid of his father to offer an alternative. He strode over to Carson, took his arm in a vicious grip, and led the little group out of the room.

Kendall caught the sly wink and smirk Rashid gave Ahmad as he passed by. Ahmad seemed to relax a bit. She realized that Rashid did have some sort of calming power on at least this son. She stored this information away.

The president was tired of the meeting. He barked, "Saaqib, take Fields *Khan* to your offices and thoroughly explain our issues."

They left the room, leaving only the president, Kendall, Rashid, and their original escort, General Omar. Shazeb looked at Kendall and motioned towards the back of the room, to an early 1900s French two-seater sofa decorated in Afghanistan ceremonial fabric. "You, go sit there while we talk." Kendall frowned and wondered what assignment she would be given and who her minder would be. She half hoped yet feared it would be the rakish Rashid Sharif.

The men spoke in low urgent tones. The president ordered General Omar to stay with him, so they could discuss short-term plans for their "guests." The Afghan leader decided that once their guests' luggage had been thoroughly searched, they would be allowed their personal belongings, sans electronic and communication devices. He figured their personal effects would bring them some measure of comfort and hopefully entice them to cooperate so as to speed up their exit plans. Mostly, he hoped this little measure of conciliation would incite Fields to come clean on Orion's technical trickery.

However, he had underestimated the depth and breadth of Orion's electronic machinations. The fact was that Orion executives couldn't afford to tell the truth. Even Orion did not fully understand the scope of the electronic tentacles that had been laid.

Omar was finally dispatched to work on the details that had been discussed.

There were now only President Shazeb and Rashid Sharif left, with Kendall still awaiting her fate at the back of the room. He leaned in toward the good-looking younger man and tapped him on the chest.

"Rashid, I want you to get to know *Kendalljan.* Be her friend. You are very good at putting people at ease. Learn her secrets. She must know a lot about Orion Premier Net Services. Find out everything about the company. Romance her, and make her see that you are on her side. Win her over.

"My sons will be mad with jealousy. They bicker enough between them. I hope this will not be a problem. You know you will have to share her eventually. Now, go work your charm on her. If you stay out of the public eye, do not be concerned with being alone with her. Since she is a westerner, we must treat her so in order to gain her confidence. Understand?"

"Yes." Sharif put his hand over his heart and gave a slight nod. The president nodded, turned, and headed for the door from which he had entered.

Sharif pondered the president's scheme and decided it would fit nicely into his plans.

# CHAPTER TWELVE

THE BROAD-SHOULDERED, DARK-HAIRED MAN APPROACHED Kendall and stood before her. She was at first nervous but then quickly angered as she remembered the Orion people were all there against their will. He stared at her for so long that she finally had to say something. Her voice was dripping with sarcasm and annoyance. She stood up.

"Well, what is my assignment? What do I need to do to go home?" She figured if they had intended to kill her, she would already be dead. So, she could afford to show her true feelings, which at the moment happened to be great displeasure. She wasn't even afraid any more. Somehow she could tell that this man was a lot gentler than his appearance. She felt safe in his presence. His countenance was one of quiet control and thoughtfulness. He certainly did not reveal a lot of emotion. Rashid Sharif was not saying a word. He was contemplating his options and sizing her up at the same time.

"Well, are you going to stand there staring at me?"

He smiled, and she realized that he was even better looking than she originally thought. He had a twinkle in his eyes that flashed and sparkled with humor. She felt the urge to laugh with him, but gave herself a mental slap.

"May I call you Kendall?"

"Yes, if it will get me out of here. Why are we here? Why am I here?"

He frowned. "Yes, it is unfortunate that you are here. It was never intended that you be brought here. You are what is called collateral damage. President Shazeb only ever wanted Paul Fields. Your presence is a problem. The only thing you have in your favor is that you are an Orion employee. I suggest that you cooperate and make the best of it, or you could be dealt with in a most unfortunate manner."

She had no doubt what he was referring to. Yet somehow, she wasn't afraid of him.

"Fine. I can cooperate—even help, if need be. What are you supposed to do with me?"

"I'm supposed to get to know you to see if you have any information that might solve our problem."

"Well, it sounds like your system has technical issues or maybe even a virus, if you believe that state secrets are getting out through your systems. Why would you think it was Orion Premier that caused this?"

"I'm not technically proficient, so I cannot begin to explain the intricacies of the issue. Let's just hope that Fields and Saaqib can solve this. Why don't you and I take a walk down to the president's stables? He has some of the finest stallions."

They exited the oval room and headed downstairs, with Sharif leading the way. As they stepped out into the bright sunlight from a side door, Kendall was blinded for a moment. She stopped to get her bearings, causing Sharif to slow to a stop. He gave her a questioning look. She decided to get the jump on any interrogation and barrage him with a lot of questions. *Two can play this game, and I can be charming to boot!*

"I'm going to call you Rashid. How come your English is so perfect? You must have been educated in the West."

"Very astute, Kendall. I attended a university in England."

"Where did you grow up?"

He threw his hands out in a wide arc. "Close to here. My father ran President Shazeb's farms. He was the manager, and oversaw the operations. My mother worked for the Shazeb family, helping with the children and doing light accounting projects. They were both very smart and loyal people. Soon after the Taliban arrived, my parents were killed when one of Shazeb's farms was set on fire and completely destroyed."

"How horrible for you! Why would the Taliban have destroyed the president's farm?

Rashid said with a wry smile, "They didn't like the crop that was being grown."

"What a waste of humanity, not to mention vegetables!"

"Who said anything about vegetables?"

It suddenly dawned on her what the "crop" had been. Poppies! *Good Lord, President Shazeb was a former drug lord.* She felt quite naïve and chided herself for being such a dolt. *You really must get out more. Hey, look at this. I already am!* She felt better and continued with her questions. "So, the president felt guilty that you lost your parents, and he took you in?"

"Something like that, only this family does not feel guilty about anything. Most things are justifiable in their eyes." He gave a long sigh as he decided that full disclosure was in order. "As a matter of fact, I also lost my four brothers and sisters and the poor excuse for a hut we lived in. The president lost his wife and two of his children. Because I got along so well with his surviving sons, Ahmad and Saaqib, he took me in more as a companion for his children. I was a little older than the boys. I would accompany them to school. Otherwise, I would never have gone to school."

"How old were you when your fam—when the fire happened?"

"I was twelve. I became a man shortly after that. There was no time for play. I soon learned that if I was going to get far in this world, I would need to listen and do as I was told."

Kendall felt sad at the events of his early life, and guilty for the easy, charming childhood she had had.

"Wow! I'm so sorry for you. That's a tragic story. And now the president owns you, and you do his bidding."

Sharif gave her a hard stare. "If that's what you think, then I have succeeded." She had no idea what he was referring to. Before she could follow up on his comment, they arrived at the stables and walked around the side to where the paddock opened into a back meadow. Several horses were grazing, their tales flicking flies off their sleek coats.

"Gorgeous, horses! They look well groomed. I wish I knew how to ride."

"If you are here long enough, I will teach you a few things."

She looked over to him, "How long do you think we'll be here?"

He kicked a tuft of grass at his feet, sending pebbles flying, "Kendall, you should know that the president is very serious. He knows there is funny business going on with your company's products. He is planning a lengthy stay for all of you, or at least Paul Fields, if need be. He's asked me to find out everything about you and your company."

She sucked in a breath and her eyes grew wide with terror. "Is my life in danger?"

"I believe it is. That is why you must please the president at all costs. In fact, if Fields angers him, he could take it out on you."

"What should I do?"

"You must become his friend. Maybe even hint that you would like to stay. Kendall, this is for your very survival."

"But he kidnapped us and murdered the crew." She shivered.

"Oh, grow up! Do something about it! Now it's your turn to pull one over on him. Just figure out how to do it."

She was shocked at his bluntness and completely puzzled as to his motives. He had gotten into her head, and she was now thoroughly confused. In a bitter and vicious tone, she spat out, "You sound very practiced, Mr. Sharif! Do you just go around killing people and getting even when you are in the mood?" She whirled around to stalk into the meadow. He caught up with her and grabbed her arm, swinging her around to look at him.

"Give me some credit, Ms. Radcliffe. What I am asking you to do is to use all of the skills you possess to help yourself."

"I have principles, and I'm not going to behave in an undignified, uncivilized manner. You're asking me to lower myself to your level. Well, I won't do it! You all can go to hell! I'll figure out a way to get out of here."

He threw back his head and laughed. "Figure out a way out of here? You need to figure out how to keep your head! At the moment, you mean nothing to the president other than a pretty face. He could order your death tonight! I suggest you get down off that high horse and learn to play the game."

She considered her options. "Fine! What do I do right now ... today?"

He was encouraged. "Well, I can help. Do you cook?"

"Yes. Western meals."

"Okay. This afternoon I'll suggest that you help in the kitchen. In the meantime, are you familiar with the Book of Judith?"

That came out of left field. Where the heck was he going with that question, she wondered?

"Yes, as a matter of fact. It was required reading during an undergrad religious studies class ... The Bible as Literature. As I recall, the Book of Judith is one of the books of the Apocrypha ... the books in the Old Testament that were not recognized as authentic or handed down from God. The story of Judith is seen as more of a legend."

"Do you remember what she was known for?"

"Absolutely! We should all be that brave! On the night before a decisive battle that her tribe was not expected to win, she goes into the other camp and seduces the leader. She cuts off his head while he's sleeping, and her tribe is saved. How do you know about it?"

"I majored in religious studies and minored in political science."

"What does the Book of Judith have to do with me? Are you suggesting that I go on the offense and cut off President Shazeb's head?" She shook her finger at him. "If so, I'm not interested. I'll take my chances on the defense."

"I'm not saying that at all. I'm merely telling you that it would be very helpful to you if you learned a little about President Shazeb. What is the saying? 'Knowledge is power.' If you get to know him, he'll let his guard down. You can seize the advantage."

"And how do I know you aren't trying to get me killed or that this isn't some big game for you? Why would you want to help me? I don't even know you. You're the enemy, you know!"

"Am I the enemy? As a matter of fact, I've been waiting for your little group for some time. The fact that you are here makes me believe that all will be right in the future."

"What are you hoping for, a promotion?"

Sharif smiled. "Actually, I am ... sort of. We will speak more later, at dinner. Now, I'm going to return you to the base, and will see you this evening."

Kendall felt deflated and perplexed. This man spoke in riddles and double-talk. While she couldn't be sure, he didn't seem to harbor any resentment toward her or wish her ill will. But she got the distinct impression that he was holding back on a key bit of information that she needed to know.

# CHAPTER THIRTEEN

"You are very quiet this evening," Rashid whispered to Kendall. She had barely eaten and was picking at her succulent lamb, basmati rice, and *naan.* Rather than the traditional *Dastarkhan* floor spread where everyone sits on the floor and eats with their hands, President Shazeb was anxious to appear enlightened and up on the latest western trends. They were seated at a large traditional dining room table, and the president, his sons and their wives, and the few military officers who knew of the Orion people joined them. The Afghan wives said nothing and appeared fearful, as if they would be severely punished if they spoke out of turn ... or maybe even if they spoke at all. Kendall had smiled at the women, but couldn't summon the strength to carry on a charade of normalcy in the form of polite conversation.

Kendall was not fond of curry, but loved the juicy *khameerbob* pasta dumplings that reminded her of the *dim sum* dishes she enjoyed at home. She took a nibble of a piece of pomegranate and turned her head towards Rashid.

"I'm just not very hungry. It's probably that I'm not used to your local cuisine."

"It's all very tasty, Kendall. I see you have not tried the *kalah chuquki* directly in front of you."

To Kendall, it looked like a blob of something that was deep fried. It looked heavy and rich. Her stomach roiled. But she didn't want to offend anyone. She poked it, and saw that it had a crispy outer shell. "It looks like large fish and chips. What is it, if I may ask?"

She noticed the twinkle in his eyes as he remarked in deadpan tone, "Deep fried bird heads". *Oh Lord,* the very thought made her want to gag.

The president sitting two seats to her left at the head of the table, noticed her small appetite. With a booming voice, he commented, "Kendalljan, I hope you are not ill too? It is most unfortunate that Carson *Khan* could not join us."

Kendall forced herself to perk up, and shook her head at the Aghan leader.

"I feel fine, sir. I'm just a little tired from the travel." She wanted to add *and the stress,* but didn't dare. After being told she was collateral damage, she couldn't afford to offend her "host."

"Did you enjoy your meeting with Rashid? Were you able to tour some of our lovely grounds?"

Shazeb's two sons sitting across from each other immediately glared at one another and listened with rapt attention. The salacious looks they cast at Kendall made her fearful and relieved that she had been paired with Rashid earlier in the day.

She could see that the two sons hated each other. They were rivals and probably competed for everything ... starting with women. But they clearly underestimated Rashid and saw him as nothing more than their loyal friend, carrying out his duties at the behest of the president. In fact, they weren't jealous of Rashid at all. Rashid never had women around him, and didn't seem to even notice a woman. What they didn't understand was that Rashid's interest was more subtle. Because he was not a blood relative, he was never going to risk the displeasure of the two brothers, not to mention their father, the president. Rashid had obligations and responsibilities far beyond the daily activities of the leader's household. Besides, the president had always looked to Rashid to keep the peace between the brothers. That was Rashid's number one directive.

What baffled her most was that the president seemed to enjoy the sibling loathing. He took pleasure at the obvious ill will between the two. One could even say that he stoked it for his own amusement.

Kendall looked up from her musings. "Yes, we went to the stables and out to the meadow." Kendall caught the not-so-subtle wink President Shazeb threw to Rashid. He clapped his hands together.

"Excellent! We are all getting to know each another. Kendalljan, you are free to visit the stables any time you want, so long as you are accompanied by someone ... preferably Rashid."

Shazeb turned his attention to Paul Fields, and his eyes darkened. "Well, Fields *Khan,* did you get a full tour of our computer systems? Are you impressed?"

Fields knew enough not to antagonize the leader. He nodded, wiping his mouth on his white-on-ivory linen quatrefoil patterned napkin embossed with the family crest. "Please call me Paul. I am very impressed. Your son has done a remarkable job in the system design."

The president turned to his eldest. "And what do you think of Fields—er, uh, Paul, Saaqib?"

His oldest son was quick to show his importance and competence and sought to embellish his meeting with Paul Fields. "Paul is an expert at computer systems, and made some good suggestions for maintaining our systems in peak order."

The Afghan leader was irritated at all the fluff and pandering. "Fine, fine, fine. But I expect a full report tomorrow on how we can, shall we say, improve our processes. If progress is made tomorrow, I think I might make time to contact your home office." With that proclamation, the president turned to Rashid.

"Rashid, my son, you should take Kendall out to the back gardens. There is a full moon tonight." Shazeb gave a nauseating laugh that sent a shiver down Kendall's spine. But for tonight, she was elated at the thought that someone might finally learn of her fate.

She knew that her friend and neighbor, Heather Jacobs, would come looking for her ... eventually. But they usually spoke only a couple times a week. They had a girls' night out once a month, and it was set for two days from now. Kendall could only hope that word got out to either Heather or Gwen Albertson soon, and that the Orion three would be saved. She didn't have much family. Her father had passed away from cancer a few years earlier. Her mother lived by herself in a beachfront cottage in the picturesque seaside community of Redondo, south of Seattle. Several times a year, Kendall took her mother to Sunday brunch at Salty's in Redondo. The nostalgia brought tears to Kendall's eyes. Would she ever see her friends and mother again? This whole surreal experience made her very angry. Her father had always taught her to dig deep when the chips were down, to fight as if her very life depended on it. She had the feeling she was going to need that strength in the very near future.

# CHAPTER FOURTEEN

KENDALL AND RASHID STROLLED OUT to the wide patio in the back of the palace. He could tell she was sad, maybe even despondent. She spoke little but was willing to listen to him. In order to take her mind off her present circumstances, he told her of the sacred shrine of the *Blue Mosque* and the giant Buddha statues in the Bamiyan Valley that were destroyed by the Taliban. He suggested that if they had time, they should visit those sites. He also regaled her with the ancient stories of *Alexander the Great,* and how his cultural influence lasted for centuries. Rashid was very proud of the fact that *Alexander the Great* spoke of Afghanistan as *"easy to march into but hard to march out of".*

"Yes. You must not underestimate the difficulty of leaving Afghanistan."

"And why is that?"

"Ah!" He was delighted Kendall was finally showing an interest in the conversation. "I am sure you noticed that here in Kabul we are in a valley surrounded almost entirely by mountains. Basically, Afghanistan is landlocked. There is no escaping via a nearby seaport."

"And why would I care about that? Are you telling me that escape is all but hopeless, Mr. Sharif?"

"Oh, please, Kendall. We are now friends, and you must call me Rashid. And no, escape is not hopeless. But you must have the right plan."

"Which is ...?"

"Afghanistan is at the center of several major trade routes. But some of our neighbors are not exactly friends. For you, they could be dangerous."

"Like who?"

"Well, Pakistan is east of Afghanistan, and Iran is southwest. The easiest way out of Kabul is through the nearby Khyber Pass. But that is mountainous and leads you right into Pakistan. The route would be too obvious. However, there are several major rivers that run near Kabul. The largest and best way out would be by the Helmand River. It's the longest river in Afghanistan. You could get to it in about an hour, but it flows right into the Helmand Province." He didn't bother to tell her that navigating that river would also mean encountering at least one hydroelectric dam, depending on which tributary one took.

"That sounds good."

"Not necessarily. Are you familiar with the Helmand Province?"

"No. Should I be?"

His voice was wry when he responded, "It's only the largest region in the world in the production of opium, which also happens to be owned by your host, President Shazeb. You would be headed straight into the lion's den ... again, the enemy."

Kendall sighed and threw up her arms. "I don't know why you are talking to me of escape. It seems impossible, and I think you're having a laugh at my expense. Why would you help me escape and jeopardize your head too?"

Rashid carefully weighed his response and intoned, "My motives are not exactly to help you, so much as they are to expedite my plans."

She was frustrated and, frankly, scared. "Your plans! Your plans! What are you referring to? What plans? And why do you have plans?" she ranted.

He realized he was getting a little head of himself. He grabbed her arm and moved close to her so that his face was only inches from hers. His voice was barely a whisper, "Kendall, you must trust me. There is more going on here than I can explain this evening. It's getting late. I shall reveal more tomorrow. Please trust me that only I can help you." He pulled her *hajib* down and stroked the escaping tendrils of hair in a smooth motion and ran his finger down her cheek in a soft caress. He smelled of exotic juices. She wanted to touch him, but didn't trust herself.

She contemplated the alternatives. There was no way she was going to accept everything he said as the truth. But she was willing to listen or at least appear as if she believed him. "Maybe. But I thought you were supposed to be finding out about me? You haven't really asked me any questions ... personally or professionally. Why? I'm confused."

He was getting annoyed. "Let's see. You travel a lot for Orion Premier, testifying in court cases. Your good friends are Gwen Albertson from Orion and Heather Jacobs, your neighbor. Your Jewish boyfriend, Jeremy Levy, recently broke up with you when his mother forced him to quit his job in Seattle to move to Florida and run the family banking business. She has also promised to release his trust funds. How am I doing so far?"

Kendall gasped, and croaked, "How can you possibly know those things? Not even my friends know about my breakup with Jeremy yet. Do Shazeb and his security people know all of this too? Why?"

Rashid knew he had shocked her and shook his head. "No. They know nothing."

"But how do you know these things, if they do not?"

He sighed, "It's very complicated, Kendall. I only told you these things so that you would believe there's a larger plan. I will tell you more tomorrow."

"I don't know if I can handle it."

"If you want to get out of here alive, you'll have to. Also, uh, there's one more thing."

"Oh God, what now?"

"You must pay attention to the sounds you hear tonight. There is a nightly ritual that was canceled last night."

She was almost too afraid to inquire further, but pushed ahead, "And what is it?"

"Punishments are handed out in the courtyard near your rooms. You can't see them, because you don't have windows, but you will be able to hear the screams. Please don't be frightened. They sound awful. But so long as you are careful and don't confide in anyone else, you should be safe."

Her eyes widened with horror. "I'm in a nightmare that I'll never get out of. I must be dreaming."

He grabbed her face between his large, strong hands. "Stop it! I'm only telling you this to save you from freaking out tonight! Punishment is a way of life around here. Shazeb thinks that it keeps the citizens—and more importantly, the military—in line ... through fear. The person is whipped and then may or may not be beheaded."

She was furious at the revelations and pushed his arms away. "And you partake of these activities?"

"As a matter of fact, I don't. But there is nothing I can do about it. There are many willing participants. This activity happens to be the highlight of Saaqib's day. He can't wait to get in there and have a go at several prisoners. The president expects me to ... again ... keep the peace and make sure the punishments do not get out of hand."

"What do you mean, 'get out of hand'?"

"That the whole process deteriorates into a killing frenzy of the guilty as well as the innocent."

Kendall was stunned beyond belief, rendering her speechless for a moment. "How can you people live like this? What are you ... a bunch of animals?"

Now it was Rashid's turn to show anger. "You call us a bunch of animals with the types of crimes the U.S. has? Don't judge this country, Kendall. There's actually very little crime here. When crime happens, punishment is handed out swiftly and severely. It's just a different way of life than what you are used to. It is actually a very effective way to maintain an ordered society."

She felt so sad, trying to take this all in. "But what do people do to deserve flogging or beheading?"

"Usually, they steal or lie or commit adultery. If they steal, a finger is often cut off."

"What do they have to do to be beheaded?"

"Kill someone, act against the president or country, or take off with another man's wife."

"Oh, is that all?" Kendall retorted with all the sarcasm she could muster. Then it dawned on her that their discussions and talk of "plans" fit within that definition. "And don't our discussions fall within those parameters, Rashid?"

"That's why we need to be careful." He grabbed her hand and led her to his parked jeep. Paul Fields had long since been returned to the military compound. They drove back to the base in silence. As she stepped out of the vehicle, Rashid came over to her side and whispered, "Please believe me, Kendall. I will not hurt you. We can help each other. Look at me! Can you not see that I speak the truth? I'll see you after the morning meal tomorrow." He gently kissed the top of her head.

***********

Kendall lay in bed turning from side to side, trying to find a comfortable position. She felt thoroughly miserable at all the events of the day. She was overwhelmed with the brutal Afghan men she had met, and the things she had been told. She was terrified of the unknown. She also worried about her mother, who would be expecting her biweekly checkin call. Her head was reeling at the things she had heard today.

But deep down, she did feel a measure of comfort with Rashid. She believed he was a good and kind person ... maybe even "civilized" when compared to the other men she had met earlier. He had apparently learned to adapt through difficult circumstances. Her instincts told her to trust him, and that he had far more resources than she could ever imagine.

***********

Her body gave a jerk at the first shriek. Someone outside was screaming in pain! Amidst the piercing cries of torture, Kendall could hear raucous laughter. The horror continued for almost an hour but seemed to last an eternity. She felt she had descended into the very depths of Hell itself. Her body was frozen with alarm, and she began to cry in huge sobs of fear and panic. She fell into an exhausted and fitful sleep.

***********

Sometime later, Rashid, too, lay in his warm, comfortable bed and replayed the day's events. He liked Kendall, and realized that she could be a useful tool for him. He knew how to manipulate her, given her current stressful existence. But he struggled with how far he should push it. He actually felt a personal connection with her, and that really bothered him. He was a professional, had no time for a woman in his life, and was not about to jeopardize his mission. He had a goal that was bigger than himself ... bigger than the president ... even bigger than Afghanistan. He must be careful tomorrow, think clearly, and practically, and above all proceed cautiously and logically. He knew exactly what he would do tomorrow. But he, too, fell into an exhausted and fitful sleep ... with dreams of a lovely chestnut-haired, green-eyed female tormenting him.

# CHAPTER FIFTEEN

Daniel Blumfeld took the call mid-morning on his prepaid disposable cell phone. He was shocked to hear that Paul Fields and Glenn Carson had been kidnapped when their plane returning to Seattle had been taken over mid-flight. The entire crew had been slaughtered. *Holy Shit!* he thought.

He was in over his head. He hadn't minded providing a conduit for information, but he never thought he would be privy to news like this. He had not heard anything on the news or in email this morning. He could only conclude that either Orion security was keeping a lid on this, or the facts were not yet known.

The caller was insistent that a third employee had been abducted as well, a Kendall Radcliffe. Oh my God, he knew her! He had worked with her when the company's remote storage datacenter was set up. He genuinely liked and respected her and considered her a friend. They had shared many meals when she traveled to the company's datacenter site.

Daniel was at the datacenter alone most of the day under tight security conditions. A few employees came and went during the day. As a condition to being hired, he had agreed to live on the premises. He had a nice setup in the loft of the oversized warehouse-type building. His mother and sister had helped him decorate, so the open-concept living area was comfortable and spacious. He was not allowed to entertain visitors on site. His family could visit, but they were restricted to his living area.

His personal computers were in his living space, and he had the latest in secure servers and network tools. He had made sure that no one could trace any of his personal messages, let alone recreate his key strokes. He hadn't received a PhD in Computer Science from MIT for nothing. He was repaying the people who funded his education, and therefore he had agreed to this "arrangement" for a few years. Since he was being rewarded handsomely and had little chance of being caught, he thought he had a pretty sweet deal. His offshore retirement account was growing at an astonishing rate.

The only drawback was that there was no night life. He was in a small town surrounded by acres and acres of farmland. There was no action to be had. Still, he felt he could handle this for a few years, and he resigned himself to saving as much money as he could until he could no longer stand the living arrangements—most particularly, the isolation. He spent his personal time playing computer games and perfecting his expertise.

In the field of computer science, Daniel was considered to be an expert in the time complexity of an algorithm. He admitted to being able to randomize the binary search-tree process, thereby hiding the scope of the resulting elementary operations. What very few people knew, including most of the Orion research and development group, was that by manipulating the IP address to send and receive at random, he could open a hidden portal or "window" on an email address, website, or cell phone. He could then instruct the personal account or number at will to stream data that should have been totally and completely private. It could not be tracked or traced back to the company, and the "victim" had no way of knowing there were eyes on its data. Further, if the unsuspecting person checked his email via a smart phone, a permanent conduit would open to all of the text messages on that cell phone and any other that it communicated with, giving the peeper access to even more accounts and data. Daniel's high-tech spying tool was code named *Prophecy.*

The *coup de gras* was the USB device that was given out as a company freebie. It was embedded with *Prophecy* and established a link to the hardware into which it was attached, and automatically streamed the entire content back to Orion Technologies ... via Daniel. It was like a creeping vine of streaming data. Truly, the gift that keeps on giving.

The streaming process took place automatically using special servers housed within the datacenter. As the massive content was received, search parameters immediately highlighted and separated out critical data. The source was reduced to an algorithm. The pertinent information was parsed through query and then forwarded on to Daniel, with the full awareness of Fields and Carson. Based on information from the executives, Daniel knew what to escalate. The beauty was that anyone reviewing the data would have no idea who it belonged to or what it all meant. They would simply think these were internal, proprietary documents of Orion Premier Net Services.

The whole process was working great, and tons of secrets were pouring in every day, much of it proprietary in nature. Orion Premier got the jump on its competitors.

But for the extreme invasion of privacy on several levels and the countless laws being broken, Daniel would have liked to obtain a patent on the process. He lamented that he had done the work under the watchful eyes of Orion executive Paul Fields, rather than as an independent operative or consultant.

As a way to compensate himself for the untold millions of dollars lost in foregoing a patent, Daniel allowed himself to decide who could know and access the streaming data. When the company datacenter was first set up and the new technology *Prophecy* activated daily, he had rationalized this as a harmless endeavor, so long as he granted it to only trustworthy people with the highest and best motives. He had even built in a safeguard whereby, should information unexpectedly get into the wrong hands or be used for evil intent, he could "lock out" the curious eyes permanently. But that would work only so long as he had the technical know-how to detect other eyes.

He also viewed his creation as a form of artificial intelligence that could literally save the world, if used responsibly. Orion executives had commissioned the project during Daniel's two summer internships under the guise of a technical security research project.

The Orion leaders were, in fact, using the "anonymous eyes," or *Prophecy* technology, for their own purposes. It was Daniel's opinion he wasn't responsible for what Orion was doing. But Daniel had not revealed to the Orion people in the know—namely, Paul Fields and Glenn Carson, the two trusted childhood friends—that he could actually view what information was being looked at, by whom, and on what date.

Daniel knew that the Orion executives had allowed another entity to routinely stream certain data from multiple sources. He tracked the information being gathered and noted the observer. He was quite surprised that the Orion principals were in bed with the devil himself and wondered how much time would elapse before the whole thing blew up and somebody went public or got caught with proprietary information.

In the meantime, he was working his own deal on the side, allowing his "benefactor" to gather information from various accounts.

Daniel was extraordinarily intelligent, but he also had a practical side. The caller, his "benefactor," instructed him to pass an anonymous message to the head of security. He had to figure out how to do it fast and in secret. He was located some 100 miles from the company headquarters. How was he supposed to get an urgent message to security in Seattle?

With some calm, focused thinking, he came up with a plan. Using a prepaid cell phone that he had purchased with cash, he phoned in an order to a messenger service, using a fake employee name but the correct company account number. He arranged to have the messenger meet him in the lobby of one of the busier company buildings. The message was all typed out, along with the customized Orion messenger slip. Daniel drove to Seattle in a little over an hour, exceeding the speed limit whenever he could. He donned a khaki jungle hat and his thick black plastic-rimmed prescription glasses that he never wore in public. He knew he would fit right in, and no one would recognize him.

The instructions for the messenger were to deliver the plain envelope addressed to Eric McDougall at the latter's building.

The plan went without a hitch. The weather was perfect, the state troopers a rare site, usually heading the opposite direction. All precautions were taken. Daniel used driving gloves when handling the envelope and messenger slip, and made it to the agreed upon meeting place with five minutes to spare. He had left the datacenter around 10:30 a.m. and told the few employees who happened to be working there today that he was out pricing hardware—something he frequently did—and would then go to lunch and be back before 1:00 p.m.

He handed off the envelope to the messenger while assuming an attitude of youth, irresponsibility, average intelligence, talk of parties and goofing off, and a good measure of English slang ... all things the real Daniel would never do. He watched the messenger get in his car and head towards McDougall's building, and fervently hoped Mickey was in the office today.

Finally, he walked out of the building, down the street, and into a nearby restaurant where he stopped at the restroom and removed his hat, glasses, and gloves and placed them in his large blue backpack. The blue backpack had been rolled up and stashed in the empty red backpack he had carried into the Orion building for his meeting with the messenger.

Daniel then walked through the restaurant and exited out back into an alley. He headed to a parking garage some half a mile away and, more importantly, out of range of the company surveillance cameras. He made sure to pay with cash, leaving no trace of his trip.

It was now noon, and Daniel was sweating bullets. He was about thirty minutes out of the city of Seattle and would be back at the Datacenter in another thirty. Now that his mission was over, with the hat, glasses, driving gloves, and the two backpacks having been stowed away in his trunk, he was replaying everything to see if he had forgotten any details. He felt like he'd just committed a criminal act, but he was simply delivering a message. This was all too cloak-and-dagger for him.

He pulled into the datacenter parking lot and drove around back to his designated spot. He entered the building from his private stairwell, grabbed a banana, and headed down to the floor where it looked as if he had been having lunch in his upstairs quarters.

Of course, if anyone checked surveillance, they would see the time his car drove in. But he felt that was unlikely. Besides, the surveillance footage was on a loop, and would record over the top of the existing data within a week. The one employee he encountered on the datacenter floor amidst the rows of servers, heading to his office, appeared bored and merely grunted as they passed.

Daniel sat in front of his computer screen and breathed a sigh of relief.

He was dying to know what would happen next and figured, at the very least, that some sort of public announcement would be made. At the same time, there was a sense of foreboding deep in Daniel's gut.

He had unleashed a piece of information that could get him fired, arrested, and even killed. If caught, he couldn't begin to tell the truth. There were too many operatives with their customized piece of information, not knowing of the others. Any of them could come after him. He couldn't tell them about each other, because some of them didn't know that he had knowledge of their existence within the Orion Datacenter world. The final complication was that Fields and Carson didn't have a clue as to the scope of information Daniel was routinely monitoring as it flowed in and out of the servers.

Each of the parties to the illegal snooping thought they were the only ones to have knowledge about and be using the unregistered, illegitimate intellectual property technology. Removed from it all was Daniel, watching and waiting ... but most importantly, keeping his nose clean. He was not doing anything with the data other than to isolate it and place it on a secure server that was used only by Paul Fields. Daniel simply observed who was doing what, and had found the whole thing amusing ... until now.

***********

Out in the datacenter ether, another set of eyes was observing the proceedings of the past two days from his shadowy world. He was fascinated at the fast-paced unfolding of this worldwide drama. He was eager to share his knowledge and knew that he would be rewarded for his work. Now, he just had to figure out how much to share and how to get it to the right people.

# CHAPTER SIXTEEN

Mickey sat at his desk in shock. He held the recently delivered note in his hand. It was short and to-the-point:

> Paul Fields, Glenn Carson, and Kendall Radcliffe have been kidnapped. Control of their plane was taken over by international operatives. International forces are working to free them. Wait for further instructions.

It was 3:00 p.m. when Mickey's admin handed him the innocuous looking plain white envelope. He frowned, and his fingers fumbled as he attempted to open it. He read it and sat back. After a few minutes—when his mind froze—he could only think, *"What the fuck?"* He didn't know if he was more surprised at the kidnapping, or that Kendall Radcliffe was part of the abducted group. And who, he wondered, were the "international forces" that were working to free them?

Mickey quickly scanned the note into his computer and fired off an email to FBI Special Agent Zanders, attaching the scanned note. He used a well-known high-level security utility that scrambled the message and attachment. Zanders, possessing the same high-tech scrambling software, received the email and attachment, both of which were then unscrambled.

Neither of them knew that the so-called high-tech scrambling security device was no barrier for Daniel's brilliant mind.

Within five minutes Mickey's phone was ringing. He answered it before the first ring, noting the caller ID, and barked into the phone, "Zanders, what do you make of this note?"

"How did you get it? Who delivered it? Do you have the envelope?"

"It was handed to me by my admin five minutes ago. The envelope looks like plain white stationery store stock."

"Okay. Please preserve it. Place it inside something, like a large Baggie or bigger envelope. Try not to touch it anymore. We'll be running it for DNA and fingerprints."

Zanders took a deep breath and continued, "I'm going to fly out there. I should be in Seattle late tonight; I'll touch base with you late this evening for any updates, and will meet you first thing in the morning. In the meantime, you need to trace the delivery of the envelope. Talk to the messenger service, the front desk of your building, and the messenger person who delivered it. Get the exact time when the service took possession of the envelope. If this is your usual messenger service, there should be some form or something that accompanies the envelope, I assume. Get that, too.

"Now, who is this Kendall Radcliffe?"

"That's what has me confounded. She's the new director of operations. It's an upper-level position, but not one that would routinely have her crossing paths with the company executives ... so far as I know."

"Damn! Do you think this Kendall Radcliffe is in on the kidnapping? Get me all the information you have on her by the time I see you in the morning. Take a look at her employee file, and let's retrace her steps for the past few months or even earlier. I want to know who her friends are—particularly at Orion Premier—any boyfriend, husband, or kids, and anything else that you run across that might be useful. I'll run a criminal background check and pull her passport records showing her international travel. I'll talk to you in about six hours."

Mickey was a bit overwhelmed, and he no longer cared that he be in charge of the investigation. It had taken on international dimensions. Why the hell had the three Orion people been taken? He wasn't through with Zanders.

"Wait a minute, Zanders!"

"What? I've got a shitload of things to do in the next hour, including lining up my ride."

"What do we do about notifying the public? I don't think we can keep this quiet any longer. The families need to know some sort of status, and the board of directors need to be involved."

Zanders frowned and rubbed his throbbing temple. "What do you suggest?"

"Let's get out in front of the issue. I'll call our Public Relations Department and get going on a press release providing a vague statement that the executives were on an international trip, and their plane experienced mechanical issues. That it was forced to land in a remote place, and that rescue efforts are now in progress."

"Hmm ... not bad. The country of origin will either be laughing that Orion is scrambling to explain the disappearance of the plane and employees, or it will realize that we may be on to them, because of the reference to an international trip.

The trip was domestic, and therefore, how would we know at this stage that the Orion people are out of the country? That'll drive them nuts!"

"Yep, I agree. I'll call the families and again give them a general update, and let them know that a press release will be issued. Zanders, if Kendall is in the clear, we need to include her next of kin in any notifications. I'm looking at her personnel file now. The personal contacts indicate her boyfriend, Jeremy Levy, neighbor, Heather Jacobs, and mother, Kathleen Radcliffe."

"Fine, but don't notify Radcliffe's people until we can clear her ... maybe in twenty-four hours."

"Okay. Also, I've checked on Fields' and Carson's cell phones. Both phones are dead, and the last calls were made in DC just before they flew out. I'll track Kendall Radcliffe's."

Mickey called both executives' families and provided a ridiculously vague update that basically told them nothing. At the same time they got the between-the-lines message that their loved one was somehow okay. Both families had been through emergency drills before, so they understood their roles. Given the importance of their husbands on the worldwide stage, they knew that everything that could be done was indeed happening. They also knew that sometimes they would not know all the details up front. That was the reality of their worlds, they had accepted that, and it had been that way for many years now.

Mickey then called the company Public Relations VP and discovered she was in her office in the adjoining building. He needed to stay in his office in the event of additional information, so she agreed to an emergency meeting in his office. He also rounded up the executive in the Investor Relations Department, and the two arrived within seconds of each other. Mickey explained the matter in rather blunt terms. He didn't dare sugarcoat or put any type of spin on the status.

***********

The two executives left his office with much on their minds. They got to work immediately by first expanding the circle of Orion executives "in the know." A short, cryptic press release was drafted. Then emergency calls were made to the board of directors, and it was agreed that calling a limited trading halt to the Orion Premier Net Services stock was the best recourse until the gravity of the situation was known. The press release was finalized and the PR agency instructed to release it over the wires to the general public.

***********

Special Agent Zanders called his contact at the NSA in Maryland, gave a status report to his superiors, and assigned several tasks to other agents, including getting back to the charter company that owned the plane. He now pressed for immediate document release and analysis on every task his team undertook.

His agency buzzed with activity as people browbeat anyone who might have information or documentation about all of the players—principal and peripheral—who might have knowledge of the events.

He was matter-of-factly preparing for his trip to Seattle and reviewing the new information. It was driving him nuts that some as-yet-unknown international agency had more knowledge about the matter than he did. Who was the agency? Which country did it involve? Why did the country want the executives? Who is Kendall Radcliffe, and why is she part of the unfolding events? Who sent the note to McDougall, and how was it delivered? All of these questions re-played continuously in Zanders' mind.

He now had other agencies involved in the investigation and was determined to stay on top of the information flow. He urged cooperation and sharing at the highest levels and fervently hoped his colleagues would respect his authority. He, of course, had no intention of sharing information ... if it could be helped. He still had ten years before retirement, and he wanted at least one more promotion and a cushy assignment at the end of this ordeal.

As Zanders climbed aboard the FBI plane, he was thoroughly irritated at having to fly to Seattle. Having grown up and spent most of his life on the East Coast, he viewed Seattle as nothing more than a remote outpost that was barely civilized and full of liberal nuts and tree huggers. The fact that Seattle experienced rain or gray skies practically every day only added to the misery of having to make this trip.

He could have sent agents from the FBI's Seattle office. But he didn't trust anyone else to size up the Orion business and its employees. He wanted to look firsthand at the company and its headquarters, scrutinize the security staff and maybe the families, and then hightail it back to DC in no more than forty-eight hours. Zanders knew how to turn up his internal turbojets and, in truth, accomplished more during a crisis than most of his fellow agents.

The one thing this investigation had going for it was Zanders' zeal. When he was on a mission he was dogged, focused, and passionate. He could sniff out the slightest lie or catch a whiff of a clue that would have him charging ahead, most times before his colleagues had time to regroup.

He gritted his teeth, ordered himself to sleep on the plane, and settled back for the five hour trip. He brought two agents with him and commanded them to do the same. He wanted a sharp, alert team tomorrow, and they were going to get answers ... one way or another. Once the others were settled and quiet, he allowed himself a Guinness and then quickly slipped into a deep sleep.

# CHAPTER SEVENTEEN

KENDALL AWOKE TO THE FARAWAY sound of the call for *Fajr* prayer. The call to morning prayer was oddly comforting to her. If she was left alone all day, she was able to tell how much time had elapsed by the ritual chanting she had now heard at set times throughout the day.

She was getting really worried and going stir crazy. She had been left in her room in isolation for two days now. Meals were brought to her room and the dishes removed perfunctorily as she finished her meal. Making matters worse, she was convinced she was being watched. A thorough search of her room only revealed hundreds of pinpoint holes in the walls, including in the bathroom. She couldn't be sure where the cameras were, but she spent as little time in the bathroom as possible, and even less in the shower stall.

Maysah, the female doctor, had stopped in for a minute each night only to ask if she had any needs. Maysah seemed timid and afraid of Kendall, or maybe of any friendship that might develop between them, and was not interested in small talk. She usually left as quickly as she arrived.

Kendall was terribly worried about her mother. She knew that her mother's neighbor would dutifully check on her every day, even if only by phone. But she also knew her mother was not strong. This dear lady had been a stay-at-home mother after her only child was born. Kathleen Radcliffe had devoted all of her time and love to her daughter and husband, and nearly died of a broken heart when Kendall's father passed away. He left her with plenty of money to see her through the retirement years, but her zest for life was slowly ebbing. It did not appear that grandchildren were even on the horizon, and she had stopped asking about it.

One time recently she made some vague reference to the temporary nature of Kendall's relationship with Jeremy. Kendall had been angry at first but then chalked it up to her mother being confused and tired and probably associating the sentiment to one of her friend's children. Now that Kendall had time to think about it, she wondered if her mother knew all along that the relationship with Jeremy was never to be. She had underestimated her mother again.

The thought made her more miserable, and she longed for the view from her mother's Puget Sound bungalow along Redondo Beach Drive, something that had always calmed her. At that moment, Kendall would have given anything to walk along the boardwalk and watch the scuba diving groups on the north end as they assembled for classes and recreational dives. The refreshing salt air energized her and renewed her until the next visit.

A loud knock sounded on her door and ended her musings. Somehow she knew it was Rashid. She was very glad to see him, but also angry that she had been left alone for two days. He had assured her that he was going to explain things the next day after leaving her on the evening of the dinner with President Shazeb. Two days had now passed. Where the hell had he been?

She wanted to fling herself and all her fury at him, but she didn't want to send him running from the room in disgust.

His demeanor was cool as he appraised her room. He quickly took in her suitcase and few personal items in view. He felt bad that he had left her alone for two days. But he knew it was necessary in order to solidify their friendship and in particular Kendall's reliance or dependence on him. It was a psychological trick he had learned during intensive military training. He was partly curious to see if it actually worked on this independent American female.

It was not in his nature to use psychological torture on anyone, let alone a young, pretty, vulnerable female who he suspected was entirely innocent and at the very least was being held against her will. During the last two days, Rashid thought about Kendall and her Orion colleagues quite a bit. He had no ill intention toward them and had actually looked forward to seeing Kendall again. He was not planning to harm her in any way and hoped he would be able to get her and the others out of Afghanistan. But first he needed to gain her trust.

Kendall couldn't help herself. She had to release some of the pent-up frustration. Her eyes blazed when she confronted him. "Where have you been? You told me we were going to talk! Obviously, your word means nothing."

Rashid turned to leave, saying quietly, "I'm sorry. I thought you would be happy to see me." He grabbed the doorknob to pull it open.

"No, wait! Stop! I'm just so angry and bored and worried about my mother. I thought you'd left me for good, and I was going to be stuck here by myself." Her voice trailed off as she realized that she must sound like one of those weak, dependent, helpless, females with a penchant for histrionics. Well, hell, she did feel close to hysteria and wasn't about to apologize for what she considered as rational behavior, given the circumstances.

He slowly turned around and waited as she took a deep breath and seemed to visibly calm down. "It is unfortunate that I was not able to see you the past two days. But that couldn't be helped. I am here now. Would you like to go outside for some fresh air and perhaps take a ride?"

Slightly mollified and straining to catch every word to analyze for sincerity, she decided that for whatever reason, his not visiting her the prior two days was beyond his control. She was also ecstatic at the opportunity to go outside and also to spend more time with him, to learn more about their previous cryptic discussions. She did not fear him and felt that if she played her cards right, she might actually glean some useful information.

Kendall donned her headscarf, and they headed out of the building. Rashid inclined his head as they passed General Omar. The general smirked and gave a wink at Kendall. She shuddered at the knowing look.

"Where are we going? I would like to see Glenn Carson. Is he feeling better?"

Rashid slowed his pace, pondered the question, and then frowned. "That will not be possible. He's not feeling better, and we're not exactly sure what's wrong with him. It may be contagious, and therefore, he's in isolation. I'm doing some research now." He stopped, realizing he was getting ahead of himself.

Kendall caught it immediately. "What? You are doing research? Why not the doctor? You are a soldier! What's really wrong with him? What've you all done to him?" She felt the bubblings of panic again. She swallowed slowly and shook her head as if to clear the cobwebs. She put her hands on her hips and demanded, "Who are you?"

He looked from left to right and then straight ahead and motioned to the jeep some twenty feet away. In a measured tone he answered, "If you are quiet and patient, it will soon be revealed. But not yet. We need to be alone and away from others." He looked deeply and thoroughly into her eyes as if searching for a sign of understanding or at least an attempt at allegiance. "Please trust me."

She hesitated and then stepped into the jeep, and the two drove away. Kendall willed herself to calm down. She felt optimistic for the first time. This quiet yet imposing man appeared capable of having a plan and seeing it through. His confidence and demeanor gave her the assurances she so needed. She considered herself somewhat worldly. She had traveled all over the world and had met many personalities. She could spot a scoundrel with ill intentions the first minute she spoke with him. Rashid was anything but that. His countenance was earnest and forthright, and he gave the impression of reasonableness. At the same time, she got the distinct feeling he would not appreciate her summing him up so. Therefore, she decided to play along for now.

"So, where are we going?"

Rashid smiled and caught Kendall's cautious—if slightly reluctant—

conspiratorial tone. He relaxed in his seat. "I thought we would go to the market in Kabul. We will buy some fresh fruit and get you something to drink ... maybe a Coca Cola?"

She broke into a cautious smile and said, "I would love to have some fresh fruit."

"Great! The market has wonderful melons, but it needs to be carefully washed before it's eaten." He frowned having to admit it and continued, "Much of the fruit is washed in the nearby *juie.* That's an open ditch that runs through the city. The water is not clean. It would make you very sick."

She nodded. "Okay. Good to know."

"Even though the country of Afghanistan is quite wealthy now with its continual flow of oil, at least forty percent of Afghan children die before the age of five due to the lack of clean drinking water. The country has greatly improved its infrastructure and living standards, but it is hard to make people understand how important something like clean drinking water is. At least the country now has a water system." Kendall shook her head in disbelief.

They drove in silence along the somewhat bumpy but paved road for the few miles to the market. As they approached the city, they passed a few donkeys on the side of the road. A large delivery-sized truck rumbled past them, and Rashid stole a glance at Kendall as she reacted to the colorful truck with a gaping jaw.

"What is that?"

"Welcome to Afghanistan! Our truck drivers are very proud of their trucks. As you can see, they hand paint little pictures over most of the flat surfaces."

Kendall noticed that in between the pictures was a border of stylize flowers.

"This particular driver is quite successful ... maybe even wealthy."

"How can you tell?"

"He's wearing a watch. Not too many Afghan men wear watches yet."

They rounded a curve and drove onto the main street. She took in all the bustling activity and the various stalls. There were groups of men hanging around. Most were smoking what looked like cigarettes.

Kendall pointed at one of the groups. "Are they smoking cigarettes?"

"Yes, cigarettes. But also *naswar.* It's the Afghan version of snuff. It's a kind of dipping tobacco that is moist. It's made from baked tobacco leaves, limewater, tree bark ash, and flavorings. At the end of the manufacturing process, water is added and then the mixture is rolled into balls. The balls are then placed under the lip for awhile."

"Ugh."

Kendall noticed there were no traffic lights. Only a uniformed soldier provided traffic control. Most of the cars were Japanese, German, and Russian models, with a few newer French cars and an occasional Ford truck. There seemed to be honking everywhere for no apparent reason.

"Why is everyone honking?"

Rashid smiled. "That's the way we drive in Afghanistan. They are telling people to get out of their way or just generally letting people know they are driving by."

"Good Lord! I don't know if my nerves can take all this racket!"

Now he laughed. He maneuvered the jeep into a parking spot. "Come! Let's walk." He had made sure to dress in full military garb and was wearing his service weapon. There was a long-handled knife stuck in the other side of his trouser. He caught her open stare at his imposing form.

"Is there a problem, Kendall?"

"No, but you do look ready for battle. Is it necessary to have all those weapons on you? This looks like a peaceful place."

He gave her an intense look. "That's exactly why I'm wearing them. I am not required to wear the weapons, but I choose to always have them on. I want people to be afraid of me or, rather, to not question my authority. It gives me respect. Does that make sense?"

She shrugged.

"Also, you notice there are only a few groups of women out and about. My appearance with you—an obvious westerner—shows people that I am your escort. They will be curious about you but will mostly not approach you."

"Do these people know you or at least recognize you?"

"Yes. I have worked hard for their loyalty and friendship. I help them when I can."

Kendall was puzzled. Why did he need to help them? Was this part of his official duties, or did he simply choose to help them? And how did he help them? *All in good time, Kendall!*

As they began to walk through the market, she observed two men look down at their feet, laugh, and quickly shake hands. She turned to Rashid. "What's that all about?"

"We Afghans are very superstitious people. It looks like their feet touched accidentally. In our culture, you must immediately shake hands or you will get into a fight with that person."

She shook her head in amazement. They stopped at a cart loaded with grapes. He bought a bunch. They also bought some succulent dumplings and barbecued kebabs. When Kendall saw the cart ladened with stacks of fresh, warm, garlic *naan* bread, she gave Rashid an imploring look.

"Oh, I love this bread!" He was pleased that she was becoming familiar with their food. He was very happy to buy the *naan.*

They came to the meat market section and she looked at the rows of hanging carcasses. She inclined her head toward the meat. "I'm almost afraid to ask what these are."

"These are mostly goat and lamb."

"Aren't they afraid of the meat going bad in this warm weather?"

"They are okay for one day. It actually helps the meat age and taste better. These will all be sold by the end of the day. People have parties and reasons to celebrate. You know, the standard of living is much better now than fifteen years ago during the war with the Taliban and, Al Qaeda, and the arrival of the Americans. People may not be able to build big houses or wear the latest in western clothes, but most can afford the local Afghan foods and are satisfied with that."

There was a moment of awkward silence, and she wanted to ask, *So, what is the problem then?* but realized this was not the appropriate place or time for a philosophical discussion on the modern challenges in Afghanistan. She noticed there were a lot of street children picking up discarded soda cans and other items and hawking everything from chewing gum to small pots of coal, which she was later informed was to ward off evil spirits. These children looked very dirty. A handful surrounded them, begging for money. Obviously, not everyone could afford even a meager life. She sighed at the ragged clothes and mournful but hopeful eyes when their arms thrust out hoping for an *Afghani* or two. Rashid looked at her, shrugged his shoulders, dug into his pockets, and gave out as many *Afghanis* as he had to the most needy-looking street urchins.

They swung back to the other side of the street toward their vehicle and nearly got run over in the attempt. Rashid grabbed her arm in a protective vise-like grip and waved off the driver. He continued to hold her arm all the way to their vehicle. Kendall couldn't tell if he had forgotten that he was holding her arm or was purposely doing it. He seemed reluctant to let go when they reached the jeep. She hastily scrambled to her side of the vehicle and climbed in, declaring, "Whew! We made it, and in one piece too!" They both laughed.

"Where are we going now?"

"We are going to have our meal at Lake Qargha Park. We can walk around in privacy and be able to talk."

As they drove up, Kendall was surprised to see a carnival-like setting, complete with rides. There was even a street vendor rolling cotton candy referred to as *cotton floss.* They gathered their food from the jeep and walked past the boisterous crowds. As the squeals of delight from the local children faded, they approached the lake shore. A young boy charged past them on his horse.

Kendall was delighted when Rashid rented a boat and motored away from the shore. There were quite a few paddle boats near the shore, but their motorboat allowed them to move further out from the shore and away from the noisy crowd. Besides, the motorboat was a lot larger, and she could move about easily.

They had their midday meal in silence. Rashid produced two bottles of water, some of which they used to wash the fresh fruit. Although the local drinking water was a lot cleaner than a few years before, it was still not safe enough for Kendall. Rashid did not want her to get sick ... particularly with the plans he had for her. She would need her strength and wits about her to survive the next few weeks.

# CHAPTER EIGHTEEN

THE CALL FOR THE NOON prayer *Duhr* sounded. Rashid and Kendall were far away from the shore. She stole a quick glance at him to see his reaction. He looked around and saw that no one was near and they were obscured by a land spit with downed trees at the shoreline. They were completely hidden from view.

She couldn't stand it. "Don't you have to pray?"

Rashid reckoned the truth telling had begun. "Well, first, not everyone in Afghanistan is a Muslim. In fact, only a quarter of the population is Muslim. The rest are various ethnic groups. I'm not Muslim."

"What?" she said in an incredulous tone that was more than tinged with rudeness. "What are you then?"

"I'm a Christian of Jewish ancestry raised in a Muslim society."

"That's a mouthful. I can't wait to hear the story. Go on!" She urged him to continue.

"My mother was Jewish and was kidnapped when she was a teenager. She was brought to my father's village. She was given to my grandfather in payment for a debt that a very bad man owed him. She was educated and beautiful, and my grandfather thought she would be perfect for my father."

Kendall recoiled in horror. "That is awful! Your poor mother! She was forced to marry your father?" Then it dawned on her that her circumstances were not so dissimilar to his mother's. "Hmm! I see there is a lot of kidnapping going on in this country! Is that how you all solve your problems?"

"Unfortunately. Her family back in Israel never knew where she was taken. She never saw them again. She and my father made a life for each other. I did not notice that she was unhappy or being held against her will. She certainly loved her children. She taught all of us to read and write, both English and Hebrew. She learned to speak our language right along with her own children."

"But she was a Christian? How could that be?"

"Her father—my grandfather—was an Arab Christian living in Israel. Her mother—my grandmother—was Jewish. According to Jewish law, the mother's religion determines the ethnicity of the children at birth."

He looked directly into Kendall's eyes. "Do you know what this means?" He fervently hoped he had not made a colossal mistake. She swallowed slowly and pondered the meaning. Her eyes widened.

"You are Jewish by birth? Holy shit! Isn't that a death sentence for you here in Afghanistan?"

"Sometimes, but not necessarily. It can certainly bring you hardship and discrimination. But it's not something you want to publicize."

"Does anyone here know?"

He thought wryly, *Here goes!*

"No, as a matter of fact. Only you! I would be in even bigger trouble for keeping this secret—particularly from President Shazeb. That is why I keep a low profile. When I was a small child, my mother constantly told us that our heritage was something to be proud of but not spoken of outside of our immediate family. She put it to us in such a way that we were fearful of our very lives and those of our family if we talked about it. She made the teachings magical and told us that no one else in the village would know these things. She said we were special and were the only ones meant to know this information. It worked great, especially for me. I couldn't get enough lessons. She taught me that knowledge truly was power."

He grabbed Kendall's arm. "Kendall, I have a lot of knowledge and plan to use it very soon. You will be helping me."

She shook her head in fear, not wanting to be involved in a wild scheme. "I will? How? Are you planning to stage a coup?" She had sought her safest refuge, sarcasm.

He wavered. "As a matter of fact, I am."

Her eyes registered the shock. "Is that why we were kidnapped? To help you overthrow the government?"

He laughed. "No. You are getting a little head of yourself. I didn't know you and your colleagues were going to be brought to Afghanistan against your will until recently. But I decided that it could fit nicely into my plans."

"How?"

"First, do you trust me?"

"I barely know you. You could be playing me, for all I know. Anyway, if you are such a good guy, then why didn't you stop this?"

"Kendall, you are only thinking of yourself. You must look at the big picture. There is much more going on than the Orion issue alone—whatever that is. It's just caused me to make some adjustments to my plans and work with what I have."

"I still don't know how I can trust you." She was clearly conflicted.

"Well, consider this. I've just revealed something that could get me severely beaten at the very least and more likely beheaded. Believe me, President Shazeb would do it to save face and for the years of lying or keeping the info from him. Knowing Shazeb, it would be for the sheer humility of having lived right under his nose and been a friend to his children and his confidant for twenty years."

"What exactly do you do for him?"

"Kendall, I'm being completely honest here. I manage his crop deliveries, oversee the manufacturing, and make sure that the end product goes to the buyers."

"You make it sound so businesslike. You are nothing but a common criminal."

Rashid felt like he had been stabbed. The pain of the words was unbearable. He really was a good person. She just didn't understand. He lowered his head. "I probably am. But I'm trying to make it right. Shazeb's business enterprise is about to close down. I have been working on that project for years. The only way for me to plan all of this is to understand the process. No one would suspect me, and I have free access to every aspect of his operation."

She felt as if there was more. "And what else?"

"Shazeb's presidency and his family are about to lose their jobs and maybe their lives as well."

She waved her finger at him. "Oh, yeah. That little thing you talked about before, the coup! Just how do you plan to do all of this?"

"I have friends."

"Oh, here it comes. And they are ...?" Her voice trailed off as she waited for the announcement. She felt like it was going to be an epic proclamation.

"I'm a member of the Mossad. Obviously, I'm part of their covert operations."

She laughed. "No way. You couldn't be. You've been in Afghanistan too long."

"Not really, Kendall. I was sent to boarding school with Ahmad and Saaqib, and then lived in England while I was going to the University. I travel a lot for President Shazeb's business enterprises."

"Well, either way, that information would be secret. No one reveals they are part of the Mossad."

"Generally, that is true. But I have nothing to lose here, and I need your help. If my plan works, this whole country will soon undergo a major change. And the world will be rid of a drug kingpin from the crop all the way to the end product."

"You're crazy! How can you possibly pull this off by yourself?"

"Israel is helping me, and you are going to help me."

"Me? I don't even like guns, and I'm not very coordinated when it comes to athletic things."

"First things first. You are going to learn to ride a horse, because that may be our way of escape. We are going to fashion a gym of sorts where you will be working out every day. That will be easy to do, because Shazeb asked me to get close to you. I can convince him that the gym needs to be in secret. That way, the other men won't both wonder what's going on and yet watch you too. That could put you in danger. I'm going to teach you how to shoot and throw a knife."

Kendall felt her head spinning. This was a lot of information to take in, and she felt overwhelmed by the enormity of what Rashid was planning.

"Is the U.S. involved in any of this?"

"Only peripherally. They know Israel is watching Afghanistan. I'm thinking that when it all goes down, the U.S. will agree to use their drones for some well-placed bombings of Shazeb's fields, manufacturing sites, and the transport vehicles. The U.S. is not happy with President Shazeb and his cruel dictatorship. But, as you know, after the long war with the Taliban and Al Qaeda, the Americans have steered clear of any military actions in the Middle East for years now. As I understand it, currently the U.S. economy has recovered nicely since the war in Afghanistan, and people just want to have comfortable lives. They don't want America to be part of any wars ... for any reason."

"Well, then, how will you talk the U.S. into helping?"

"This is where you Orion people come in. I know how important an American asset Paul Fields and Glenn Carson are. I don't think it would take much effort for the U.S. to be talked into sending a rescue team."

"So, Orion and the U.S. do not currently know where we are."

"Sort of. But Israel does ... through me. As a matter of fact, that's what I was doing the past couple days. My traveling around and overseeing the drug operation gives me plenty of time alone to get on the satellite phone and converse with my Israeli counterparts. They are actually pleased at the Orion event. They realize that it will be the impetus to force the U.S. to get involved."

"When do you tell the U.S.?"

"When we are just about ready for the revolution."

"What needs to happen first?" Kendall absentmindedly squished a little spider that was moving toward her on the seat.

Rashid stated matter-of-factly, "The Shazebs—father and two sons—need to die. Here's where you can be of help."

"Oh, no! I'm not shooting or stabbing anyone!"

"That's not what I had in mind."

"My God, I know I'm going to regret this. What are you thinking?"

"This is where the Book of Judith comes in. You can wreak a lot of havoc by cozying up to all three Shazebs. It will be most important for you to get along well with the sons and play them off each other."

Kendall was furious at what she thought she was being asked to do, and stood up in the boat. It began to sway from side to side. "I will not be your Judith! I'm not seducing those men and then cutting off their heads. That was only a story, and probably nothing more than an urban legend. After all, it never even made it into the Protestant bible!"

Rashid grabbed her arm and pulled her back onto the seat. "Lovely, as it sounds, that's not what I had in mind. I was thinking you could make them jealous of each other. If they think they are the only ones you are interested in, they would gladly fight for you."

Kendall put up her hands. "Hold it! These men are all married. They are not looking for women!"

"Kendall, you are being naïve and shortsighted. These are brutal men. They are always looking for women and maybe even another wife. In their minds, you would be a great addition to their households, although you would probably be killed by the other women or wives." He chuckled.

"Very funny! So, you want me to draw out each of them separately, make them feel special, and get them to kill each other."

"That's exactly what I'd like to have happen."

With excessive sarcasm she spat out, "No problem! Except I don't want any part of this. I want to go home. In fact, I demand to be taken home at once ... right now! I'm tired, and I want my bed and my clothes. I need to pay bills. I have a life to live. I need to check on my mother!"

She had to admit that at least the little matter of her boyfriend breaking up with her had slipped her mind. After all, she was having an adventure! That's what she had always told herself when she was in a jam. The best way through it was to view it as an "adventure." Well, she was certainly having the "adventure" of a lifetime, and she didn't want any part of it!

She put her head in her hands and looked down, not uttering a word. She would not give this man the pleasure of seeing her break down. She had to pull herself together, now! *Okay, I've had my few minutes of a nervous breakdown, and I need to suck it up. You're strong, and you can do this.*

Rashid was uncomfortable. He didn't know how to comfort her or assure her that his plan would even work. In fact, it could get them both killed. Then he had an idea.

"Kendall, I can get a note to your mother by tomorrow. I can also make sure that your bills are paid."

She rolled her head to the side and peered up at him. "How? How can you possibly do those things?"

His voice was both soothing and apologetic. "I'm asking you to trust me!"

She just looked at him expectantly. He took it as a sign of encouragement and continued. "Why don't you write a note to your mother as soon as we get back. We'll go now. I'll have it delivered via wire within twenty-four hours." He scratched his head and then said, "I'll have money put into your account. I saw that you have your luggage and purse."

"Yeah, minus my cell phone and laptop!"

"It was necessary. You must understand that. But you have your purse with your financial information, correct?"

"Yes, but how does that help?"

"Just give me your account number, and I'll have money wired into it."

Her wheels were turning. "Oh great! I can see it now! I'll go from the frying pan into the fire. You'll empty my account."

"It doesn't work that way, and you know it! Banks don't mind if money comes in, but they will make you jump through a few hoops to withdraw it. Like, ensure that the person has authority to withdraw it. Correct?"

She nodded. "Okay, fine. Let's do it. I want to leave now, so I can write that note for my mother."

They were back in her room in thirty minutes. Rashid rounded up a sheet of paper for her, and she quickly penned a note to her mother. As she handed him the neatly folded note and provided her bank routing and checking account number, he asked, "Does your mother need money too?"

"You know, you can't just pay everyone off, and then it's all fine! No, my mother does not need your money."

He was getting angry. "Listen, Kendall. I'm going out on a limb for you. This note business is risky and could get me shot, not to mention discovered. My counterparts are going to be angry with the request. But if it means you are willing to help us, they'll do it. So give me a break!"

"Great! I'm the victim, and you're making me feel guilty! Get out of my room! I want to sleep. Maybe when I wake up, it'll all have been just a nightmare. Leave ... now!" She lay down on her bed and rolled toward the wall and away from him.

Rashid was furious and stalked out of the room. He was also worried that she wouldn't be able to go through with his plan. She seemed so terribly distraught, fragile, and vulnerable. Even if she did help, how could he trust that she would hold up her end of the plan?

His father had taught him that Muslims believed that everyone would be tested during their lives. He had often quoted verses from the *Koran* that "God is with those who patiently persevere" and "And be steadfast in patience …." His mother told him about the trials of the ancient Jewish people as they wandered through the desert on their way to Mt. Sinai. The wisdom that inspired him the most from his mother was that the Christian bible had one hundred and forty-four references to the virtues of patience.

His heart was heavy and his mind raced as he made a mental list of the things he must do in the next day. Getting the note to Kendall's mother would be tricky. He couldn't believe that he had promised to do this for her. He wondered if he was going soft. He had never before let a woman interfere in his life. He saw how much trouble they could cause and had made a decision when he was younger not to take them too seriously or get involved until he was ready for a family life. But he bore the responsibility for a nation and maybe even the world. He couldn't possibly include a woman at this time.

He had to acknowledge, though, that he felt a stirring in his heart for Kendall. He didn't understand it, and it made him furious. For the first time in his life, he was thinking about something or someone else than his single life's mission of righting a wrong and destroying Mujtaba Shazeb and his sons.

His goal really centered around the father, and he knew that it wasn't the sons' fault their father was such an evil man. But they had grown up in his shadow and held his same violent views. They had been raised to be catered to and obeyed at all costs. Rashid had stepped in many times when he came upon mainly Saaqib meting out some violent punishment for a perceived slight against him or his father. Several times Rashid had not arrived in time, and the poor victim was not able to be saved. Rather than own up to the sadistic deed, Saaqib simply had the body buried, and no one—least of all the victim's family—ever knew what happened to the poor guy. It particularly sickened Rashid that, once or twice, Saaqib's prey was a woman who would not submit when he took a liking to her. It was well known around Kabul that if a woman wanted to keep her virtue—not to mention her head—she should stay away from Saaqib and basically cover up so as not to be noticed by him.

Rashid decided that he needed some time to himself to think and plan the next couple of days. He had built a very simple hut nearby within a grove of trees that provided seclusion. Since it was a couple miles from the palace, regular citizens did not venture out there. The farmlands, pasture, and meadows ran the other direction from the palace. This refuge was in a lower part of the lands owned by the president. None of the Shazeb family took long walks or got much exercise outdoors, including riding the horses they so prodigiously collected, and therefore Rashid had the full expectation of privacy.

A little stream ran by about fifty feet outside the front door, and he often sat there for hours in quiet contemplation, listening to the gentle winds and slow-moving water as it lapped against the smooth rocks and grassy streambed. It helped him focus his energy on the matters of utmost importance and gave him the wisdom and strength he needed for the next step. He would go there now.

But first, he must seek out Paul Fields. Rashid had a request that only Fields could carry out.

# CHAPTER NINETEEN

Special Agent Anthony Zanders and his associates had been working with Orion Premier's head of security, Eric "Mickey" McDougall, for several days now. They had pored over every personnel file that might be even remotely related to the current crisis, and nothing of significance stood out. They were now sitting around a conference room in the Orion executive offices, reviewing what they knew so far.

Zanders and his crew were planning to return to DC in the morning. He had kept in constant contact with his DC office, and had, for the most part, kept the NSA and his liaisons within the various military agencies up to speed. Electronic eavesdropping had been stepped up. The only thing that stood out was that it was uncharacteristically quiet in the Middle East. The only thing of import was the increased availability of heroin. The distribution seemed to have reached an all-time high, and the conversations there centered on an impending massive production and the need for better, more efficient shipping methods. The product was about to hit the markets within months. While this was all interesting for the DEA and Zanders' FBI counterparts in drug enforcement, he was frustrated they weren't any closer to finding answers to their immediate situation, the kidnapping of the two Orion Premier executives.

They had visited each of the families again, including Kendall Radcliffe's mother and neighbor. The neighbor, Heather Jacobs, promised to let them know if she received any communications regarding Kendall or Orion. She also agreed to check on Kendall's unit every day and pick up her mail.

The visit to Kendall's mother, Kathleen Radcliffe, had not gone well. The mother was fragile and became very upset. The more they probed about Kendall's background and whether she harbored any resentment against Orion or the executives, the more agitated the mother became. The thought that her daughter might be involved in something so heinous and criminal was too much for her to bear. Zanders and Mickey had driven together out to the mother's place at Redondo. Shortly after arriving, Zanders was regretting his desire to meet the mother. She was such a nice and decent woman, and she seemed to shrink in size and stature right before their eyes. At first, she rushed around trying to serve coffee and cookies, but then abruptly sat down on the couch to catch her breath when the few known facts were presented to her. It was soon obvious that she knew nothing and would be of no help at all. They promised to keep her apprised of the situation and then quickly backed out of her front door and scurried to their car. As they pulled out of the driveway, Mrs. Radcliffe shut the door and promptly collapsed in a heap.

The phone conversation with the boyfriend, Jeremy Levy, was bizarre. It turned out they had broken up a few days earlier, and Jeremy, while concerned, was not overly disturbed. He did think it was odd that she was missing, but he also said that she was independent and could easily take care of herself. As Zanders figured it, that could be taken several ways. The question was whether she was independent enough to have planned or been part of this kidnapping scheme. Since it had been several days now with no demands for money, none of the investigators knew what the objective was. That part drove them crazy, because they couldn't then think a step ahead. Knowing who the bad guys were would have been of tremendous help, they thought.

In any event, Levy seemed to backpedal on any committed association with Kendall ... minimizing the relationship and chalking it up to nothing more than buddies and weekend sex. It was clear that Jeremy now wanted to distance himself from Kendall and whatever distasteful deed she had done. All he could think of was what his mother might say. On that thought, he was instantly relieved that he had broken up with Kendall. She was clearly not the woman he thought she was. His mother had been right all along. Zanders clued in on Levy's type right away. Jeremy Levy was a cad and a jerk. He was obviously self-centered and incapable of loyalty. In fact, Zanders pegged him as a probable "momma's boy."

Each conversation about Kendall brought more suspicion and intrigue. Her friend and co-worker, Gwen Albertson, appeared to be a staunch ally. She assured the men that Kendall would never be involved in the disappearance of Paul Fields and Glenn Carson; that Kendall was excited about her recent promotion and loved working for Orion Premier Net Services. She vouched for Kendall's character and strenuously objected at the implication—no, the outright accusation—that Kendall would be capable of such a criminal act.

She admitted that Kendall had been quiet and preoccupied on the day she agreed to travel to DC. Mickey and Agent Zanders knew that was probably due to the breakup with Jeremy Levy, but they kept that information to themselves. Obviously, Gwen did not know of the recent breakup. In their minds, she might not have been the good friend of Kendall's that she thought she was.

Gwen argued that Kendall had no clue she was going to DC that day. The trip was sudden and unplanned. The two men conceded that was indeed strange. Had Kendall's presence been a mere coincidence? But that didn't make sense either, because the executives rarely traveled together for security reasons, and they almost never had a junior executive in tow. It really defied logic that it would be Kendall, as her job did not overlap with theirs at all. It made more sense, however, once it was discovered they had all stayed at the same hotel in DC. But that's where the similarity ended. Fields and Carson were testifying on the Hill while Kendall was meeting with Orion's outside counsel and the FTC. The attorneys who accompanied Fields and Carson to the Hill were from a different law firm with a completely different specialty.

Somehow, Kendall got on the Orion charter flight. But how did she do this? And where the hell were they now?

Agent Zanders' phone rang. He spoke for a few minutes, scribbled furiously on a notepad, and then hung up. He didn't speak for a while, and the others around the table looked at him expectantly.

Mickey couldn't stand it any longer. "Well, who was it?"

"That was my DC office. A $10,000 deposit was just made to Kendall's checking account via wire transfer."

"A wire transfer from which bank?"

"At first glance, it looks like a bank in New York, but traces to Paris, London, Switzerland, and Israel."

"Israel? What the hell?"

There was stunned silence in the room. No one could even imagine where Israel fit into the unraveling mystery.

Zanders mulled the revelation. "So, the payment originated in Israel, then went to Switzerland, London, Paris, and New York, where it was finally deposited into Kendall's bank account." He looked at Mickey. "Is Kendall Jewish? Does she have family there?"

"No. I don't believe so."

"Well, then, we need to get Israeli intelligence in the loop. I need to be in DC ... now!"

He instructed one of his DC junior agents to stay behind in Seattle and basically shadow Mickey. That agent was to learn all he could and pass anything new back to DC at once.

***********

The media had finally picked up the news of the disappearance of Fields and Carson. Nothing was said about Kendall Radcliffe's involvement. Because no one knew anything, there wasn't much to report. It was a simple article about the men having disappeared from DC on their way back to Seattle. It wasn't clear how they disappeared or their manner of travel. Since the Orion people did not know the actual details, and there were no pilots around to verify the facts, there was only speculation. It was front page news, particularly since trading on the Orion stock had been halted.

The market did not seem to be reacting in a dramatic way, so the board—having been somewhat apprised of the details—decided to resume trading of the stock the next day.

***********

Mrs. Radcliffe lay in the hospital bed and appeared quite frail and weak. The IV pole stood solidly next to her bed as if on sentry duty. A nurse came in and checked her vitals and adjusted the dials on the IV unit. She smoothed the older woman's hair, sighed, and walked out to the nurses' station. The night nurse, Katie, was about to go on duty and patiently awaited any updates.

"So what's the status of Mrs. Radcliffe? Has anyone been able to get a hold of the daughter?"

"Unfortunately, no."

"Aren't there any other relatives that can be notified?"

"Not that we know of."

"I feel awful. That poor woman ... in here all by herself. I can't believe the daughter isn't answering her phone."

"I hear ya, Katie. The daughter's cell message says the phone is not in service ... whatever the hell that means! I'm just glad Mrs. Radcliffe's neighbor saw her lying there and called for an ambulance."

"What's her status now?"

"Her vitals are stable ... no change ... but she's still comatose. She's lucky to have survived the heart attack. I just hope we can locate her daughter in the next day."

The two women continued to discuss Kathleen Radcliffe's medical condition. The requisite thrombolytics had been prescribed as soon as she reached the hospital, but it was clear she had lain on the floor awhile before she was discovered. Heparin would be continued for at least another twenty-four hours.

Katie shook her head in puzzlement. "I don't understand what happened to her. She shouldn't be comatose. It's almost as if she received a shock. She should be awake by now."

The other nurse nodded. "I agree. Just keep a close eye on her, and notify the doctor immediately when she wakes up. You might sit with her awhile or have one of the volunteers sit with her. I sat with her for thirty minutes this afternoon, and just held her hand. She seemed to calm down a little."

A few hours later, Kathleen Radcliffe opened her eyes. As her eyes adjusted to the surroundings, she realized that it was night and she was in the hospital. She had a slight headache from the bump on the head when she fell. But the stabbing pain in her heart and soul eclipsed any medical issues. "Oh, Kendall," she whispered. "What have you done?" The violent turn of events had been too much for the elder Radcliffe.

She knew she should call the nurse, but she didn't want to bother the staff. She had heard them quietly moving around her during their gentle ministrations. She couldn't bear the idea of talking to strangers about her daughter. She just wanted to block it out and make it go away. *My lovely Kendall,* she thought. *What could have happened to her? There must be a logical explanation.* Even if Kendall had not done anything wrong, the fact that she was missing was too frightening for Mrs. Radcliffe to comprehend. She closed her eyes and retreated back into that deep, wonderful, soft place between worlds where she didn't have to deal with any harsh realities or perplexities. There was a light at the back of that dark, comfortable world. She thought about heading in that direction. Her body relaxed as she took a step forward on the secure and untroubled pathway that suddenly opened before her.

# CHAPTER TWENTY

Kendall and Rashid had settled into a routine of spending most of the day together. After her meager breakfast, he picked her up, and they went to a rundown, abandoned military warehouse about five miles away. Two years earlier, it had been overrun with flood waters during a flash flood. The military decided it was too close to the nearby river and abandoned it. Rashid decided that retrofitting the warehouse would be the perfect solution.

He brought in a handful of local day laborers and had the warehouse floor cleaned out in a couple of days. He had them build a crude workout facility using extra lumber from the military stock that he provided in small increments. No one at the base seemed to miss the few pieces of wood that disappeared every day. The day laborers never asked questions. It just looked to them like the military was trying to save money. Either way, they were being paid and weren't about to ask questions.

Rashid devised a series of daily workout routines for Kendall. He constructed homemade weights by filling plastic jugs with sand. Wood planks and plastic piping were used to construct an abs bench.

His favorite creation was a soundproof indoor shooting range. He had the men wall-off one section of the warehouse. The two lanes that were constructed ran the width of the warehouse in the back. Rashid again "borrowed" bags of cement from the military stash, and had his workers pour concrete blocks. He managed to secure some defective sheet rock that had been discarded and was awaiting pickup and delivery to the local refuse area.

He researched the construction of a gun range and dutifully used a double thickness of sheet rock, being careful to have the first layer nailed vertically and the second horizontally. He did the best he could to plug any seams where excessive noise might escape. He fervently wished he had sound-deadening paint, but that was not possible in this part of the world. A crude ventilation system was jerry-rigged to provide the required negative air flow to trap any airborne contaminants.

Finally, bags of combined sand and semi-soft cement were laid against the back wall of the firing lanes, from floor to ceiling, to deflect spent bullets.

Rashid stood back and marveled at his resourcefulness. The workout facility was quite functional. He was anxious to have Kendall begin her training in earnest. Up to now, she had done a lot of walking and running, and improved her swimming skills in the nearby river. A few times she had used the president's pool, but she was uncomfortable wearing the required full-length gauzy swim costume worn by Afghan women. He had her run up and down the nearby hills to strengthen her legs and increase her endurance. But it was time to step up the training.

He had learned some unsettling things involving Kendall and the Orion executives, and he felt like a traitor not being honest with her. But he knew that if he told her, he would unquestionably face her wrath and lose all hope of a combined effort at ousting President Shazeb and his sons and securing the freedom of the Orion executives. Rashid was torn, but had a job to do. He had no choice but to keep these damning things secret from Kendall ... for now.

Through the technical genius of the Orion datacenter guy, Daniel Blumfeld, the Mossad was able to track the investigation by Orion and the U.S. agencies. The new technical "eyes and ears" *Prophecy* was sending a constant stream of information to the Mossad. That agency was kept scrambling to change course and head off any untoward action by the U.S. that might get in the way of the Mossad's intention ... the downfall of President Shazeb. The destruction of the poppy fields and downstream manufacture and distribution of the heroin—from the manufacturing facilities to the trucks and tankers—was the highest priority for them. Intercepting a few hundred million dollars along the way, just to teach Shazeb a further lesson, would simply be an added bonus.

It was a blessing and a curse that the Orion people had been taken. This threw a wrench in the Mossad's carefully planned operation. But the proud and tenacious agency was a master at flexibility and adaptability and had regrouped to incorporate the extra dynamics.

The most worrisome details haunting Rashid's dreams were the medical situations of both Glenn Carson and Kathleen Radcliffe ... Kendall's mother. Carson's situation was deteriorating. He had now contracted malaria. Even though Kabul was considered a low-risk province for malaria as compared with the rest of Afghanistan, Carson had managed to contract it. The medical facility that housed Carson did not have the proper medicine and sterile environment to combat the disease. The on-site limited laboratory was able to isolate the malaria strain to *P. vivax,* but it didn't have the requisite antimalarial medicine *Primaquine.* The disease was slowly ravaging Carson's body. If nothing more was done, he would be dead in a week. President Shazeb had shown no concern, and it appeared the despot would let Carson die.

On his own, Rashid had his sources check on Mrs. Radcliffe. They discovered she had suffered a heart attack and was in the hospital. For some reason, she wasn't improving, and her situation appeared dire. He couldn't possibly reveal this to Kendall; she would lose all objectivity and might even reveal his plans during an emotional outburst. No, there was nothing he could do with the information. But it was clear the mission needed to be stepped up.

The one bright spot in all this was that Rashid's conversation with Paul Fields had gone very well ... almost too well. He was choosing to view his unexpected departure from society as an escape from reality in the form of a vacation to an exotic locale. The only thing that bothered Fields at the moment was that he didn't have his passport.

When Rashid went looking for Fields, he found him alone in the president's datacenter, from which all Afghan business was conducted. Rashid was surprised that Fields had been left alone in the facility. He soon learned that Saaqib often left him alone under some guise of national security business. Rashid suspected he was going to meet one of his mistresses. Fields said that Saaqib was usually gone about ninety minutes at a stretch. In fact, he had just left when Rashid arrived. Fields and Rashid were able to have a long talk.

Rashid quickly explained who he was, his background, and the planned mission. He needed Fields to become intimately knowledgeable with the country's technical infrastructure, and when the time was right, to render it inoperable ... preferably permanently. This included the movement of funds out of Afghanistan and the shutdown of the oil refineries. This would create a diversion and wreak enough havoc to set Rashid and the Mossad's plan into effect. Fields was more than willing to do this. He was tiring of the amusing diversion of tinkering with the Afghanistan technical superstructure and thought it was timely to discuss their exit strategy. Rashid had the distinct impression that Fields didn't exactly live in the real world. He was concerned that Fields viewed this whole thing as a virtual game, and that he was just a player.

For the moment, President Shazeb believed that Fields was helping isolate their technical issues, e.g. prying eyes and ears, because no other shipments had gone missing nor funds disappeared. In actuality, since Rashid knew the source of Afghanistan's spies and double-crosses by virtue of Blumfeld and his technical weapon of at-will, real-time streaming data via the Orion datacenter, the Mossad had simply gone quiet for the past week as it restructured its mission and refocused its short-term goals.

Rashid couldn't believe he was dealing with these unknown quantities. He knew that in the end they would either engineer a grand escape, plus take down a major drug supplier and dictator, or get themselves killed in the most gruesome of ways and possibly start World War III. Rashid was not one for drinking a lot of alcohol, but he had taken to throwing back one or two stiff belts at the end of the day—anything to help him relax. The bottom line was that once the warning bell was sounded and the first domino fell, there was no turning back. It all had to be executed flawlessly in order for the Orion people and himself to survive ... and the Afghan leadership to fall.

***********

Kendall was lifting makeshift weights when Rashid hurried into the facility. He had routinely left Kendall for short periods of time during the day when he had to run his errands, e.g., checking on Carson and Fields, contacting his Mossad counterparts, and having the occasional meal or tea with the Shazeb family. President Shazeb and his sons had left Kendall alone, as they were concerned she might carry the same sickness as Carson. They certainly did not want their families contracting any illness, even though they had been told it was only malaria. They were no longer anxious to be near her, and they thought Rashid was the most loyal of servants to agree to look in on her, and see that her needs were met. Truth be told, they were apprehensive of being near Rashid too, as they felt he could be a carrier by virtue of his daily contact with the Orion people. Rashid found it both amusing and maddening. In his opinion, these people were small-minded and ignorant. Well, it worked in his favor. He could spend more time with the Orion people, putting his plan into place, and less time in the presence of the Shazebs. It actually worked perfectly on both ends.

Rashid walked up to Kendall and handed her a bottle of water. He grinned. "I have good news."

"Wonderful! Tell me that I'm getting out of here."

His eyes twinkled and he gave a playful shrug. "Sorry. It's not that good. My sources tell me the Orion people and the U.S. government agencies know you are part of the missing group. In fact, it's front page news. Also, your mother has been assured that everything is being done to locate you, and your neighbor is picking up your mail."

"Wonderful! Now, when do we get out of here?"

"Not so fast, Kendall. Also, $10,000 has been deposited into your checking account." He wrinkled up his nose and said, "I don't see how that is going to help you, because you aren't home to make any payments."

She grinned. "Oh, I'm much more technical than that. I don't write checks any more. My bank account is set up to automatically pay certain bills periodically. I just need to make sure there is enough money in the account to do that. For instance, in a couple weeks, my annual car payment and homeowner's insurance are due. Those are lump sums and usually run close to fifteen hundred dollars. Normally, I would move money around from one account to another, but now that you have deposited funds, the payments will be made, and all will be well."

She felt immense relief at his news, particularly knowing that people knew that she was with the missing Orion executives and that her mother was doing okay.

Rashid couldn't look her in the eyes. He felt like such a louse for not telling her about her mother's heart attack, Glenn Carson's being at death's door, and that the Orion people and the U.S. government thought she was part of the master plot against the executives.

He grabbed her arm. "Let's have something to eat, and then let's do some target practice. I want you to be a fairly good marksman by the end of the week. We are going to step up your training in that area, until you get it right."

She searched his eyes, detecting a change. There was something disquieting about his demeanor. "What's wrong? Has something changed?"

He looked down and stuttered, "N-N-No, I just want you to get better at holding and shooting a gun."

"You are a lousy liar. What's going on, Rashid?"

In search of something to fill in his reticence at all the missing details, he blurted out, "I've got Fields in the loop. He's agreed to help. I'm kind of nervous about him. He seems a bit odd. Can we count on him?"

"For what?"

"To keep his head! If he blows this, we're all dead."

"He's a really smart guy. And he wants to go home. I'm sure he would do just about anything right now to get out of here."

"I'm just saying that he'd better come through for us. A lot depends on him doing his part."

They had a quick meal and then worked on Kendall's shooting skills. She hated the rifle; it was heavy and loud. The discharge was deafening and she felt it to her core. They didn't have the luxury of ear plugs, and she figured she would surely be deaf by the time she got home. She was a decent shot when lying prone during sniping rounds. Her shots were accurate, and she liked that after firing, the rest of her body absorbed the recoil. When she stood, the rifle was awkward and she instinctively pushed the butt of the gun away from her cheek. That caused her a lot of pain when the butt jumped to her bicep and left a noticeable bruise. It took her several days to finally learn the proper cheek weld. She was relieved to find that when she held the gun tight to her cheek, her shoulder pocket could easily absorb the shock of the rifle discharging a round.

They practiced stress firing outdoors, where Kendall would run a ways and then stop and shoot immediately. She learned the art of compensating for twitching muscles. She had never been so aware of each breath she took. She felt uncoordinated and could only imagine how bad her technique was.

She really liked the handgun ... mostly because it was not a rifle. She felt like she had more control. It was smaller and easier to hold. The clip was easy to load and ram into place. It was so much lighter than the rifle and easier to conceal. She would rather have carried just one or two handguns. But Rashid insisted she learn the art of sniping. She had no idea how she was going to carry all these weapons. For that matter, she wondered if she would survive the whole escape ordeal once it went down.

When Rashid brought Kendall back to the military compound, he pulled a folded khaki military field bag from under his jacket. It was ringed with side pockets for spare ammo. "Let's look at your things. This bag needs to be ready at a moment's notice."

Kendall was mortified when he started pawing through her personal belongings. She was near tears as he discarded one item after another that she considered a necessity. "Can't I at least have a toothbrush or hairbrush?"

"No. Hopefully, we won't be in an isolated predicament for very long. We'll rendezvous with my counterparts as soon as we can. You just need to be dry and warm or cool ... depending on the weather. We will mostly be carrying food, water, and weapons. If it helps, my bag will be larger."

Kendall was now terrified at the rash act on which they were about to embark. In a similar vein, although Rashid tried to be optimistic, in reality he was beyond fearful. Kendall was obviously not an athlete and uncomfortable around weapons of any kind. The only thing she had going for her was that she was loyal and would take direction. He didn't have to worry about her turning the gun on him. He was her only Afghan ally, and she would stick with him to the end ... for her own preservation. She was just petrified enough not to start thinking on her own.

Rashid had not counted on the added Orion element. He could only surmise that it was a gift from the Divine. His mother had taught him that a devout Jew must participate in repairing the world by being a part of *tzedakah* ... justice. She also said that Christians believed that, if it is God's will, then the mission will succeed.

Rashid sighed and refused to worry about it any longer. He did not believe in rash acts and martyrdom. For this situation, he had thought things through and planned and organized the Shazeb downfall, rendering inoperable the Afghan infrastructure, and getting the hostages out of Afghan. There was nothing left to do except choose the moment.

But he had not been honest with Kendall. What he had in mind for her could get her killed. In fact, it would most likely get her killed. The probability of her survival had to be very small. But that couldn't be helped. In the overall scheme of things, he needed a backup ... someone he could count on to look over his shoulder and be his "second." She certainly wouldn't be his choice in terms of physical and military abilities, but she was smart and he knew she wouldn't fall apart under the stress.

Now, Rashid just needed to light the match of rebellion and watch the flickering sparks ignite.

# CHAPTER TWENTY-ONE

The young Mossad Agent Shane Menard was bent over reviewing the newest information streaming courtesy of *Prophecy.* He had just finished doing the same with the info pouring out of the Pentagon in Washington, DC. He frowned. This was not good. Things were heating up in DC, and Israel needed to make a decision. They were close to their final operation and could not afford to have DC interfere or thwart their plans. They had worked too hard on this long investigation that had been years in the making. Nothing would get in the way of the mission. That meant they needed to take action ... and now!

He stormed into the director's office and waved the latest downloads at him. There was tension in his voice. "Benjamin, you've got to see this! It's happened. The Americans know we're associated with the Orion kidnapping. They just don't know in what way."

Benjamin Zimmerman slowly reviewed the information and then sat back in his squeaky chair. "We knew this day was close. It's time to put the diversion into effect." He consulted his watch and declared there would be a meeting of the team in sixty minutes. All available traveling agents were to be linked in via satellite. He got out a sheet of paper and scribbled the pros and cons. He was about to provide the U.S. Intelligence agencies with a red herring that he hoped would keep them busy for a day or two.

While the pros-and-cons exercise seemed elementary, it helped Director Zimmerman zero in on the viable options and fairly quickly discount the foolish, unwise ones.

Six agents sat around the conference table while four more traveling agents were linked in by satellite to the private, secure Mossad network. Two more agents in the field were connected via their cell phones and a reverse link to the base center in Israel. The customized scrambling software was automatically running, and the routine check for unauthorized eyes and ears had been deployed.

In Afghanistan, Rashid felt the gentle pulse emanating from his father's silver tribal ring that he wore on the middle finger of his left hand. The ring was inlaid with green malachite. It had been modified and customized by Israeli scientists. Thick veins of fiber-optic wire posed as silver. The wire delivered a subtle throb when communication by his counterparts was desired. Any unauthorized wearer of the ring would feel nothing if communication was attempted by the Mossad. The technology had included a biometric element, and it only recognized Rashid's middle finger.

He went directly to one of his safe, isolated places and found a text message in Hebrew on his hidden cell phone about the conference call.

He established the secure link to the requested Mossad conference call precisely on time and used a tiny wireless, colorless earpiece. He hid the cell phone on one of the corner beams that made up the roof of a nearby sheep shed and stuffed dry grass around it. He peered out through a small opening between wooden slats and could see anything approaching within a mile. Because the microphone was supercharged, Rashid could stand across the room and still be heard. He usually checked both sides of the hut when he was "in conference."

In the past week, he had emergency, unplanned "conferences" every other day. He knew that was pushing the limit. If this whole mission was not brought under control, a slip-up would occur and then they would all be exposed. There was far too much scurrying around and too many back-up plans being considered. It was all due to the Orion people's being kidnapped. The fact that one of them was gravely ill only added to the imminent danger and uncertainty. Rashid absentmindedly adjusted the leather straps on his knife sheath.

Mossad Director Benjamin Zimmerman entered the conference room and consulted his watch. The atmosphere was tense but quiet. "Let's get started, people. The Americans know about the money deposited into Kendall Radcliffe's account. We knew it was risky when we made it, and we knew it would only buy us a few days. That's exactly what it did ... bought us a few days. But it was the only way to secure Radcliffe's help and get her to believe us. She's now on board, thanks to Rashid's quick thinking. Let's move on to the next step."

He looked around the room and then at the split screen of faces. "U.S. intelligence is about to contact us and demand an explanation. This is what we're going to do. I will contact my friend at the CIA and tell him that we've paid a small sum of money for information involving an important operation we have been working on for some time. If they press further, I will reluctantly reveal that it involves large scale drug smuggling." He looked around the room and continued, "It cannot be helped, but unfortunately it will look like this Kendall Radcliffe is involved."

A spurt of static sounded over the wires. Rashid reacted. "You cannot do this! It will make her look bad and will surely get her killed. Plus, it will damage her reputation and she could lose her job and even be accused of treason! What are you thinking? This is going too far!"

Director Zimmerman furiously spat out, "Enough! Agent Sharif, you have lost your focus. Don't tell me that you have feelings for her? You are a professional and a high-ranking member of the Mossad ... the most elite intelligence agency in the world! You are dangerously close to throwing it all away for nothing more than sentiment. Have you not been taught to look at the big picture? I have seen you destroy families in the name of the ultimate goal. What is it called? Right! Collateral damage. That is what Ms. Radcliffe will be. It cannot be helped. She and her Orion bosses have unfortunately landed right in the middle of our mission. In order to save that mission, we need to throw them to the wolves. Or at least throw her to the wolves."

He paused just long enough to take a breath and continued in his tirade. "Making that deposit into her account was a stroke of genius! The American intelligence agencies will be all over her and every aspect of her life. We've bought ourselves a couple days. The plan will have been set in motion by the time the Americans rethink the kidnapping episode."

The director was very worried about Rashid. "Agent Sharif ... Rashid, are you with us?" And then in an attempt to mollify Rashid, he allowed himself a somewhat soothing tone, "We will do everything we can to rectify the situation at the end of the mission. Be assured that a full explanation will be given to the Americans. Ms. Radcliffe's reputation will be restored. The current scenario is simply a short-term solution to direct the Americans away from our mission."

To take the focus off Rashid and minimize any further embarrassment to his favorite agent by having singled him out, Zimmerman pointed his finger at all of the agents present. "You all need to remember that our single most important goal is the destruction of the poppy fields and the related upstream manufacturing and distribution. Secondary and perhaps even as important is the complete annihilation of President Shazeb's dictatorship and the end of his family rule. He and his sons will be destroyed. No ... must be destroyed ... for the good of the entire region!"

He continued his tirade. "Israel is not unsympathetic to the Afghanistan people. But if we do this right and expose Shazeb's evil ways, the people will be thankful. We will help them find a new leader who will rule with fairness and by democratic principles. And the whole of the Asia and the Middle East will be much more stable."

Zimmerman didn't dare tell the group—and particularly Rashid—that he had big plans for Rashid down the road. That he saw Rashid assuming a critical leadership position once the country of Afghanistan was reorganized. Just how high Rashid went up the ladder of leadership was up to circumstances and how he conducted himself through the present mission. He'd worked very hard to gain the loyalty of the Afghanistan military and had allies in every city. Rashid was generally known as an honorable and fair military advisor.

Oh, yes, the Americans would want to be involved. But it had exited Afghanistan years earlier and since then had not taken an active role in managing it or helping it grow. Its capitalistic enterprises had been burned and run out of town. Because America's taste for war was long gone, it turned tail and ran. Its subsequent years of political infighting and move towards isolationism had allowed a sleeping giant to grow beyond an acceptable position.

Israel had picked up the mantle of policing the Middle East through covert means. It was dealing with Afghanistan in the most back-door manner. Once Rashid Sharif had become known to Israeli operatives through his then university roommate, Rashid had been in their back pockets from then on. The hatred Rashid had for the Afghanistan way of life, and the Shazeb family, who had destroyed his own family, fueled the disloyalty. It had been relatively easy to lure Rashid over to their side. He had always been interested in his mother's background and wanted to connect with the country of which she had such fond memories.

He remembered his mother as a gentle soul. She had spoken of her family back in Israel with such sadness and devotion. But she had come to love her Afghanistan husband, and once she bore children, could see no way to live in both worlds. She had reconciled herself to the Afghan way of life and convinced herself to be the best wife and mother she could.

What Rashid didn't realize was that Director Zimmerman wanted him installed as the new leader of Afghanistan so that Israel could begin to assert more control and power in the Middle East. Israel believed it could manipulate and control Rashid just like it had done to several other international leaders whom Israel had backed.

They were underestimating Rashid. He had values, ethics, and honor, and would never agree to be a puppet at the hands of a self-interested Israel with ulterior motives ... even if he had blood ties. Rashid wanted Shazeb out so that a fair and honorable leader could be installed in Afghanistan. The leader would look out for the country's best interests, starting with its citizens. He would promote good will with the neighboring countries and seek to raise Afghanistan's status as a world leader. Those might be lofty goals for such a backward country, but with the right leadership great strides could be made in the next ten years to help Afghanistan. It certainly had the resources, and now it only needed the right people and organization to move it forward.

Director Zimmerman began pacing before the group. "Agent Menard will step up the monitoring. Get one of the new hires to assist full time. I will have him reassigned to tactical monitoring for the next month." He looked over at Menard. "I cannot emphasize enough how important it will be to employ the countermeasures on the Orion communication wave stream. You know the American intelligence community probably possesses the same abilities that we do, to establish a one-way ear from whatever source we are inclined to monitor. But we have the added advantage of having our Orion protégé Blumfeld on our side. He will let us know if others are on to our abilities."

He grabbed the sheet of paper on the table and ticked off the remaining items in pedantic fashion. "Agent Sharif, you will set the Afghanistan mission on its course in two days' time. It will begin in the evening. The Paris team will run into their American counterparts at an outdoor café in Paris and will let slip through vague reference that it is working on a drug matter that will be eradicated soon. The London team will request an immediate meeting with British intelligence and seek their assistance in tracking a large-scale drug smuggler thought to be operating in the Mediterranean Sea ... possibly out of Lebanon. This will stroke the English egos and focus its teams on the Mediterranean Sea. I am hoping England will send a couple ships to patrol the Mediterranean. In the meanwhile, our mission will go forward in the Arabian Sea."

Zimmerman began pacing again. "Lastly, the Iranian team will stay close to the border and be ready to assist with the extraction of the Orion people. That should take place the morning after Rashid has begun the operation." He stopped pacing and looked between the agents and the screen. "Any questions?" he barked.

No one spoke. In fact, it was deathly silent. This moment had been coming for a long time, and the agents were moving into their combat-like roles. They knew exactly what was expected of them. They were but a cog in the wheel of this mission. Every last detail was to be attended to. Every agent's role was critical to the success of the mission. Rashid's was the most vital and dangerous. He was to give the electronic signal once the Shazeb family had been neutralized.

***********

Rashid practiced his rhythmic breathing. He was having to do it a lot these days in order to appear calm and "normal." In reality, he felt agitated and stressed. His senses were heightened, and he realized that the time for action had come. He was considered a young Mossad agent. This was basically his first and only assignment. He was not in the employ of the distinguished agency for any purpose other than to see the Shazebs obliterated. But he understood that the destruction of the drug manufacture and supply operation was as important an undertaking.

He doubted that Director Zimmerman realized the extent of his hatred for President Shazeb and his boys. Rashid had lain low for so many years now that he often feared that the ruination of the Shazebs would never take place. In the interim years, Rashid had learned a lot about patience and that timing was everything. He couldn't believe that he let slip his concern about Kendall during the conference call. He was wise beyond his years, and very rarely showed his emotional side. He made a mental note to guard against future irrational displays of emotion.

That was one reason he was drawn to Kendall. When he was with her, he could be himself. He let his guard down, allowed himself to smile, and even enjoy himself. Upon meeting her, he had realized that the only way to establish a personal connection with her was through emotion and truth. The more truthful he was, the more she was drawn to him and trusted him. The only way to deal with her was through straightforward communication. That is what he had done. Kendall was very good at sizing people up and determining their authenticity. She could also spot the dangerous souls who crossed her path.

The few but huge lapses in information that he kept from Kendall were not to be helped. Right now, Rashid needed to think through every detail of his plan. It involved Kendall in a major way. His plan had better be perfect. He would sell it to Kendall as her only way out. Unfortunately, he would need to use Glenn Carson's current critical medical condition in order to instill a sense of urgency. At this point, Rashid was not even sure that Carson would survive any rescue attempt. But at least he could be brought home.

Rashid left the sheep hut, carrying all of his Mossad tools. He stowed them away in a couple of hidden compartments he had made in the jeep. Because he drove an older model, somewhat battered military jeep, no one ever asked to borrow it. In fact, he was often teased about his lowly broken-down jeep. Even President Shazeb accused him of making him look bad. The leader had offered a brand new jeep to Rashid several times, but each time the young man had declined. He said that he preferred to remain the humble servant that he was. Thankfully, Shazeb was not too up on his English literature, or Rashid was sure he would have conjured up an image of the *David Copperfield* character *Uriah Heep*. He had to be careful not to feign too much humility.

Rashid figured he had learned most of his patience from the years of living amongst the Shazeb clan. He was well liked, didn't outshine the Shazeb boys, could easily manipulate them to stop squabbling, and teased and cajoled the Shazeb women. They all thought highly of him and welcomed him in their presence and their household.

He drove back to the makeshift gun range and prepared himself to be as honest as he needed to be in explaining the situation to Kendall. He gave a big sigh as he bounced over one of the many potholes on the road. He enjoyed the ride along the slow-moving creek. He wished the drive would last forever.

There was so much responsibility on his shoulder. He must succeed. Anything less than complete success would be fatal to the Orion people and himself personally and to the mission and possibly the Middle East and the rest of the world. He quickly recited the Jewish *Prayer of Protection* that his mother had taught him. After a few minutes, he felt the anxiety leaving him. It was replaced with a sturdy resolve and determined mindset.

# CHAPTER TWENTY-TWO

IT HAPPENED VERY UNEXPECTEDLY. THE pulsing beat on the cardiac monitoring device was rhythmic and steady. Without warning the cardiac telemetry registered a flat line. A high-pitched alarm sounded, and the nearby physicians and nurses came running. A crash cart was brought in and every attempt was made to resuscitate the patient. The patient was blue and registered no heartbeat, and the pupils were dilated with no corneal reflex. Several attempts were made to shock the heart back into normal sinus rhythm. After three defibrillation attempts, Mrs. Radcliffe was declared dead.

The night nurse felt particularly bad. In the past couple days, no relative had been located. It was clear Mrs. Radcliffe was loved. Her neighbor had called for an update, but the hospital declined to offer a status for privacy reasons. Mrs. Radcliffe had died alone and without her daughter beside her. The daughter wasn't even aware that her mother had suffered a heart attack and was currently in the intensive care unit.

Mrs. Radcliffe's body was sent to the morgue in the basement of the hospital. The cause of death was straightforward: myocardial infarction.

The night nurse felt helpless. It was the end of her shift. Mrs. Radcliffe's room had been cleaned and readied for the next patient. The nurse was about to go off duty and was staring at the computer screen trying to make sense of the tragedy. She didn't know why this particular death was hitting her so hard. People in the ICU die all the time.

A nondescript man in an ill-fitting business suit hurried past her and stopped at the doorway of the now empty hospital room. She did not recognize him as having visited any of the other patients. He was obviously not following the ICU protocol of suiting up in protective gown and booties. She moved toward him. "Excuse me, Sir. Who are you looking for? I think you are in the wrong place. This is the ICU, and you shouldn't be here."

He was abrupt and borderline rude. He pointed toward the empty room.

"Where is the patient who was in this room?" His eyes flashed concern but only in a professional context. The nurse could tell he wasn't a caring relative by his demeanor, or lack thereof.

"There is no one assigned to this room yet, Sir. Who are you looking for?"

He was impatient and barked, "I am looking for Mrs. Radcliffe. Where is she? I see you have moved her out of ICU. Answer me!"

Just then, a young volunteer hurried up with a clipboard and handed it to the nurse. "The morgue needs you to sign off on the Radcliffe transfer order."

The unpleasant man looked aghast, "Mrs. Radcliffe died? No! That can't be!" He quickly turned toward the exit and strode down the corridor.

The night nurse looked exasperated. She called after him, "Wait! Who are you? How do you know Mrs. Radcliffe?" She was about to summon Security, but he turned around.

His manner had changed, and he was now calm, soothing, and pleasant. "I will speak with the people in the morgue. Please let them know I am on my way down now."

"What is your name, Sir?"

He hesitated for the briefest of moments. "Uh, Mr. Jones."

A flash of doubt passed through her mind, and she pushed it away, thinking her paranoia was getting the better of her. She was glad he was going to the morgue to sort things out. She alerted the morgue that Mr. Jones would be there in a few minutes. He never arrived but walked straight out of the main lobby and disappeared into the misty morning rain.

Rashid was awakened shortly after that. He was given the news of Mrs. Radcliffe's untimely demise. He wondered if things could possibly get any worse. But he knew the answer to that. Yes, of course. Nothing in this mission had gone smoothly, particularly after the introduction of the Orion people. He cursed their existence but then thought of Kendall. He was very fond of her. She was nice to look at and had an appealing personality.

Now what was he going to do? He couldn't very well tell her about her mother's death. He felt like a traitor and vowed to tell her at the first opportune moment ... after the rescue had been effected. Either way, he couldn't win. She would probably take out her anger and sorrow on him. She hadn't asked for this. But then neither had he. His involvement in the mission had been his choice from the beginning. Hers was not a choice. There was just no way around it. She would end up hating him once she was told.

He brooded in silent frustration at his dilemma and eventually resolved to work that much harder to succeed. He also vowed to do whatever he could to protect Kendall, even if it cost him his life. He took his responsibilities seriously.

From this point on he must focus like never before. He must shut out all emotions and center his thoughts and actions on the ultimate goal. He would do this, or die trying. He would draw from his mother's most inspirational Jewish and Christian teachings.

He whispered a prayer and set out to find the Orion CEO, Paul Fields.

As usual, he found him alone in the main datacenter at the palace. While the offices of the Afghanistan Infrastructure Data Center, or the AIDC, were housed in two side-by-side, ten-story buildings in downtown Kabul, President Shazeb had insisted that he have ultimate control over the datacenter. He had installed his son Saaqib to oversee and monitor all computer activities. No major changes could be made to the infrastructure or Datacenter without Saaqib's sign-off.

Rashid coolly strolled in to the small but impressive datacenter and looked around. "Where's Saaqib?"

Fields rolled his eyes and shrugged his shoulders. "The usual."

"When did he leave?"

"Thirty minutes ago."

"Shit! He could be back soon. We don't have much time." Rashid pulled a chair up next to Fields.

Sensing a major shift in the wind, Fields raised his eyebrows. "What's up?"

"We're moving forward in two days. You will start the process by jamming all Afghanistan radio signals and interrupting the power grid."

Rashid explained in detail that it must be an interruption that cannot be explained and easily reversed. Fields was concerned at his obvious exposure. He had also heard the nightly screams from punishments handed out to a collection of prisoners on a regular basis. He had a right to be fearful.

"What if I am accused of causing this?"

Rashid nodded. "Oh, you will most certainly be accused! Think ahead. Plan for it. Can't you explain it away as a solar flare? That was the cause when Canada's power grid went down."

Fields nodded. "Maybe, but that was in 1989. We've come a long way since then."

"Yeah? Well, Shazeb isn't that computer savvy or up on historical references. He won't know that. Just make him think it was recent. Talk fast!"

"Wha-what do I do if he wants me to fix it?" Fields stammered.

"Stall! Tell him you must check all of the internal systems, including visiting the AIDC offices in downtown Kabul. That would totally make sense."

Fields perked up. "That's good! I can do that!"

"Then we'll meet you at the AIDC offices on the rooftop, where hopefully a helicopter will be waiting."

"Oh, God, that sounds too good to be true! Do you think it will work? It's got to work." Then his thoughts turned to Glenn Carson. "What about Carson? How is he? Can he be moved?"

"I'm damn well going to figure out a way."

Now Fields was exasperated. "Just wonderful! You haven't thought that far ahead!" he said with much sarcasm.

"Leave that detail to me. I'll figure it out."

"Do you even have any friends here who are helping you?" The consequences of a negative response were not lost on Fields. His eyes widened at the thought, and he didn't even wait for Rashid to answer. "Oh my God! We're all going to die!"

"Don't get ahead of yourself Fields! Everything's under control. I am not without resources. Yes, I have friends. They're just not physically present at this time."

"Fine! I guess since we haven't made much progress towards a departure time, we have nothing to lose. What do we do first?"

"I'm going to arrange for a dinner for you, Kendall, and the Shazeb family ... and me, of course. It will be two nights hence."

"Why? How will that help us?"

Rashid was impatient. "If you'd let me finish," he spat out through clenched teeth."

"You will tell Shazeb how frustrating it all has been, but that you and Saaqib have isolated two viruses and detected several malware strings or whatever computer maladies you can think of. Saaqib will beam and naturally take credit. He will never admit that he wasn't watching you at all times. You must let President Shazeb see how clever you are that it has all been cleaned up and removed. But then tell him that his systems are not operating at an optimum level, and he needs to upgrade his mainframes."

He paused and made sure Fields was listening. "Here's the critical part. You then tell him that the current system is being stressed and could lose functionality at any time. Today, start dropping hints of this to Saaqib."

"Won't that piss President Shazeb off?"

Rashid nodded. "Exactly! That's what we're going for. Between you, Kendall, his sons, and a lot of drinking, we are going to push him over the edge."

"God help me!"

"God help all of us!"

Just then Saaqib strode in and, catching sight of Rashid and Fields in conversation, grinned and remarked, "You two plotting the overthrow of the country?"

Rashid got up slowly, laughed, and went to Saaqib, giving him a brotherly hug. "Oh, Saaqib, how I've missed you these past few days!"

"Few days? We haven't spent any time together in weeks. Have you spent all of that time with the American woman?" Saaqib winked.

Rashid felt sick at the inference but buried it. He gave Saaqib's arm a light punch. "You old dog! Leave it to you to blame the females."

Saaqib was pleased at the reference to his coarse reputation. Rashid continued, "Where have you been, or should I ask if you have a new conquest?"

"Rashid, I am a married man, devoted to my wife."

"But?"

Saaqib was perturbed at the probe and chose to view it as good-natured banter. It abruptly entered his mind that Rashid might be wondering how long Fields was left alone. He ushered Rashid from the room and out of the hearing of Paul Fields. "I, uh, I haven't been gone long, you know. I would never leave this man alone with our systems unprotected like this."

Rashid nodded good-naturedly and assured him that he had only just arrived.

"Ahhh! So, you were looking for me?"

Rashid raised his eyebrows, "Who else would I be looking for?"

Saaqib laughed nervously. "Of course."

Rashid continued smoothly. "I'm planning a celebratory dinner for two nights from now. Let's get the whole family—children included—and the Orion people."

Saaqib nodded. "Great! A party. What's the occasion?"

"I've just missed all of you and the children."

"And why do we need to include the Orion people?"

"Well, it's just Paul Fields and Kendall Radcliffe. I have spent a lot of time with Kendall in the past couple weeks. She is sad that she is not home. She misses her mother and friends. I have come to really like her, and I think you would like her too." Rashid poked Saaqib in the chest, his eyes twinkling. Rashid was quite alarmed and even nauseous at the debauched look that could be seen in Saaqib's eyes.

"Really, me?"

"Yes, she has your wit. I think you two would hit it off great! So, how about it? Are you on for the party?

Saaqib was positively salivating. "Absolutely! We'll all be there. Do you need my help?"

"No, as a matter of fact. Kendall is apparently quite a good cook and has been wanting to bake something in the palace kitchen. She's planning the menu with the palace chef.

"Saaqib clapped his hands together. "Well, this should be interesting! Count me in, brother!"

Rashid was quite pleased with the exchange. He knew right where to find the younger brother, Ahmad. Rashid had been avoiding him. Ahmad was quite intelligent and with little thought would figure out what was going on with his ferret-like senses.

As usual, Ahmad was in the nearby barracks browbeating some new recruits. He was demonstrating the proper stance for hand-to-hand combat and encouraging the men to be quite physical with each other. Rashid was furious. He could see that a couple of the men were hurt. They were feigning enthusiasm but hung back from the crowd. He was glad he was interrupting.

Ahmad was pleased to see Rashid. He greeted him and said, "Come look, brother, at the new recruits. Do you think they'll give me a challenge?"

"No way! If I know you, you'll have them in shape by sundown!"

"Ha! You know it!"

Ahmad barked an order at the young recruits for vigorous courtyard exercise under his second-in-command and walked a few steps away with Rashid.

"What is it, my brother? I haven't seen you here in days."

"You and Saaqib! I didn't know you were that interested in my boring daily duties as ordered by your father."

"Not interested in the least. Better you than me, taking orders from the old man. Just wait until I'm in charge."

"Whoa there, Ahmad. You're getting ahead of yourself. Saaqib is older. Maybe he will be the chosen successor."

Ahmad shoved Rashid playfully but none too lightly either. There was a scheming gleam in his eyes. "Not if I have anything to say about it." He looked as if he knew something that no one else did.

Rashid wasn't sure he should recognize it out loud. "Eh?"

"Well, I'm just saying that you never know what might happen. Anyway, whose side are you on?"

"Ahmad, I love both my brothers equally! You have been my friends since childhood. Please don't ask me to choose."

"Fair enough, Rashid, but one day you just might have to choose." His eyes narrowed as he focused on Rashid. He lowered his voice, and Rashid stepped closer to hear. "And I know you'll choose wisely."

"Oh, Ahmad, don't talk of such unpleasantness. I have news!"

With that segue, Rashid explained the plans for dinner. Ahmad wasn't about to miss anything his brother and father might also be involved in. The younger brother readily agreed to the dinner plans. After a few more jokes, Rashid excused himself, citing the need to speak to the president and then the kitchen staff. Ahmad sent him on his way, laughing at the menial tasks Rashid often undertook.

Rather than feel sorry for Rashid, Ahmad instead was very glad that he was the actual son of President Shazeb. Yes, Ahmad was quite fond of Rashid and even preferred him over the older brother, Saaqib. But Ahmad knew that Rashid would never be president. He was not part of the Shazeb birth lineage. All that stood in Ahmad's way was his older brother. Ahmad constantly looked for ways he could undermine his older sibling. He just kept watching and waiting, biding his time until the moment arrived. He wasn't sure what he would do, but he would be ready and seize the opportunity.

Ahmad had done everything he could to point out to his father how emotionally immature and unstable Saaqib was. Of course, all of it was true, but Ahmad fit under those labels as well. Ahmad was just better at hiding it. He could see how angry his father got when he heard of Saaqib's latest exploit. The two brothers were actually very similar in intellectual capacity. But Ahmad was wiser ... only to the extent that he rarely got caught. Saaqib didn't even try to hide his brutal and sexually sadistic proclivities from his father. Ahmad, on the other hand, always considered the time and place ... and most importantly, the audience. He knew how to play to those present. If the father was in attendance, Ahmad was on his best behavior ... showing just enough viciousness tinged with civility and wisdom to earn his father's respect.

The only difference between the two sons was shrewdness. Ahmad was clever and Saaqib wasn't. To make matters worse, Saaqib wasn't intuitive enough to recognize what his brother was doing. He was too busy brutalizing women, playing with the country's data systems, and feeling more important because he was older and in charge of the infrastructure, the very heart and soul of Afghanistan. He made the erroneous, if not naïve, assumption that the mantle of leadership would fall to him naturally because of birth order. He was caught up with self-importance and exploited the none-too-little power that was afforded him in his position.

It was only a matter of time before a decisive event fractured this family for good.

Rashid didn't want to be far away when this happened. He wasn't sure how it would come about, but he had no doubt that it would ... and very soon. The fires of hatred, ambition, and lust for power had been stoked. The only remaining component was the metaphorical spark. Rashid planned to provide that during the dinner, with Kendall's help.

Lastly, he went in search of President Shazeb. Rashid found him on the phone, where he had just been told that this latest crop of poppies looked to be the largest harvest ever. He motioned for Rashid to enter and close the door. Shazeb continued his phone conversation ... ordering the raw material, a brownish-black gum that had been bundled into bricks, to be delivered to the morphine refinery outside of Jalalabad some ninety miles to the east. He was informed that the sap was still being collected and milked from the poppies. The deliveries were being made to the refinery on a rotating basis and would continue for the next week.

The first kilos of manufactured heroin would soon be ready for transportation through Pakistan via Khyber Pass to the southeast of Karachi on the Arabian Sea. The transshipment arrangements had been made, and the appropriate local officials in Pakistan and along the Indus River bribed. A cargo ship was now on its way to the rendezvous point at Port Qasim outside of Karachi and would arrive in three days.

Transshipping through Port Qasim, where the opium was loaded onto the cargo ship, was always the trickiest to negotiate. This time, Shazeb readily agreed to the local demands. He thought he was quite generous, given the profits he would soon be enjoying. But he made it clear to the Port Authority official that this was a one-time "gift," because at the moment he had other pressing business to attend to; but that if this unreasonably high demand was made on future Port business, there would not be a good outcome. Shazeb's partners and middlemen were well aware of his penchant for violence and retribution. They would not press their luck next time.

The president was in a great mood. Business was going well and his sons were not at each other's throats. He owed much of the good will to Rashid. He kept the peace between the sons and enlightened the father on a routine basis.

Shazeb looked at Rashid appreciatively. "Ah, my son, Rashid. How is my blessed son today?"

Rashid explained that he was organizing a dinner, and Shazeb heartily approved. Given the tens of millions of dollars he was about to reap from his current harvest of poppies, he was ready to celebrate. He didn't even mind that the Orion people were being included. It was high time he browbeat Fields on the state of Afghanistan's computer infrastructure and that perceived issue of unknown eyes and ears having access to Afghanistan confidential business. He understood when explained about Kendall's homesickness and anxiety, and even managed to find a spark of guilt at being the source of her current predicament. He thought it would be very interesting and entertaining to have Kendall work with the kitchen staff to prepare the meal.

He even thought that perhaps Kendall could be persuaded to stay on permanently. She would make a perfect third wife for him, having lost his first wife to the great fire that also took Rashid's family. Shazeb had quickly remarried a young woman who promptly provided him with two girls. But he had not been blessed with any more sons. He reasoned that Kendall might be able to produce sons. He wasn't so sure that either of his grown sons were the men he intended them to be. Shazeb shuddered at the thought of either Saaqib or Ahmad leading the nation once he was gone. He figured that Kendall's surprise presence on the Orion plane was providential. She was a gift to him, and he would acknowledge that gift wholeheartedly. He knew he would have to deal with an angry wife, but she would fall in line ... just like the rest of Shazeb's family once he issued an important edict.

He sent Rashid away with his blessing to prepare an evening that would be memorable to all in attendance. Rashid headed to the family's quarters and felt a slight unease at what lay before him in the next few days. The more he pondered the future, the more nauseous he became.

He finally arrived at the kitchen, one of his favorite rooms in the palace. It was bright and warm and smelled of fresh *naan* and a gentle, simmering, and fragrant lamb and vegetables for the evening meal. He vowed to put his anxieties aside and focus on the day's events. The Head Chef, Taheem, was very happy to see him and greeted him like a son. They bantered back and forth for a few minutes as Rashid inquired after his wife and children. Then he explained the purpose of his visit.

Normally, the fastidious Taheem didn't let anyone interfere in the preparations of the meal. He knew how diabolical the Shazeb men were. Without the slightest provocation they would cut a member of the household staff down. Taheem had never given them a reason to. Instead, he had gone out of his way to cook succulent meals for the family and special treats for the children. His *yema* dessert was their favorite.

Rashid explained that he would speak with Kendall and find out what ingredients were needed from the market. Taheem and his staff would go to the Kabul market the next day. But Rashid made it very clear this was a celebration, and that there should be several selections of wine for dinner. Even the older children would be allowed to have a glass.

They discussed the seating arrangements and theme.

Finally, an exhausted but triumphant Rashid went in search of Kendall. Of course, he knew where she was. He had left her alone now for three hours while he ran around locating people and arranging the upcoming evening affair. Given her state of mind the last time he left her alone for a couple hours, he was wondering in what emotional state he would find her this time. Well, either way, he knew that as soon as he explained the gravity of the next few days and the demands that would be placed on her for the dinner event and beyond, she could make things very difficult for him ... for all of them. *Did he know her as well as he thought,* he asked himself? Yes, and that's precisely why he was nervous about facing her now.

# CHAPTER TWENTY-THREE

Mossad Director Zimmerman sat at his desk at home that evening, pondering his next move. He was steeling himself for the story he was about to recite. Lying was a part of his business, and he accepted that. But it took its toll. One had to be on the highest alert to keep track of the false information being imparted. Further, if he spoke with an associate of the first recipient of lies, he had better remember what was said, or his fabrications—and by association, his character—would be called into question. Within the international intelligence community, though, lying and deceit was not surprising and actually was quite necessary. Still, a measure of loyalty and integrity was expected among "friends."

In this instance, Zimmerman had known his CIA "friend" for over ten years. He considered her a worthy counterpart. They had worked together on many investigations and had jointly solved several of the most high-profile cases that had them traveling together and spending a great deal of time pursuing the same elusive suspects.

He sighed as he picked up his phone. This time it couldn't be helped. He had to deceive his "friend" and even possibly make a fool of her. It was in Israel's best interest. But it would surely cost him the friendship. There would be no going back. The days of old would be gone. They would no longer share information and insight once the full details came out. Zimmerman would be despised as a traitor to the intelligence community, and he would have trouble seeking favors in the future. He was not in the least naïve. He knew that this would be his last assignment. He would need to move on from leading this team. All of the good will he had so carefully cultivated would be gone in a flash.

But he perked up at the thought that he might even be named to a ministerial position within the popular Israeli party currently in power. If this mission was as successful as he dared hope, nothing would be out of reach for him. He could name his price ... and position, for he would be held in the highest esteem. Even his counterparts around the world would be in awe of his success and daring.

He was startled out of his reverie by the beeping of the phone line. He drew a deep breath and made the call.

"Candace Lawrence," a cool voice intoned over the line.

"Good morning, Candace, this is Ben. How the hell are you?"

Candace sat up in her chair. She detected an ever-so-slight edge of nervousness in Ben's voice. Since she had never heard this from him before in all their years of working together, her senses were immediately on high alert. She hit the record button that would save the conversation permanently to the archives. This was hardly ever done, but something told her this would be an appropriate time.

She cleared her throat and tried to sound nonchalant. She was a master at the art of appearing composed when she was actually anything but. She shook an errant wavy black tendril from her eye and continued. "Oh, I'm fine. As a matter of fact, I'm having a little down time at the moment and am planning on taking a much-needed vacation in the next couple weeks."

"Oh, really? Where will you go?"

"Haven't decided yet, but definitely somewhere warm. This past winter was brutal in Virginia. Even though we're almost through spring, I'm sick of the cold. I'm envisioning a private beach, never-ending supply of gin, and seafood of every type and flavor."

"Sounds great! Maybe I will join you—ha, ha!" Agent Zimmerman sat back in his seat and relaxed. This was going well. Since her mind was on personal matters, she would probably not even notice the ever-so-slight tension in his voice.

"What can I do for you, Zim?"

This was even better than he hoped. She had used the pet name she had casually started calling him during a very long and bloody investigation in Lebanon a few years back.

He cleared his throat. "I'm calling with a small personal favor. I'm working on a drug investigation and have come across an American name. I'm wondering if you would run the name through your databases and let me know if she's on the up-and-up?"

"Sounds intriguing. Is she an informant or a principal?"

"She came to us as an informant, but I suspect she's actually a key part of the operation."

"And what's the location of the investigation?"

"I don't know yet. We think somewhere in the Middle East ... or possibly Turkey or Egypt. It involves the worldwide distribution of large amounts of heroin. The transshipment appears to be via the Mediterranean Sea."

Candace assumed a bored toned. "Doesn't sound like you have much info yet. How do you know it's even true?"

Agent Zimmerman was feeling quite cocky now. "We've seen the stuff. The American girl gave us a sample brick. It's high quality. We've had it analyzed, and it's cut with cow's blood. Apparently, the end result is a more pliant textured product. It's easier to cut and results in less wastage. This is incredible stuff that's about to hit the international market ... including the U.S."

What's the name of the girl?"

"Candace, do I have your word this is just between you and me?"

She feigned a reluctant tone, "Agreed ... for now ... or until it becomes a national security issue."

He paused and thought, *Well, here goes.*

"Kendall Radcliffe."

Agent Lawrence's antenna hummed. She had heard that name recently ... but where? "Hmm! Can't say that I've ever run across her name before. Do you know which state she's from?"

"No. I haven't met her. A low-level investigator came across her."

"I'll do a quick check on her, Zim, and will call you back in an hour or so. Okay?"

"Sounds great! Talk to you then. Bye."

He planned to be far away from his phone when she called back—if she even called back. Agent Zimmerman figured his call would trigger a massive wave of activity within the American intelligence community. They would have tons of questions for him, and he was not about to supply any answers. In fact, he planned to avoid any further communication with his American counterparts in the near future. He hoped Rashid's operation would be well into play by the time the American intelligence mobilized for all-out war. They would be so far behind in gathering the facts that it would be over before they could interfere. Unfortunately, the collateral damage might not be so good for the Orion people, but the Mossad operatives would at least do their best to rescue them.

Agent Zimmerman was fairly confident that the two Orion executives would be saved. Hopefully, the sick one would survive his illness. But, in the agent's eyes, it would work better if Kendall Radcliffe didn't survive. It would be easier to let her involvement die with her. Questions would go unanswered, and the Mossad and Israel could offer any explanation that suited their purposes. She would be unable to refute anything. Just for good measure, they could even add fifty thousand dollars to her bank account at the end and call it a "down payment" from Shazeb. It would surely seal her fate of guilt by implication.

The first wire transfer had been a really stupid move on their part, Zimmerman thought. This time they would make sure the wire transfer began and ended in Switzerland. There would be no tie to Israel. It would look like she was in cahoots with the Afghanistan drug suppliers and distributors. If America put up a fuss, the Mossad would plant a story in the West that Kendall died at the hands of the American intelligence community during rendition. That would cause such an uproar in the U.S. that Israel would be left to its own devices. Granted, rendition didn't usually happen to U.S. citizens when at home in the U.S., but that was just a technicality. If enough innuendo and disinformation hit the press, the public would eat it up and not notice the inconsistencies.

Zimmerman sat back at his desk at home and smiled. Yes, he thought, the phone call had gone well. And he had high hopes for the remainder of the operation.

CIA Agent Candace Lawrence opened the national intelligence database and ran the name "Kendall Radcliffe." That triggered an internal alert that had her phone ringing in two minutes flat. As the name and background popped onto her screen, she realized where she had heard that name: in association with the two missing Orion Premier Net Services executives. The proverbial fat was about to hit the fire.

She picked up her phone and answered in the most officious tone she could muster: "Agent Lawrence."

The call was from a conference room within the Pentagon where a joint meeting of various agents of the NSA, FBI, Secret Service, and Defense Department were present.

The caller identified himself and those present. "Agent Lawrence, you just ran Kendall Radcliffe's name through the system. Do you have information on the missing people or Radcliffe specifically?"

Agent Lawrence thought fast. It was too late to invent lies at this point. She would surely get caught up in the inaccuracies that were bound to result. No, she reckoned. She couldn't keep the Mossad phone call from this group. Knowledge was power, and she hated imparting her information before she could work it up.

"Agent Lawrence, are you there?" an irritated voice sounded.

"Yes, Sir. I—uh—received a call a few minutes ago from Israeli intelligence inquiring about Radcliffe's background."

"I see. Was this agent a Mossad Agent?"

*Damn,* she thought. She was not going to be able to push anything into the grey area. It was going to be all the facts up front ... now.

"Yes. It was Benjamin Zimmerman."

At the news, there was a murmur of voices in the background. This was no low level agent. Director Zimmerman was well known within the upper echelons of the international intelligence community as a son-of-a-bitch in the Mossad. In fact, if one needed to contact the Mossad to seek assistance or cooperation, it was only after first securing the approval of the director. He was a hard man to get close to. He trusted no one outside the Mossad and only rarely shared bits of information—never the entire piece. How interesting that the tables were turned and it was he that now requested information.

"Why you, Agent Lawrence? Do you know him well?"

"We have worked on some of the same investigations ... obviously from different angles ... over the past several years."

There was discussion around the table about anyone else having a professional relationship with the Mossad or Zimmerman. A few heads at the table had worked with Zimmerman on one or more occasions as he rose through the Mossad leadership ranks. But it was decided they needed to minimize the interest of the U.S. intelligence community for the time being, while very little info was fed to Zimmerman. In fact, he would be getting basically public info.

"Agent Lawrence?"

"Yes?"

"What else did he reveal in his conversation?"

"He said they were working on a large scale investigation involving heroin manufacture and distribution."

"Where?"

"His exact words were somewhere in the Middle East ... possibly Turkey or Egypt with transshipments via the Mediterranean Sea."

The meeting of intelligence experts confabbed and a faceless voice finally summed it up. "We know that Kendall Radcliffe went missing on a chartered flight that also involved the two top executives at Orion Premier Net Services, Paul Fields and Glenn Carson. What do the disappearances have to do with a major, possibly Middle East, drug investigation and Israel? And even as important, what is Radcliffe's role? She received $10,000 recently via wire transfer from an Israeli offshore corporate banking account, most likely the Mossad. How could the wire transfer trail be so transparent? Why was it so sloppy? Did they want us to find it? Possibly. But why?"

Again, many theories were put forth. It was finally decided that Agent Lawrence needed to be brought into the inner circle of the investigation. She would begin by calling Mossad Director Zimmerman. She would reveal that Radcliffe worked for a high-tech company in the Pacific Northwest as the director of operations. That she had no criminal history, and she appeared to be an ordinary American citizen. If the Mossad director pressed for more info or expressed irritation that she was holding back, she could reveal the company, its business, and the city in which it was headquartered.

The committee rang off, after receiving Agent Lawrence's assurance that she would send a scrambled coded email *"For Your Eyes Only"* providing the details of the conversation.

As the meeting attendees from the various U.S. intelligence agencies filed out of the secure conference room venue at the Pentagon, three agents from the NSA stayed behind. Two of the members had not offered any comment during the meeting of the larger group. They sat amongst the others and observed, with technical administrative functions only. As agreed upon prior to the meeting, two of the smaller group (Alex and Ping) were secretly recording an audio of the meeting. The other individual, Frank Reynolds, had arrived early and installed several hidden video cameras that were feeding everything to a private computer not associated with the massive U.S. intelligence network.

They now sat at one end of the large conference room. None of them were taking notes.

"What is *Prophecy* telling us, Alex?"

"There is nothing unusual happening anywhere, except at the Orion offices ... which is to be expected. Even there, they don't have a clue what's happened to their people."

"*Prophecy* has been a godsend for us," Frank stated. "But I can't help wonder if it isn't somehow related to the Orion people's disappearances."

Alex nodded. "Do you think it's time we reveal *Prophecy's* existence?"

Both Ping and Frank vehemently countered at the same time, "No way!"

Frank, the leader of the group, was the elder of the three and a former fraternity brother and good friend of Paul Fields. He was emphatic: "We can never reveal Orion's secret technical tool to our fellow agents or even to anyone ... ever! You both know that. This would not only be on our shoulders ... in the form of treason and spying, but it would turn the domestic and international intelligence communities on their collective ears. No one would trust anyone. The mere existence of such a technical phenomenon would cause other countries to seek the like, just knowing that it was possible. The bottom line is that a lot of people would go to jail, starting with us. More would lose their jobs, and a very large U.S. company—a major asset—would go out of business, just like that."

Ping was the quiet one of the trio. His job was to make sure the data feeds coming from Orion were clean, and to modify the code to establish new feeds outward. He nodded and said, "It could also turn country against country and companies against companies."

Alex, the youngest of the three, was frustrated, and threw up his hands. "I can't believe there isn't a way to use *Prophecy* to locate the Orion people. Do we know who at Orion wrote the code for *Prophecy?* If so, we could enlist their help!"

Frank Reynolds shook his head. "Nope. That was the deal I made with Paul

Fields at the very beginning. In exchange for getting access to and being able to use *Prophecy* for U.S. investigations, we were not to know anything about its development ... or developer. He has to be one smart bastard, though! I would love to meet him ... or her."

Ping, the brilliant mind of the group, was curious. "Does the *Prophecy* developer know about us having knowledge of and using *Prophecy*?"

"I don't believe so."

"What was its original purpose?"

"You're asking that now?"

"Well, it might help us to understand its technical capacity."

Frank was wired. "Oh, how I wish I had asked Paul Fields more questions way back when. I was just so excited that I had a tool that could quickly get intelligence answers. I reasoned that it would not hurt anyone ... just the bad guys. I was too busy climbing the proverbial ladder, looking for any way I could to further my NSA career."

Alex laughed. "Well, it worked! You're only a level below a cabinet position, and you have the ear of the State Department. You are well thought of, and people trust your judgment."

Ping snickered at the irony that Frank's judgment or intuition was in reality due mostly to *Prophecy.*

Agent Reynolds looked at his team. "Here's what we're going to do. Ping, you make sure the feeds are open and establish any new ones ... like to Israel ... so we can monitor their waves. Then help Alex analyze the data for any reference to Middle East drug investigations or the Orion people. Call me on your burned phones if you find anything."

The men left the room after removing their various planted devices.

Agent Reynolds sat in his office and contemplated the events of the day. He knew that he didn't need to issue warnings to his two young NSA agents. They were both loyal and beholden to him for their jobs. He had basically rescued them from obscurity or at the very least, from the back room of some institution or corporation that promised to be the most boring job in the world. He had brought Alex on board when *Prophecy* was first up and running. He realized he needed someone to analyze the info coming in. He had made Alex believe that *Prophecy* was a secret tool he had been commissioned to develop for the nation's intelligence community. After a few years, Alex had figured out that no one else used it. He had also learned that Frank and Paul Fields were best buddies. It didn't take much intelligence to put two and two together.

Ping, on the other hand, was rescued from his own self-destructive tendencies. He had first come to Frank's attention as a possible intern shortly after Frank was introduced to *Prophecy.* Ping was a brilliant math and science student at Stanford University. He had a dark side, though. He had been adopted at birth and could not reconcile that his mother had given him up. He partied hard and managed to rack up a couple of misdemeanor charges involving alcohol—Minor in Possession and a DUI—before Agent Reynolds learned of him and plucked him from his destructive pathway. Frank gave him a purpose and offered him a new life doing what he liked best: intelligence work that involved high-tech tools. *Prophecy* was more than Ping could ever have hoped for. He was excited to come to work each day, and couldn't wait to learn more about the individuals and companies under investigation. It helped him forget about his personal issues. For the time being, he was content to have relocated from Stanford, California, to the Virginia suburbs.

Reynolds wondered what Paul and Orion used *Prophecy* for. Since Orion seemed to always come out ahead of its competition, he surmised that *Prophecy* was being used to check out the competition's latest technical advancements. He and Paul never discussed *Prophecy.* It was a done deal that worked well, and nothing more needed to be said. The computer and network to which the data was streamed was not housed in any of the nation's intelligence offices. It was situated in a large fortified commercial warehouse along Chesapeake Bay. The exterior of the building was one of marked disrepair, including tons of rust and dented exterior walls. Any attempts at determining ownership met with overlapping holding companies and trusts.

With the help of Ping, it had been easy to set up the companies and purchase the building by diverting money during a deliberate power surge in the midst of a multi-agency transfer of funds. In the ensuing internal investigation, chaos reigned, and the political party in power buried the story about the missing funds to save face. Needless to say, since then Agent Reynolds was a believer in big government.

He was quite concerned about his frat buddy and good friend, Paul Fields. Where was he? How could he just drop off the radar? Why didn't any of the cell phones ping from a tower close by? Worse, what if the disappearances related to *Prophecy?* The horror of that info getting out was too much to contemplate. On the other hand, if no one else knew about Frank's involvement, and the Orion people turned up dead, then the secret would be buried with them. Frank might lose his technical ace if the data link unexpectedly closed up, that is, if *Prophecy* stopped working. It wouldn't be the worst thing that happened. But it might affect his career going forward. He still had another ten years before retiring.

Agent Reynolds was weary from his scattered thoughts replaying different scenarios. He knew he was overthinking the situation. It was going to have to play out on its own. He could only hope that *Prophecy* revealed more details. But the failing of *Prophecy* was that he didn't know where to direct the data streaming ... to or from. He was anxious to get more answers but even more fearful of what might be revealed.

***********

CIA Agent Candace Lawrence hung up the phone and sat back. She thought it very odd that her phone call had gone to voice mail. She expected Mossad Director Ben Zimmerman to be literally waiting next to the phone for her call. But he didn't pick up. She had an uneasy feeling that she had been played. *But why? For what purpose? Well, two can play this game,* she thought. She set about working on a plan to further engage Ben Zimmerman. In the meantime, she duly notified the multi-agency investigative team of the upshot of her attempted phone call. Candace desperately wanted to be part of the investigation, and she was determined to get ahead of the others, even if it meant a little underhanded dealings and withholding of essential details.

Mossad Director Benjamin Zimmerman smiled as he let the last ring on his phone go to voice mail. He was in charge. Things were developing as planned. Those who thought they were "in the know" were frustrated and shut out.

# CHAPTER TWENTY-FOUR

Rashid walked into the improvised workout facility and was instantly pissed and anxious to find that Kendall was not there. He searched both inside and outside the crude building and found no trace of her. He was beyond concerned at the possibility she had been discovered and taken by the military or, worse, some passing soldier who just happened to stop and satisfy his curiosity about the strange, run-down building barely visible between the trees.

He ran his hand over his stubbly chin and willed himself to think about the options. He decided to drive back to the military compound, just over five miles away, on the off chance that she was there. He couldn't imagine she would have returned to the compound on her own, but nothing about Kendall surprised him these days. He drove like a madman toward the compound and found it busy and bustling, with jeeps driving in and out of the entrance and troops assembling in the courtyard for the next shift.

As he entered the main gate, General Omar was giving instructions to several soldiers nearby. The general put up his hand to stop Rashid and walked over to his jeep. The younger man could not mistake the twinkle in the general's eyes. "Are you perhaps looking for your lost girlfriend, Rashid?"

Rashid was very careful and cautiously threw back his head and laughed. "You caught me. Is she here?"

"Oh, yes, Rashid. She looked like she had been on a long distance run and came through here about thirty minutes ago. I'm glad she's made herself at home here on the base. She looked tired, but was smiling. She waved at me and went right to her room."

"Thank you, General Omar. I'm greatly relieved that she is here and okay."

*"I'm going to kill her!"* he thought.

"Tell me. How did you two become separated? Weren't you supposed to look out for her at all times? Why did you leave her alone?"

Rashid wracked his brains for a quick and appropriate answer. "As a matter of fact, I am helping in planning a special family dinner tomorrow and needed to stop by the palace kitchen to speak to Taheem. I left her with the royal horses in the meadow and expected her to wait for me."

General Omar laughed at the younger man's unease. "Well, you better reign her in, Rashid. She seems to have a mind of her own. It is not a good idea for her to be literally running around the countryside by herself."

Rashid thanked him again and headed toward the barrack housing the Orion people's rooms.

"Hey, Rashid, where are you going?"

He looked confused and pointed towards their rooms. "You told me she went to her room."

Omar nodded. "Yeah, she did. And then she came out and went into the infirmary."

"*Shit!*" Rashid thought. He, too, didn't want her wandering around the place. But he was also nervous that she might pick up a bug in the infirmary. He ran toward the two-story building and headed to Glenn Carson's room. He saw Kendall before she saw him. She was talking to a nurse. He didn't know if he should hug her or shake her. He was so relieved, yet angry. Kendall caught the motion of him hurrying towards her, and turned to look at him. She was quite alarmed when she saw the spark of anger in his eyes.

The nurse turned away from them to go look for the doctor.

Rashid grabbed her arm and hissed, "Where have you been? I looked everywhere for you. Do you know how worried I've been?"

Kendall yanked her arm away. "I'm sorry, Rashid. But I had such a good workout and practice at the range, that I decided to run back to the base. You constantly leave me for extended periods of time. This time, you left me for hours. I had no idea when or if you were coming back. So, I jogged back."

"Did you run into anyone on the road coming back?"

"Yes. Several times. Each time, I could see them coming, and I hid behind a tree or boulder. See, I can take care of myself!" She was indignant.

"Well, you could have been killed, kidnapped, or worse!"

She looked at him defiantly, and her eyes blazed. "I don't know what's worse than what I've already been through. People have been murdered before my eyes, and I hear men being tortured almost every night. I don't think I have much to lose, Rashid."

He knew he wasn't going to win this round with the level of emotion she was displaying. He was just too glad to see her to stay mad. He gave her another intense look. "What are you doing here, anyway?"

"I've come to see Glenn Carson."

"And? Have you seen him?"

"I just got here. I'm waiting for the doctor. I think they want me to put some sort of mask and gloves on before I go into his room."

Rashid quickly thought of something. "Oh, perfect! Keep them occupied for the next few minutes. Ask a lot of questions."

"Wha—Why?"

The doctor and nurse reappeared. The nurse was carrying the gown and mask. Rashid hurriedly blurted out, "I'll just run along then." He turned to Kendall, winked, and indicated he would be back for her in a few minutes. She shrugged. He was getting really pissed at her nonchalant attitude. She had no idea what she would be in for in forty-eight hours. She had better get mentally prepared, or he wouldn't be able to save her. Her very life was at stake.

Rashid ran down the hall and turned into the room that housed the infirmary drugs. He shook his head in disgust when he saw there was no one guarding the place. The door was wide open. He knew what he was looking for ... a soporific. He wanted to induce sleep, and nothing more. He went down the few rows of pharmaceuticals and saw three bottles of Valium. He quickly grabbed the front bottle and pulled the other two to the front so that no empty space was visible.

Pushing the bottle into his side pocket, he looked around, and then seeing that the coast was clear, sauntered back to Kendall and the medical staff. Because he was considered part of the Shazeb "family," Rashid pretty much had the run of whatever place he visited. People did not question him. He never overstepped his bounds or mistreated others. He treated them with respect. Consequently, both men and women were very amenable to let him wander around as he saw fit. They were eager to gain his trust and sought his friendship. He knew that someday he would need their loyalty too. So, he, in turn, often brought bread, nuts, fruit, or some treat for their children. Rashid was well liked. He fully intended to use that loyalty when the time was right. He would need all the loyal friends he could find in the very near future.

The doctor was arguing with Kendall. He had urged her not to see Carson, and now that she had, she was extremely upset. She looked like she was going to cry. She saw Rashid and ran to him, grabbing the front of his jacket with both hands. "Rashid, Glenn looks terrible! He looks as if he's going to die in a few days."

"Oh, Kendall. I'm sure it's not that dire. The doctor is very competent, and Mr. Carson is getting the best attention."

"Then why is he in a coma?"

Rashid grabbed her arm and spun her around toward the exit door. He quietly hissed into her ear, "I don't know, but perhaps there is something we can do about it. Follow me!"

With that declaration, she was curious about his statement and followed him mutely out the door. He walked so fast ahead of her that she had to break into a run to catch up with him. He climbed into his battered jeep. "Get in!"

Kendall was so curious about his comment that she let pass the bossiness of his order. Rashid drove out the main gate, passing a genuinely amused General Omar at the guard house. They drove to the palace stables, and Rashid declared that they were going riding. "Do you know how to ride, Kendall?"

"Barely." In fact, she was terrified of the horses' giant heads and large bodies. A horse had kicked her in the knee once, and she had been careful to avoid them after that.

"Well, let's see how you do."

They walked into the barn. He chose an Arabian stallion for himself and a young female cross mare for Kendall. "Your mare's name is "*Laleh.*" That means tulip in English. She is sweet natured and gentle. She is not too young and will not be easily startled. She will hold her head and do as you command if you show confidence. Can you do that?"

"I'll try."

"Good. My horse's name is *Papaver,* which means poppy in English." He rolled his eyes at the irony. "*Papaver* is Ahmad's horse. He rarely rides it. That's fine with me, since he doesn't take good care of it."

The young stable boy, Poya, helped saddle up the horses and lead them out of the barn. Both horses were ready, and Rashid helped her mount *Laleh*. He winked at Poya, produced a soft drink from his pocket, pressed fifty *Afghanis* into his hand, and ruffled his hair. Poya responded with a huge grin and a look of devotion for Rashid.

They walked the horses out to the pasture, and then broke into a gentle canter. Rashid could see that Kendall was inexperienced and unsure of the proper seat. He urged her into a trot, and that only looked worse. She almost fell, but righted herself at the last second. Well, now he knew. He would not plan on using horses during their escape. They slowed to a walk and headed to a nearby stream just over the rise. This would give them plenty of privacy, plus they could hear anyone approaching from quite a distance.

They were sitting on a couple of large rocks by the stream, with the horses grazing nearby. Rashid produced two pieces of *naan* bread from his pack, along with a container of the savory lamb stew, and fresh fruit. Kendall could not believe how flavorful it all tasted. She turned to him.

"What did you mean by your comment that perhaps there was something we could do about Carson's condition?"

"The time has come, Kendall, for us to act." He decided to emphasize the seriousness of Carson's health. He felt like a heel, but it couldn't be helped.

He needed her fully on board to support him all the way. "Carson needs more medical assistance than he's getting in Afghanistan. We've got to get him moved very soon."

Her heart skipped a beat at the news, but she totally agreed with him. "I agree, but I'm almost afraid to ask. Wha-what do you have in mind?"

"We are going to have a dinner with the Shazeb family in two nights. One way or another, the president and his two sons will die. While the rest of the family is indisposed, we will move Carson out of the military infirmary."

"What about Fields? Where will we all go? What's going to happen to the rest of the family? Are you planning to murder the president and his sons?" She stopped long enough to draw a breath.

Rashid jumped in. He held up his hands. "Stop! I've got everything planned. Yes, Fields will be with us. He knows and is ready to assist. I have the finest medical team standing by, and without them, Carson will not survive the next week."

He spun her around and grabbed both of her arms. Her eyes got wide. "Kendall, you must trust me. Do you?"

She reluctantly stated, "Yes, but I'm scared about how it will all play out."

He nodded. "Good. So am I. That means we'll be extra careful and watchful as it plays out. I have friends everywhere. They will not hesitate to help me. You must believe me. It'll all work out okay."

What he really thought was that if they die in the process, it will have been for a good cause. He doubted that President Shazeb was planning to keep the Orion people much longer. Given the number of people that had already been killed just to bring them to Afghanistan, it wouldn't work to simply let the Orion people go home. There was already the distinct possibility that Carson would not survive the rescue attempt.

Kendall weighed his words and slowly came to the realization that there was really no other choice. She swallowed the lump in her throat and declared, "My mom will be so glad to see me. I hope she's doing okay."

Rashid looked away, uncomfortable with the topic. "Yes. You'll feel much better once you are home."

She thought his response was odd. No mention of her mother. She went white. Something's happened to her mother. He knows. That's why he didn't respond appropriately. She felt herself choking. "What's happened ... t-t-to my mother? What haven't you told me?" she demanded. Her eyes were wide and she was breathing hard.

He couldn't believe that his body language had betrayed him. He was a spy ... a member of the Mossad. He was a practiced liar. Damn! He was disgusted that his personal feelings were going to betray him now ... just when he needed her to keep her wits about her. He quickly analyzed the situation, shifted his focus, and took a deep breath.

He looked her right in the eyes, "Yes, Kendall, your mother had a heart attack and died yesterday. I'm so sorry. I wish there was something I could've done."

She collapsed to her knees and held her head. The tears flowed freely. She looked up at him with rage and spewed, "I hate this awful country, your people, and you. Look what you all have done to me. My mother didn't do anything to deserve this. I didn't do anything either. I wasn't even there when she needed me. In fact, she probably had the heart attack from worrying about me." She collapsed into sobs.

Rashid frowned and remained silent. He let her cry for five minutes before he handed her a wrinkled tissue. It was thick and scratchy, but Kendall wiped her eyes and blew her nose. She hiccupped and looked up at him. In a bitter tone, she said, "I have nothing now. My mom was everything to me. You've ruined my life! It can't possibly get any worse."

He sat down beside her, and they both stared at the flowing creek. "Kendall, I'm sorry these things have happened to you. But we've all had tragedies in our lives. My parents died when I was young. I'm trying to fix things for you and the others. Can't you see that?" He didn't dare tell her that things could indeed get worse. The U.S. intelligence community suspected her of collaborating in the disappearances of Carson and Fields, and she could very well get herself killed during the escape. Oh yes, things could get worse.

They sat in silence for fifteen minutes, as she watched the stream flow at its constant gentle pace. A *cyprinid snow trout* native to Afghanistan lazily made its way past them, swaying with the current. At that moment, Kendall wished she had no more cares or concerns than that fish. Her world was weighing way too heavily on her shoulders. She was overwhelmed with her feelings. She was in a faraway, mysterious country with strange customs. She had witnessed brutal behavior and a lack of respect for the most basic rights. Soldiers and ordinary citizens were routinely physically abused. They mistreated each other and anyone who got in their way.

Kendall wasn't fearful any more. She was angry. She tried to contain the rage and bitterness. Rashid was sad to see that piercing irate look in her eyes, but he also knew that he had to tap that emotion and feed it. It would keep her senses sharp and keen. She just might survive the next few days if she could focus on that. But what would happen if she did survive? Where would all that rage go then?

He pushed that thought away as he realized the best option for Carson's survival was to split up the Orion people. Carson would need to be rescued first. Because he would not be able to help himself, his rescue would take time and care.

Rashid would need to cause a diversion to afford him the time for Carson's rescue. He pondered his options and the loyalties of his friends. Could they be trusted? Would he be putting their lives in jeopardy? When he looked up, he realized there had been silence between him and Kendall for some time.

Kendall seethed and fumed. Finally, she stood up and stomped around Rashid, circling him as if he were prey. "Well, say something! What great plan do you have to get us out in one piece?"

Out of the blue a pair of beautiful, full-grown peafowl came into view. The male peacock with its greenish iridescent tail and brilliant markings strutted towards them, followed closely by the female peahen. Kendall sucked in her breath. "Oh my God, they are so beautiful. Where did they come from?"

"They belong to Ahmad. He has a lot of animals ... the horses, hunting dogs, these peacocks, a *markur* goat, and even a snow leopard." His voice trailed off, encouraged at her interest in something other than her own present dismal and uncertain circumstances.

"Are the peacocks native to Afghanistan?"

"No. Ahmad bought them from an Indian merchant, but you can buy them at the Kabul market."

"Are they safe here ... just running around the meadow?"

"As a matter of fact, no." Rashid frowned. "It looks like they're hungry and looking for their usual cracked corn. They are kept in a large pen behind the stables. Obviously, they've gotten out and are on the loose ... just like everything around here. We'll tell Poya when we return. In the meantime, we can drop the rest of our food in crumbs, and entice them to follow us. I don't want to be blamed if something untoward happens to Ahmad's damned peacocks."

Kendall looked over at Rashid, who was still sitting on the bank of the stream, and shook her head. What a contradiction this man was. Obviously, a man of action ... not afraid to kill or plan killings. Yet willing to consider the lives of a pair of peacocks, fairly meaningless in the scheme of things, she thought. He had clearly seen a lot of misery in his lifetime and been dealt a great deal of unfairness, yet he persevered with plans and goals for the future.

She resolved to get through the next few days doing what she could to help Rashid in securing the safety and freedom of the Orion people and most importantly, medical assistance for Glenn Carson. She would set her fears aside. After all, she had lost everything—first her boyfriend and now her mother—in just a matter of weeks. She figured that if she died during the escape attempt, she would go down having done her best and fought her hardest. She would do this for her mother. *No,* she told herself. She would do this in memory of her mother. She would use her wonderful childhood memories to be strong and be the bravest leader and warrior she knew she could be.

*I've learned to fire a gun, throw a knife, and fight with my hands and feet*, she rationalized. *I'm getting the hell out of here as soon as I can ... and on my terms!*

Rashid was watching her, trying to decipher the strange expressions that crossed Kendall's face. He was almost afraid to ask. He could tell she had come to some decision ... but about what?

# CHAPTER TWENTY-FIVE

THE DAY BEFORE THE PLANNED dinner event passed quickly. Rashid spent the morning reviewing Shazeb's scattered financial accounts associated with the "business." He sought out Fields and once again found him alone. *That damn, lazy Saaqib*, Rashid cursed. Fields helped Rashid set up several alternative international banking accounts using the various aliases Rashid had already carefully created. While these days it was virtually impossible to open a completely anonymous bank account, it would still provide Rashid with a measure of secrecy, because no banking establishment would agree to reveal the account holder's name unless there was proof of deliberate fraud.

He wasn't worried about Fields' knowing his personal business. Fields would not have access to any of the numbers, and was only too willing to assist if it meant he was closer to getting rescued and saving his head in the process. Fields was ready to get back to the U.S. and home and was therefore quite eager to be a part of whatever plan was proposed. The faith he put in Rashid's abilities was a bit daunting in the latter's eyes. Fields asked few questions. He seemed to know that if anyone could make this *coup d'état* happen, it was Rashid.

Rashid's issue with Fields was that for the first time since arriving in Afghanistan, Fields was able to interact technically outside Afghanistan's computer network. He begged and pleaded for Rashid to let him contact his family or get a message to Orion. But Rashid was resolved that this could not happen. The events needed to play out his way. He strenuously objected to the insistence of a short email message; he sympathized with Fields but held firm that the U.S. intelligence community must not learn of his whereabouts or the upcoming plans. Rashid had worked too hard on the details, and any interference by a third party not already in the works would surely be a disaster. Rashid didn't need or desire help from the U.S. Fields was angry that his seemingly reasonable request was rebuffed. The continued loss of control was fraying Fields' nerves. Good God, he ran a multi-billion-dollar company, he thought. He was at the edge of the abyss. He was on board with the plan, but just barely. He was no longer really thinking clearly. The captivity was affecting his reason. The sooner the plan went into action, the better for all.

Rashid tried to explain to Fields that he didn't want the U.S. getting their hands on the business's finances, by physical or technical means. Rashid had already deceived the Mossad about the finances. He figured that the Mossad wasn't worried about his future, so he had resolved to put most of the money aside, allowing him to disappear and assume one of his other aliases. Yes, the Mossad would get a measly ten million dollars, but nothing compared to what it expected.

Rashid and Fields had overlapped the alternative financial accounts and created enough confusion that the Mossad would not be able to pin any missing money to anything Rashid did. The Mossad would simply think that some of the money had been moved by Shazeb's operatives and associates prior to the chaos created by Rashid. The latter had never been completely forthcoming on those associations. In actuality, there were no others than President Shazeb, his sons, and Rashid. The President had trusted no one outside the family except Rashid.

The Mossad was given to believe there was a network of financial operatives working on behalf of President Shazeb, personally, who continually moved the business money between accounts and countries. This disinformation was what kept Rashid in control.

He considered himself to be a man without a country. His family had been murdered long ago, his second family was led by a dictator to be feared, who abused his citizens, funded terrorist networks around the Middle East, and was nothing more than a crook. The despot didn't care about the country of Afghanistan or its people, but only the money flowing into his private accounts. Furthermore, Israel and the Mossad had not shown any personal interest in Rashid or his well being, by virtue of his mother's having been a kidnapped Israeli. Instead, they milked that facet in order to seek Rashid's loyalty to further their own interests, stopping the flow of drugs out of Afghanistan and into and through much of the Middle East, drying up the millions of dollars flowing to Middle East terrorists, hand-picking the new Afghan leader, and re-directing and claiming the massive amounts of Shazeb's personal ill-gotten gains for Israel.

Rashid was hoping that by the time the Shazeb men were dead, the business had been destroyed, the Orion people were rescued, and the country was in turmoil, there would be no paper trail.

One of his fortes was explosives. With his background, international associations, and holdover childhood issues, he had no choice but to learn the art of finessing his exit by leaving no trail and ensuring complete destruction in his wake.

It took him a few hours that last day, but Rashid managed to assemble and hide what he needed to cause mini-explosions in the palace after the Orion people left ... if they succeeded. He couldn't bring himself to even contemplate anything less than full success in the form of the deaths of the president and his sons.

Rashid was not without sympathy for the Shazeb women and younger children. Some of them had treated him fairly and looked after him soon after his parents died. He hoped and expected they would retreat in a panic, flee the scene, and re-appear well after his group had left the palace. But in his business, things didn't always turn out as planned. He had learned long ago to keep what little emotions he had left—except anger and rage—at bay. Those intense feelings were excellent primers and offered plenty of encouragement and foolhardiness for the most risky of undertakings and ill-advised schemes. But collateral damage was a distinct possibility. Rashid rationalized that if that happened, it was for the best—fate, if you will—and not something he would spend time regretting.

***********

Kendall got in a four-hour workout in the afternoon, complete with target practice on the homemade gun range. Rashid was out of Kendall's way for most of her workout. When he dropped her off earlier in the day, she promised him she would not run back to the base on her own. He, in turn, gave his word that he would return within a few hours. He was back on time and drove her to the palace to meet with the Head Chef, Taheem.

She and Rashid sat in the large, inviting kitchen at the palace and helped Taheem with the details of tomorrow's dinner. Two fatted lambs were in a pen outside the back door of the kitchen. They would be slaughtered after this evening's meal. They would be seasoned with lemon juice, orange juice, balsamic vinegar, olive oil, garlic, oregano, and basil, and the body cavities would be filled with lemons, oranges, onions, garlic, and dry wine. The cavity would then be stitched shut. The lambs would be placed on the spit early in the morning, and would roast for ten hours.

It was agreed that Kendall would arrive early afternoon and help make the dessert ... a favorite recipe of Kendall's ... chocolate cheesecake pie. The Shazebs were particularly fond of chocolate desserts, and this dish would satiate them, lulling the president and his sons into a false sense of contentment.

Taheem had a great sense of humor. That was the main reason he had stayed in the employ of the Shazeb household for some ten years now. He knew how to make himself scarce and assuage hurt feelings and flared tempers with kind words and mouthwatering dishes. His meals were loved, and his company was delightful. The children were always in good spirits when he was around.

More than that, Taheem was smart and intuitive. He knew something was in the works. Rashid had never before shown such interest in a particular dinner. Taheem could sense that change was in the wind. He just wasn't sure which way the wind would blow. So, he resolved to stay quiet and in the background, but watchful.

Rashid teased Taheem about his dyed red beard that was a custom of older men. They, like Taheem, used henna to dye their beards red, because the Prophet Muhammad was believed to have done so. The beloved head chef was also highly superstitious. With a twinkle in his eyes, he stated that the hennaed beard also helped against his constant headaches.

"But Taheem," Rashid said with a straight face. "If you've had a red beard for years now, then why are you still getting headaches? I thought the henna keeps the headaches from coming back?"

"Oh, no, Rashid. The headaches are under control so long as my beard is red. If I didn't dye it, then the headaches would be worse."

Rashid and Kendall laughed. Who could argue with logic like that? They enjoyed the bit of levity, even if all too brief. They talked Taheem into fixing them a quick dinner in the kitchen. Kendall could not get enough of the *naan*. It seemed to always be warm, soft, and fresh. She decided that was the one positive experience she would take away from her time in Afghanistan ... if she happened to get out alive. She was introduced to and immediately loved the taste and texture of *naan* ... especially when it was seasoned with fresh garlic. She spread a liberal amount of tangy hummus on the warm bread and licked her fingers.

When she looked up, Rashid was regarding her with amusement. "I'm so glad you like our food."

She nodded and proclaimed, "Absolutely! It's tasty, I'm sure, because the cooking is excellent!" She winked at Taheem, who was prepared to be shocked and left wondering if he had just been propositioned. But he was wise enough to chalk it up to a cultural moment. He wondered what Kendall's role was in the coming days, but prudently kept that thought to himself.

Rashid brought Kendall back to the base an hour later. His manner was serious and all business as he instructed her to go through her things. She would be taking only the one military field bag filled with the items she needed the most. They agreed that her laptop and clothes would stay behind. He brought in Glenn Carson's bags. She was mortified at having to go through the executive's personal belongings. But she did her best at packing his bag.

Rashid agreed to destroy a suitcase full of proprietary documents and electronic devices, including hard drives, thumb drives, and memory chips that would not be going with them. He planned to stop near the workout area and blow the suitcase up. Anything remaining would be set on fire. He exited her room, carrying Carson's bag. Tomorrow they would carry Kendall and Fields' bags.

He left Kendall sitting on the edge of her bed. She was both excited and afraid of what would happen the next day. She just hoped she would be able to get a good night's sleep. Rashid stopped at Fields' room and helped him pack a small bag of things. Fields became very angry again, at the affront of having been kidnapped, held against his will with no contact with his family or business, and now being forced to choose what little to take for what he saw likely as tomorrow's descent into hell ... leaving the remaining items to be destroyed. *Somebody is going to pay*, he thought.

***********

It had been twenty-four hours since the Mossad had contacted CIA Agent Candace Lawrence, and the U.S. intelligence community was no closer to getting answers about the missing Orion people, Kendall Radcliffe's role in the events, or Israel's supposed large-scale drug investigation. In NSA Agent Frank Reynolds' mind, something was not right. Israel was too quiet. It was almost as if *Prophecy* had been silenced over the Israeli intelligence networks; that a curtain had come down on *Prophecy,* preventing its routine cyber-stalking eyes.

But Reynolds knew that was not feasible. His good friend and fraternity brother, Paul Fields, had assured him that no one else had knowledge of *Prophecy*. Why then, he surmised, was he hearing only the most inane, routine chatter out of Israel? It felt staged, like the information was being spoon fed to the U.S. That notion both enraged and unnerved him. Thoughts raced through his mind. Had Israel, through its cyber spying expertise, stumbled across *Prophecy* and now begun using it for its own purposes? *Impossible*, he thought. His gut was telling him that something big was going down, and that the missing Orion people were smack in the center of it. Reynolds wanted to be a part of it.

He was so perplexed and intrigued about Israel's secret investigation that he decided to take matters into his own hands. Telling himself that he was being proactive and tenacious, he picked up his regular office phone and dialed Mossad Director Zimmerman. He was glad Zimmerman's phone number had been circulated during the debriefing by CIA Agent Candace Lawrence.

Zimmerman answered on the third ring. He recognized the unique caller ID info as scrambled and from the U.S. He could tell that it was not from the CIA—or more particularly, from Agent Lawrence.

He hoped these U.S. intelligence department probings into Israel's current activities were not going to cause a problem. Israel was so close now to its goal. He tried to keep the irritation from his voice.

"Zimmerman!" he barked into the phone, almost daring the caller to speak.

"Agent Zimmerman, this is Agent Reynolds in the U.S." Reynolds was nonplussed.

"I didn't catch your agency, Agent Reynolds?"

"I didn't say. I'm a consultant working with the CIA." That statement was true and allowed him to gloss over his NSA affiliation.

There was a pause while Zimmerman quickly ran the phone number and name through his database. Neither produced an exact hit. Puzzling, but he could discern that the number came from within the U.S. intelligence community. The Mossad director was disgusted that a U.S. intelligence agency would outsource its business to a mere contractor. He figured this was done to keep the full-time employee numbers down and to avoid paying benefits. He shook his head at the thought that the quality of the U.S. intelligence community really was going downhill. He chalked it up to budget cuts and the current U.S. preference towards nonaggression and isolationism. He doubted Reynolds was even an actual agent ... probably just some off-duty police officer looking for more interesting work after hours.

He finally responded cautiously. "What can I do for you, Reynolds?"

"I'm following up on your phone call with Agent Lawrence. I'm working on an investigation in the U.S. involving Kendall Radcliffe. I would like to share information."

"Like what?"

"Ms. Radcliffe's whereabouts are currently a mystery. Do you happen to know where she is?" Agent Reynolds' heart pounded and he held his breath awaiting the response.

"Not exactly."

Reynolds felt deflated. "What exactly do you know, Director?"

"Not much."

Reynolds had had enough. He was done with the small talk. "Director Zimmerman, what kind of game are you playing? This is a real missing person. Her family is very distraught. It is obvious that you have a lot of information. If you don't tell me, then I have no choice but to deduce that Israel is behind this. If so, why would Israel take her? I want answers now!"

An uncomfortable silence followed. Agent Reynolds half expected the connection to cut off. He could literally hear the wheels turning on the other side of the line. "Zimmerman? Are you there? Say something!"

Zimmerman was not about to be backed into a corner. If Reynolds wanted answers, then he would provide an explanation of sorts. "Agent Reynolds, I am trying to protect your U.S. citizen. As a matter of fact, you are putting her life at risk. I am not in a position to give you more information at this time. But I am willing to reveal everything in forty-eight hours."

Reynolds mind raced ahead. Whatever was going down would happen in the next day. It must be big if Israel didn't want the U.S. involved. Yet it involved U.S. people, or rather, a U.S. person. The first rule of intelligence gathering was not to reveal anything the other person didn't already know. Reynolds had therefore conveniently left out the two Orion executives' names. Likewise,

Zimmerman had not referenced any other persons than Kendall Radcliffe. They were at a stalemate. *Damn it,* Reynolds thought. *I need more information.* He fell back on the fellow comrade-in-arms approach.

"Agent Zimmerman, what can I tell Ms. Radcliffe's family? Is she being rescued soon, or is she currently in danger?"

There was an ever-so-subtle intake of breath on the other side of the line, and Reynolds knew he was on to something.

"To be kind to the family, Agent Reynolds, I would advise them that you are still investigating. I find that false promises of a safe return are futile and will often prove you wrong."

Reynolds was horrified. "Are, are you saying she is in imminent danger? And there is nothing you can or will do for her? We can help you. Let us provide some logistics for you. It's too late to send ships. But as you know, the U.S. has military bases all over the world. We can send in an unmanned aerial vehicle, a bomber, electronic surveillance aircraft, a WASP drone, or even military personnel, if that would help."

"I'm sorry, Agent Reynolds, but it's not that simple. Those things would only add to the existing confusion." Zimmerman adopted a conciliatory tone. "Please trust me, Agent Reynolds. We have things well under control. If it helps, I promise that you will be the first person notified once we have possession of Ms. Radcliffe."

Reynolds was mildly pleased about that but pressed one more time. "Can you at least tell me this, Director Zimmerman: Is Ms. Radcliffe the only U.S. citizen involved?"

"I won't know until I see her. But I will, of course, inform you." Zimmerman adeptly let that line of questioning end. He was not about to open the door for discussion about the missing Orion executives. He continued in a smooth tone, "I will be in touch with you no later than forty-eight hours from now. Is there anything else, Agent Reynolds?"

"Yes. Is Ms. Radcliffe involved in something illegal?"

Director Zimmerman sighed. "We don't yet know, but suspect she may be involved with something criminal. She is certainly in the company of and communicating with known criminal elements."

"Fine, I appreciate your speaking with me. I will expect to hear from you in the next day or two." Before ringing off, Agent Reynolds provided a cell phone number for a brand new burner phone. When this was all over, Reynolds knew he would need to destroy that phone.

He leaned back in his chair, staring at the phone. He replayed the conversation in his head, wondering what it all meant. If his team of three just had a country or location of the Orion people's whereabouts, he could direct *Prophecy* there. It might take several hours, but Ping's cyber probing talents were unmatched. He'd locate the bastards. But Reynolds had no names or even regions.

He reviewed the things they did know from the Mossad. It all seemed to center around a large-scale drug distribution network. Reynolds knew there was a marked increase in the supply of heroin all over the world. It was reaching a crisis point and was also believed to be funding terrorist networks in the Middle East. But Zimmerman referenced transshipment via the Mediterranean Sea in his conversation with CIA Agent Candace Lawrence. He even pointed the finger at Turkey and Egypt.

Agent Reynolds sat up. Having spoken with Zimmerman, he knew there was no way Zimmerman would have revealed the true transshipment point or involved countries. Therefore, that info was nothing more than disinformation to lead the U.S. intelligence community on a proverbial wild goose chase. It had always been known that most of the large-scale and high-valued heroin came out of Burma, Columbia, or, at one time, Afghanistan.

*That's it,* Reynolds thought wildly. He deduced that it was either Burma or Afghanistan. They could rule out Burma within hours. That country spoke freely over the wires and never took security precautions. He would have Ping immediately get to work on pointing *Prophecy* towards the Burmese governmental offices. At the same time, *Prophecy* would also begin cyber-stalking the Afghanistan seat of power in its governmental offices in Kabul, listening for discussions of drug shipments or harvesting and manufacturing. At the same time, they would poke around the Afghanistan finances to see if unexpected monies were flowing into or out of the governmental accounts.

Agent Reynolds was hopeful. He knew that he was on the right track. He just needed to narrow it down to the country and the operatives. He was still puzzled about the involvement of the Orion executives. Why had they been taken too? Why did Kendall Radcliffe need them for her high-level drug associations? A horrified thought crossed his mind. She didn't need the Orion executives. She needed their plane to get to wherever she was going. If that was true, they were most certainly dead. That thought was very depressing and caught Reynolds off guard. Not only had he genuinely enjoyed his friendship with Paul Fields, but Fields' death would inevitably affect his team's ability to use *Prophecy*. As Orion's systems and networks were upgraded through the years, it only stood to reason that *Prophecy,* if not upgraded too, would eventually cease working by sheer incompatibility. Since Reynolds had no other contacts within Orion, and he believed that only a few Orion employees had knowledge of *Prophecy,* he surely would be out in the cold in no time.

He was now really concerned for purely selfish reasons. There was no way Paul Fields was alive. Reynolds' days with *Prophecy* would soon be over. With a heavy heart, he texted Ping and Alex and requested an immediate meeting. While he waited for his team, his thoughts turned to Kendall Radcliffe. He was irate. She had ruined his plans. He hoped she died over there in some big drug bust. Now he didn't care if the Mossad got their hands on her. He just couldn't figure out how someone like her, with no criminal record or known associations with international drug operatives, could somehow be in the middle of an international drug ring. Well, he told himself, she must be really important within the organization and good at what she does if she was able to fall under the radar as she'd done.

Ping and Alex, Agent Reynolds' minions, arrived at the same time and hurried into his office, closing the door after them. The older Agent's face looked grim, but his eyes burned with knowledge and strategy.

# CHAPTER TWENTY-SIX

The early Afghanistan day broke with bright sunshine and the promise of a most interesting day. Kendall had tossed and turned through a good part of the night, falling into an exhausted but restful slumber several hours before dawn. As she lay on her small bed, she recalled the particularly disturbing cries she had heard the night before. A young boy was being whipped for stealing bread from a Kabul market vendor. He was undoubtedly one of the thousands of homeless children who could be seen on the streets of Afghanistan.

At the height of the war with the Taliban, and after three decades of continuous war, there were fifty to sixty thousand homeless children in the streets of Kabul alone. In the ensuing years, through the newfound and exploited Afghanistan resources of oil and natural gas, plus international donations, non-profit organizations, and the United Nations programs—using outreach workers—hundreds of millions of dollars were earmarked for the children. Programs were set up to get the children back to school and provide housing, play areas, and other shelters. Modest schools were constructed. But the best of intentions would never eradicate the entire problem.

Kendall wondered what this young boy's story was. In her uninformed, naive mind, she told herself that he was probably a hungry orphan who hadn't eaten all day. As she lay on her bed, she could hear his high-pitched screams for *Allah*. She would have been very surprised to learn that this young thief was a former child soldier forced into the Afghanistan subculture of *Bacha Bazi*. This dark world of sexually exploiting young boys by local police and powerful warlords, including the Taliban during its day for its own amusement, had been a part of the subculture for so long that the practice of these "dancing boys" was still continuing to this day.

Kendall had just cracked the surface of the horrors of Afghanistan. She would soon see firsthand the extent of wretchedness this country held for its citizens and surrounding lands.

To deaden the sounds of the boy's screams, she had finally resorted to rolling into a fetal position, putting her hands over her ears, and pulling the one shabby blanket over her head. Yes, she told herself again, she would put her all into the plan in the morning. She would not look back but would throw herself wholeheartedly into Rashid's exit strategy by using all the skills she had learned in the past few weeks.

There was a soft knock on her door. She rose and opened the door, and there stood the young stable boy, Poya. He ran many errands for the palace and was often seen with Rashid accompanying him on one of his tasks. This time he was carrying a breakfast tray. Poya was now twelve years old and without family. When Rashid came upon him one day a couple years ago and saw those big, dark, mischievous twinkling eyes, he couldn't resist helping the then ten year old. Poya was a happy child, and about as loyal a friend as one could ask for.

He was a great jokester and loved to pull pranks on Rashid. Rashid had come to love the little guy with the big, round eyes, and to trust him implicitly. Poya never questioned Rashid. He knew that Rashid would never harm him or put him in harm's way.

One day shortly after going to work for the Shazebs, Poya was at his usual post at the palace stables. The Shazeb grandchildren—Saaqib's children—wanted to go riding. Poya saddled up two ponies, and the children began to ride them around the corral. One of the saddles broke, came loose, and slipped off the pony, taking the child with it. The child fell off and broke his arm. The nanny was terrified she would be whipped, and blamed it on Poya. Rashid had just arrived at the palace, and he came running when he heard the high-pitched screams, shrieking sounds from the nanny and the child's mother, and Saaqib's irate voice.

When Rashid got there, he quickly sized up the situation. Saaqib was about to strike Poya with the nearest object he could lay his hands on, a priceless antique bronzed statue. Rashid grabbed the statue and shouted, "No, Saaqib, the statue! Your father would be angry." Saaqib came to his senses and realized he wouldn't want to risk his father's ire. He was relieved and thankful that Rashid had stopped him. But his eyes darted back to Poya, and he grabbed the young boy by the arm. "Come with me!"

Rashid stopped him and asked to see the still-wailing child who had fallen. He shushed the child with his gentle ministrations and soothing tones. The child stopped screaming at once. Rashid had a little medical knowledge and could see that the break was not bad. It just needed a quick x-ray to confirm the exact location of the break and then the arm measured for a cast. Rashid explained this to Saaqib and, with a twinkle in his eye, he turned to the tearful boy and said, "You will be quite a hero, young man. You will get a wonderful cast on your arm for all to see what a warrior you are."

The child was now content and happy to be seen as a hero. Rashid offered to take the boy and his mother at once to the nearby military infirmary. He also stated emphatically that he had noticed a weakening of the saddle strap a week ago and apologized profusely for not saying anything; that it was certainly not Poya's fault, and, if anything, he—Rashid—should be blamed.

Mollified, and now tired of the entire scene, Saaqib grunted his acceptance of Rashid's generous offer. He whirled around, muttered a few choice words about wailing women and children, and went back to the palace offices, but not before sending a withering look Poya's way. The young boy visibly shrank.

From that point on, Poya was eternally in Rashid's debt. There was nothing Poya would not do for Rashid. He viewed the older man as honorable and kind ... and quick thinking.

***********

Kendall saw that there was a lot of food on the tray ... way too many fruits, nuts, and breads for her to eat. She asked Poya to join her. His eyes lit up, and he nodded shyly. He eagerly took a piece of bread and a handful of grapes. She motioned him to sit beside her, and they chatted. Kendall drew him out by asking the name and pronunciation for the various fruits and nuts on the tray, and the furniture around the room. As she stumbled over the unfamiliar words, he laughed at her poor or incorrect pronunciation. She, in turn, had him repeating various English words, and was pleasantly surprised at how many words he already knew ... obviously due to Rashid's careful tutelage.

Kendall didn't care for the local sour cottage-cheese-tasting yogurt made from goat's milk called *quroot*, but Poya readily consumed the raw balls.

He visibly relaxed in her presence and thought this nice, American lady was beautiful and kind. He imagined that his mother—if she were alive today—would have been just like Kendall. She wanted to hug Poya so badly but didn't dare, fearing she would frighten him off. He beamed up at her, his eyes shining with happiness and the knowledge that he was in safe company. She would also have liked to take a warm, soapy washcloth and scrub his hands and face. *All in good time*, she told herself, but immediately felt regret that there was no time left to help Poya.

Because of his presence at the base this morning in her room, Kendall surmised that Poya was part of the escape plan tonight. After they had eaten their fill, Poya produced a storage bag used for fresh vegetables, and put the remainder of the nuts and bread in it. He then placed it inside Kendall's bag that was to accompany her later in the day.

As Poya prepared to leave, he confided that Rashid asked him to help the doctor overseeing the sick American today. He was excited to be doing such important work in the infirmary for a day, although he loved the palace animals.

She hoped that came with a shower and fresh change of clothes. *This godforsaken place*, she thought.

Over at the palace, the Head Chef Taheem already had the lambs rotating on the outdoor spit. He had ordered the formal state dinner flatware and china from France to be scrubbed and polished. The linens were being freshened and readied for the immense formal dining room table.

Taheem hummed to himself as he stuffed and rolled onions using his special family recipe. The spiced chutney sauce had been made. As usual, fresh *naan* was baking in the new electric *tandoori* clay oven—or *bhatti*, of which Taheem was so proud. He was excited that he would be working with Kendall in a few hours' time.

Rashid made a side trip to the military base and stopped to speak with General Omar. He found the general red-faced and scolding a new recruit, who Rashid noticed had a missing front tooth. He looked as if he was going to order a flogging for the young soldier, or at least limited rations for a week. Rashid swore under his breath. He felt like he was always coming to someone's rescue. But he had to be careful in how he interfered, or it might be seen as a sign of weakness on his part, or worse, obstructing the duties of a superior officer. No one quite knew what Rashid's rank was. But the fact that he was a favorite of all the Shazebs, even the children, afforded him a great amount of leeway. No one questioned his authority. Besides, he was so good-natured and non-confrontational that most people did not realize he had manipulated them and stopped their barbaric actions. Rashid had saved many a soldier, servant, or government worker from a flogging, caning, or worse.

Rashid vigorously pumped the general's hand and gave a hearty laugh. The general wondered what all the frivolity was about. He was curious, and the laughter was infectious. He smiled and nodded at Rashid. The younger man explained that he had good news, that there was to be a celebration of sorts tonight at the palace, and that the president was feeling very charitable. The general's eyebrows rose and he eagerly awaited further details. He pushed the wayward soldier away and ordered him to rejoin his comrades. The young soldier could tell that Rashid was an important man and had certainly a conspiratorial wink. That confirmed the soldier's thought, and he vowed to pay him back someday.

Earlier in the morning, Rashid had urged President Shazeb to allow the military base to have its own celebration of sorts, complete with barbecued meat, imported beer, and music for dancing. The base would relax its hours for the evening, forego the usual nightly punishments, and allow the men to sleep in an extra two hours the next morning. Shazeb was surprised and quite irritated that the troops would be afforded such luxury. He demanded to know why he should be so generous. Rashid had a moment of uncertainty that this time he had overstepped his bounds. He was really going to need to talk his way out of this one.

He smoothly explained that since the harvest had been so plentiful, that he should share in the fruits of his enterprise with his fellow countrymen. While it was not practical to share with all of the Afghanistan people, he could at least share with those most important, the military troops who keep his family safe.

The president had reluctantly agreed but was still piqued that he had to be told to do this. He responded impatiently, "Yes, yes, yes. Go tell General Omar that there will be a feast for the troops at the base tonight. That it includes several cases of imported beer from my private stash. You will have to take care of all the arrangements." Shazeb was feeling his importance and power. He continued, "You must assure the general that this benevolent act is to show my gratitude to the troops for their loyal service." Rashid wanted to gag at the utterance of the word "benevolent." He knew that Shazeb was anything but.

As the general and Rashid were discussing the details, a large delivery truck drove up. Rashid nodded towards it. "Ah, here are the goods now." General Omar quickly waved the truck past the guard gate and followed it toward the Base's kitchen to supervise the unpacking. In actuality, he wanted a quick look-see to grab whatever succulent he could requisition for himself. Rashid chuckled and shook his head as the general disappeared from view.

***********

Paul Fields had been instructed to remain in his room for the morning. He would be allowed to visit and sit by Carson in the afternoon, but he needed to be ready for the palace affair by 5:30 p.m. when his ride would come for him. He would spend a few minutes with Kendall in the palace kitchen and then join the Shazeb men for drinks at 6:00 p.m. Because the children were being involved in the dinner, the meal would be served a little earlier than usual, at 7:00 p.m., so they could eat, bathe, and be bundled off to bed by 9:00 p.m.

***********

The palace was abuzz with activity. Fresh flowers were being placed around the primary rooms where the guests and family would be assembling.

The president returned to the palace from the Afghanistan governmental offices in downtown Kabul in the afternoon. He was in high spirits and, much to Rashid's surprise, had given the government workers the afternoon off. He was feeling on top of the world. The Afghanistan governmental affairs were in order. The oil wells were pumping thousands of barrels a day, and the country was producing enough natural gas to sell to neighboring countries. Yes, the president felt very good about Afghanistan. It was going places ... mostly up. And so was he. He was going to fill his coffers to overflowing, so that he and his family for generations to come would never want for anything.

The Afghanistan government was running so smoothly and efficiently that he did not need to oversee the daily governmental business. It fell to his advisors and ministers. Shazeb was able to spend a lot of his time on his own business enterprise, that most close to his heart: his poppy "farming" business.

The president was quite pleased with his life and very glad of the timing of this celebration. The ships hadn't quite come in yet, but he knew that was all going to happen in the next week. He intended to push the limit tonight and thoroughly enjoy himself. He made a mental note to give Rashid a little bonus and a raise for all he had done for the Shazebs over the years. He wished Rashid had been his bona fide son. He refused to think about the shortcomings of his own sons, Ahmad and Saaqib. At least he had the devoted servant Rashid Sharif to keep his sons from each other's throats, maintain order in the household, and see to the smooth operation of Shazeb's business.

The only thing President Shazeb regretted about the day was foregoing the routine evening corporal punishment. When he was feeling enraged and angry in the night time, he often joined his officers to observe the beatings. There was nothing like the infliction of pain to assuage the tension in his shoulders. Hearing the cries of pain brought Shazeb a measure of peace that he could not find anywhere else. Sometimes he even volunteered to show the men the best techniques. It wasn't that he'd had the most experience. He was just more passionate about it. Even his boys had felt the sting of a whip on occasion during their hell-raising youthful years.

***********

The Shazeb clan was in high spirits as the evening festivities began. The children were excited and had run out back all afternoon to peek at the roasting lambs and watch the basting process. The dripping juices gave off a heavenly scent of lamb, herbs, and fruit juices. Every so often, Taheem would cut off a slice to check the tenderness. He would wink at the children and give them a tiny morsel to taste. They couldn't wait for the evening meal.

Several bottles of Pinot Noir had been consumed by the Shazeb men and the Orion guests, Paul Fields and Kendall Radcliffe. Kendall moved freely between the sitting room where the men had congregated just beyond the formal dining room and the kitchen. President Shazeb was delighted that Kendall had taken such an interest in the dinner preparations. He was brimming with optimism that Kendall could be persuaded to become a permanent resident of the palace.

His mind was too fuzzy from wine to figure out all the details of where she would fit in the household hierarchy. Kendall would certainly never agree to be a servant. She deserved to be no less than a wife. But he did not want tension and jealousy to descend among the palace women should she be installed as one of his favorites. He then ruminated about the possibility of setting Kendall up at the palace in one of the back suites that was not presently used. She could be a sort of *Khala* or aunt to the children. Of course, he would visit her often. *Yes*, he thought. *This would be perfect.*

He would need to keep his boys away from her, though. He had seen them ogling Kendall. He looked up to find both of his sons talking to her about the horses. She was complimenting Ahmad on how beautiful and strong his horse, *Papaver*, was. Rashid stole a glance at Kendall over the rim of his wine glass. She seemed to know exactly what to say to have Ahmad eating out of her hands.

The latter began regaling her with the tale of how difficult it was to break *Papaver* when it was first acquired. Ahmad was quite proud of the fact that he had *Papaver* broke in one week when it usually takes several weeks. Even though patience and hard work were essential for breaking a horse, Ahmad waved his hand dismissively and declared that his methods were much better. He looked quite handsome in his dress uniform complete with sidearm. And he acted every bit the soldier.

Kendall was following the conversation closely and listening intently. Ahmad leaned in. "You've got to show the horse who's boss. Don't let them decide when and where to behave. Get him introduced immediately to the whip. Once he's felt the sting of that whip he'll fall in line. That's why they call it 'breaking in a horse.'" He winked at Kendall. She flushed, and her eyes flashed. Rashid was furious at Ahmad's comment but relieved at Kendall's response. It was perfect for Ahmad. If Rashid hadn't known her so well, he would have taken the flush for sexual encouragement. But knowing her as he did, he knew the flush and the flashing eyes were masking intense anger. He could tell that Kendall was infuriated at the proposition of harsh treatment of a prized animal like *Papaver*. That brute, Ahmad, didn't have a clue.

Rashid kept the men's wine glasses full. It had not escaped notice either. Saaqib greedily accepted more wine and helped himself to an hors d'oeurve of *Bolani*, or stuffed flat bread. He leaned over to Rashid and said with much derision, "What are you doing, trying to addle my brain so I don't tear Ahmad's head off? Can you believe the boasting and obvious flirting?"

Rashid threw back his head and laughed ... a little too loud. "Nonsense, Saaqib. I've seen you operate with women before. You have lots of charm and many stories. Go tell Kendall some of your war stories."

Saaqib watched Ahmad and Kendall as they traded laughs. He beamed at Rashid's comment, and with newfound courage tinged with anger he strode over to the laughing pair. "Ahmad, shame on you. You are keeping Kendall to yourself. Let the poor girl breathe." As Rashid rushed over to re-fill Ahmad's glass of wine, Saaqib moved in and put his arm around Kendall's waist. "Kendall,

I see you were admiring our horses. Did you happen to see the peacocks?"

Kendall's eyes lit up and she clapped her hands together. "Oh yes, Saaqib. They were beautiful the way they strutted around owning the meadow."

"Well, I bought the peacocks as a gift for Ahmad. I knew how much he liked animals."

Kendall touched his arm. "That was so nice of you. What a thoughtful and unique gift. You are a wonderful brother." She was laying it on thick.

Ahmad, watching this exchange and wondering how Saaqib had suddenly gotten in the middle of their conversation, was enraged. He had been outmaneuvered once again by his older brother. When this dinner was over, he told himself, he was finally going to tell Saaqib off and maybe even show him with his fist. Just because Saaqib was older didn't mean he always got the girls.

Ahmad started to push his way into the center of the group when the rest of the family burst into the room. It was quite a commotion as the children and wives rushed in all at once. The children were excited about the unplanned party and that they had been allowed to help Taheem in the kitchen.

President Shazeb loved his grandchildren. He especially loved sharing meals with them. This evening, their constant chattering and changing of subjects created enough chaos and normalcy to stifle the men's growing annoyance toward each other.

The group moved into the formal dining room and began their feast. President Shazeb naturally sat at the head of the table, with Kendall to his right, followed by Rashid. The Afghan leader had purposely placed Rashid next to Kendall, keeping his sons away from her. He knew he could trust Rashid. But Rashid was teasing a couple of the kids and they begged him to sit with them. He looked at the proud grandfather, shrugged his shoulders, and acquiesced. The children squealed with delight, their mothers quietly shushing them. Rashid pointed over to Ahmad to sit in his place. While Ahmad was overjoyed at sitting next to Kendall, Saaqib and the president were furious. Only Rashid could have gotten away with altering the seating arrangement. But in the end, it looked as if the children had done the maneuvering, when, in fact, Rashid had masterminded the entire scenario. The children were just pawns, and very easy ones at that.

Paul Fields was sitting at the president's left, with Saaqib on his left. Fields was not adept at the dangerous scene that was playing out. He was uncomfortable and found it hard to be jovial. Fortunately, he did like fine wine, and readily accepted glass after glass ... just to take the edge off. Fields and the president began to discuss the computer network system of the Afghanistan government, and Fields explained that he had cleaned out quite a few viruses and malware, but had not seen any signs of a monitoring device or any unauthorized accessing of information. Saaqib, not having been present most of the time when Fields was working, simply nodded and concurred with Fields' opinions.

Fields wanted to emphasize that he was not in the business of IT cleanup, but felt that might not be too good for his overall health. He had agreed to play this game and was going to see it through so he could escape tonight. Rashid had told him that under no circumstances should he call anyone out, like Saaqib, to degrade or criticize the current systems. Fields was ordered to be genial, pleasant, and courteous. While those qualities were not in his nature, he genuinely missed his family and had agreed to do just about anything to see them again ... or at least to get out of this godforsaken country.

Rashid was enjoying a friendly banter with the children at the end of the table while keeping a watchful eye on the other end. President Shazeb was politely but just barely listening to Paul Fields. The Afghan leader was more intent on keeping an eye on his younger son who was shamelessly and loudly flirting with Kendall. In the president's eyes, Kendall was only being polite, and was needlessly suffering through Ahmad's extreme forwardness and boorishness. Rashid deftly and covertly signaled the pouring of more wine. Shazeb absentmindedly took another drink and shoved more succulent lamb into his mouth. His eyes narrowed, and he would have liked to use the whip on Ahmad at that very moment.

As the main courses came to an end, Rashid arose and announced that Kendall had made a special dessert. She followed him to the kitchen where Taheem had already dished up the dessert onto delicate china plates. Rashid grinned at Taheem. "This looks wonderful Taheem. I'll help Kendall serve it. This is her masterpiece. Would you please have the coffee served?"

With that, Taheem turned away and began supervising the coffee service with the help of his staff. Rashid quickly reached into his pocket and produced a vial of powder. When Kendall caught sight of it, she sucked in her breath and had a brief stab of fear. She looked at him for reassurance that it would not hurt anyone. He nodded and quietly assured her that it would only make them sleepy. He put a small dose on each of the desserts intended for the children and a slightly larger dose on the women's plates. The men received their desserts completely unaltered. Kendall did not understand what Rashid's plan was and had no choice but to trust him. It seemed to her that the men should have received the sleeping powder and not the women and children.

Kendall and Rashid served the dessert, carefully placing the correct dishes in front of the intended person. Saaqib was disgusted and irritated to see Rashid helping. "Really, Rashid ... women's work now? Don't you have any pride?"

Rashid chose to view the comment as a lighthearted jab. He laughed and responded, "Normally, I would agree with you. But I've already tasted this wonderful chocolate cheesecake, and I couldn't wait for you all to try it."

President Shazeb's eyebrows rose at all the fuss over a dessert. Rashid continued smoothly, "You know that we hardly ever have chocolate. It is such a rarity, and I wanted to watch all of you—especially the kids—enjoy something incredible."

The coffee was served, and they all began to eat the sumptuous treat. The room got very quiet as everyone nodded and exclaimed at the exquisite taste. The children finished quickly and asked Rashid if they could have another piece. He looked over to their mothers who smiled and agreed so long as the piece was small. Rashid retrieved several "seconds" while effusive praise was being bestowed on Kendall's cooking abilities.

The Afghan leader had eaten and drunk copious amounts and was beginning to stumble on his words. "Kendall, dear, perhaps you might consider staying on and overseeing the meal preparation and management of the kitchen?"

The men's wives had said very little during dinner. One look at Shazeb's wife, and Rashid thought he'd better collect the palace knives. Ahmad and Saaqib, though, thought it was a wonderful suggestion and heartily approved. As the bantering continued, the children began to yawn and nod their heads. The president noticed immediately and ordered the women to take the children away for their evening baths and to put them to bed. Often the women would signal that they would like to stay and would simply summon a servant to see to the children. But on this evening, the women were unusually compliant and seemed to be nodding off themselves. They gathered up the children and shuffled out of the dining room without the usual grumblings and beseeching to stay up later.

President Shazeb was puzzled and irritated. "What is all this sleepiness? Those women had better not have overindulged on wine, or there will be hell to pay." He was still itching to take the whip to someone.

Rashid proposed they move into the sitting room overlooking the meadow, and have a glass of brandy and a cigar. He hesitated quite openly and the others looked at him wondering what the issue was. The president said, "Yes, my son?"

"Sir, do you mind if Kendall joins us, since she's the only female left at the table?"

Shazeb waved his hand and said, "Not at all. Kendall, my dear, come join us. We are quite civilized. There is no reason you cannot enjoy a drink with us."

While the Afghan constitution prohibited the consumption of alcohol by its citizens, President Shazeb chose to view the law as intended for the ordinary Afghanistan citizen but not himself. Being the leader of the country, he was expected to entertain international guests. He reasoned that it was therefore necessary to keep a well-stocked supply of liquor for those esteemed occasions.

The men stumbled into the sitting room and Rashid poured the brandy. The president's humidor was full of imported hand-rolled Cuban cigars. Shazeb and his boys helped themselves to a cigar and a snifter of brandy.

Fields looked downright scared, his eyes wide and wondering. Rashid was livid and forced a glass of brandy into his hand, glaring at him in the process and willing him to calm down. If he looked any more guilty, they would all be beheaded before the night was through.

The Afghan leader slowly ambled across the Persian rug with a drink in one hand and a cigar in the other. He walked over to the French doors leading out onto the large courtyard. He looked over to Kendall and inclined his head, "Come here, my dear. Why don't you and I take a walk in the gardens. They are very fragrant this time of night."

She froze and didn't dare look at Rashid. A million thoughts ran through her head. She gave the president a brilliant smile. "I would love to see the gardens." She moved towards him, and he opened the door. As she stepped out onto the terrace, she saw there was a rather large gazebo-type building several hundred yards from them, off to the side. It had huge marbled columns and was obviously meant for privacy. President Shazeb put his hand on the small of her back and urged her toward the pathway leading to the small structure. *Oh, Lord, what am I going to do?* She walked very slowly toward the gazebo, chatting amiably and stopping to ask about various unique flowers they came upon.

In the sitting room, the brothers glared at each other. There was a tense silence while the two fumed and stalked about the room. Rashid feigned trouble with his guillotine cutter and cigar. It looked as if he was going to cut into the cap a little too deeply, causing damage to the body of the cigar. This would most assuredly cause the wrapper to unravel, and the pricey cigar would be ruined. Saaqib was watching the awkward sequence, when he strode over and angrily grabbed the cigar and guillotine cutter from Rashid. "Here, give it to me. You'll ruin it for sure."

Ahmad had had enough of Saaqib's sanctimonious bluster. "Saaqib, you are such an ass!" They were both itching for a fight. It had been in the making for weeks now and had finally reached the boiling point. The now expertly-cut cigar was roughly shoved into Rashid's hand, and it promptly split in the middle. This enraged Saaqib, and he flung the guillotine cutter at Ahmad, hitting him across the bridge of his nose ... as if it was his fault the cigar broke.

Saaqib was on a roll, not to be deterred. "You bastard! Haven't you done enough for one night? First, you interrupt me when I was talking to Kendall, then you tell her some stupid story to impress her, and finally, you monopolize her during dinner and shamelessly flirt with her in front of your wife and children."

Tears of pain were streaming out of Ahmad's blazing eyes. He sneered, "You're jealous because she likes me better. Just because you're the oldest doesn't mean you always get what you want."

Both Rashid and Fields unconsciously took a step back. Fields' eyes were wild with fear. Without warning, Saaqib pulled his sidearm from his dress uniform and fired directly at Ahmad. Ahmad's eyes widened, and he fell to the floor, bleeding profusely from his gut. Upon the loud discharge of a weapon, President Shazeb whirled around in confusion and panic and ran back to the palace. As he flung open the French doors, he saw Saaqib with a still-smoking gun, and Ahmad lying dead on the carpet. Both Rashid and Fields looked appropriately shocked and distressed ... frozen in place.

Not thinking but only reacting, the president let out a roar, ran over to the prostrate body of Ahmad—his favorite son—grabbed his gun, turned, and shot Saaqib in the chest, but not before the older son shot his father right between the eyes.

# CHAPTER TWENTY-SEVEN

The U.S. intelligence community was still in the dark. They were stumbling around checking all angles, including conversations with their international counterparts. They were no closer to locating the Orion people who had been gone for weeks now. None of the three missing people had attempted to access their bank accounts or use their credit cards. Nothing made sense. No ransom note had been received and no crash site had been located. The only communication was that suspicious cryptic note delivered to one of the buildings at the Orion campus. FBI Agent Zanders wondered how, in this high-tech day and age, three people and an airplane could go missing.

Of course, no one spoke much of the two pilots and the flight attendant. Their pasts had been thoroughly researched and scrutinized. Nothing stood out. They all led fairly ordinary lives. One of the pilots was going through a divorce, but even then it was not contentious. The couple had filed jointly and already divided their assets. The soon-to-be ex-wife was as distraught as any loving, caring wife.

There was just no explanation for a plane and its passengers to disappear out of the sky. This fact alone baffled the aviation industry. They were the experts. They should be able to provide a logical, rational explanation or at least research the events leading up to it, and then offer a plausible theory.

The press was having a field day. Rumors were rampant, and the public and Orion's employees and shareholders demanded answers. People were sure that the truth was being withheld. Conspiracy theories abounded and investors panicked. The Orion spokesperson assured the public there was no factual basis in the stories that an airplane crash had occurred. But no one, including the FAA, Orion, or the charter jet company, could provide a reasonable explanation for how the plane could fly under the radar without detection. Obviously, the emergency beacon and communication systems had been deactivated, but the plane should have still shown up on radar.

The families of Paul Fields and Glenn Carson were in a continued state of shock. Their lives were in limbo as they awaited the critical information on the whereabouts of their loved ones. The wives were convinced their husbands had died and were steeling themselves for the ultimate news. They were already planning the funeral services and memorials, all while assuring their children that their fathers would be home soon.

No one, however, worried about Kendall Radcliffe, except her friend at work, Gwen Albertson, and her neighbor, Heather Jacobs. The company investigators had learned that the elder Mrs. Radcliffe had unexpectedly died of a heart attack and didn't know what to think.

Kendall's two bank accounts and her cell phone were being monitored. Nothing was seemingly amiss. Nothing stood out except for the $10,000 that the Mossad had wire transferred into her account. The local FBI picked up Kendall's mail daily and read everything. Eric "Mickey" McDougall personally opened Kendall's work mail and emails every day. His team also monitored all business-related correspondence and communications to Paul Fields and Glenn Carson. Security patrols had been stepped up the last couple weeks, and additional surveillance had been set up.

They were also no closer to finding the author of the mysterious note that had been delivered to the Orion offices.

Jeremy had been re-interviewed several times and stuck to the same story that he had broken up with Kendall just days before she went missing. On second thought, he decided that she had indeed been acting strangely the weeks leading up to the breakup. He was effectively throwing her under the bus. Although nothing was amiss or irregular with her bank accounts or cell phone records in the weeks or months leading up to her disappearance, the authorities could not rule out an international bank account. If one was smart enough and flashed enough money, it was fairly easy to get around the international banking laws. The authorities surmised that she could have created different aliases and opened international accounts under those names. But there was nothing of an incriminating nature pointing to that on her home laptop. The hard drive had been thoroughly searched, and it was clean.

Both her friends, Gwen and Heather, strenuously objected to the inferences that were being made about Kendall. But Gwen was beginning to falter. She admitted that Kendall was very upset the day she traveled to DC, and Gwen never inquired why. She was beginning to think that Kendall was not the person she thought she was. Maybe there was this hidden side to her. Either way, in the event Kendall was implicated in the disappearances, Gwen needed to dump her fast. She had her career to think about. She now downplayed the friendship label and defined it more as a business association that sometimes extended after hours. And even then, any socializations were due to an office function or celebration of some sort.

Law enforcement had mixed feelings about Gwen. She was obviously looking out for her own interests at the expense of any so-called friendship. Gwen told herself that in the event Kendall came back and was found not to have been involved in the disappearance, then Gwen would make it up to her and become the best friend she could. After all, Gwen reasoned, it's possible that if Kendall was a victim in this mystery and survived, she could end up being a hero. Gwen would want to share in the limelight with Kendall and help her through the difficult transition back to a normal life.

***********

The NSA and CIA offices were busy and focused but not making any headway. There was much discussion and theorizing about the missing plane and its important passengers. International chatter spoke of shipments of high-valued heroin that were currently in transit both at the manufacturing stage and ultimately to their unknown destination. The most crucial pieces of information missing related to the farms, manufacturing facilities, and transshipment points.

Frank, Alex, and Ping were monitoring the international law enforcement communications using *Prophecy*. They had already ruled out South America, and specifically Columbia, as being the source of the much-anticipated shipment. That left Asia. They started with the obvious culprit, Burma. But Burma had never produced as much as the mysterious massive shipment that the Mossad had implied was currently in process.

While nothing out of the ordinary appeared to be occurring in Burma, Frank caught a thread of a heated discussion regarding Afghanistan. A known major drug manufacturer in Burma was complaining that Afghanistan had cornered the heroin market and was driving the prices higher because of the high-quality end product. Frank took a quick gulp of coffee and allowed himself to get that familiar fluttering in his gut. He knew he had stumbled on the answer. But what exactly was it? He was sorely lacking in details, and it was driving him nuts.

He directed Ping and Alex to focus strictly on Afghanistan but to program *Prophecy* to kick out any communications anywhere in the world that referenced heroin. He found it puzzling that strings were trickling in from everywhere except Israel, where it was strangely and noticeably silent. *Those bastards*, he thought. *They must have discovered* Prophecy *and figured out how to shut it out.* He made a mental note to discuss this with Paul, when or if he returned.

In the meantime, Frank rose from his desk and began pacing his office. He absentmindedly scratched the two-day growth of beard on his chin. He wondered how high the knowledge of the heroin production, manufacture, and distribution went in the Afghanistan government. Was it even possible that President Shazeb himself, or one of his sons, had knowledge of the criminal enterprise? Frank intended to find out. But that meant the missing Orion people were probably in Afghanistan. But where? In some remote military outpost? And why would they have been taken to Afghanistan? Even if Kendall Radcliffe was involved somehow in the heroin distribution, why would she have involved the Orion executives? And what was her link, if any, to Afghanistan?

These unanswered questions got the better of Frank. He was desperate to find the answers, both for Orion and for the international community that would soon feel the effects of tons of premium heroin or "H" working its insidious evil way through the frail, hungry humanity all over the world that barely kept it together as it was.

He even wondered if Israel was behind the whole thing, having commissioned the "H" for its own use in purposely affecting the terrorist countries and basically turning them into drug-addled, barely functioning humans. Frank surmised that wasn't such a bad idea, but it really didn't make sense. He shook the cobwebs from his head and set that theory aside. Israel didn't have the contacts or land to set up such an operation. It would take someone with a tremendous amount of resources. Someone who easily moved about the international arena using the many contacts they had all over the world.

*Oh my God*, Frank thought. *That's it*! The person behind the entire drug operation had to be President Shazeb. He kept to himself these days and seemed content to run his country and lie low. *Exactly!* Because he was busy running his drug business.

The international community had been praising Shazeb and Afghanistan for years now, because it seemed to be on a course of expansion and growth. While a democratic system of government was still elusive to the country, thanks to President Shazeb's iron fist and dictatorial tendencies, the country's oil and gas enterprises were profitable and expanding. The country no longer requested financial assistance from the international community and in no uncertain terms had politely escorted the foreign business interests to the border, shutting the proverbial door behind them.

Frank highly doubted that Afghanistan didn't need financial assistance or an investment of international resources. It desperately needed an infusion of scientific resources and brilliant, educated, creative minds to bring the socially struggling country into the modern era. But Shazeb and much of the Afghan populace didn't want these "outsiders" to interfere with their hundreds of years of culture and tradition that they would know nothing of or respect.

Afghanistan, or primarily Shazeb, had chosen to go it alone for several years. Now, it totally made sense to Frank. The upshot was that the natural resources were being exploited and turned into personal profits for President Shazeb. Frank could only imagine how much money Shazeb had stashed or funneled into personal accounts all over the world.

But how was Frank going to prove this? He imagined what a hero he would be if he could crack this whole enterprise, save the Orion people, and take down Shazeb and his illicit enterprise. The *coup de gras* would be for the U.S. to get its hands on Shazeb's drug money.

Amidst the plausible musings, he suddenly got a chill. *The Mossad!*, he thought. It must know this too. If that's the case, then they know exactly where the Orion people are. And they know their relevance or connection, if any, to the drug operation. If so, then why had the Mossad been so coy during communications with U.S. intelligence? In fact, the Mossad did everything it could to point them to the Middle East and the Mediterranean Sea.

Frank got his large worldwide map out, tacked it to the wall, and zeroed in on Afghanistan, and specifically, the closest ports of trade. He surmised that manufacturing would be done close to the poppy farms. The logical route then for getting the heroin out of Afghanistan would be via the long-established Silk Road black market network through Khyber Pass, using trucks traveling into Pakistan. Numerous people would need to be paid off along the way, but only if the trucks were stopped. Frank figured that Shazeb probably owned a melon farm somewhere in northern Afghanistan as well. Since the best time to harvest the hard-seeded melons was summer, the shipments of heroin were probably loaded with stacks of melons as they made their way into Pakistan. Afghanistan shipped melons into Pakistan daily during the summer. It made complete sense that Shazeb would use melons as a cover for the heroin, once it left the refinery.

He was not sure of the route the trucks would take once they entered Pakistan. But since Karachi was the largest city in Pakistan, and the Port of Pakistan was the country's busiest seaport and in close proximity to the major shipping routes like the Strait of Hormuz, Frank theorized this was the final destination for the Afghanistan trucks.

The NSA agent directed Ping and Alex to look for communications in Pakistan and Karachi to or from Shazeb or Afghanistan for shipments leaving in the next week. All they had to do was plug in key words—as many as they wanted—and wait for the information from *Prophecy* to return the data almost immediately.

In the meantime, Frank picked up the phone and called his friend, Secretary of Defense Quinn Pendleton. The latter's office administrator answered the phone in an efficient, clipped tone and, upon informing Secretary Pendleton who the caller was, put him through at once.

"Frank, you old dog, how are you?"

"I'm doing great, Secretary Pendleton. Thank you for asking. How is your family?"

"Couldn't be better, Frank. We need to go to lunch soon, eh?"

"I agree. When all this Orion mess is figured out, I'll schedule it."

"Good idea. Speaking of Orion, what's the word? Is that why you're calling?"

"Well, obviously you're getting all the updates and monitoring the situation."

The Secretary of Defense could not tell if Frank was stating that as a fact or a question. But he straightened in his chair and anticipated something newsworthy. "Absolutely! Are you on to something?"

There was a slight pause as Frank decided on the best approach for the delicate manipulation he was about to wangle. "I'm only hearing rumors and the usual chatter. I believe something is about to happen around the Arabian Sea. I can't tell yet if it's Pakistan, Iran, Afghanistan, or just who the players are. I was wondering about the location of U.S. warships there?"

"There is a warship patrolling off Somalia in the Indian Ocean and another one patrolling just off Oman and Yemen. What exactly do you know, Frank?"

Frank frowned. *God this is hard*, he thought. "Mr. Secretary, Sir, it's better that you don't know the specifics of these rumors just yet. I'm strongly urging or recommending that one of the warships be moved closer to Pakistan to enable the rendering of quick assistance or targeted precise strikes if needed."

"Frank, I can't just order the Navy to move ships based on a rumor. That's madness. I need more information so I can adequately inform the Cabinet, National Security Council, SECNAV, and everyone else in the Chain of Command. Tell me exactly what you have."

The NSA agent quickly reminded himself to reveal only the facts that could be substantiated through the usual covert channels. He didn't want any slip-ups causing *Prophecy* or its abilities to accidentally be exposed. "I—uh—I'm hearing chatter from Asia—specifically, Burma—that large amounts of heroin are about to be distributed via ports in the Arabian Sea. What's interesting is that the Burmese are angry about this. Apparently, they are not the source."

The Secretary was frustrated. "So, who is, and what does all this have to do with the Orion people disappearing? Quickly, Frank! I'm a busy man." He was running out of patience.

Frank was beginning to sweat. This was not going as smoothly as he intended. "Mr. Secretary, the Mossad told the U.S. intelligence community that Kendall Radcliffe, from Orion, provided information about a heroin distribution that is believed to be considerable, possibly the largest distribution ever. If that's true, and we know it's going to occur in the Arabian Sea, then why don't we try to intercept the shipments by simply being at the right place at the right time? Let's be opportunistic and place a ship in a strategic location that will surely cross paths with any outbound ships. My suggestion would be off the coast of Pakistan. It's central to the other possible parties involved. If this Kendall Radcliffe is indeed involved, then the Orion people are somewhere in that area. The U.S. will be able to insert itself very quickly."

The Secretary slowly nodded. "I get it. That makes sense. Let me talk to my people. Thanks for laying it out for me, Frank. If you hear anything else or things change, please let me know."

They spoke for a few more minutes while Secretary Pendleton scribbled on his note pad. The latter finished with, "It was good talking to you, Frank. We'll get together for lunch in a few weeks." The Secretary of Defense studied his notes and then rose and went to his door. He popped his head out of his office and barked at his executive admin to round up the Cabinet members for an emergency meeting and to invite the Secretary of the Navy.

NSA Agent Frank Reynolds sat at his desk, sweating profusely. He replayed the phone conversation in his head, making sure he had not said too much. If the Orion employees are rescued, then he will be a hero—at least to Secretary Pendleton. He did feel a little guilty at directly implicating the Radcliffe woman as being involved, but it was the Mossad who first mentioned that angle. And $10,000 was wire-transferred into her account. So the not-so-subtle inference didn't seem to be a stretch. Frank just didn't want to be involved in perpetuating a rumor, particularly if it ended up being pure fabrication. *Blame it on the Mossad*, he told himself. *I'm just passing on factual leads, and that's what this is.*

The U.S. was several steps behind the current happenings in Afghanistan. President Shazeb and his sons were dead, and the world did not yet know. Even the Afghanistan people, not to mention the military, had no knowledge of the horrific events of the evening. It would all spiral out of control within hours. Those who acted first and had the most knowledge would benefit the most. But only those who survived and were proclaimed as heroes would make their mark. Time and circumstances would ultimately reveal the fate of the missing Orion people and Rashid Sharif.

# CHAPTER TWENTY-EIGHT

KENDALL RADCLIFFE HURRIED INTO THE sitting room through the open doors and stood in stunned silence at the carnage that lay before her. She wasn't sure who had shot whom, but looked over at a grim-faced Rashid. Fields looked as if he was about to lose it. His eyes were wide and his mouth was agape with horror. Rashid quickly grabbed Fields' arm and squeezed it, causing the latter to grimace and come to his senses. Rashid ran over to the three men and checked each for a pulse. He looked at Kendall and shook his head.

The sound of rushing, thumping, footsteps brought the president's security with guns drawn. The head of Palace Security, Waleed, looked at the bloody scene before him and then at Rashid. He shook his head. "I knew those boys would kill each other one day. I just didn't realize they'd take their father with them. What do we do now?"

Rashid took charge. He instructed Security to take photos and notify the Afghanistan military police at the base. As the photos were being taken, he instructed the other members of the security detail to gather clean white sheets to place over the bodies, according to Afghanistan custom. Five officers were dispatched to the living quarters to notify the wives. Officers were posted all around the perimeter of the house, guarding against God knows what, since the only threats to the Shazeb family had just massacred each other.

Once the women had been allowed to begin their traditional mourning and the general overseeing the military police released the scene, the bodies were to be removed to the nearby military hospital for customary cleansing.

As everyone scurried around with their assigned tasks, Rashid pointed over to Kendall and Fields. He said in a loud, efficient voice, "Come; I will take you back to the base. Waleed, don't move anything until the general gets here."

Waleed nodded and stepped aside to let the small group pass. He then redirected his attention back to the bodies. As the group made its way to the front doors, they could hear shrieking and wailing coming from the grand staircase in the back. The wives had been told and were on their way down the stairs to view the scene of destruction for themselves. As the intense caterwauling came nearer, Rashid rushed the group out the door. "Come quickly." His voice was full of tension, and he was completely focused.

He nodded and saluted several young officers standing post as the jeep casually but directly made its way down the driveway. At the main road, he turned left to go to Kabul instead of right to head back to the base. At a distance, in his rearview mirror, he saw the general's caravan approaching the road to the palace. He sped off into the dark night.

The trio bumped and wound along the darkened stretch of roadway heading into Kabul. As they pulled into the parking garage of the semi-darkened building housing the seat of Afghanistan government, they were greeted by a lone security officer. Rashid knew the man well and nodded his head. "Greetings, Imran. There's been some trouble at the palace. The Shazeb boys shot each other. I'm here to secure the government offices. Do not let any vehicles enter the building except for a military ambulance van that should be here momentarily. When it arrives, the doctor will need assistance in moving the patient to the rooftop."

Imran was not accustomed to taking orders from Rashid, but he knew the latter had the run of the government offices, coming and going as he pleased. He assured himself that he would not be in trouble, since a crisis was apparently happening at the palace. Rashid's presence at the government offices made sense to him. After all, the president and his family trusted Rashid, although, he acknowledged, one could not be too careful that some sort of sabotage might be attempted during a traumatic event.

Grabbing their respective field bags that had been stashed under the jeep's floor, Rashid, Kendall, and Fields ran into the Afghanistan Infrastructure Data Center building and headed directly to the heart of the country's network center. Things were very quiet as expected, and they ran into no one as they turned on various computers and communication devices. Rashid entered a password into one desktop screen and began sending secure, scrambled messages. He motioned to Fields to sit down next to him and begin shutting down the country's radar detection system. Rashid watched as Fields moved through the system network, adeptly opening files and keying in commands. As they got to the oil and gas fields, Rashid instructed Fields to program the shutdowns on a delayed timer. He hoped it would monopolize the military's focus, once the discovery was made in a few hours.

He figured General Omar would come looking for him in the next hour or so if he didn't return. And once the Orion people were not accounted for—particularly Glenn Carson—the general would certainly send out search patrols.

Fields was able to program the electronic grid—supporting radio, TV, and wireless communications networks, towers, and cell structures—to shut down in two hours. While Fields was busy shutting down the Afghanistan internal structures, Rashid pulled a piece of paper out of his field bag and began transferring hundreds of millions of dollars out of President Shazeb's various personal and business accounts into the newly established accounts all over the world, leaving a scant few million dollars in several of the Afghan leader's accounts.

Finally, the hard drives were then programmed to self-destruct in three hours.

The trio had been at the Afghanistan government building now for over an hour. Fields was drenched in sweat. The door burst open, and a young security guard stepped in and informed them the ambulance van had arrived. The patient and doctor were now on the roof. He was a little concerned, because he thought he heard an approaching helicopter. They had received no warning from Base Command that a helicopter was being sent to their building. Rashid patted his shoulder and assured him that it was expected. They all headed to the roof.

As they burst out of the door onto the windy roof of the ten-story AIDC building, they saw Maysah Siddra, the female doctor who visited and saw to Kendall's needs every evening. She was standing next to a rickety-looking gurney on which Glenn Carson was lying. His IV bag had been carefully lain on his stomach, with the lines precariously arranged over his shoulder.

Just then a swirl of cool air churned about the group, and the outline of a dark, modified and elongated AH-64D Apache Longbow helicopter descended from the starless night and slowly set down on the rooftop. Using the onboard Forward-Looking InfraRed, or FLIR, system, the helicopter was able to maneuver a relatively smooth landing in the dark. The unmistakable Star of David insignia stood out proudly affixed to the side of the chopper. The Apache's side door slid open, and two uniformed soldiers jumped out. They rushed over to the gurney and quickly loaded it onto the helicopter. Paul Fields, Dr. Maysah Siddra, and all their bags were ushered on board.

Suddenly the heavy metal door out of the building onto the rooftop squeaked, and everyone turned to look as the door was shoved open. Imran stepped out, carrying an automatic weapon trained on the group. "Stop, I say. General Omar has ordered that no one has permission to leave. He knows nothing about a helicopter landing." Imran was shouting to be heard over the downwash and rotating blades. No one moved.

Rashid yelled back. "Imran, let these people go. They were kidnapped. General Omar will have them killed. We are not like this. We are not violent."

Imran was confused as he stared at the Star of David emblem. "Why is an Israeli helicopter here? Are these people Israeli?"

Rashid's voice was loud but soothing. "The people are Americans. These are good people. I know you will not shoot them. Israel is helping to rescue them."

With that, he shoved the soldiers into the copter and closed the door. The helicopter immediately rose into the night sky and flew out of sight.

Kendall was furthest from the helicopter and got left behind. She was terrified and angry. "What about me?" she shouted to Rashid.

He lowered his voice. "I'm sorry. It couldn't be helped. If we'd wasted any more time talking, Imran would have followed his orders. As it is, he's in big trouble."

Rashid looked at Imran, whose eyes were wild and blazing. "Why did you do that? I'll be punished for sure."

Rashid walked towards him. "No, Imran. Just tell them that by the time you got up here the helicopter had taken off."

He inclined his head sharply toward Kendall. "Yeah? Well, how do I explain that she wasn't on board?"

"She's with me now. I'll take care of her. You need to go quickly, Imran. This building is about to blow up ... in the next minute. Go! Now!"

Rashid tapped his earpiece. "Damn it!" he violently uttered. He grabbed Kendall's arm and propelled her to the end of the gusty roof. They looked at the other building ten feet away. It dawned on her what he was planning. She shook her head. "No way! I can't jump this high up and that far. I'll never make it. I'll fall."

"No you won't. I'll help you. Quickly! We don't have much time. A missile's been launched."

He backed up and threw their field packs onto the roof of the other building. Kendall's eyes were wide and her heart was pounding. They retreated some distance from the edge. Before she could utter another protest, Rashid grabbed her hand, and they began to run toward the end of the roof. They picked up momentum and broke into a full run. At the absolute last second when they were at the edge of the roof, they leaped into the air. Rashid yanked Kendall's body up and towards him. As they were in the air, a huge flash of light flared, and the ten-story building on which they had just been standing collapsed in a cloud of hazy dust and smoke. The sound was deafening.

The concussion from the explosion propelled Kendall the rest of the way over the ten foot chasm. They fell onto the rooftop, just barely clearing the edge. Both were momentarily stunned and deaf from the blast. Rashid hit the rooftop and rolled, as he had been trained. The violent impact sent his earpiece flying. He didn't notice.

Rashid recovered first, but Kendall lay there a minute while she collected her wits and her breath. Her ears were ringing and her head was banging. She had bruised her knees and felt like every bone in her body was broken. She couldn't believe she had made it. But now what?

In the dark and swirling dust, they heard voices coming from below. General Omar had sent a convoy to the government building. Quite a few of them were in the building and about to burst onto the rooftop when the missile hit. Most of them were now dead.

Rashid poked Kendall's arm and indicated to be silent. He and Kendall quietly picked up their field bags and located the rooftop door. They stealthily made their way down to the parking garage that sat below both buildings. Rashid had purposely parked under the side of the empty building, knowing it would not be bombed. Still, the remaining building had sustained heavy damage and would most likely soon collapse. All the lights had gone out in the building and garage. A huge cloud of dust engulfed them; they could not make out Rashid's jeep and were momentarily disoriented.

They heard voices on the other side of the wall and hugged the corner where they huddled in the pitch dark. The soldiers were speaking in excited tones, wondering where the helicopter had come from. The Afghanistan military radar system had not detected any approaching aircraft. The soldiers radioed back to General Omar that a helicopter had landed and taken off and then the main government building had been bombed. General Omar uttered several choice epithets and tried to maintain his composure. After all, he was now in charge, as he figured it. He instructed the soldiers to wait for him, advising he would be there in ten minutes. One of the men suggested they take a look around the other side of the building to see if anyone was there. They also wanted to give the general a report on whether the building could be accessed at all. They briefly peeked into the building where Rashid and Kendall were huddling. Looking right at the two, the soldiers could see nothing through the dense and dusty air, and they turned away.

As their voices receded around the corner, Rashid and Kendall, having now become accustomed to the dark, and the dust having somewhat dissipated, saw the jeep. They quickly rushed to it and got in. The vehicle punched its way out of the garage and flew past the astonished soldiers at the opposite end of the building. The vehicle was too far away to fire upon, but they ran toward their military cargo jeep. The soldiers realized they could never chase the jeep and catch up with it. They dreaded explaining this to General Omar.

The soldiers stood there helpless, awaiting orders, when several fire trucks rushed by. They looked at each other, wondering why the trucks hadn't stopped at the government offices that had clearly been bombed. "Look!" shouted one of the soldiers, pointing toward the area where the military base was. An unmistakable glow could be seen in the distant night sky.

Five miles ahead, Rashid was driving like a man possessed. In the chaos of the moment, he wanted to put as much distance as possible between the Afghanistan military and the jeep. He knew they needed to head somewhere safe where the locals would help them, far away from Kabul, the palace, or the base.

He looked over at a visibly frightened Kendall who was gripping the side of the jeep with white knuckles. "It's okay! We're safe ... for now. Why don't you try to get some sleep? We're going to be on the road for several hours."

She was having none of that. She wanted answers. Her eyes blazed. "Did you plan this whole thing?" she said in an accusing tone.

He sighed. "No. I went with Plan B."

"Plan B? What the hell was Plan A?"

"I was hoping that all of us would have gotten on the helicopter, but obviously that was not to be."

She continued with her vehement castigation. "Why did they blow up the building? That wasn't necessary."

"You're telling me! I had no idea they were going to do that. The infrastructure network systems were set to deactivate on a timer. Once the building and computers were blown, everything went down at once. Look!" Rashid pointed out the eerily darkened streets of Kabul.

Kendall nodded. "What were those sirens behind us? They seemed to go past the government building?"

Rashid frowned. He had seen the fire in the distance. It seemed to be coming from the area where they started. He didn't want to think about what it could be. But in the pit of his stomach, he knew it was bad. "I don't know, Kendall. It doesn't make sense. God, I hope the Israelis haven't blown anything else up. That's not what I signed on for."

He carefully and expertly wended them through the heart of the city and on a northwest course through the Parwan Province. They were soon out of the city and rumbling along a crudely paved narrow highway. They were headed some eighty miles up into the Afghan mountains via the Shibar Pass. Rashid looked in the rear view mirror and, seeing that they were not being pursued, pulled over. He ran to the back of the jeep, grabbed something and returned to his seat. He donned a pair of night vision goggles, turned off his headlights, and pulled back onto the roadway.

Kendall was startled, "What the hell?"

Rashid laughed. "Night vision goggles. I can see the road ahead very clearly. No one can see us, except from the back if I brake. If any vehicle approaches, I'll see it from far away, and we can find cover ... either another road or a large rock or tree."

Kendall looked dubious. Rashid responded with a grim look and said, "It's the best I can do right now."

They bumped along doing forty-five miles an hour. While the road was newly paved, it was of poor quality and quite dangerous at that speed. They soon began to climb. One small error in judgment would send the jeep tumbling down the steep mountainside. Kendall finally relaxed from sheer exhaustion, leaned against the door frame, and fell into a deep sleep.

Rashid pushed himself on in the darkness of night. About halfway to their destination, he saw approaching lights as he came around a curve. He quickly slowed the jeep and pulled over behind an overgrown hawthorn bush. He held his breath as the approaching vehicle came closer. Kendall was fast asleep.

A rickety delivery truck finally came into view. It appeared to be wandering the entire width of the roadway. Rashid uttered an oath under his breath. He was glad for more than one reason that they pulled off the road. The delivery truck driver had obviously been drinking. There was nothing Rashid could or would do if the truck careened out of control and toppled over the edge. He just hoped it would travel enough of a distance away from them not to attract too much attention to that area. Finally, the truck was far enough down the road that Rashid felt safe enough to pull back onto the highway.

He settled into a tense but even pace as they continued on their way. As they proceeded into the night, Rashid reviewed the events of the evening. Everything had gone according to plan until they got to the rooftop of the AIDC building. He still could not believe the building and the computers had been bombed. He was very worried that the blast had affected the international wire transfers. He was going to be without any resources if they failed, and the Israelis would be the benefactors of hundreds of millions of dollars of President Shazeb's ill-gotten gains.

On the plus side, he was relieved that Glenn Carson was finally safe and would receive the best medical care. Rashid just hoped Carson would survive to see his family again. He thought about Kendall and wondered what was in store for her. He wasn't sure that enough of a bond had been created between Kendall and the Orion executives for them to come to her defense should any accusations be cast her way. He wouldn't think about that now, though. He skillfully swerved to avoid a huge boulder in the middle of the road. He could hear the roar of a nearby waterfall as he pressed forward.

He would have preferred driving eastward across the Khyber Pass and into Pakistan. But there were numerous obstacles for that route, beginning with the lack of a passport for Kendall. They would never get by Torkham, the government crossing station from Afghanistan to Pakistan into the gateway of Khyber Pass. Given her light hair and obvious Western looks, she would have certainly stood out. By the time they even reached the pass, Pakistan would have been notified and been on heightened alert. The fact was that route was too obvious, it would be the first place General Omar looked, and it was frequented by military convoys.

Rashid also knew that with the light of the next day Israel would be precision-bombing the Afghanistan-to-Pakistan highway route at the pre-designated farms, manufacturing sites, and transportation vehicles. It all had to be done before the trucks entered Pakistan territory, or Afghanistan would certainly have a war on its hands.

President Shazeb had been persuaded by Rashid to have the truck transports outfitted with the latest in GPS tracking system, so they could monitor each truck for its exact location and ensure its safe delivery to the Port in Karachi. The president had marveled at how smart and loyal Rashid was. He knew that if his own sons had been in charge, a delivery or two might have gone missing ... on purpose.

No matter how Rashid played it in his mind, heading to Khyber Pass and Pakistan was not a viable option. It was certainly the most direct route taking them out of the country. But most Pakistanis still hated the West, and particularly, the U.S. Americans were not welcome and their lives were actually in danger while in Pakistan. Since the Afghanistan war had ended and the U.S. and all other U.N. troops had left, Pakistan was not seen as quite the important partner it once believed it was.

It was no longer the beneficiary of billions of dollars in foreign aid from any country. It had descended into chaos, with various factions of the military claiming they were running the country. There was continual bloodshed at the top, and after each such incident, a new "leader" would be announced. The world took note but refused to get involved.

***********

Rashid snapped to attention when a blinding white light suddenly appeared before him. For the first time, he panicked. He looked over at the steep incline on Kendall's side of the jeep and immediately contemplated driving right off the road. He knew they would never survive the now eight-hundred-foot drop into the swollen river below. But a quick end would be preferable to being taken prisoner by General Omar. Rashid turned the wheel sharply and braked hard. Kendall's eyes flew open. She let out a bloodcurdling scream.

# CHAPTER TWENTY-NINE

The AH-64D Apache Longbow helicopter with the Orion executives and the Afghanistan doctor safely on board flew south through the night air. It stayed within Afghanistan territorial boundaries and then continued south, hugging the Pakistan-Iranian border all the way to the Arabian Sea. It flew low, below radar, hoping to escape the detection of either of the "hostile" nations of Pakistan or Iran. Once it reached the open ocean, it rendezvoused with the newly commissioned Israeli aircraft carrier positioned offshore.

On board the aircraft carrier, Glenn Carson was immediately taken to the ship's hospital, where he was found to be in grave condition. Within twenty-four hours, though, he was out of danger and had improved enough to be upgraded to "critical" status. He remained in a medically induced coma, and it was decided that for the next few days he would stay on board the ship. For that reason, Fields was informed that he, too, would be continuing on the carrier for the time being. Israel needed to complete the long-awaited mission.

Paul Fields was not happy about it when he was so informed by the commander. He paced back and forth like a caged tiger. "Fine! I understand that I need to remain on board for a few days. But I would like immediate access to a telephone and computer to contact my family and my company."

The Israeli commander frowned and shook his head. "I'm sorry, but that won't be possible for at least twenty-four hours. We will be running sorties all day. We have worked very hard to rescue you. Our troops and aircraft have been put in harm's way. We have a mission to accomplish, and we will succeed. Tomorrow, or rather later this morning, we will be running combat missions all day. But rest assured that the people who need to know about your recovery have been so informed."

Fields was not assured at all. "Why? We've been rescued! Well, except for Kendall Radcliffe. What happened to her, anyway? Where is she?"

"Unfortunately, your rescue helicopter was about to take small arms fire.

There was a platoon of soldiers in the building on its way up to the roof. The pilot had no choice but to take off with those already on board."

Fields was uncomfortable having been rescued at the expense of Kendall's being left to her own devices on the roof of the AIDC building. He had the decency to be embarrassed. He got rescued, but one of his employees, a female at that, got left behind.

"So, what's happened to her? Is she dead? I saw the explosion. You blew up the goddamned building right after we took off! Why, in God's name?"

The commander took a deep breath and maintained his composure. "Mr. Fields, it was necessary to take out that building. You have no idea what was going on in that building."

"And you do? How?"

"We are not without our resources. I'm sorry, but that information is classified."

"And what about Kendall Radcliffe? Is she classified too?" Fields barked with as much sarcasm as he could muster. He was shocked when the commander muttered under his breath, "Possibly."

"What did you say? Is there something I need to know about Ms. Radcliffe?" Fields was a little taken aback at the subtle implication that Kendall's being left behind might not have been an unfortunate or unplanned event.

"We'd like to speak with you about her, as well as the time you spent in Afghanistan, as soon as you've had some rest and a meal. Now, if you will follow Captain Abrams, he will show you to your suite on the lower deck."

Fields was getting the distinct impression that he had gone from one kidnapping situation to another ... of sorts. But this time he had a few more resources at his disposal.

As Fields turned to follow the captain, the commander spoke one last time. "Oh, and Mr. Fields, we will be posting an officer outside your room, should you need anything. Please don't plan to wander about."

Fields was furious and utterly deflated. That was precisely what he had planned to do: wander about. Now he knew for sure something was amiss. As he lay on his bed, he alternately worried about Carson, Kendall, Orion, and his family, in that order. He vowed that when he got out of there someone was going to have some explaining to do.

He was also intensely curious about Kendall. What was her role in all this? Was it just happenstance that she ended up on their charter flight? He replayed the events in his head. She hadn't mixed her luggage with theirs. But she could have engineered it from behind the scenes, he reasoned. He was letting his imagination get the best of him. He fell into an exhausted sleep full of images of shootouts, chase scenes, computer hacking, rooftop rescues, bombings, fire, and death. He awoke bathed in sweat.

***********

As rescues go, Mossad Director Benjamin Zimmerman was pleased. Those that counted had been rescued, and Israel would look like a hero in the world's eyes. The ones not rescued would not be missed should they perish in Afghanistan ... like Rashid Sharif, who no one knew about anyway, or Kendall Radcliffe, who if need be would be made to look like an instigator or willing participant with the drug kingpin, the late President Mujtaba Shazeb. The AIDC building had been destroyed, and along with it, the critical Afghanistan computer network that kept the infrastructure going on a daily basis.

The country had been brought to its knees and would soon descend into chaos. The president and his sons were dead ... presumably. With a quick communiqué from Rashid during the time he and Paul Fields were deactivating the AIDC network, the Mossad had received the passwords and financial accounts to President Shazeb's personal business enterprises. The Mossad had now liquidated and closed all of the president's personal accounts. Zimmerman was a little surprised how few millions had been in Shazeb's accounts, and had a queasy feeling in his stomach. He chose to ignore it ... for the time being. All evidence of those accounts had also been destroyed as a result of the bombing. The only other location of the personal account information was at the Shazeb Palace. And the Mossad had craftily taken care of that ... unbeknownst to Rashid.

Director Zimmerman knew that he had to be patient for the first communication from Rashid ... if he perchance survived. In his mind, the execution of the rescue plan had been flawless. He could not imagine that Kendall was still alive. There was no way she would've been able to jump the ten feet between buildings. He knew that Rashid could do it, but doubted that Rashid would have stayed behind and been blown up with her ... no matter how much he liked her. And if he had remained with her, then it would be a shame, as he was a valuable Israeli asset. A lot of investment had gone into his training. Ultimately, he had done his job. He had masterfully orchestrated the events leading up to the rescue, the president and sons were dead, the Afghan government offices destroyed, and the personal financial accounts siphoned off. The only remaining task was the strategic bombing of the poppy fields, manufacturing locations, and all transport trucks before they reached the Pakistan border the next day.

For the good of the nation of Israel, the Mossad and Israeli leaders had made a strategic decision that no word would leak out about the rescue of the Orion executives until after all the bombing was through the next day. That would only amount to a delay of twenty-four hours. After that, a huge PR event would be set in motion, complete with the appropriate fanfare and parade of heroes.

The plan was for the Orion executives to be displayed on live TV ... or at least Paul Fields to be on camera. Carson would hopefully have sufficiently recovered so that his rescue would be seen by the world as a godsend as well. The Orion families and the U.S. would certainly understand and forgive the holdup on the announcement, so that Israel could complete the planned day of bombing without interruption or delay.

***********

The various international spy agencies were abuzz. Covert operatives all over the world had detected that Afghanistan had gone dark. That meant either an upgrade in Afghanistan's internal network that caused a severe country-wide shutdown that included the military's systems, or that something unexpected and possibly disastrous had happened at the top of the leadership chain of command—with or to President Mujtaba Shazeb.

No one was particularly worried at either scenario. While the Afghanistan computer systems were considered to be sophisticated due to the last five years of heavy-handed modernization attempts, it was generally viewed that there were not enough computer science experts within the Afghan government and military to maintain those systems in prime working condition. If those in charge did not know what they were doing, as was suspected, it would not be hard to envision a catastrophic shutdown.

Certainly eyebrows were being raised within the whole international intelligence community. No one wanted to think about the alternative, that something untoward had happened to President Shazeb. It was generally believed that he'd become nothing but a tyrant and brutal dictator. His unsophisticated PR attempts had shown the world a somewhat modern society, with every citizen benefiting in some small way financially, through the sharing of oil and gas revenues. But for the past couple of years, the word was that Shazeb was hoarding hundreds of millions of dollars for his private coffers.

The future of Afghanistan was in doubt. Shazeb looked to be nothing more than another dictator who would run the country into the ground while the world pretended not to notice. But because it had stayed out of other countries' businesses primarily by minding its own business and curtailing or brutally repressing any would-be home-grown terrorists for export, the country of Afghanistan had uneasily and reluctantly earned the begrudging respect of the international community. That translated to being left alone to run its own country as it saw fit. While it was true that the Afghanistan leaders kept its youth and young men within the borders of the country, President Shazeb had contributed tens of millions of dollars personally toward supporting terrorists in the Middle East. But the rest of the world had no inkling of that. So long as it wasn't bombing any other country directly or exporting mayhem and disillusioned youth to exact vengeance and rage on other countries, the world had left Afghanistan to its own devices.

The same begrudging respect could not be said for the Shazeb boys, Saaqib and Ahmad. Their brutality and ruthless actions were legendary. Most countries avoided any attempts at crossing them or engaging them. As far as the world cared, those boys bore watching. If and when one of them succeeded his father, it would most certainly become an international issue. But with the current worldwide climate of aversion to interfering in any country's governance, not to mention directing it toward the head of the country's own kin, the boys' behavior was observed and cautiously ignored ... for the time being.

Nevertheless, the international intelligence community was on heightened alert. All available eyes were directed toward Afghanistan to get an idea of what was happening. The U.S. Department of Defense sent up Unmanned Aerial Vehicles, or drones, over Afghanistan to surveil the country. The smaller UAV *MQ-9 Reaper* was used for reconnaissance, to get closer to the ground for real-time pictures. The *MQ-9 Reaper* captured the first images of the destroyed AIDC building, followed by the burnt-out shell of President Shazeb's former palace.

The Secretary of the Navy noted that Israel had an aircraft carrier positioned in the Arabian Sea just off Pakistan ... in international waters. This was the ideal location if one were to launch an action in Afghanistan. While that was not unusual, as it patrolled those waters several times a year, it was more than coincidental that it was in perfect position for any strategic military activity in Afghanistan.

The U.S. leaders contacted their appropriate counterparts in Israel to find out the reason, if any, for the aircraft carrier's presence at that precise location in the Arabian Sea. Of course, Israel denied any pending military action involving Afghanistan.

With the confirmation that the AIDC offices had been destroyed and Shazeb's palace gutted, it was pretty clear that the president was either dead or on the run. Since he or his boys were not beloved around the world, the U.S. decided to observe from afar. At the same time, the Department of Defense raised the alert status for all the U.S. military branches.

A warship, destroyer, and aircraft carrier were deployed to the Arabian Sea, with several more standing by in the Indian Ocean, ready to assist. But it would be at least two days before any U.S. ship reached an area within striking distance of Afghanistan. In the interim, the U.S. would need to rely on its small contingent of troops at the al-Masanah Base, northeast of Muscat, in Oman.

As a result of the financial disaster of 2008, followed by a decade of high unemployment and recession, hard times were felt all around the world. There were simply not enough resources to keep all the U.S. bases running at full capacity. Many bases had experienced downsizing or even closure as funding dried up and congress refused to continue pouring money down the drain.

The U.S. had effectively stepped back from the world, choosing to isolate and regain its strength internally. U.S. presence around the world was not as visible, and it was no longer expected to automatically come to the aid of a struggling country every time it was needed. Nevertheless, this time the feeling was strong that U.S. military assets needed to be close at hand should they be required.

The U.S. intelligence community was already edgy over the mysteriously missing Orion people and the inability of the experts to locate them. There was an overwhelming feeling among the U.S. spy agencies that the Afghanistan events gave rise to a foreboding state of affairs. This time the U.S. could not afford to ignore world events. Besides, it had not had a naval exercise in over six months, and this would serve that purpose. But the irregularity of not informing the nearby countries, as was the standard operating procedure, would need to be adroitly handled by the most experienced and diplomatic of the U.S. top brass.

The U.S. scrambled to understand what was happening in Afghanistan and position its military to render assistance or intervene should whatever was occurring in Afghanistan spill over into the neighboring countries. It was definitely behind the eight ball and knew it. It sorely lacked critical intelligence and for the first time felt helpless as to the seemingly major events that were unfolding. It had been reduced to that of a spectator. What would be the upshot?

In the meantime, within twenty-four hours things disintegrated as strategic bombing and military sorties were begun in Afghanistan. Every U.S. spy agency and its international counterparts and nations sought to pore over the images coming to them from their respective countries' drones. Nothing made sense. Why would ordinary farms, warehouses, and trucks be bombed with such precision and forethought, and all within one area of Afghanistan? It soon became clear that this had to be the major drug operation that Israel had referenced days earlier.

But why had it necessitated the destruction of the Afghanistan government building and presidential palace? There was only one answer. The president and possibly elements of the Afghan government were the operatives behind the Afghanistan drug business.

Even if some or all of that was true, why hadn't Israel just told the international community of its plans? Why the secrecy? Why the deception and outright misdirection by Israel?

There was definitely more afoot than the international community realized. By the end of the next day, the rest of the world would be reeling at the rapidly unfolding events. Even Israel would be taken by surprise, as the result of its strategic mission devolved into lawlessness and more bloodshed.

# CHAPTER THIRTY

Braking hard in an effort to control the swerving and out-of-control vehicle, Rashid finally brought the skidding jeep to a halt. He then reached over and grabbed Kendall's arm to silence her scream. She hadn't even realized she let out a sound. Rashid quickly pulled the night vision goggles off his head and turned on the headlights.

As they blinked in the harsh light, a young figure stepped out from a confusing movement of dark bodies on the road. Rashid looked closer and realized it was hundreds of goats. A young boy of maybe fourteen approached their vehicle. He apologized for being in their way and shining a bright light at them.

He explained that he and his cousin were herding the goats up a little higher into the mountains where the prime meadows were. This was the best time of night to move the large herd, when few vehicles were on the road. They had run into a large rock face that forced them to move into the road for a few hundred feet. He assured Rashid they would be off the road and out of their way in five minutes. Rashid was very relieved at the simple explanation. He lapsed into casual conversation with the goat herder as the jeep crawled along behind the rambling animals. Rashid translated for Kendall as he chatted with the goat herder at the back of the pack. The boy smiled shyly at Kendall. He stopped to talk to them but then darted about to redirect a wayward kid.

Apparently, the boys were in charge of some four hundred twenty-five sheep for twenty-two families. Kendall was fascinated. She did not see any brandings and asked how they could tell the sheep apart. The young goat herder proudly proclaimed that he had learned over the years how to distinguish each family's goats. He was easily able to tell them apart.

Rashid rooted around in the back of the jeep and offered the young man a bottle of water and a chocolate bar. The goat herder eagerly accepted but would not stop to indulge himself until he could share his treats with his cousin. For the children in Afghanistan who had nothing to speak of, any act of charity was met with delight and thankfulness.

The goats and herders turned to proceed up the steep mountainside. Rashid and Kendall continued on their way west. The young goat herder at the back of the pack smiled and waved as the jeep rolled past. Rashid decided to leave the headlights on.

Kendall was now wide awake and wanted to talk. "Rashid, where are we going?"

"We're going over the Shibar Pass into the Bamiyan Province or Valley."

"Why there?"

"I have a friend, Jangi Khan, who is a farmer. I know he will help us."

"How do you know you can trust him?"

"Because one day when I was traveling in the Bamiyan Valley for President Shazeb, I came upon Jangi. His truck was broken down on the side of the road, and he was on his way home. I was driving a military transport truck, so I towed him home."

"That was nice of you. You helped a complete stranger."

"Yes, I did. I always try to help. You never know when you might need a friend. He was so thankful and urged me to think of him if I ever needed help. We kept in touch and became good friends. I often stayed there when I was traveling from or to Bamiyan. So, here we are ... on the way to his house."

"How do you know he'll help us?"

Rashid grinned. "You aren't very familiar with the Bamiyan Valley, are you?"

"Sorry. Not at all. Tell me."

"Well, the Bamiyan Valley is quite famous. In ancient times, Bamiyan was a crossroads for caravans traveling the Silk Road trading route. The famous Buddha statues are carved into the cliffs overlooking the Bamiyan Province."

Kendall sat up as her memory was stirred. "Yes, you mentioned that the day we were at the bazaar in Kabul. Didn't the Taliban destroy some of the statues and paintings a couple years before the U.S.–Afghanistan war in 2001?"

He was pleased that she knew something of the history and nodded. "Yes. They thought the statues were nothing more than idols that the infidels worshipped. The Taliban ordered the Afghanistan military to destroy them."

"That's awful! Those statues were cultural landmarks."

"Yes. The whole thing was sad to watch. Anyway, one of the other reasons we are going there is that the Bamiyan Valley is the safest place for us in Afghanistan."

"Really? Why?"

"The Valley is home to the Hazara people, like Jangi. They have always been outsiders and faced much persecution. They are pretty much left alone.

But they are very poor, since the government does not sponsor any improvements there. As long as they don't make any trouble, the rest of Afghanistan leaves them be." Rashid grinned at her. "Doesn't that sound like the first place we should go?"

Kendall looked and sounded relieved. "Absolutely! We're going to friends ... or at least to a friendly place." She settled back in her seat with the knowledge that they weren't headed into a dangerous area. She even slept a little.

The remainder of their trip was uneventful, and they reached the Bamiyan Province as the morning light was just coming into view. It was still dark out, and Rashid was relieved that their arrival would be in darkness. This thirty-forth and largest province of Afghanistan was centrally located and far enough away from where the bombing would take place all day long. As day broke, the jeep sped past the Bamiyan University and nearby hospital. Finally, they turned into a pomegranate-tree–lined private road leading to a medium-sized farm in the Hazarajat region within the Bamiyan Province. The farm was situated in the lush fertile Bamiyan valley.

They circled behind the modest house and pulled into a makeshift barn. A middle-aged man ran into the barn followed by three teenage boys. He greeted Rashid like an old friend. Rashid was obviously acquainted with the man's sons as well. They all nodded shyly at Kendall, who quickly donned her headscarf. The man was introduced to her as Jangi Khan.

Their meager possessions were removed from the vehicle, and the boys then surrounded the jeep with a wall of hay. All evidence of the jeep was effectively erased. They entered the house where the man's wife was completing the cooking for the morning meal. Kendall was relieved to see they had indoor plumbing. Sitting on a large rug, she and Rashid joined the family. The men spoke in *Dari* for a long while. Kendall watched Rashid's face as his expressions alternated between anger, rage, sorrow, worry, and even some fear. She was dying to ask him what was being said, but knew she had to wait until they were alone.

Jangi and his wife could see that the travelers were weary and in need of sleep. Kendall was surprised when, after the meal, they were ushered back to the barn and shown two low beds in the upper corner of the barn. The makeshift beds had been quickly erected from wooden slats and hay, with a thick blanket over each cot. The cots were situated under the sloping roof and were, for all intents and purposes, invisible. They both sank onto their freshly made beds and fell fast asleep.

Kendall stirred occasionally and caught the sounds of a working farm all around her as the daily chores were attended to. She could hear Jangi talking to his children. Although she didn't understand the local language, Jangi had instructed two to work together in the nearby potato fields, and the other to attend to the animals they kept. The sons were very polite and respectful to their father.

The boys ran in and out of the building all day, as they sought some needed farm implement. Periodically, the sound of kids' laughter rang out. It was soothing and musical to Rashid and Kendall's sleep, but every so often Rashid would think about Poya and wonder if the little guy had stayed out of the line of fire.

The sound of several donkeys braying was a little distracting to Kendall, but she preferred that over the sound of soldiers overrunning the place.

Towards evening, both sleeping visitors awoke. Kendall looked over at Rashid and was at first embarrassed at how she must look. She sat up and attempted to smooth her tousled hair. But when her thoughts turned to her now-deceased mother, she couldn't have cared less about her appearance. Rashid half-smiled, reading her thoughts. He was glad they were safe and quite happy that she was with him. He thought she looked beautiful as the last rays of sunshine shone into the barn.

Her demeanor changed when she thought about their predicament. She looked over to Rashid. "What were you talking about during the meal? You seemed upset."

Rashid contemplated the question and how much he should reveal. He decided that he had withheld enough information over the past weeks. Since they could be separated by accident at any time, she had better know the truth; that way, she would be better able to deal with the present. He gave her a stern, direct look. "Our faces and names are all over the news."

She was alarmed, and interrupted his carefully unfolding revelation. "All over the world? Everyone knows where I am now? I'll soon be rescued? Will the U.S. rescue us, or the Israelis?"

She stopped to take a breath, and he cut in sternly. "No, Kendall. It's not good. General Omar has assumed control over Afghanistan. He is saying that you and I killed the Shazeb family and burned down the palace. Our faces are all over the Afghanistan news. I don't know about the rest of the world." He let the words sink in.

Kendall was stunned into silence. Finally, she sputtered, "But how ... why ...?" and became silent once again.

After a few moments of collecting his thoughts, Rashid continued, "I do not understand what happened. Bombing the palace was never the plan ... so far as I was told. As to why General Omar is saying that we did this, my guess is that he's afraid the people will be loyal to me. He wants them to blame us."

She frowned. She knew there was more bad news and sighed. "So that's where the fire trucks were going last night. What else?"

"The Israelis have been bombing all day, so the poppy fields, manufacturing sites, and trucks have most likely been destroyed. That's good."

"So, let's communicate with your Mossad contacts and get out of here."

Rashid shook his head. "We can't for several reasons. I lost my communication piece on the roof of the AIDC building. I do have a satellite or SAT phone, but I don't dare use it until we get some place where the signal won't be picked up by General Omar and the troops loyal to Shazeb."

Kendall didn't understand. "Who cares? We can take off ... you know, leave before they arrive."

Rashid was angry. "I will not put this farm or my friend, Jangi and his family, in jeopardy. They could lose their farm and their lives if we were discovered here. As it is, they are taking a huge risk."

"Okay, okay, I get it and agree. But I thought Fields disabled the infrastructure?"

"Possibly, but it was never more than a short-term solution to buy us time to get away. It could very well be operable by now, since it's been twenty-four hours. But I don't want to chance it."

"I thought Fields changed the passwords and deleted files. And wasn't everything lost or damaged from the bombing?"

Rashid shook his head. "Not necessarily. Those things can be recovered from other computers located elsewhere."

Kendall was beginning to think things were hopeless ... and then it got worse. "Why did the Israelis, or the Mossad, bomb the palace?"

He was bitterly angry. "I don't know, and I'm really angry about that."

"Do you think the whole family died ... even the women and children?"

He nodded miserably. "I don't see how they could have survived. I just don't understand why it was bombed. The only answer I can think of is that they could tell the troops were on the way to the AIDC building, and decided to create a catastrophic event that would keep most of the troops focused at the palace. It seemed to have worked. We got away very easily."

She could tell there was more and prompted him, "So, what's bothering you about how it all played out?"

"I also don't understand why they destroyed the AIDC building. They could have just killed Imran and stopped there. It's a miracle that you and I survived!"

Something dawned on her. "Do you think they believe we're alive?"

"That's what's bothering me. I don't know if they were planning for us to perish in the blast. I'm almost afraid to contact them."

Kendall looked at him with eyes wide open and whispered, "What do we do?"

Rashid looked grim, and his face was drawn with worry. "We wait for another twenty-four hours. We're safe here at least for that amount of time. But I have to decide if I want to contact Israel or someone else."

"Who?"

He ignored that question and asked her, "Kendall, how well did you know Fields and Carson? Will they vouch for you?"

She frowned, "As a matter of fact not well at all. Our paths only crossed before by chance. We never spoke directly, though I attended meetings where Paul Fields was present. They know nothing about me, my life, my friends, etc. I just happened to stumble across them as we were all leaving the hotel separately in DC."

She was looking down contemplating the darkness that was enveloping them. She wasn't sure if she should voice it, but decided to forge ahead. "It's possible they might think the mix-up at the hotel was planned."

"What? Why? My God, we can't have you Orion people against each other!"

"Well, that may not be helped. The fact is, we didn't run in the same circles. You said you wanted to get things out in the open, so here it is. I don't know where I stand with them."

"So, you don't know if they'll back you up or throw you to the dogs?"

She was becoming frightened and yet angry too. "This is ridiculous! We can sort all this out once we get to a safe place."

He grabbed her arm and gently shook it. "That's the problem, Kendall. We need to be able to distinguish our enemies from our friends."

Her face contorted in confusion, "Why would I have enemies? In fact, how do I figure into any of this? I'm just an innocent party caught in the middle of shit happening!"

Rashid shook his head violently. "Not anymore! Israel, Orion, General Omar ... any of them could and would throw you to the wolves."

Kendall seemed to shrink from the thought. "But why?"

"Because they want to deflect any blame away from them."

"Not Orion! It hasn't done anything!" She was indignant now.

He spat out, "Don't bet on it!"

She was surprised. "What has it done? Tell me!"

"All I know is that it has to do with secret spying and somehow finding out things about others through the computer."

Kendall gasped, "You think Orion is involved in some sort of technical spying?"

"Let's put it this way. Its technological capability is apparently more than people think."

"I work there. I can't believe Orion would be part of something illegal. Besides, the U.S. government would never allow that to happen."

"And how do you know that the government isn't also involved?"

She stood up and angrily put her hands on her hips. "Now you're just talking crazy! Someone's brainwashed you, and unfortunately, you believe them. The international community is always accusing the U.S. of things."

He stood up too and put his arms out, "And yet, here we are."

"What's that supposed to mean?"

"We'll get to the bottom of it ... just not today. Have patience, Kendall."

"I'm sick of hearing that. I've been patient for weeks now. Where has it gotten me? I'm now on the run, being accused of unspeakable crimes by a country or people I don't even know ... and where I was kidnapped and brought to forcibly."

He turned and gently pushed Kendall towards the ladder from the hayloft. She burst into tears and put her hands over her eyes. He stopped and said, "What is it?"

She looked at him and tearfully said, "I don't even have my passport!"

Rashid almost laughed. That was the least of their worries. He gave her a hug and said, "Let's go! The passport is something we'll worry about later. We need food and hot water."

She nodded and moved to the ladder. They quickly descended and saw Jangi talking to his sons on the porch of the house. He was explaining the tasks to be accomplished the next day out in the field. The fields would be tested for their hydrogen ion concentration or pH levels. Because the crops were not rotated as much as they should be in an effort to farm as much of the land as possible, Jangi knew that his field could be highly alkaline. If that were the case, it would affect the skin quality of his potatoes, and he would need to deal with the resulting micronutrient deficiencies.

Jangi broke off when Rashid and Kendall approached. "Come, my friends. Let's have supper." He smiled at Kendall.

As they were halfway through the meal, Jangi suddenly bolted upright. Everyone froze. "Someone is coming up the drive. Come quickly."

While he ushered Kendall and Rashid into a hidden space behind the wall of a closet of sorts, his wife removed their plates, cups, and silverware. The children spread out the family's settings evenly on the table.

Kendall was terrified in the small, dark space while Rashid was curiously calm. She grabbed his hand. "Why aren't you afraid?" she hissed.

"Shh! Wait!" He was holding his breath.

It seemed like they waited forever. Suddenly there were heavy footsteps in the hallway ... approaching them. The closet door slid open and the hidden panel was yanked out of the wall.

# CHAPTER THIRTY-ONE

Daniel Blumfeld felt sick to his stomach at the things he was hearing and seeing courtesy of *Prophecy*. He may not have been on the front lines and certainly wasn't privy to all of the details, but he got the gist of it. Paul Fields and Glenn Carson had been rescued. Carson was very ill but was expected to recover. Kendall Radcliffe got left behind, and it was possible she was dead. The Mossad couldn't tell if she had survived some huge blast to the building from which the prisoners had been rescued. There had been continued strategic bombing the entire next day. Even the Afghanistan president's palace had been bombed. The chatter amongst the Mossad and Israeli leaders was that all of the president's family was dead, including sons, wives, and children. That was beyond their wildest expectations.

Blumfeld felt responsible for all of it. He had created a monster, *Prophecy*. Now it was being used to kill people, which might even include his own friends. He just couldn't imagine that Kendall was dead. She didn't deserve this. The situation looked to be even worse than it appeared.

The Mossad was implying in not-so-subtle ways that Kendall was somehow involved in the drug trafficking. That thought was so ridiculous that Daniel wanted to use his burner phone and call them to refute the rumor. If it was anyone else, he wouldn't get involved. He would ordinarily tell himself that it wasn't any of his doing, and he wasn't to blame. But because it was Kendall, his friend and co-worker—and, goddamnit, a really decent person—there must be something he could do.

Daniel knew the Mossad had altered its pathway technologically to and from *Prophecy* to ensure that no one could see into the Mossad's communications ... or so it thought. But Daniel had allowed for that possibility so that he, and he alone, would receive notice via an encrypted message that a technical modification had been made. Daniel simply followed suit, applying the technical "fix" so that he could continue to see everything from the new iteration. He might have created this monster, he told himself, but he wasn't going to be left in the dark and lose control. His mentors were forgetting that this technological tool was, after all, his brainchild. Did the Mossad really expect him to roll out his crowning achievement and then go away? Not for all the millions they were paying him.

Blumfeld also knew the Mossad had the power to destroy him. They could attempt to close the link, effectively disabling *Prophecy,* and then give him up to the Feds if things got too hot. So, it was paramount that whatever he did, it needed to be done covertly. Not even the slightest hint must point his way. But what could he do? Who could he talk to?

He sat back in his chair, tapping his pen against the desktop out of nervousness. He knew that eventually he would need to act. But for the time being, he would need to just watch and continue collecting data and sorting through the actions of the *Prophecy* power users.

***********

It was evening in the Middle East at the end of the bombing missions. Mossad Agent Shane Menard had been monitoring the Afghanistan communications. The electrical grid was back up, but shaky. Blackouts were occurring at regular intervals. General Faisal Omar was about to address the Afghanistan people and the world.

Menard jumped up and yelled for his boss, Benjamin Zimmerman, to activate his dual flat-screen computer-monitor/TV and turn to the twenty-four hour international news channel. The fairly new channel had been introduced a year ago by the U.N., and it broadcasted live simultaneously in the fifty most spoken languages and dialects around the world. The location of the viewing pre-programmed the broadcast language. Conversion to the requisite desired language was instantaneous.

Menard could hear sudden shuffling going on in Director Zimmerman's office next door, followed by a thud, papers falling onto the floor, and some choice expletives. Finally, the sound of a news broadcast and a man's voice filled the room and hallway in stereo. Both men sat in their respective offices, amazed at what was being said and shown on the screen.

General Omar was telling the Afghan people for the first time that an assassination of President Shazeb had taken place at the palace; that, in fact, the entire Shazeb family was dead, and the palace bombed. He also explained that the Afghanistan computer network controlling the critical infrastructure had been sabotaged and severely damaged through the bombing of the government offices in the AIDC building in Kabul.

Mossad Agent Zimmerman shook his head in astonishment as General Omar went on to cast the entire blame on a diabolical plot by President Shazeb's beloved adopted son, Rashid Sharif. He implied that initial signs pointed to a well-thought-out and long-planned conspiracy that included American operatives ... most likely the CIA.

He conveniently altered the reality of the strategic bombing of drug labs and distribution sites, and instead referenced those destroyed locations as "government facilities and vehicles." In truth, he had no idea what had been bombed or why. He had not been privy to President Shazeb's drug empire, though he had heard rumors. The day's events were a mystery to him, but he wasn't about to admit that. He reckoned that if he spoke with assurance and authority and acted like a leader, the people would fall in line, like the willing sheep they had always been.

The general assured the Afghanistan people that he was now in charge, and that the significant damage had been contained. Their lives would continue as before, and that he would protect them and seek vengeance on Rashid Sharif and his co-conspirators. He promised that the government systems and electrical blackouts would only be a minor inconvenience for a few days, that Afghanistan would come back stronger, and that he would work for the people to build a safer and better fortified nation.

As for the rest of the world, he implied that he knew exactly who was involved. Once the investigation was through, he was confident that it would reveal the full extent of the scheme, and that the parties who plotted with Rashid Sharif would not get away with it. The mighty Afghanistan military would exact its revenge at a date, hour, and place of its own choosing. General Omar looked directly into the camera and with a voice full of confidence bordering on bravado, issued a proclamation of war against its as-yet-unnamed enemies.

General Omar had convinced himself that the Orion people were actually CIA operatives working with Rashid. The kidnapping had been staged, and they had planned all along to kill the president and his family. Rashid's engineering their escape confirmed in Omar's mind that the young man was working with the CIA.

Mossad Director Zimmerman paced around his office and pondered General Omar's speech. The former had certainly not anticipated this reaction. He was trying to decide if this was good or bad. Since there was no mention of Israel, and any witnesses to the touchdown of the obviously Israeli-owned helicopter on the AIDC building rooftop were dead, it was not hard to imagine now that Israel had somehow escaped the notice of the Afghanistan military ... starting with General Omar. Zimmerman wondered if Omar knew the truth but was choosing to blame Rashid until it could act against Israel.

This war of words complicated matters and put Zimmerman and the Israeli leaders on edge. The problem was that once Fields and Carson's whereabouts were revealed, the facts and ultimate truth of the involved parties would follow. But Israel had not done anything wrong.

The conundrum they were faced with was that no one now could seemingly prove how President Shazeb and his boys died. Because the Israelis bombed the presidential palace, any evidence of the original murders was reduced to bits of bones and tissue. The heat of the blaze and violence of the blast resulted in the destruction of the guns and spent cartridges—basically the necessary evidence. Metal subjected to a high degree of heat resulted in the alteration of its form. The structure of the metal would undergo thermal expansion, an increase in volume. The best detective in the world would not be able to reconstruct the scene of the crime.

For the first time, Director Zimmerman had to concede that the bombing of the presidential palace had not had its intended consequence. Yes, the Israelis had escaped detection, the Americans who counted had been rescued and Israel would be the hero, and the drug labs and distribution network were destroyed. But what was Israel getting out of this debacle now? The much anticipated hundreds of millions of dollars didn't seem to exist. Zimmerman entertained the idea that someone had gotten to it first. If that were true, he knew who that someone was.

He frowned as he sought a way out for them. It may be that Israel would have to serve up Rashid Sharif and Kendall Radcliffe as the instigator and partner. Because being a member of the Mossad was not exactly publicized, the agency would need to categorically denounce or debunk any notion of Rashid's association with the agency ... if it ever came up.

Zimmerman perked up when he realized that he might be on to something. The world would never believe that a man of Afghanistan descent would in actuality be a Mossad agent. No one knew Rashid's past ... or his mother's, for that matter. So long as Rashid and Kendall died in Afghanistan, the truth would die with them. And when Rashid contacted the Mossad in the next few days, Zimmerman would discreetly inquire as to the meager coffers that were discovered by the Israelis following the rescue. He hoped that Rashid would shed some light on the whereabouts of the bulk of President Shazeb's financial fortune derived from his heroin business. He would even suggest that perhaps Rashid was trying to help liquidate the money, and that now they needed to consolidate it.

It troubled the Mossad leader that he had heard nothing from Rashid in twenty-four hours. Unless he was dead—which was highly unlikely—he should have been in contact with the Israelis by now. Why would he not contact them? They would be the ones to look to for another extraction ... if needed. Yes, Rashid was perfectly capable of looking after himself ... but why not contact the Mossad?

Zimmerman was letting his imagination get the better of him. If Rashid had diverted that much money, why would he ever contact the Mossad? He certainly would be the winner in all of this and could quietly disappear.

The Mossad director contemplated the consequences of voicing this scenario and decided against it. He was the one who had vouched for Rashid's loyalty and gone out on a limb for him when he was still at the University in London. Most of the high-ranking Mossad agents had been against Rashid's joining their ranks; they didn't trust him.

Zimmerman suddenly felt ill. At the very least, he had a blinding headache. If it turned out to be true that Rashid couldn't be trusted, then Zimmerman's stellar career would be destroyed. Especially if it came out how much money Rashid had siphoned off ... if he had indeed diverted monies.

The elder Mossad director decided he must do everything he could to contact Rashid. He would act on his own. Once he determined if Rashid had profited from any diversion of money and was not going to turn any of it over to Israel, then he was immediately expendable. Thank God for drones, he thought. In the "fog of war," no one would know who actually killed Rashid. He would use a massive weapon that would reduce Rashid to dust.

Director Zimmerman felt somewhat better. He shut down his computer and headed for the door. It had been a long and trying day with several ups and downs.

He was glad he didn't need to worry about the communication to the world about the rescue. He had been in charge of the strategic thinking and planning of the bombing and rescue. Everything he was tasked to do had been done. As far as everyone knew and the results showed, he had pulled off a perfect plan. Rashid had done what he was supposed to—deliver the hostages, plan the Shazeb dinner and instigate a vicious fight, provide accurate info on the heroin manufacturing status and location, and lastly, communicate the personal financial account numbers and location of Shazeb's ill-gotten gains. Zimmerman had been in charge of Rashid. A successful mission had been accomplished.

As he hit the light switch in his office, he felt a lurch in the pit of his stomach and a sour taste in his mouth. Mutinously, he ignored the feelings and decided to stop at the nearest bar for a quick *beera shchorah*—or black sweet beer. That always relaxed him and made him feel better ... or at least pushed away the nagging doubts and worries.

***********

Commander Tzuk Reichenfeld, onboard the Israeli warship currently anchored in the Arabian Sea and to which American hostages Paul Fields and Glenn Carson had been brought, was on the phone with his superiors back in Israel. They had watched General Omar's address to the Afghanistan people and the world, and were now scrambling to provide a response. It was time to communicate the rescue of Fields and Carson. But it would be a delicate balance as to how much information to reveal and what to blame on others.

After much discussion, it was agreed that a press conference would begin in three hours. That would give Fields plenty of time to clean up, be debriefed, and then be paraded in front of the cameras. The commander requested that Fields be brought to him within forty-five minutes. He was to have received a shower and be provided with a clean set of clothes.

Orion Premier Net Services CEO Paul Fields was groggy when he was unceremoniously commanded to awaken, take a shower, and follow the accompanying Israeli officer to the captain's quarters for a meeting. He frowned at the ridiculous pajama-like outfit and robe he was given. He had been left alone all day, and aside from the regular meals that were brought, he had slept most of the time.

His dreams had been bizarre and littered with a regular staccato of blasts from the vertical takeoffs by the fighter jets on the deck of the carrier all day, and then returning at the end of their missions. He felt grumpy and out of sorts, but he kept telling himself that he was alive and had been rescued. He reasoned that maybe it was finally time for the Israelis to reveal his whereabouts. He missed his children terribly and was hoping he would be allowed to contact his wife soon.

Paul Fields was seated at a small round conference table when Commander Reichenfeld, accompanied by two of his officers, strode in. His entrance was anything but quiet. He threw the door open and immediately made eye contact with Fields. The commander barked for refreshments and then sat down opposite Fields. "Well, Mr. Fields, you look somewhat rested. How are you?"

"I'm alive. How is Glenn Carson?"

Reichenfeld cleared his throat. "He's improving and will recover. The Afghanistan doctor who accompanied you is competent and is being allowed to assist in Mr. Carson's care."

"What will happen to her?"

"She is seeking asylum and wishes to relocate to the West. She will be detained pending the outcome of our investigation."

Fields' gaze shifted back and forth from the commander to the officers, "What's the news on Kendall Radcliffe? Where is she? Did she survive the bombing?"

The commander held up his hands from the barrage of questions. "We don't know. We've heard nothing from her and unfortunately seriously doubt she survived. In fact, we'd like to ask you a few questions about her."

They discussed Kendall's background, length of employment, and any other information Fields had about her ... like how she came to be kidnapped with the Orion executives. Fields was not helpful at all. He was as much in the dark as anyone else. He had not worked with Kendall and knew nothing about her background. He went on to explain that he had not seen her during his stay in Afghanistan, except at two dinners. He didn't know what she was doing during the day.

"Why were you kidnapped?"

Fields frowned and tried to keep his impatience in check. "I have no idea. We weren't allowed to communicate with our families or business."

"Where were you kept?"

"It looked like a military base. It was several miles from the presidential palace."

"What did you do all day while in captivity?"

There was a long pause as Fields searched for the appropriate answer. He wasn't about to reveal *Prophecy* or President Shazeb's not-so-paranoid concerns about his computer network.

The commander of the Israeli aircraft carrier wasn't stupid. He knew when he was about to be lied to. He raised his eyebrows, "Was that a difficult question, Mr. Fields?"

Paul Fields had had enough. He decided to go on the offensive. He raised his voice and spoke in the caustic tone of voice usually reserved for co-workers who raised idiotic ideas. His eyes blazed as he stabbed his finger into the air, "I was a prisoner, Commander Reichenfeld. I was not there on vacation. I am the victim here. As far as I could tell, my being there served no purpose. You will need to ask President Shazeb."

The commander's eyes twinkled, and Fields couldn't tell if he was about to explode in anger or laughter. He held his breath. Reichenfeld slowly spat out, "That would be a little hard now, wouldn't it?"

Fields shrugged, and the tension eased a bit. The commander changed course. "Who is Rashid Sharif?"

Fields relaxed. "As far as I know, he's some sort of adopted son of President Shazeb's."

"And what was your interaction with him?"

"Practically nothing. I saw him at the two dinners at the palace. And he drove us to the Afghanistan government building where we were rescued from the rooftop."

Fields felt no compunction to provide all the information about their prior conversations or the extent of their activities at the AIDC building. At this point, he wasn't sure who his friends versus enemies were. The fact was that Rashid had looked out for all of the hostages' interests and had engineered a brilliant exit, complete with slowing down any Afghan military pursuit through sabotage of the Afghanistan infrastructure. As Fields saw it, if Rashid had transferred the bulk of President Shazeb's personal money into his own accounts—which, of course, he had done—he certainly deserved it. In fact, he would need it to set up a new life. There would be no going back to Afghanistan after the Shazebs died, the AIDC building was destroyed, and the prisoners were rescued. If he was caught in Afghanistan, it would certainly be a death sentence or worse for Rashid. The young man had Paul Fields' undying gratitude for getting them out of that hostile country. Fields was not about to give him up.

Commander Reichenfeld had been observing the emotions play out on Fields' face. "Was there something else you wanted to tell us?"

"As a matter of fact, yes. I do not have to answer any of your questions. I haven't done anything wrong. I demand to speak to the U.S. Government at once."

The commander gave Fields a cold stare. "Do not play games with me, Mr. Fields. If you are hiding something, I will find out. We have every right to keep you for as long as we wish. May I remind you that you arrived here without the proper documentation. You are not in possession of a passport, correct?"

Paul Fields returned the commander's steely gaze. "And I, too, am not without resources. I bet the U.S. already knows we are here. Israel is playing a dangerous game. The world will not be on your side." Fields hoped to hell that *Prophecy* was being used at this very moment to track them down.

That statement gave the commander pause. Perhaps he had pushed a bit too far. He sat back and changed his demeanor, "Oh come now, Mr. Fields. We are on the same side. Let's be friends. I have something to show you."

The Israeli naval officers re-played the evening's speech by General Omar to the Afghanistan people and the world. Fields' mind reeled at the news. He was astonished that the entire Shazeb household was dead, that the palace had been bombed, that Israel's presence somehow escaped undetected during the pandemonium, and that the Orion people, Rashid, and the U.S. was being blamed for the destruction and ensuing chaos. Fields was, for the first time, at a loss for words.

Commander Reichenfeld gave a conciliatory smile. "So, you see, Mr. Fields, that Israel has seemingly had no part in the events of the day in Afghanistan. All we did was rescue some American hostages after receiving a distress call. We have no knowledge of who bombed the AIDC building, killed the Shazeb family, or destroyed their palace." He sat back with a smug smile.

Fields didn't know what to think about the speech by that raving lunatic, General Omar. But he certainly knew that Israel had been behind their rescue ... and its planning. However, he wasn't about to argue the point with Reichenfeld.

Fields got the distinct impression that Israel was about to serve up Rashid's head on a platter. What the hell had the young man done to earn Israel's wrath? Of course! It was the money. Israel had counted on getting hundreds of millions of dollars and instead came away with maybe ten million dollars, just like Rashid planned.

"Commander Reichenfeld, why is your carrier in the Arabian Sea, off the coast of Pakistan?"

"We were patrolling in international waters, and came to the kidnapped Americans' aid."

"Did you notify the U.S. of the distress call?"

"Time was of the essence, Mr. Fields. We were told there was a critically ill or injured American who was in need of immediate medical attention. We stepped up to assist after ascertaining that we were not walking into an ambush. We are now ready to hold our own press conference."

The commander looked pointedly at Paul Fields and said, "Mr. Fields, for the good of the world, you must not discuss the facts that you believe you possess. There is more going on than you realize. For that reason, the less you say the better. A lot of people will be harmed—maybe even countries—if you go into detail. General Omar is threatening war on any parties to the bombings and deaths in Afghanistan. May I remind you that every nation now has nuclear weapons."

Fields understood the gravity of the situation. He wished he was privy to more. "But what about Kendall Radcliffe?"

"She will be an unfortunate casualty to the events. Basically, collateral damage. I know. It's terrible and certainly wasn't intended. But what's done is done. Let's move on!"

Fields just wanted the whole thing to end. He was sick of the politics and the endless lies and machinations. He would do anything, play any part, if it got him off the damn carrier and home to his family and Seattle. He toned down his petulance and quietly asked, "May I see Glenn Carson now?"

"Absolutely! You may go with First Officer Baum."

Consulting his watch, he continued, "The press conference will take place in about an hour."

Paul Fields rose and followed the first officer to the door. "Mr. Fields?"

The Orion CEO turned and looked at the commander. "Do I have your word that your knowledge of the facts as relayed to the world will be broad and brief?"

Fields looked as if he was going to say something but didn't. "Yes, Commander. You have my word." Under his breath, he muttered to himself, "... for now."

With that, the two men made their way to the carrier's on-board hospital. Fields was vastly relieved when he saw a little color in Carson's cheeks. Carson was even partially conscious and squeezed his hand. He couldn't speak, but Fields could see that he was getting excellent medical care and would most certainly survive.

Fields looked over at the two doctors discussing Carson's care, and saw that one was the Afghanistan doctor, Maysah Siddra. He was struck at how happy and content she seemed. She must have really wanted out of Afghanistan.

He stayed with Carson for thirty minutes and then was ushered back to his room for a brief snack and to prepare for the press conference. As he munched absent-mindedly on his cheese, crackers, and grapes, he vowed to do everything he could to find out what happened to Kendall—after he got back to Seattle. But for today's show, he would be a gracious guest of Israel and, as requested, feign no knowledge of the details of the kidnapping or rescue other than the obvious.

As for Afghanistan, Fields hoped the country exploded in a rage at the mismanagement and brutality of the military advisors and ruling party at the top. He would personally do everything he could to foment that rage. The ravaged country deserved an honorable and just leader who loved his country and treated its people and land with dignity and respect. It was a sad and courageous country that had seen too many wars since ancient times.

Fields pledged to put *Prophecy* to work as soon as he returned to the States. He stared at his reflection in the mirror. His face was very sore after shaving for the first time in weeks. He was provided with a slightly large but new pair of jeans and a starched oxford shirt.

He was not the same man who had gotten on that ill-fated flight from Washington, DC. No one would be after what he had been through. He could still hear the horrible screams from the prisoners in the courtyard beyond his room. He was going to do something about it. Somehow, the Orion day-to-day business no longer mattered. He might even give up his CEO title.

A knock sounded at his door, and his escort appeared. Fields sighed and followed him out the door.

He felt like he was about to "walk the plank." His footsteps were heavy in the narrow corridor. As he stepped into the well-lit, plush executive conference room, he had a moment of fright at the number of Israeli officers that had been summoned to witness the event. The video equipment was ready and standing by for hookup to the remote satellite feed. Paul Fields, CEO of Orion Premier Net Service, stood next to Commander Tzuk Reichenfeld at the podium, with his subordinates flanking him and Fields on the right and left. The countdown began, and the screens around the room activated.

Fields wanted to turn and run.

# CHAPTER THIRTY-TWO

Kendall's eyes were squeezed shut, and she was pressed into the back of the hidden closet space as far as she could go. When the door slid open, her heart skipped a beat. Rashid let out a whoop as Poya's grinning face appeared before them. There were cheers all around, and Rashid and Kendall scrambled out of their dark refuge.

Poya gave them each a big hug. Rashid knelt down and put his hands on Poya's shoulders. "Boy, am I glad to see you! I was so worried you were caught in the fire."

Poya nodded excitedly and said, "Did you think I was the *babalu*?"

Rashid laughed and ruffled his hair. "No, I didn't think you were the bogeyman. But how did you get away? How did you survive the fire? What happened?"

Jangi insisted that they return to the evening meal. The table was reset to include the three of them. Poya was obviously starving. He dug right in, and for once, was not shy about it. He tried to speak and eat at the same time, and finally Rashid insisted that he finish eating before he told his story. Finally, the meal was over and the dishes cleaned up.

Poya was feeling right at home and began tussling with Jangi's boys. Rashid could hardly contain himself. He wanted the details of Poya's escape so badly. "Poya, come over here and sit next to me. Tell us what happened at the palace!"

The boy sobered dramatically as his mind took him back to the last evening. His eyes got wide as he looked at Rashid. "I was on the other side of the stable when a bright light burst in the sky. It came down with a boom right on top of the grand house. There were flames everywhere."

Rashid grabbed his arm and began to examine him. "Were you hurt?"

Poya laughed and scrambled out of his grasp. "No, Rashid. I was very brave. There was much commotion. I put the rest of my stuff in the car and took the back road—like you said—that came out on the main road a ways down from the palace. It was so dark, and I kept the headlights off, so no one saw me. They weren't paying attention anyway. There were little fires everywhere.

Kendall was astonished at his story. "But you are only twelve. And you can drive?"

The men and boys gave a collective laugh. Jangi, feeling comfortable around the strangers, burst into the conversation with, "But Miss Kendall, all boys learn to drive after ten ... especially around here. They must help their fathers on the farm. They learn to drive the tractor first."

She gave a nod of understanding but remarked reprovingly, "But so far, Poya. You drove for hours!"

He nodded, very pleased with himself. "Yes, I did, *Khala-Auntie* Kendall. Rashid told me to leave as soon as you all left. I was hanging out by the back door of the kitchen and heard the gunshots and yelling. Then you all left, and I ran through the dark gardens back to the stable, where my car was pretty much ready to go."

Jangi's eldest son was very impressed with Poya's independence and sense of self at such a young age. He was eager to hear more. "What did you do then? Did you come straight here?"

Poya laughed, engagingly. "No. I went to the house of the palace's butcher in Kabul, Yuhannis. He supplies all the meat for the palace. I am often the one to go pick it up. I know him well. Yuhannis and his family are friends of mine. I eat there all the time."

Rashid winked at Kendall and smiled knowingly. It dawned on her that Rashid had purposely brought about the relationship and then stoked it, so Poya would always have a "friend" to run to. He was watching her, and added softly, "That's also why I made sure he had a car that was sturdy and reliable, so he could run errands."

Now Jangi's youngest son—who was near Poya's age—was impatient to hear more. "Keep going. When did you leave Kabul?"

Poya scratched his head, remembering the details. He appeared wise beyond his years. "Rashid told me not to start my trip until first light. The butcher made sure I had a full tank of gas, and then I headed straight here. I didn't stop once."

Kendall wanted every detail and looked at Rashid. "You must have arranged for Poya to come here before we even knew we weren't being rescued?"

He nodded. "Yes, I did. I needed to make sure Poya would be looked after by good people." He smiled at Jangi and his family. "This is the best Afghanistan family I could think of. I knew he would be safe here and that he would not be mistreated."

"But how did he know how to get here?"

"I drew him a map awhile back and explained exactly where to go. I also gave him Jangi's name."

"But weren't you afraid he would be stopped and searched or taken into custody and interrogated?"

"Yes," he replied solemnly. "I was terrified of that." But his face broke into a huge, relieved grin that made his eyes crinkle. "God kept him safe. I am thankful."

But there was one question he had to ask. He was very serious when he sighed and began, "Poya, what happened to Taheem? Did he get away?"

The young boy shook his head. "I don't know, Rashid. He was in the kitchen when I went into the garden."

Poya couldn't bear any more sorrow. He looked at Jangi, and with much respect stated, "*Kaka*, I have brought you a gift. It's in the car."

Rashid was glad that Poya referred to Jangi as *Kaka*, or Uncle. The young man was clearly accepting the elder as the respected member of the family. In his young life, Poya had met many a man who was not worthy of being called *Kaka*. They all trooped out to Poya's car, and Kendall was surprised to see that it was a white old Toyota Corolla.

Before long, Kendall would realize that half the cars on the Afghanistan highways were Toyota Corollas, many with over two hundred thousand miles on the engine. Used Corollas were shipped from Canada, Germany, the U.S., and Japan to Dubai where they were then delivered to Afghanistan. During the war with Russia in the 1980s, people didn't want to be seen driving cars from the West. They first drove the Russian Volgas. Japanese cars were considered an acceptable alternative. To this day, the Toyota brand still dominates the automobile industry.

Jangi's eldest son was envious and lovingly stroked the dusty hood. "It's nice, Poya ... and white too!" White was considered the choice of color because it showed the least dirt. One paid more money in Afghanistan to purchase a white car.

There was a squawk from inside the car. One of Jangi's sons said, "What's that?"

Rashid rolled his eyes. He knew exactly what that was. He pointed to Poya and sighed, "Go ahead, show them!"

Poya quickly opened the back door and out popped Ahmad's peafowl. Jangi's children were delighted and clapped their hands. Jangi was a bit taken aback but quickly recovered. He instructed his children to give the peafowl some cracked corn. They were obviously hungry and followed the boys around the farmyard, as bits of corn were offered. A pen of sorts was hastily constructed adjacent to the barn, where they would be safe from predators.

Jangi thanked Poya and remarked, "This is excellent Poya. They will keep the insects down and the snakes away." Poya warned the children that they would need to pick up any bits of paper or the birds would surely eat it and possibly die.

Kendall gave Poya's shoulders a squeeze. "You are so smart, Poya. How do you know these things?"

Poya nodded towards Rashid. "Rashid's taught me everything I know. He's my best friend."

Kendall looked at Rashid with a new light. This man was truly a marvel. There was not much he couldn't do. He was so resourceful. Tough, yet gentle. A man of mystery and depth. But she quickly sobered when she thought of their predicament. Her mind also suddenly flashed back to Jeremy. She shook her head in wonderment at how long it had been since she saw him. It seemed like months ago when he was part of her life. She hadn't thought of him in days. He seemed pretty one-dimensional now that she had met Rashid. In her estimation, Jeremy didn't even rise to the level of Poya or Jangi. He wasn't worthy of any of the Afghan men and boys who stood before her.

Suddenly the front door opened and Jangi's wife yelled for them to come and watch something on the television. They all hurried into the house and settled before the rickety television set. There was the face of General Omar raging before the cameras. Kendall could not tell what was being said, but she saw their pictures flashed in front of the camera several times. Finally, the speech ended, and the men lapsed into a long conversation in *Dari*. Every once in a while, the boys would look over at her. They seemed alternatively sad and frightened for her. She was impatient to know what was being said but remained silent.

It was time for bed, and Jangi led Rashid, Kendall, and Poya to the barn. First, they moved Poya's car to the outside of the barn and covered it with a tarp. They made up Poya's bed next to theirs, and Jangi said goodnight. He patted Rashid's arm in a comforting way. He then turned, closed the big barn door behind him, and retired for the night.

The moon was full, and a surprising amount of light shone in through the side window above their heads. Poya had had a long day and quickly fell asleep. His gentle snores were soothing and childlike. He looked happy and content. Rashid was pleased he was here. He would find loving people with whom to make a life. Still, Rashid would worry about him, hoping he was thriving and growing into manhood with the right mentors. Rashid recalled the anger that had consumed him as a young man in the early days of living with the Shazeb family. He fervently hoped and prayed that Poya would never know such anger and rage. He made a silent promise that he would consider all of the options when it was time to leave Jangi the next day.

Rashid turned his attention to Kendall, who was quietly staring at him in the moonlit night, waiting to hear a recap of General Omar's speech. Even though they'd only been up half a day, Rashid was weary and would have liked to drop his head on the soft blankets and sleep, but he knew that Kendall was expecting an explanation of their circumstances and what would happen on the morrow. He gave a general account of Omar's rantings. Omar was blaming Rashid and unnamed persons, possibly Americans, for the bombings and deaths of the Shazebs. He was calling it a *coup* that had been planned for some time.

Kendall's face was shown as one of the so-called co-conspirators. It looked like an enlarged picture from her driver's license. The image was fuzzy and not at all clear. It was not a flattering picture. The expression on her face was serious and downright fierce. She thought she even looked like a criminal type.

Kendall reached out and pulled Rashid's arm. "What does all this mean?"

Rashid frowned but decided to be truthful. "It's not good, Kendall. We were made to look really bad. Anyone who loved the president is going to be gunning for us. It will be imperative that we keep a low profile." He stared at her lovely chestnut colored hair.

"What is it?"

He sighed. "It's your hair! You stand out as a foreigner. Everything about you stands out. We can't very well dress you like a man, because it just wouldn't work."

"Can we contact someone now to come and rescue us?"

He shook his head violently. "Absolutely not! Once we activated the SAT phone, our presence could be detected by radar. Omar's troops would find us."

Kendall's eyes were wide and she felt helpless. "What are we going to do?"

He saw the concern in her eyes and relaxed, saying soothingly, "Don't worry, Kendall. We'll be fine. We just need to be careful, stay off the main roads, hunker down, and keep to ourselves for a few days."

"Why can't we just stay here? It seems safe."

"Because Jangi has already put his family and farm at risk. He could lose everything and end up in jail, all just for helping us. I will not stay any longer than is necessary." He looked at Kendall and stated emphatically, "We leave tomorrow, Kendall. Get some sleep."

She lay down but found sleep elusive. Her thoughts alternated from wondering how Glenn Carson was to where her mother's body was to finally how she could ever go back to a nine-to-five job after all that she had seen and been through. She finally fell into an exhausted sleep.

Sometime after midnight, Kendall began moaning and uttering the name, "Rashid, Rashid," over and over. She awoke to find Rashid gently shaking her and cradling her in his arms. He stroked and lightly kissed her hair, saying, "Shh, you're having a bad dream, Kendall."

She was trembling and looked distraught. Their dire situation and unknown future had gotten the best of her. "I'm so afraid, Rashid." He quickly grabbed his makeshift bed and pulled it over next to hers. He lay down beside her and she rested her head on his shoulders. They both fell into a sound, peaceful sleep, their bodies pressed warmly against each other.

Rashid and Kendall woke up to the sound of Poya laughing and pointing out the window. Jangi's boys were feeding the peafowl, and there was much bedlam as they chased the birds around.

After the morning meal, they discussed their plans with Jangi. Poya was outside with the other children, helping with the daily chores. The adults watched the Afghanistan National Television station for the morning news. They were stunned to find out that General Omar was appealing to the Afghan citizens for information on the whereabouts of Rashid Sharif and Kendall Radcliffe. A reward of 10,000 Afghani, or just under $200, was offered to enlist the public's help. Alternatively, anyone found to be harboring the fugitives would be publicly beheaded. That warning extended to their immediate family as well. Jangi gasped at that news.

While Omar was not certain that Kendall was the second person in the vehicle seen speeding away from the bombed AIDC building, he was fairly certain it had to be her. Omar had seen them together every day for the past few weeks, and they seemed thick as thieves, in his eyes. His jealousy at Rashid's closeness with the Shazeb family and how he had tricked him the night the Shazebs were all killed, drove him crazy with rage. His single-minded purpose to track down and punish Rashid in the most heinous way was evident to Rashid. The only bright side was that nothing was said of Poya's going missing.

The message to the Afghanistan public was that military troops were being sent to all the major cities, and a house-to-house search was to be conducted. Roadblocks were to be set up, with all vehicles inspected. When Rashid and Jangi saw that Bamiyan was one of the first cities to receive troops, they looked at each other knowingly.

From the look of fear and concern in Jangi's eyes, Rashid knew they must leave at once, within the hour. He also knew that Poya must go with them for the time being. Once the troops had left Bamiyan, it would be safe for Poya to return to Jangi's farm.

Rashid explained the situation to Kendall, and everyone went into action. Quick showers were taken, and Rashid's jeep was filled with food, drink, and more ammunition. Jangi's wife shoved several clean headscarves and a *chadrei,* or long headscarf providing full coverage, at Kendall. They were stowed away. The license plate from the Toyota Corolla was removed, and several large machines, bales of hay, and miscellaneous equipment were casually placed around it. It looked like a broken-down vehicle that had been sitting there for some time. No attempt was made to hide it.

Jangi and Rashid pored over the map of the Bamiyan Province. They discussed the options, and there was much pointing northwest into the mountains overlooking the valley. As the jeep sped away from the house and made a beeline for the higher hills, a convoy of military troops was headed toward Jangi's house. The procession of military vehicles was five minutes away. His house was on the edge of town. It made sense that his farm would be one of the first to be searched.

The jeep headed north into the hills where thousands of caves stood watch over the Bamiyan Valley. They drove for about thirty minutes on a winding dusty backroad that was not well traveled. They found a secluded spot behind a row of large boulders to park the car. Kendall was instructed to remain in the jeep. Rashid and Poya went in search of an abandoned available cave for their short stay. Before they left, Rashid had pointed out the many large boulders and shrubs nearby. He informed her that if she needed a toilet, she would have to find something amongst the natural landscape. She was aghast.

After walking for half an hour and seeing many families squeezed into the confines of a red stone cavern, they chose one on the third level of caves up a dirt pathway. The cave had a particularly narrow opening that looked hardly habitable, which was probably why it had been abandoned. They rushed back to the jeep, and the three of them carried as many of their possessions as they could. Kendall wore a large headscarf pulled low that covered all of her hair and half of her face. She walked with her head down and basically blended in with the other women. The weary trio looked like they carried all of their worldly possessions on their backs.

Kendall was shocked at the tight, dark space that was to be their living quarters for the next day or two. Rashid explained that he and Poya would need to speak *Dari* when in the cave, so as not to rouse the curiosity of their neighbors. When she wanted to speak English, she would need to stand close to him or Poya and whisper. She nodded.

She had never been so miserable or scared in her life. She sank down onto the floor of the cave. She longed to listen to her iPod or turn on the radio just to relieve the terrible tension. It was almost unbearable. But she knew that world full of expensive toys and worldly must-haves, which she had so taken for granted a month before, was well beyond her reach here. She looked out towards the small vertical band of light barely shining into their eight feet of living space. It was really just a hole cut into the rock by rain and wind. Kendall leaned her head against the wall of the stone chamber. A single tear slid down her face.

Rashid stood sentry at the narrow opening of their temporary "home." He allowed Poya to roam around nearby and talk to the other cave-dwelling families, but cautioned him not to stray too far away. Poya was not to discuss where he was from or how they traveled. He was told to shrug and change the subject.

They needed to hear the news, and decided it was the most expedient and practical to have Poya wander around and interact with the others. He would not raise suspicion like an obviously educated Rashid.

People were curious, though, and at one point a man poked his head into the cave and asked if they would like to join his family for tea. As Kendall averted her head, Rashid declined, pointing to her and saying that she was not feeling well. The man quickly backed out of their cave, not wanting to catch any sickness from the new people. Rashid was immediately sorry that he had used that excuse. Around these very poor, uneducated people, they would not take kindly to a stranger introducing an illness to their population. He was really hoping there would be no gossip about them; that they would just blend in.

Poya quickly learned that the main living in the caves was eked out by the children. The caverns were only a mile from the Bamiyan morning market. During the day, the children would run around the countryside, picking up grass, hay, and other fruits, nuts, and potatoes, and either bring them back for their families or sell them at the market.

The ceilings of the caves were rounded and about seven feet high. In the seventh century, the Buddhist monks had occupied the caves, using them to meditate. The caves could accommodate a small fire near the entrance. The children gathered dung from the countryside to stoke the fires. Many of the caves had makeshift or crude doors made out of discarded wood or a rug that had been hung up.

In the early evening, Rashid made a fire and they had a meager meal of bread, melon, and nuts. Rashid had plenty of money with him, but it was imperative that they hide from the troops now scouring the nearby countryside. Poya offered to go out to the Bamiyan morning market first thing in the morning pretending to find some day labor work. He would listen to the news and bring back word to Rashid. Kendall was afraid for his safety but knew that was the most practical solution for them.

Rashid could see that Kendall was miserable. He decided that based on what Poya learned tomorrow, they would determine their next course of action in the evening. But he told himself that they would leave as soon as it was safe.

As the evening wore on and the stars shown brighter, Rashid and Poya sat on either side of Kendall. They decided to distract her by telling her what they could hear from the other caves. Voices carried in the tunnel-like tombs, and many conversations swirled around them. An excited teenager above them was telling his family that when he was walking back from the market, he came upon a police commander and two officers who had rounded up a family of eight at the side of the road. The teenager hid behind a piece of old, rusting farming equipment to hear what was being said. The patriarch of the family of eight was accused of murdering two local brothers when he could not pay his debt to them.

The police commander explained his mission and then promptly killed all eight family members to avenge the deaths. The young man waited behind the tree for an hour as the policemen searched every body ... rifling through their clothes and belongings ... taking what they wanted for themselves.

The large extended family living on their one side was loud and boisterous. The father was railing against the local government, because last week his ten year old had stolen a loaf of bread from the market. He was caught, and two fingers were cut off. The youngster was going to recover, although he also had a bad cough. The parents were angry that he had not been able to scavenge in the streets and countryside for a week now.

Kendall had been sipping some tea and choked when they recounted the story. “Stop!” she hissed. “I don’t want to hear any more.”

She was surprised how well Poya adapted to their bleak existence in the cave. He was happy to be with Rashid and away from the palace. He missed the horses, but was glad that he was no longer being mistreated by the Shazeb family. He curled up and slept with a smile on his face.

Kendall took one last walk under the watchful eyes of Rashid out to the boulders to relieve herself by the jeep and then settled in for the night. She tried not to think about how dirty her hands and face were. As she drifted off to sleep on the hard surface of the cave’s floor, on which only a thin pad had been hastily thrown down, she kept waking to voices all around her. It was the oddest thing she had ever encountered ... living in a space with no front door ... completely at the mercy of her neighbors’ whims. The thought was so surreal that she actually smiled. She told herself that it was probably hysteria.

Rashid lay on his bedroll thinking about what he hadn’t told Kendall. People were talking about him, having heard from trips to the Bamiyan market about the deaths of the Afghan leader’s family. The people thought how wonderful it would be to get the reward money. So long as Kendall kept out of sight, and Rashid’s jeep wasn’t recognized, they would not be discovered. But it was too much to hope for. In reality, the trio with their clean clothes and quiet ways, who kept to themselves as if they were better than everyone else, was attracting attention. It was only a matter of time before someone tossed a match onto the perfectly built haystack.

# CHAPTER THIRTY-THREE

The U.S. intelligence community and government leaders were reeling. Along with the world, they had just watched the Israeli video about the rescue of the Orion Premier CEO and CFO. The Israelis paraded Paul Fields in front of the cameras. He looked well enough but seemed stunned and, for once, at a loss for words. Glenn Carson was reported to be in serious but stable condition, now that he was receiving the best medical care.

There were scant details on the "rescue." Israel simply stated that its carrier was in nearby waters on a routine mission and had received a distress call from within an Afghanistan government building. After confirming the source and accuracy of the report, it sent a helicopter that landed on the rooftop and rescued the two Orion executives. No information was given about Kendall Radcliffe or Rashid Sharif. But the Israeli spokesperson did say that the helicopter was forced to take off abruptly and use evasive maneuvers to get back to the awaiting ship in the Arabian Sea. Nothing was said about the Afghanistan doctor that accompanied the Americans.

The world was stunned. Nothing made sense. Afghanistan had a competent military complete with its own capable air force that should have responded. Israel should never have been able to fly into Afghanistan airspace, let alone land on a government rooftop. The only conclusion was that the Afghan military communication network and radar had been jammed, deactivated, or destroyed.

The bombing that was seen by satellite during the day did not target the military. But the images showed the presidential palace had been bombed. No one was sure what the story was. Israel wasn't saying anything and appeared to know little beyond the rescue.

The worldwide intelligence community wasn't buying it. There was much more to the story. The U.S., in particular, was furious. Why hadn't it been told of the planned rescue, even if it was an emergency? In the old days, Israel would never have taken such steps without consulting the international powers.

On the face of it, the American citizens, Seattleites, Orion employees, and the Fields and Carson families were ecstatic. They didn't ask for further explanation. They were just glad that their loved ones and citizens had been rescued.

The press event concluded with a statement that in the morning the Orion executives would be flown to Tel Aviv, where Glenn Carson would be transferred to the top trauma center there.

The cameras went dark, and the tension in the executive conference room onboard the Israeli carrier eased. Israeli officials at the podium shook hands and congratulated themselves. Officers approached Paul Fields and fawned over him, asking if there was anything they could do for him. He was offered a refreshment and chose coffee, strong and black. Fields was momentarily overwhelmed and uneasy at all the attention. He soon recovered and asked for a phone and a computer.

Commander Reichenfeld agreed to the phone and computer, and asked that the computer be set up at the back of the conference room. He wasn't about to let Fields have a private computer. Whoever he communicated with was going to be the business of Israel. All phone conversations would be taped, and the computer would capture the network activity by history and content. Reichenfeld and his crew, of course, were not privy to *Prophecy*. For that reason, the commander had been warned that the Mossad would be keeping an eye on Fields' computer activities, from afar. Naturally, the commander was curious about the process but valued his elevated position more, and therefore said nothing.

Paul Fields began a marathon of phone calls starting with his family. He assured them he would be fine and that his wife did not need to meet him in Israel. He would be home in the next few days. He did not have his passport with him and would be working with the U.S. embassy in Jerusalem to procure a replacement. His wife thought he was subdued and kinder than usual. For once, she was anxious to have him home.

He then called his head of security, Eric "Mickey" McDougall.

"Hello, Mickey, this is Paul."

"Oh, thank God, Mr. Fields, Sir. You're all right! I just saw the press conference. What would you like me to do?"

"Is the company plane back in the air?"

"Yes, Sir, it is. Standing by, awaiting orders."

"Good. Please bring it to Tel Aviv to pick me up. Arrange for Mrs. Carson to travel with you. She will want to see her husband. I'm hoping that just hearing her voice will help him recover faster."

"Anything else, Mr. Fields?"

"Please, Mickey, you always call me Paul."

"I know, Sir. You've just been through a lot. We've all been so worried."

"More than you know. But I want to be out of this fucking circus and back in Seattle as soon as possible."

"Understandable, Paul, Sir."

"Is that it?"

"Yes. Please patch me through to my office."

"Okay."

There was an awkward pause as Fields waited to be transferred to his executive administrator. But he wasn't put on hold. Finally, he said, "Mickey, are you still there?"

Mickey blurted out, "Uh, yes. What about Kendall Radcliffe? What's happened to her? Was she with you?"

Fields thought quickly and then answered carefully, fearful of unknown ears. "Yes, she was with us by happenstance. Carson and I ran into her at the hotel in DC. That's how she came to be on our charter."

It didn't sound like he was going to offer anything further. Mickey just had to press for more. Too many people had inquired about her. His face was beet red as he whispered into the phone, "But why wasn't she rescued when you were?"

"I don't know, Mickey. We were about to take fire, and the helicopter just lifted off the rooftop."

"Was she with you?"

Fields felt terrible. He hated admitting that Kendall was left behind while he was rescued. "Yes, she was behind me when we were loaded onto the helicopter. Troops came storming out of the building."

"What happened to her? Is she still alive?"

"I don't know, Mickey. I didn't see her after that. Now will you patch me through?"

"Absolutely, Paul. Right away."

Fields spoke with his executive admin for thirty minutes, assuring her that he was fine and that he would be home soon. He told her that Mickey would be bringing the plane to Tel Aviv and that hopefully Mrs. Carson would accompany the security detail. He asked her to get him a new cell phone and laptop and have the latter set up exactly like the old one. He requested that Daniel Blumfeld personally oversee the configuration. Since it was early morning in Seattle, Daniel would have time to drive to Seattle and get the laptop ready before the flight left later in the day.

Fields had to repeat everything twice, because his executive admin kept interrupting him with sobs. She had written him off as dead, and couldn't believe that the ornery, ruthless, sonofabitch had survived. She was happy, for her sake. She wondered how his wife had taken the news that he had survived. Finally, Fields outlined the emergency meetings he would need to conduct upon his return, starting with the board of directors and Orion executives. Once he knew his upcoming schedule better, he would have her start filling up his calendar.

The Orion CEO hung up and sat back to take his first breath. He felt satisfied that he had spoken with everyone he needed to for the moment. He looked around, and saw that the room was mostly empty. The furniture had been efficiently rearranged to its original configuration. His eyes traveled to the two men sitting at the nearby conference table. He locked eyes with Commander Reichenfeld. The latter quickly looked away.

"Commander?"

"Yes, Mr. Fields?"

"I'm tired, but I would like to use the computer. Can it be moved to my room?"

"I'm sorry Mr. Fields. I understand you're tired. But the rooms are not equipped for computer hookup. The ship was configured that way on purpose, so the men would not be tempted to have personal computers in their rooms. You understand. We'd never get them out of their rooms. Any time you want, you can use the computers in the resource room."

Fields frowned and nodded. And the commander did not bother to inform him there were rooms wired with network lines. Fields just wasn't assigned one of those rooms, on purpose. He looked directly at the commander. "Any update on Kendall?"

Reichenfeld had the decency to look uncomfortable. He shook his head. "I'm sorry, no word."

"From Rashid either?"

The commander shrugged, "Nothing."

Fields requested to be taken back to his room. He was given something to help him sleep. He awoke sometime in the middle of the night trying to catch his breath. He had been dreaming that as the helicopter rose from the rooftop, Kendall had been shot in the back by the soldiers and then blown up by whoever bombed the AIDC building. He then lay there and replayed the rooftop events in his head.

He was puzzled, wondering if the helicopter he was on had bombed the building, and he just missed it in all the chaos? No, he was certain there was no gunfire or missiles shot from his helicopter. It was all they could do to maneuver vertically and head south for the Arabian Sea as fast as they could. But then who destroyed the building? He sat up and had a brief moment of terror, wondering if Israel was going to cut Rashid loose. Kendall, by mere association, would once again be in the wrong place at the wrong time.

Fields fervently wished he knew Kendall better. She had been very relaxed at the dinner at Shazeb's palace. She and Rashid appeared to be playing a part. Fields had detected an underlying theme or plot to which both Kendall and Rashid seemed to have assigned roles. Looking back on the evening, one could even say that Kendall and Rashid had played both sons against each other in the presence of their father. But how could they have known the brothers would turn on each other, be killed, and the father would be forced to avenge his favorite son? They couldn't possibly have known that. President Shazeb wasn't even in the room when Saaqib shot Ahmad.

The Orion CEO fell back onto the bed into an exhausted sleep, woozy from analyzing the different scenarios in his head.

In the morning, Fields requested a visit with Glenn Carson. The CFO was awake and alert. He had a lot of questions about where he was and what had happened in the past weeks. Fields brought him up to speed in a non-specific way, saying that they had been rescued by the Israelis from the rooftop of a building in Afghanistan. Carson could not believe he had been unconscious for so long. Within an hour, Carson was overly stimulated and exhausted. Fields was asked to let him sleep. He went back to his room in much better spirits.

Early afternoon brought the helicopter that would shuttle the Orion executives to Tel Aviv. Carson was moved without incident into the helicopter, along with his accompanying attending physician and the Afghanistan doctor, Maysah Siddra. Carson was strapped into place together with the medical supplies and machines he required. Finally, Paul Fields was summoned and settled into his seat.

The chopper, a Chinook CH-47F, was more suited for the transport of passengers. The sleek design and high-tech modernized digital control system made for a smooth, quick, and safe transport to the Tel Aviv naval station, where Carson was whisked off to the nearby world-famous trauma center.

Fields was ushered into yet another conference room, where he was subjected to an additional debriefing by the Israelis. There was nothing more that he could or would tell them they didn't already know.

Finally, toward early evening, his Orion security detail was allowed onto the naval base where they retrieved him and drove to the nearby Carlton Tel Aviv. He was overwhelmed when he got a look at the luxury suites his executive admin had booked for him and his staff. They had half the suites on one floor. He was overjoyed when he saw luggage for him that included all of the clothes and shoes he needed to replace the ones left behind in Afghanistan.

He was informed that Mrs. Carson, as expected, accompanied the security detail to Tel Aviv. After checking into the hotel, she was taken to the trauma center, where she was now refusing to leave her husband's bedside. One car and security guard remained with her.

Fields felt rejuvenated. He couldn't get over the unbelievable luxurious comforts the hotel offered. For weeks he had worn soiled clothing and slept on a bed that was really nothing more than a cot. His security detail ordered sushi for him while he took a hot, steaming shower. He remained in his room for the evening, where he could relax and look out onto the Mediterranean Sea below.

He was anxious to get onto the corporate network and work on emails and review key documents awaiting his critical analyses. It was morning in Seattle, and he was pleased he would be able to connect with his employees at corporate headquarters. After several hours of intense work, he was completely exhausted and had lost all desire to get up to speed any further on events at work. He marveled at how quickly he tired at the slightest attempt to focus. Of course, he had no idea he was suffering the effects of an extended period of stress and trauma.

Fields dismissed his security detail for the night and sent them to their rooms. He watched a little news and called his family. His children gave him such comfort and brought him back to the realities of family life. They updated him with the trivial happenings at school and on the soccer field. He loved hearing their banter. He really and truly appreciated his kids for the first time.

He vowed that he would repair his marriage when he returned. As soon as he was caught up at the office, and the board of directors and shareholders were assured that nothing untoward had happened to him and that things could get back to "normal," he would take his wife on a vacation.

His wife came on the line and asked when he would be returning. He told her he would not leave until Carson was able to travel in a matter of days. He hoped that within a couple days there would be word of Kendall and maybe even another rescue. It would be just perfect if they all traveled back home to Seattle together. But in the pit of his stomach he knew that would never happen.

His last call was to Daniel Blumfeld. Using his new cell phone, he plugged in the scrambler for a secure, direct line that he was assured would not be heard, recorded, or streamed real time by third parties. The young man was shocked to hear his boss's voice on the other side of the line when he answered the phone.

"My God, Mr. Fields, are you and Mr. Carson okay? Are you back in Seattle?"

"Yes, Daniel, we are fine and are in Tel Aviv. Glenn is in the hospital for a couple more days, and then we'll fly back to Seattle together."

"Wha—wha—what about Kendall Radcliffe?" he stuttered. "Is she with you?"

"Unfortunately, no. But that's why I'm calling you. Daniel, I need you to concentrate on looking for any word about her. Focus your efforts on any communication dealing with her, her body, her whereabouts, any rescue, etc."

Daniel was alarmed. "Her body? Do you think she's dead?"

"I don't know, Daniel," Fields stated, feeling miserable. "But if there's the slightest chance you and I can find her, we're going to do it."

"I'll get right on it, Mr. Fields. Do you know where she might be?"

"The last time I saw her, she was on the rooftop of the Afghanistan government AIDC building. So, if you could use *Proph* to monitor General Omar or any other Afghanistan government leader, that should give us an update."

"Anything else?"

"Yes. Include Israel in your monitoring. They are definitely not telling me everything. Also, a young Afghan by the name of Rashid Sharif was instrumental in getting us rescued. He was left behind also. If you find Kendall, you will also find Rashid. He needs to be rescued as well. Daniel, we would not have been found if it wasn't for Rashid. He's a good guy. But for now, don't reveal anything to anyone about Rashid. Okay?"

Daniel was well aware of the U.S. intelligence connection with *Prophecy* too, but Fields didn't know that Daniel knew. So, the young man had to tread lightly. "Absolutely. But Mr. Fields?"

"Yes?"

"Are you going to tell anyone else about your theories of Kendall?"

"I don't know what you mean."

"What about the FBI or CIA? Is there anyone you know that might be able to help us?"

"Possibly, Daniel, but not yet. When you find more information, I'm going to shake every tree I can to get someone in DC to jump in."

"Excellent, Mr. Fields. I'll start right away."

"Good. I'm going to bed now, so I'll talk to you at the end of your day."

They rang off, and both men sat at their respective desks—Daniel in the office and Fields in his hotel room—lost in thought. Daniel was greatly relieved that something was going to be done about Kendall. He was also reassured that his full-court press of snooping via *Prophecy* was sanctioned by the boss. Maybe *Prophecy* could finally be used for good. It occurred to the Orion site and IT manager that Fields was obviously feeling guilty about an employee having been left behind, while he managed to get rescued. He had never known Paul Fields to care about anyone or anything but business. He had always been considered ruthless and cold.

Daniel roused himself from his musings and rose from his desk to go refill his coffee mug. He was going to need a lot of caffeine fortification for the next couple of days. He was determined to be the driving force behind uncovering the whereabouts of Kendall Radcliff. As he walked to the kitchen, he pondered

Israel's current role. He, too, agreed that something odd and seemingly sinister was developing between the Mossad and/or Israel about what to do with Kendall and Rashid. From what Daniel had already gleaned from observing communications within Israeli intelligence, it believed that Rashid might be alive, but Kendall not at all. Daniel's heart fell to his stomach in a thud at the thought that *Prophecy* might have been used to eliminate one of his friends and a valued co-worker. He gave a big sigh as he grabbed a larger cup from the cupboard and filled it with steaming black coffee.

Paul Fields sat motionless at the little desk in his hotel room, staring out at the Mediterranean Sea. He had never second-guessed the development and use of *Prophecy*. He had rationalized it as a brilliant high-tech business device that gave him an edge. He told himself from the very beginning that it was a necessary business decision. That in order to get ahead in this day and age, one had to make sacrifices and make difficult decisions as the head of the company.

He found it interesting that during the conversation with Daniel, he could not bring himself to utter *Prophecy's* whole name. He felt kind of sick now about his slick high-tech masterpiece. After all, wasn't it the existence of *Prophecy* that started this whole nightmare scenario into which he had been thrust against his will? His conscience—something he took prize in controlling and ignoring or at the very least suppressing—reminded him that Kendall Radcliffe hadn't even known about *Prophecy*, and yet she was caught up—and possibly even dead now—as a result. It was likely that as a result of his "business decision," an employee had gotten caught in the same vicious web as he, but through no fault of her own. The worst thing was that people had been quick to cast blame or responsibility on her. *Guilt by association*, he thought wretchedly. In actuality, he was the "guilty" party, and yet he got rescued and she didn't.

Fields walked into the bathroom, looked around and suddenly stopped. For a moment, he basked in the luxury of the modern amenities. But he was soon beside himself with self-loathing. Here he was, about to brush his teeth in the most amazing glittering suite, and God knows what was happening or had happened to Kendall Radcliffe. Was she living like a rat? Was she hurt? Did she even know who she was? Was she even alive?

Fields had to stop himself, because there was nothing he could do about Kendall's situation at this very moment. He and Daniel were going to do everything they could to find her and Rashid. He just hoped it would be in time.

As he crawled into bed and sank into the luxurious down comforter and pillows, he found that he couldn't sleep. The bed was too soft. The covers were too many, too heavy, and too fine. His silk pajamas had him sliding all over the bed. He felt like he was falling or out of control. He tossed and turned all night with images of Kendall in his mind either lying dead ... without her head ... or running for her life with a crazed look of fear on her face. He wasn't so far off on the latter. Things would rapidly go downhill for Kendall in the coming days.

In the morning, Fields' security detail found him on the floor of his hotel room next to the King-sized bed in search of more solid ground ... having yanked a pillow and the comforter off the bed. He had finally found a comfortable position and was sleeping soundly.

# CHAPTER THIRTY-FOUR

RASHID PEERED OUT OF THEIR Bamiyan cave at first morning light. People were beginning to stir and move about. Poya ate a quick morning meal with green tea and then took off for the nearby Bamiyan village. He followed close behind a group of children, so he would know the safest route to the morning market. The children knew where the landmines were and how to avoid them.

While much of Afghanistan had been cleared of the ten million landmines from the combined Soviet occupation, Al-Qaeda, and the Taliban, hundreds of thousands still dotted the Afghan countryside. The country still possessed the unfortunate honor of being one of the most heavily-mined in the world ... the result of prolonged wars. The ordnances ranged in size from smaller than a cigarette lighter to the size of a saucer. The greatest number of children in the world killed by landmines was still in Afghanistan. Poya needed to keep that in mind and be very careful to pick a well-traveled, known path to the market.

Kendall and Rashid stayed behind and fretted the entire time he was gone. Occasionally, Rashid walked about outside, listening to his neighbors' conversations and keeping abreast of the news. Kendall was going stir crazy in the cave, particularly when she was left alone. Most people walking by their cave peered in out of curiosity. Kendall had no choice but to keep her headscarf low so that it virtually covered her entire face. She was also not used to sitting with her legs crossed for an extended period of time. Her legs were alternately cramping and stiff.

Finally, after four hours Poya arrived back at the cave all by himself. Rashid had taken care to tuck money into Poya's pockets and inside the lining of his light jacket before he left in the morning. He had been warned to be very careful when retrieving any money from his clothing. It was imperative that he not be seen with even a little cash. He had been mindful of that as he went from tent to tent and made a few purchases. He came back with his pockets full ... having carefully folded and hidden the clothing that he bought Kendall.

She was surprised when he pulled out a *Kuchi* tribal metallic embroidered belt and gypsy silver hoop earrings with glass inlays for her. Rashid had told him to purchase a couple *Kuchi* nomad items for Kendall, as that might be their next role should they need to ditch the jeep. He didn't want to tell Kendall that it was only a matter of time before they would lose it.

A *Kuchi* nomad was an *abadi*—a free person that was not aligned with any particular tribe. They were independent and self-sufficient, mostly traveling from place to place. They were a tough, hardy strain of people who could easily kill you or offer you a place to stay for the evening, depending on how you treated them or what you had to offer. Some got involved in illegal activities—like heroin trafficking—while others chose a much simpler, more peaceful nomadic life moving their sheep and camels from one pastureland to another. They sold their wares at the local bazaars and bartered and traded their goods, eking out a small subsistence living for their large, extended families.

Because they were so capable of looking after themselves, they had the respect and ear of the Afghanistan government. They moved around so much that they generally knew what was going on wherever they went. While President Shazeb had scoffed at the notion of their usefulness, regular government officials routinely sought them out when ethnic tensions resulted in sudden bloody skirmishes and uprisings within Afghanistan. The *Kuchi* nomads saw everything and were often helpful in getting to the truth during fact-finding missions. As Rashid saw it, the *Kuchi* nomads were not loyal to Shazeb, and could even be said to dislike the despot. But it would behoove him to keep in mind that they were loyal to the few government officials who sought them out. Rashid was more than willing to assume the risk.

He hoped to blend right in if need be. While they were only a group of three—and the normal *Kuchi* family had extended members—Rashid figured he would pass them off as a young family on the way to meet relatives in the next village. *Kuchis* often traveled together, but in small bands, maybe a few hours behind their other family members. He would just need to lie convincingly.

Kendall laughed when Poya pulled out a small sack of *lur* and offered her a lump. He immediately popped a piece of the hard candy made from brown sugar into his mouth, and a slow smile spread across his face. He was clearly relishing the taste.

He recounted that some children asked him to play *mosa* near the market, and he did. But he was older and taller than the other kids and soon lost interest. Rashid explained to Kendall that *mosa* was like horseshoes but with the use of a rock instead of a horseshoe.

Poya had not learned anything critical about their predicament or the government situation. He had only seen a few soldiers who seemed to be strolling about rather than hunting for someone or something. He watched a little news on a flat-screen television at a shop inside a tent at the market, but was shooed off by the owner for loitering.

Rashid asked him where the other children were, and why he came back alone. Poya broke into a huge grin and said they all went to watch a game of *buzkashi* at a nearby field. Rashid had seen most of the men leaving the caves, and now realized where they'd gone. *Buzkashi,* he explained to Kendall, was a game like polo played on horseback, but using the carcass of a *kokpar*—a headless goat or calf instead of a ball. The game was very violent and frequently resulted in severe physical injuries. Riders, or *chapendaz,* were often at the mercy of other player's whips and boots. The whips, carried in the riders' teeth, were used to fend off opposing riders and horses. At least a day before the match, the *kokpar* or carcass is beheaded, disemboweled, with its limbs cut off at the knees. It's then soaked for twenty-four hours in cold water to toughen it. The preference was to use a calf over a goat, because it was less likely to disintegrate during the game.

Kendall was once again horrified to learn the details of this seemingly barbaric game. Poya was eager to watch the game, and asked Rashid to come with him. The latter thought it might be the perfect opportunity to blend in while scoping out any tension around the city. They quickly ate the *pulao*—a rice dish with mutton and vegetables—that Poya also brought back from the market.

Rashid and Poya set off for the field mid-afternoon. The game was halfway through the first forty-five minute half when they arrived. They decided to walk around the field to a place that had no spectators. That way they were safe from scrutiny and could enjoy the spectacle. Poya had never watched a game of *buzkashi* before, and thought it was thrilling the way the eight horses galloped by and how quickly the *kokpar* changed sides. The young boy shrank back when a rider got hit by his adversary's whip. The crowd whooped and cheered loudly when one side scored in the opponent's *kazan*—or goal.

At the fifteen minute half-time break, they walked around keeping to themselves. They did not notice the man with a pair of binoculars trained on them. They walked a little further out on a small path heading away from the field, so that Poya could relieve himself. All of a sudden, that same man who had been watching them started waving his hands and yelling at them. Rashid heard the loud voice over the din and was startled to see the man running towards them ... arms flapping.

Thinking the man recognized them, Rashid yelled for Poya to run further along the path into the shrubs along the hillside. He took off towards Poya and looking back over his shoulder at the man who was now capturing everyone's attention, missed the short red stake that had been driven into the ground to his left to indicate an unsafe minefield that had not yet been cleared of the landmines.

The blast knocked Rashid off his feet. He lay unmoving on the hard ground. The crowd and players reacted by scattering the opposite direction. The man finally reached Rashid and helped him to his feet and brushed off the dirt that covered him. Rashid was shaken and momentarily disoriented and deaf. After a few minutes, with the sympathetic man telling him that he had tried to warn him of the nearby minefield, Rashid understood for the first time that the man had been trying to help him. He gave the man a grim smile, looked around at the clearing smoke, dust, and debris raining down on them, and shouted Poya's name.

As the air cleared and he regained some of his bearings, he saw the heap of bloody clothing first. He quickly ran over to the boy and grabbed Poya up in his arms. The boy had detonated the landmine when he stepped directly on it. Hundreds of metal fragments had torn through his body. He never had a chance.

Rashid turned when he heard the roar of an engine, and saw a pickup truck of Afghanistan National Police headed their way. The police were probably coming to help, but he couldn't take the chance of being recognized. He gently laid Poya's lifeless body on the ground. He then reached into his pockets and pulled out a wad of *Afghani*. He shoved it at the kind man and asked him to give Poya a proper burial.

With tears streaming down his face, and his head down, Rashid quickly ran past the approaching truck. He stumbled, blindly, back to their stone dwelling, still trying to clear his head, and burst into the cave. He threw himself at a surprised Kendall. Through his stilted speech, she got the gist of the horrific events. He sank onto the hard earthen ground pulling her down with him. He wrapped his arms around her, completely consumed with grief and guilt. How had he missed the clear sign of a nearby landmine? How could he have let his guard down even for a moment? Poor Poya. He hadn't deserved this.

Kendall held him tight and shushed him quietly, because he was speaking in English. She was afraid others would hear. But their neighbors were already suspicious. Some had seen Rashid and Poya at the game and thought it was odd the two stood where they did, near an uncleared mine field. All of the locals knew better than to stand there. These two people sharing their caves were obviously strangers. Now, word was spreading that they spoke English. Two men quietly went to summon the local authorities or soldiers, whichever they came across first.

Kendall could feel they were now in danger. She extracted herself from Rashid's prostrate form and efficiently gathered their things. She then knelt down and grabbed Rashid's arms. She looked him directly into his eyes and said in a stern low voice, "Rashid, stop! There is no time to mourn. What's done is done! It's terrible, and we'll deal with it later. We are in danger. People have been looking in at us. I think they are talking about us. We must leave now!"

She stood up and yanked his arms as hard as she could. He seemed to snap out of it, and scrambled to his feet. She took one of Poya's shirts and wiped Rashid's face. It took two trips to get all of their stuff back in the jeep.

As they drove out of the cave area, they could see lights flashing in the distance, coming towards them. Their way was clear in the opposite direction. They headed away from the oncoming lights. Rashid's face was rigid and tense. He constantly looked in his rearview mirror. For the moment, they were safe. But he figured the authorities were only thirty minutes behind them. He made a split-second decision to head to the Band-e-Amir Lakes. The road to Band-e-Amir was crudely paved, while the infrastructure around Kabul and the government offices had been upgraded to very passable roads. President Shazeb had not welcomed visitors and tourists. Many of the tourist destinations had fallen into disrepair from lack of funds.

It was now dark, and they had to climb two thousand feet to the ten-thousand-foot elevation of the lakes. Again, Rashid was worried about their headlights being seen. He stopped the jeep, and they put on their night vision goggles. While he drove slowly and carefully in the darkness, Kendall rummaged around for something to eat and drink. They ate on the run. This was beginning to be a habit for them.

Rashid gripped the steering wheel like he was hanging on for dear life. Kendall couldn't stand it anymore. She reached out her warm hand and placed it gently over his arm. He could feel the heat radiating the length of his arm. He instantly relaxed and eased his grip. He looked over at her and his eyes were wide and intense with anger.

"Why Poya? He didn't deserve this! He was just a boy. I had hoped he would have a stable life with Jangi. I was planning to check on him and make sure he was happy. Once I made a new life for myself, I would gladly have brought him there if his situation wasn't working out. He deserved to have a new a life. He never had a stable life until he came to live with me. Even then, he was in constant danger from the Shazebs. I wanted him to get educated and go to college."

Kendall let him ramble until his voice gave out. She patted his arm. "I'm so sorry, Rashid. I know he meant the world to you."

His voice cracked, "I couldn't even stay to arrange for a proper burial."

She murmured soothingly, "It couldn't be helped."

He shook his head. "But if I'd only known. I'm used to the rocks painted red on the sides of the road. That's how I know of an uncleared minefield. I missed it."

His voice faltered and gave out. They rode in silence for a long time, each lost in thought to the unexpected events of the day. Kendall wondered at the passing barren landscape. There were no trees on the sides of the road. But she could clearly make out large reddish-looking lumps along the way.

Finally out of curiousity, she pointed to one and said, "Rashid, what are those red mounds?"

He frowned at the distraction to his brooding. "That's moss. The village men come up here with their donkeys and use pick-axes to harvest it."

"Really? What's it used for?"

"It's stored on rooftops and used as kindling for fires."

They drove by a stone building close to the road. Before she could ask, Rashid pointed it out, "That's a tea stop. During the day, we could stop there for a cup of green tea. The men sit outside on a piece of carpet and talk." She shook her head at the comparison to a Starbucks store back home. What a different world she was in. She wondered if she'd ever see home again.

As they drove on and began to climb, Kendall could see the clear demarcation of the sedimentary rock in the hillsides. At one point, they drove by a place with poles stuck into the land. Atop each pole was a flag. "Rashid, is that a cemetery?"

"Yes."

"Way out here in the hills?"

"Yes. Those graves belong to ancestors of the nomads that roam the mountainside."

"How do they make a living?"

"They have herds of sheep and goats."

"Oh, like the boys we almost ran into when we left Kabul?"

"Exactly."

Two hours later they arrived at the first of the six lakes that comprise the Band-e- Amir Lakes. The full light of the moon reflected off the clear smooth water. The sight was breathtaking.

"Rashid, tell me about the lakes."

"Hmm. They are in the Hindu Kush Mountains west of Bamiyan. The water is so clear you can see the fish from one hundred feet up the cliff. And the water's very cold." He pointed at the obvious rock face. "There's a natural dam formed by mineral deposits. In fact, it's one of the few rare lakes in the world formed by limestone and mineral springs. Did you know that it's considered one of the wonders of the world?"

"No, I didn't know that." She saw a row of tents. "It looks like a bazaar of sorts."

"It's a small bazaar by the largest lake. Most of the population is the same as in Bamiyan. They are *Hazaras*. The only industry is the flour mills below the dam and the old tourist buildings and monuments. The millstones are turned by using the power of the water."

Kendall nodded. "Where are we going now?"

"To the lake at the far end. We're going to camp."

"In the car?"

Rashid laughed. "No. It's not exactly a *kaidi*, but it'll do for us."

"I'm almost afraid to ask. What's a *kaidi*?"

"A *kaidi* tent is a large tent that the *Kuchi* nomads use. Mine is just a light brown—sort of khaki colored canvas tent used for sleeping. We'll barely be able to sit inside it."

"Yikes! So, we're out in the open most of the time then?"

"Yep. We should be good unless it rains."

"Wonderful! It keeps getting better," Kendall said dryly.

"Is that sarcasm I detect?"

"Sorry. I'll be a better companion once I've had a little food and sleep."

They passed a lot of caravans and broken-down cars, a few camels, and horses. Each campsite had a fire around which a family sat. Rashid finally found an isolated spot a little out of the way and pulled over. He explained to Kendall that they had a lot of creature comforts in the jeep, but he didn't want to call attention to them, so they were going to set up a bare campsite. He thought it was best that they re-group in the morning and make their plans. He was just too tired to think any more.

Rashid skillfully set up the tent, after which Kendall laid out the bedrolls inside. When she was through, she turned to the next task, and was surprised that Rashid had a roaring fire going. He quickly heated water for tea, and they ate nuts, fruit, and dried mutton from the supplies Jangi and his wife had given them. Kendall felt much better after having some hot tea. She hated the inconvenience of not having a bathroom.

"Rashid, do you have a flashlight?"

He frowned, "Yes, but we're not going to use it now."

"Why? I need to find a bush!"

He laughed. "Oh, that. Well, let me come with you, and I'll give you the smallest light I have. But we'll need to walk a ways, because I don't want anyone to see our light. We can't afford to draw attention to us."

"Do you think we're in danger here?"

"Actually, no. This is a tourist place. We have to go back towards Bamiyan in order to find another route to other cities. General Omar's people should not look for us here. It wouldn't make sense. Unless someone recognizes us or we do something to stand out, we should be able to blend in."

"Okay."

"Would you like to bathe tomorrow?"

Kendall was momentarily confused. "Did you say bathe?"

"Yes. There is a women's beach behind the tomb of the *Amir*. The tomb overlooks the largest lake. From what I understand, there is a structure half built into the water where women can bathe in private. If I take you there, you must wear the local dress."

She nodded excitedly, "I know, I know ... I need to blend in."

They scrambled over the ground and after walking a few minutes, found some large boulders. He handed her the small flashlight, but wouldn't let her turn it on until she was around the back side of the first large rock. She found that with the full moon, she didn't need the flashlight after all.

They made their way back to the campsite, put out the last embers of the fire, and climbed in the tent. From the other side of the lake, they could hear singing and laughter.

They were both exhausted, with nerves frayed. But neither could sleep. Kendall could hear Rashid's breathing and knew he was thinking of Poya.

"Rashid, are you okay?"

He sighed. "Yes, I'm thinking of Poya. He would have loved camping here."

Because of the elevation, the nights were very cold. During the winter, the temperature could get as low as minus twenty degrees. Halfway through the night, they awoke to find a bright blinding light shining in their tent. Rashid opened his eyes to see a large leathery face with several missing teeth looming over him. The man was speaking *Pashto* and seemed to be yelling at Rashid. He reached into the tent and practically yanked Rashid out. He quickly stumbled out of the tent. Kendall hid her head and thought they were caught for sure.

The man grabbed Rashid's arm and pulled it hard. Kendall was frozen with fear at all the commotion. She peeked out of the tent flap, and couldn't tell if Rashid was leaving on his own or being dragged away by the man. She lay in the tent for hours, not daring to move, while voices could be heard shouting all around her. The tent was surrounded. She wasn't actually sure she had been spotted when the man first poked his head into the tent. She was curled up next to Rashid, and the man might have thought Rashid was surrounded by blankets and other travel items.

The noises finally abated, and Kendall held her breath, wondering what she should do. She lay there for hours, waiting for the morning light. Suddenly, she could hear the thud of heavy footsteps approaching the tent. The tent flap was drawn back, and a tall figure in silhouette stood before her.

# CHAPTER THIRTY-FIVE

Paul Fields didn't want to eat alone, so he had asked his small security staff to order for all of them. It was comforting to have noise and chatter around him as he enjoyed his sumptuous breakfast while looking down on the sparkling waters of the Mediterranean Sea below. He felt safe.

After breakfast, he asked Mickey to take him to the hospital to see his partner, Glenn Carson. He was feeling generous and gave his staff a few hours off to explore while he was gone. When Fields arrived, Carson was dressed in pajamas and robe and was walking about the corridor. Mrs. Carson was at his side. She looked exhausted. Fields immediately ordered her security guy to take her back to the hotel for some hot food and a nice long nap. Surprisingly, she didn't protest too much. She was just so relieved that he was going to be fine, and that Fields and her husband had been rescued.

After she left, the doctor came in and announced that Carson could be released into a doctor's care in twenty-four hours. He would be allowed to fly back to Seattle so long as he was seen by a doctor as soon as he arrived. The physician was particularly glad that Carson would be flying back in the company jet, a much more comfortable environment than a commercial jet. The latter would have been impossible.

Fields had a sudden idea that if he could get the U.S. and Israeli government officials to agree to it, Afghanistan doctor Maysah Siddra could attend to Carson on the plane. But that would involve a lot of red tape in a short period of time. Dr. Siddra was not in trouble. It was a matter of finding out if she wanted to go to Seattle, and getting the Israelis to release her. Fields walked Mickey out to the nearby waiting room and asked him to make a series of phone calls to the Israeli officials they had met the previous day and to round up the U.S. embassy official, State Department and intelligence officers who were waiting to speak with him. He would get the ball rolling.

The CFO got back into bed and looked very relieved. Fields paced about the hospital room for a few minutes at the foot of Carson's bed.

"Paul, what is it?"

Fields didn't beat about the bush. He closed the hospital room door. "Glenn, I've asked Daniel to use all his resources to find any news of Kendall."

Carson's face wrinkled up as he tried to recall her status. "Oh. We don't know where she is?"

"No!"

"Paul, tell me again why she wasn't rescued with us?"

Fields did his best to recount the facts.

"Was it just an unfortunate series of events, or was it purposeful?"

The CEO didn't want to blame Glenn, and certainly didn't want to make him feel personally responsible, but Kendall's getting left behind was because the concern and focus was on getting the sick man into the chopper. He hedged, "Glenn, I don't know. Why would it have been planned? Though the Israelis have suggested she was involved in the plot against the Shazebs."

"Was she?"

Fields scoffed at the notion. "I can't imagine it. She's a corporate type, and a local girl to boot. I say no way." He continued pacing and then whirled around and wagged a finger at Carson. "My guess is that by blaming her, it somehow helps Israel ... probably by deflecting events away from them. That's my theory."

"The poor young lady. What she must be going through."

Fields shook his head. "I can't even think about that. You have no idea what those barbarians did every night in the courtyard of the military base just beyond our rooms." He shuddered recalling the proceedings that replayed each evening. "I don't think I'll ever get the sound of those screams from my head."

Carson looked as if he was going to relapse. Fields strode over to the side of the bed and patted his arm. "There, there. Don't think about it. You just need to concentrate on resting today, so we can get the hell out of here and head home tomorrow." Carson nodded and sank back into his bed.

Fields was ready to leave, and Mickey informed him that representatives from the U.S. State Department, U.S. embassy, intelligence, and Israeli officials would be coming to the hotel right after lunch. A conference room had been reserved. Fields was quiet on his way back to the hotel as he strategized about the meeting. He would control this meeting, not the Israelis or the U.S. officials. He would need to tread lightly, though, because the U.S. State Department was already irritated that he had given them the slip from the Israeli military base and ignored their phone calls earlier in the day. But he hadn't been ready to meet with them yet. Now he was.

He almost hummed to himself. Things were going his way, and he was certain he would find out what happened to Kendall. He always felt better, more centered, when he was calling the shots.

Mickey was allowed to attend the conference that afternoon. True to his word, Fields marched into the conference room after everyone was seated and took command of the meeting. He got right to the point and laid out his plans. At first, the official from the State Department was taken aback. He explained that the Afghanistan doctor did not possess the proper papers and that she would need to be thoroughly checked out both to ascertain her motives and to ensure she had no ill intent toward U.S. citizens.

The Israeli operatives jumped in and said they were also conducting a background search on Dr. Siddra, and for the time being would be hosting her stay in Israel.

Fields allowed himself to get angry. He looked around at the group of men in their comfortable business suits appearing relaxed and satisfied with their respective lives. He stood up and barked, "Do I need to remind you what my colleague and I have been through?" He began to walk around the large conference table. "This woman, Dr. Siddra, helped take care of Glenn Carson when he was in a critical state. She was instrumental in keeping him alive! She agreed to put her life on the line, walk away from the comfortable world she had in Afghanistan, in order to help us. I don't think there's much dirt you will discover about Dr. Siddra. She's a professional woman who cares about this world and knows she can do better in the West, particularly because she's a woman. It's as simple as that!"

One of the U.S. State Department men spoke up. "Aren't you getting ahead of yourself, Sir?"

"How so?"

"Your loyalty is admirable, but we have—all of us around this table—have an obligation to our citizens to keep them safe."

The State Department official jumped in, "Another thing is, you don't even know if she wants to go to the U.S., or to Seattle, for that matter."

Ever the CEO, Fields with hands on hips responded with, "As a matter of fact, I do. She told me on the rescue flight from Kabul how proud she was to help us, and that she hoped to go to America someday, where she had relatives living in Fremont, California. So, there you are. That's her motive. And I say she deserves it. Let's make it happen."

Mickey cut in smoothly as planned. "Mr. Fields, doesn't Fremont have the largest Afghan community in the U.S.?"

"Yes, Mickey, as a matter of fact it does. After 'hosting' her in Seattle while the State Department and Immigration and Customs Enforcement complete their comprehensive investigation, she could resettle in Fremont and live the life she desires."

He was on a roll and his enthusiasm was bubbling. "Here's my plan, gentlemen. I will personally vouch for her character, and will pay all of her living expenses to put her up in Seattle, complete with a full-time guard or companion to help her assimilate into the Western culture. Mickey will help me set this all up. I'll also pay all of her tuition to bring her education current to allow her to practice as a physician in the U.S. or whatever else she wants to do."

Fields had slowly circled the table while he was speaking and was now back at his chair. He stood with feet wide apart and proclaimed, "I will assume the responsibility for and guarantee the assimilation of this young woman into her new life. That is my commitment to you." He sat down.

No one said anything for a moment. Finally, the gentleman from the State Department said, "Well, you sure are going out on a limb for her. I know that you have money, but this would be a long-term project of sorts. It's not something you could simply throw money at from time to time. You run a multinational Fortune 500 Company. For you to take on something of this nature doesn't make sense. I'm wondering what your motive is, Mr. Fields."

Paul Fields tried to sound as sincere as possible. "To be honest, I wondered that myself at first. I couldn't believe I was even entertaining this seemingly harebrained scheme. But I'm not the same selfish, ruthless, greedy bastard that I was two months ago. I have several billion dollars in personal assets, and I am determined to do something decent with it before I die. This would be a great start at that pledge. Don't you all agree?"

He looked around the room, making eye contact with every person at the table, and heads were nodding. Mickey tried to suppress the smile on his face. He admired his boss at that moment and had never been prouder.

The U.S. State Department official turned to his Israeli counterpart. "I don't see why we couldn't speed things along. What can I do to help make this happen?"

Fields clapped his hands together and stood up. "Gentlemen, why don't you meet separately and work out the red tape. I need to make some phone calls."

A sour-faced U.S. official who hadn't uttered a word so far, suddenly held his hands up. "Hold it. Hold it, everybody." He turned to Paul Fields and pointed accusingly at him. "We are not going to simply grant asylum and release this woman into your custody at your say-so."

Fields was nonplussed, "And I don't expect you to. Your Immigration people—or whoever you so designate—can accompany us back to the U.S. and work out the particulars with Washington, DC and the local office in Seattle. Once they are satisfied with the plans to monitor her activities and conduct a full investigation, then and only then should they release her to me or Mickey, my head of security." He put his hand on Mickey's broad shoulder, and the young man nodded in agreement.

"Fine. But I'll be one of those on the plane back. I want to see for myself that everything's on the up and up." He seemed very put out.

Fields was growing tired of these paranoid government types who saw conspiracies and plots behind every good deed. Never mind that Fields had his own plans for Dr. Maysah Siddra.

The group split up, with the Israeli and U.S. State officials heading off to the nearby military base where Dr. Siddra was being temporarily housed under tight security. The plan had been to move her to the newly modernized, fortified refugee detention center for those seeking asylum, at the sand dunes complex in the Negev Desert. That facility had been built about eight years ago at the Ketziot Prison facility. Dr. Siddra's status was currently an "Administrative Detainee."

Israel would need to wrap up its debriefing of Maysah Siddra and assure itself that she knew next to nothing about the politics of Afghanistan, the government—or Shazeb—or any plans and schemes involving Israel. She had been speaking openly since arriving the day before, and had shown no guile or pretense. She did not appear to be sophisticated or worldly and seemed to be nothing more than a pawn.

The only people remaining in the hotel conference room were Fields, Mickey, and two U.S. intelligence officials. They requested their own debriefing of the Orion CEO. He agreed and patiently answered their questions for hours. There was not much more he could tell them they didn't already know, except about Rashid. They were curious about him and wondered about his role and his background. Fields knew little of Rashid's personal life or background. They asked for his opinion on whether Rashid was a good guy or bad guy. Fields' instinct was that Rashid was good, that he had no interest in overthrowing the government or taking over. He seemed to have had a personal grudge against the Shazebs, and was only too willing to help the Orion people escape. Fields voiced the thought that their rescue had answered that question.

The questions then moved to Kendall. The men were clearly frustrated that Fields couldn't shed any more light on her status. They seemed to understand how she got left behind, but Fields knew he was the last person they would confide in. He gladly filled them in on the limited background he knew and her role at Orion.

Fields wasn't interested in asking them any questions or seeking their help. He had his own sources. Not only did he have his contact at the NSA—Frank Reynolds—he also had a wide circle of influential mover-and-shaker-type friends starting with Senator Robinsford from Washington State. The senior senator chaired the prestigious Armed Services Committee, which included the Subcommittees on Strategic Forces and Readiness and Management Support. The Senator could be pressed into pushing for more resources in the Arabian Sea, if need be.

The men finally ran out of questions—or sapient answers from the Orion CEO—and headed to the hospital to speak with Carson. As they rose to make their exit, Fields warned them that Carson had been in the hospital almost the entire time while in Afghanistan, much of that time sedated and out of it. He suggested they would be wasting their time. They agreed in theory, but declared that protocol dictated they at least run through the usual questions.

Only Fields and Mickey were left in the conference room. As they walked back to their hotel rooms, Fields sent Mickey on to his room to begin dealing with the personal living arrangements of Dr. Siddra. Mickey already had a two-bedroom condominium in mind. It was in his brand new complex on Lake Union. Only one-third of the complex remained for sale. The two-bedroom was next to his on the sixth floor and had a breathtaking view of Lake Union. While Dr. Siddra may not appreciate the large bodies of water in and around the Seattle area, having lived her entire life in a landlocked country and being used to a dry, arid climate, Mickey felt she would soon acclimate out of sheer relief at getting away from Afghanistan, if nothing else. He and his staff would be there to help. He had to admit he was intensely curious about this mysterious woman who was the cause of much of the discussion and activity of the day.

Mickey fired up his computer and dispatched an email to his real estate agent to prepare to make an offer on the available unit.

Paul Fields sat at his desk alone in the spacious hotel room and ordered dinner. He looked at his watch and silently cursed. He realized his family was still sleeping, as was Daniel. *Damn time zone*, he thought. His meal arrived hot and sumptuous. He had eaten cold and decidedly utilitarian meals for weeks while at the Afghan military base. He didn't know what bothered him more, the lack of choice or the unfamiliarity of the flavors and spices. Before Afghanistan, he had everything, he thought. But he had been brought to his knees. He'd lost his freedom and the basic comforts of life.

He sat before the large window at his hotel room desk and enjoyed the sparkling water below. Before he powered up his computer, he reveled in the quiet and peaceful feeling that came over him. He searched for the reason for his sudden contentment, and realized he had gotten used to a solitary existence while in Afghanistan. This day had been filled with confusion, chaos, and many different moods and personalities, just like back at the office. It was a lot to process. The newfound freedom to move about and make even the smallest of decisions had not been lost on him. He liked this sudden spirituality that allowed him to slow down and reflect on every aspect of the day, his participation, and how he could make the greatest difference the next day. He could either decide to be an asshole—as he'd been in the past, running over people and getting his way at all cost—or use his money for good.

His mind wandered to the obscene amount of money he made. He'd been a co-founder of Orion Premier Net Services and therefore owned the bulk of the shares. When the company went public, it was such a huge financial success that he had doubled his portfolio in six months. His annual salary was eight hundred and fifty thousand dollars, and he was usually awarded a six million dollar bonus plus at least ten million dollars' worth of stock options. He shook his head at the outrageous benefits package he had and could find no justification for it.

He was intrigued by this sudden crisis of conscience, and made a personal vow to make things more equitable at the company. He reasoned that he and Glenn should make far less, and the employees should make a lot more.

He wasn't sure what to do about the shareholders. Those self-serving wannabes that hitched their wagon to his and constantly clamored for action, answers, and money, was something he would deal with, but not today. That would require a lot of thought to arrive at the best way to handle them. But one thing he did know was that they would no longer make his life miserable. He would not bow to them or run his company based on how they'd react. He would be honest with the public, and if people didn't want to invest in Orion, then fine. The company's success and fast-track to Fortune 500 had been meteoric. Its product line was solid, contemporary, and high tech. The future was golden.

The one thing the CEO drew the line at, though, was *Prophecy*, his baby. He would not give it up. It was too valuable to let it die. Instead, he would continue to use it to monitor his competitors, giving Orion the business edge. But he would also begin using *Prophecy* to do good things all around the world. He would use it for his new, personal "projects." In the past, he might not have cared what people thought of him, though he was always mindful of his reputation. The new Paul Fields pledged to alter his standing in the world.

Fields ate his dinner, appreciating the fine wine that accompanied it, and then sat back with a satisfied smile. It was now late enough that his family should be awake and eating their breakfast. He picked up his phone and turned on the computer.

The next day saw more red tape and stalling from both the U.S. and Israeli governments. It was clear the Orion plane would not be leaving this day. That was just as well, since Glenn Carson was not quite ready for a lengthy airplane ride. He was allowed to check out of the hospital shortly after Noon, with strict orders to remain in his hotel room to rest and recuperate. Fields visited him once in the late afternoon and was struck by his normalcy, except for the obvious medical condition.

Of the two of them, the whole kidnapping incident from beginning to end had obviously affected Fields more than Carson. it was almost like Carson had experienced nothing more than a medical event. Yes, he had seen the flight attendant murdered in his presence. But the CFO had not heard those nightly screams and lived the drama of daily uncertainty and unending boring days and nights alone, locked in a room that was nothing more than a hovel.

Glenn Carson noticed the change in Paul Fields. The latter was more thoughtful and less self-centered and, frankly, less self-serving. Carson was glad of the change, but wondered how it would affect the business. Had Fields lost his edge? Was the ruthless businessman who outmaneuvered his competitors in business gone? The CFO was particularly concerned when Fields commented that he was a changed person and planned to conduct his life and business under the new-and-improved version of Paul Fields. Carson wondered if Fields had either gone off the deep end or was suffering some type of temporary post-traumatic-stress event.

At one point during their discussion, Carson sent his wife out with a security person in tow to do a little shopping. He and Fields continued their discussion about the future. Carson realized everything would be fine once he heard that Fields would never give up *Prophecy*. He breathed a sigh of relief and almost chuckled out loud. If Fields really wanted to turn over a new leaf, he should begin by ridding himself of *Prophecy*. But the temptation was too strong, and the results too evident. *Prophecy* was secure and here to stay—for the time being.

***********

Dr. Maysah Siddra had been put through the ringer at the Israeli military complex. She was delighted at the opportunity to travel to the U.S. and was willing to have Paul Fields sponsor her once she was investigated and released by U.S. Immigration.

Israeli officials finally tired of the interrogation, and the Mossad, too, signaled its lack of interest in questioning her further. She was promptly turned over to the U.S., where government officials put her up at a hotel a short distance from where the Orion executives and staff were staying. Protocol mandated that she stay at the U.S. embassy under guard until her paperwork had been completed. But since the U.S. embassy was in Jerusalem, that wasn't possible.

Dr. Siddra was checked into a room with two beds and an adjoining room. A female FBI agent was posted to her room and would be staying with her for the duration.

The sour-faced U.S. official turned out to be very efficient, and he managed to secure replacement passports and the necessary paperwork for Dr. Siddra to travel the next day.

While U.S. intelligence operatives interrogated her basically all day, it soon became apparent that she had no secrets to reveal. Her background was nothing short of boring. The government—needing female doctors to treat female patients—paid for her medical education in France. Her only relatives were a band of *Kuchi* nomads who had left her behind at a hospital in Kabul when she became very ill. They needed to get out of town fast, because of involvement by one of their members in a particularly gruesome car bombing. Maysah Siddra had been fifteen at the time. She barely remembered those wild, fiery people, other than her two little sisters who had died when they ventured out of their camp and into a mine field.

With striking long black, sleek hair and piercing brown eyes, she had been noticed right away by a government official's wife, who saw the intelligence and independent spirit of a strong-willed female. The wife had recommended the government sponsor Siddra for the remainder of her education and subsequent travel to France for medical studies. As soon as Siddra had recovered from her illness, she was immediately sent to a boarding school, where the rigorous education process began. She quickly learned French and English. She knew that without hard work, her life was sunk. In order to make something of herself and to help other Afghan females, she had promised herself to study hard and excel. She did just that, and finished at the top of her class. When she was released back to Afghanistan, President Shazeb's wife met her, reviewed her credentials, and promptly snapped her up to be the children's physician. From time to time, the palace women had availed themselves of her services as well.

Dr. Siddra was appalled that after immersing herself in the educational process for so many years, she was forced to work for the one man she despised: Mujtaba Shazeb, the Afghan dictator. Everyone knew he was corrupt and personally responsible for so much suffering in Afghanistan. The whole time she was in France, the locals had shown nothing but contempt for Shazeb. The French government knew he was evil but kowtowed to him because of the parallel business interests. Shazeb had no end of Afghanistan money to spend on military weapons and the latest, most high-tech fighter jets. The French were only too happy to oblige and asked few questions.

She had only been at the palace for six months when the Orion people arrived. She was intensely curious about all of them and looked for an opportunity to help them and herself. She was shrewd and careful and had purposely stayed an arm's length away from Kendall. Dr. Siddra made no effort to seek her out or appear interested in the least. She knew there were hidden cameras and listening devices in the Orion people's rooms, and wasn't about to blow a chance to escape to a better life. Dr. Siddra was all business whenever she went into Kendall's room. Her questions were methodical and efficient, and she exited without lingering for even a polite, personal exchange of pleasantries.

Maysah Siddra could not sleep her last night in Israel. She was too excited about her new life. It was more than she had ever expected. She thought she must be dreaming and that she would wake up to find herself back in Afghanistan. But before she was through, she might wish she was back in Afghanistan leading her simple, mundane life. For her, nothing would be the same. She would soon be introduced to a strange culture that would have her longing for the comfortable childhood days of dancing the *Kuchi* tribal dances around the nightly campfire.

# CHAPTER THIRTY-SIX

Kendall slowly reached for the heavy handgun lying on her side of the tent floor and pressed the safety button. She didn't dare activate the lighted scope. As she was about to raise it up toward the looming figure, she heard a low voice, "Kendall, are you okay?" It was Rashid. She was never so relieved in her life.

"Yes, but you almost weren't! My God, I was going to shoot you. What happened?" She was now wide awake.

"The grandfather—the tribal elder—lost his grandchild. The five-year old got up to pee, and didn't come back. The mother was hysterical, and the whole tent full of relatives woke up to start looking for him. As you saw, they enlisted my help," Rashid said dryly.

"Well ... did you find him?"

"Yes. He was playing. The moon is so bright, that he saw something interesting and stopped to investigate."

"Why all the hysteria?"

Rashid frowned. "I would think you would know by now."

"What?"

"There are landmines everywhere! One must remain alert at all times!"

"Oh, that. I keep trying to forget the ugliness around this country."

"Did you know there was one, just twenty feet from where we went behind the boulder last night?"

"No. Why didn't you tell me?"

He shook his head. "You have to be alert around here, Kendall! I may not be with you the whole time. At least be able to look out for yourself."

"Fine! Then tomorrow please show me again what they look like, so I'll know."

Rashid vowed to do more than that in the morning. He was very concerned at her naiveté and willingness to just follow his lead. Her trust was rewarding but misplaced. It could get her killed. She was in an unfamiliar country, and needed to get up to speed as quickly as possible on how to stay alive—by herself, if need be. More than anything, she needed to be alert and always have a plan. He lowered himself to his bedroll and lay back down. The education process would begin in the morning. He could take care of himself, but she certainly couldn't. He had purposely not pointed out the landmine near the boulder last night, because he didn't want to scare her. But he now saw that was wrong. If she was going to stay alive, he would need to immerse her in all the unpleasantries they encountered.

He closed his eyes and began to slide into that wonderful state of calmness and tranquility that takes over as sleep approaches.

"Rashid?"

He was feeling grumpy now. "Yes?"

"Why wouldn't you be with me?"

He was thoroughly confused. "What?"

"You said you may not be with me the whole time. What did you mean by that?"

"Can we talk about this in the morning? We have about two hours more of darkness. We had a big day yesterday and moved around a lot. I'm exhausted. How about some sleep while it's still dark?"

Kendall was mortified at her insensitivity to his state of exhaustion and everything he had been through, not the least of which was watching Poya get blown up by a landmine. She rolled onto her side and quietly whispered, "Okay." Rashid knew she wouldn't be able to sleep if she lay there worrying about their circumstances, so he moved his bedroll up against her and threw his arm over her body. He gave her a squeeze and heard a soft sigh. Soon they were both fast asleep.

In the morning, Rashid rose first and made a fire. When Kendall crawled out of the tent and took in the scenery around her, she was awestruck. She stopped cold, taking in the magnificence. The morning sun was shining on the lake, and it sparkled like millions of diamonds. Their campsite was only twenty feet from the shore, and though they could hear muffled voices in the distance, they had fortuitously found the perfect, isolated spot. She could not get over the pristine waters and azure color of the lake and the mountains surrounding it like a sentry standing guard.

Rashid had wanted to see her expression when she first saw the lake. He smiled. He was not disappointed at her reaction. "Did you know the lakes are referred to as the 'lakes of jewels' and are one of the wonders of the world?"

"Yes. You told me so yesterday."

"Oh. Well, imagine that ... here in the savage country of Afghanistan."

She peered at him, as he handed her a steaming cup of green tea. "You're making fun of my ignorance."

"No, I'm not. I just want you to be safe, and aware of your surroundings."

With that, they launched into a discussion on what she needed to be aware of and how to spot the unmistakable red-topped dirt or stakes in the ground, indicating the presence of a landmine. The opposite were the white-painted rocks that meant the area had been de-mined and was clear.

After a meager but nourishing meal of fruits, nuts, and dried meat, Rashid helped her into one of Jangi's wife's full *chador* and headdress worn by the local women. The only skin showing was her face. She had now been in the sun so much the last week that her skin was warmly tanned. She blended in nicely with the Afghanistan locals, and didn't need to hide her face other than to avoid eye contact with other men.

They drove to the tomb of the Amir, where Rashid left her at the women's beach. He walked to the nearby bazaar to purchase more goods and some fresh biscuits. He listened to the men talking. Apparently, the fishing was good. Since hand grenades were no longer allowed for fishing, he had to purchase a small, rickety fishing pole, which already had a reel and line attached. The toothless merchant pressed a shiny lure into his hand. Rashid's mouth watered at the thought of fresh, hot fish for dinner.

There had been two women leaving the women's beach when she arrived. She hurried past them. She appreciated having the place to herself. Kendall luxuriated in the cold lake water. It was close to Noon, and the sun was high and the air hot. She didn't have a care in the world as she washed her hair with the little bottle of hotel shampoo she had shoved into her field bag and splashed about. She didn't even mind that she had no bath towel. Rashid had given her a small, but clean, piece of cloth to use as a towel. When she was through and re-dressed, she washed out the soiled clothes she had been wearing since she left Jangi's. Looking back, she thought, that hurried departure seemed like a lifetime ago.

As she looked out over the spectacular reflection of the mountain range over the jeweled lake, her eyes brimmed with tears at the thought of her mother. The sweet lady would have basked in the hot dry air and turquoise waters of the lake and would certainly have appreciated the otherworldly landscape. Kendall sighed and gathered her clothes. She wiped her eyes with the back of her hand and turned to rejoin Rashid.

He was patiently waiting for her when she came down the path around the corner of the mosque-like tomb. He tried to suppress a smile at the awkwardness of Kendall's gait under the cumbersome *chador* that flapped about her legs. In truth, she would have liked to grab onto both sides of the *chador* and hitch it up, so she could walk unencumbered.

His eyes twinkled as he guessed her thoughts. "You look well scrubbed. Let's have some tea at the Hotel Dir over there," pointing down the unpaved road towards the dusty-looking stone building. They seemed to blend in with the locals. They stowed her newly-washed clothes in the jeep and headed to the hotel. Kendall was delighted there was a somewhat modern restroom down the hall from the lobby.

The proprietor rolled out little rugs for them on the floor and brought them *chapatti* or flat wheat bread. As they sat in the dark and dingy dining room enjoying their tea, Rashid noticed the big screen TV on the far wall in the back. He asked the proprietor to turn it on, and they moved—with their rugs—to the back table for a clear view of the TV. Rashid was anxious for the news. Given their local Afghan garments, he was not concerned they would attract any attention. But he noticed that Kendall kept looking around out of curiosity. Since Afghan women would never be so bold—at the risk of being severely punished by their husband or other male family member—he had her sit facing the television with her back to the rest of the room.

Kendall was restless and wanted to look around, but Rashid distracted her. "Did you know this place is called a *chaikhana*?"

She shook her head. "No. What's that?"

"It's a tea house that also provides meals. Some have rooms to rent, like this place. The name '*chaikhana*' is very old and came about even before the invention of a café or restaurant."

Finally, the television came on, distracting Kendall again. Sure enough, the news was all about them. They were thought to have been spotted in Bamiyan, where it was reported they had disrupted a local sporting event by setting off a bomb near the field and causing the death of a young boy. Locals were urged to stay away from this dangerous pair, and to turn them in for a handsome reward. Rashid translated for Kendall. She was amazed at how the facts had gotten twisted. They were being portrayed as dangerous criminals to be avoided at all cost. They were last seen heading west in his jeep. A photo of the jeep was flashed before the cameras. Rashid quickly scanned the room to see if anyone else was watching. The only other patrons were sitting close to the door ... out of sight of the television.

Rashid suddenly felt uneasy. They were going to have to lose the jeep. It stood out, was unusual, and would most certainly call attention to them ... if it hadn't already. *My God*, he thought. If they were spotted in Band-e-Amir, they would be cornered. There was only one road in and out. He had banked on the idea that the thick-headed and not-too-bright General Omar would never contemplate Band-e-Amir as their refuge due to its remoteness and isolation. Since they had been spotted in a city, Rashid hoped Omar would believe they were staying in cities, to blend in.

He decided they would ditch the jeep in the morning. In the meantime, he would cover it up and go looking for an alternate means of transportation. He knew what that would mean and was afraid to tell Kendall. He tried not to be obvious about hurrying them through the afternoon tea and light meal, but he wanted to get them and the jeep back to their campsite at the end of the road.

Finally, they were back at the campsite, and Kendall hung up her wet clothes on the nearby brush. Rashid removed quite a few of their belongings from the jeep and shoved them into every nook and cranny of the already much-too-small tent.

He announced that he was going swimming and would wash his clothes nearby. Kendall was surprised to hear that women were not allowed to swim in the lakes. With hands on her hips, she looked like she was going to give him a piece of her mind, but he held up his hands to stop her. “Don’t lecture me! It’s not my law. I just live here. I was hoping we could keep our heads for another day.”

At that ridiculous notion, she stopped and laughed. “Oh, go have your swim.” She stalked off to find some brush she could pee behind, and see if she could identify the minefield. She was shocked to see how close it was to the campsite.

After his much-needed and refreshing swim, he set about to fish, hoping they could have something hot for the evening meal. He climbed up on a nearby cliff ledge with steep walls descending right into the lake. He was delighted to see hundreds of fish swimming in the clear cold water below. Within fifteen minutes he caught his first fish.

Kendall ran up to see and wrinkled her nose at the strange fish. She didn’t recognize it ... being used to salmon, trout, and halibut, back home. “What kind of fish is that?”

“The locals call it ‘milk fish’. You know it as carp.”

“Is it good?”

Rashid nodded. “Yes, you will find it soft and tasty.” He hesitated, deciding not to finish his thought. Before the afternoon was over, he had caught ten fish. He cleaned them and then set aside one large one for dinner. Kendall watched with interest as he hung strips of the meat in the hot sun of some nearby bushes and then salted them and covered them with netting to protect against local wildlife. He didn’t know if that would work, but they would need food for their journey ... the one he had yet to tell her about. He cooked up the fish, and threw in some of Jangi’s potatoes and a wild onion he picked from the area close to their camp. Kendall finally had her fill and finished with some dried fruit.

She sat back with her hot green tea and looked over the lake. It was still fairly warm out, and she squinted as her eye caught something moving further down the lake towards the visitor-type center. She pointed to the strange-looking bird thing, “What’s that? It looks like a gigantic swan!”

Rashid laughed. "Yes, it's a *pedalo*. You know, one of those paddle boats. Motors aren't allowed on the lake, but these *pedalos* are. People rent them."

"That's amazing, because you'd see a sight like that in the U.S. too. Sometimes we're not so different."

He nodded and then asked, "So, how did you like the fish?"

"It was good. It had a funny aftertaste, but I figured it was just new to me."

"Sometimes it can have a muddy-like taste, particularly if caught in freshwater, which is why it is not a favorite in the U.S. It's really an Asian fish. We don't have a lot of choices here, particularly when it's free. So we just adapt and don't complain."

"Oh, I'm not complaining. Aside from the warm food that Poya brought from the market, this was very tasty. Besides food is the least of our problems."

Rashid nodded. "Yes, and that's why we need to discuss what our next plan is."

Why was she suddenly fearful of the news? "And where are we going tomorrow?"

He decided the direct approach was best. "We're ditching the jeep tomorrow."

Her brow furrowed. "Oh. So, we'll take one of those tourist minibuses? But how will we carry all of our stuff? We have a lot of things." Logic told her there was no way they were getting on public transportation.

"No public transportation for us, Kendall. We're going to buy a camel tomorrow, and maybe a donkey."

She laughed at the absurdity, because it sounded so foreign to her. "What are we going to do with them?"

"They are going to carry our goods as we walk to Mazar-e-Sharif. We're going to travel like nomads. From there, we'll be able to use an Internet café. We'll be close to the Uzbekistan border and should be able to get out of Afghanistan."

Kendall was stunned. "How? I don't have a passport."

"I don't know, yet. But we'll figure it out when we get there."

She was silent for a moment and then continued with her grilling. "How long will it take us to walk to Mazar-e-Sharif?"

"I figure about ten days, maybe longer. It's about 245 kilometers or 152 miles. It's a little further than when we went from Kabul to Bamiyan. It will be slow going, because we're going to walk over the mountain ridges and the alpine meadows. We can't stay on the main roads. It's too dangerous. Didn't you see on the television yesterday what General Omar was saying about us?"

"Yes, but why must we make it so hard on ourselves? Can't we just drive to Mazar-e-Sharif?"

"No way! There's one main highway, and there'll be police checkpoints along the way."

She looked miserable, as if he had asked the impossible. He grabbed her arm, trying to understand her reluctance. "What's the problem, Kendall? It's practically like going on a camping trip. Don't you like to camp?"

Her eyes were blazing. "You know it's way different than traditional camping—which, by the way, I detest. It's one thing to go one night without a shower. But anything more than that, and I'm miserable. Let's not even talk about the landmines."

"It's not going to be that difficult. We'll follow the Balkh River pretty much all the way to Mazar-e-Sharif. You'll have fresh water to drink and bathe in every day."

"But what will we eat?"

"We've got some dried food with us. And we'll eat wildlife along the way, maybe fish in a few streams or the river. Kendall, I can take care of myself and you. Don't you trust me?"

She nodded. "Yes, but …." Her voice trailed off. She sighed at the prospect. "What are we going to do with the jeep?"

"It's a four-wheel drive, and we're going to take it as far as we can over the land and into the hills, and then we're going to blow it up." He loved that jeep, and would find it painful to destroy. It was kind of like him—rugged but looking a little worse for wear. But they had no choice. If they sold it—probably to the camel merchant in a trade—General Omar's men would know how they were traveling.

She looked around them at the steep cliffs and narrow valley heading into the mountains. "I don't think we'll be able to take it far."

"You're probably right, and I didn't expect to. I just want to get it off the beaten path, so we can get rid of it with as little notice as possible."

"What about the landmines? They seem to be everywhere."

"They are. We'll just be careful and always on alert. The higher and deeper we get into the Hindu Kush mountains and the further from the main roads, the safer we'll be."

Kendall looked around at all their belongings. "Do you think we can take everything?"

"Absolutely! A camel can carry about three hundred pounds. I think we have about one hundred and fifty, so we don't have to buy a young, sturdy camel."

"Oh, great! And what if we get a lemon?"

Rashid looked at her like she'd lost her mind. She laughed and waved at him. "Never mind! It's just my perverse sense of humor. I'm thinking about what if you were buying a used car, and it was not sound. It might break down, and we'd be stranded."

He got the joke. "Well, I'm not planning on purchasing a 'lemon,' as you say. I've watched these types of purchases before. I know not to purchase a plain or sand-bred camel. It needs to be used to walking on rocks."

"What else, Mr. Camel Expert?"

He grinned. "You can tell the camel's condition by the firmness and size of the hump, the fullness of its quarters, and how solid its neck is. A camel's strength is in its forelegs. Its quarters are actually fairly weak. The breast pad lies under the withers, or shoulders. That's where it would carry its load."

"I know something about camels."

Rashid laughed, "Okay. Dazzle me with your knowledge."

She proudly proclaimed, "Camels store water in their humps."

He hated to burst her bubble, but corrected her. "No, Kendall. That's not right."

She looked shocked. "Really?"

"Sorry, but camels store fat in their humps, not water. Sometimes the hump leans over. That means the camel hasn't eaten in quite a while."

She shook her head in wonderment. "That makes absolutely no sense. Why would fat be stored in the humps?"

"It reduces the need to insulate its body. They can withstand a wide range in temperatures. This helps the camel survive in hot and cold climates. It's also why they can go so long without drinking."

"Okay, you win. But where are we going to find a camel?"

"You don't notice much around you, do you?"

"What do you mean?"

"Didn't you see the camel train or group of nomads camped behind the huge outcrop that has those cave formations at the bottom?"

"No. I was too busy looking at the lakes. I can't get enough of that gorgeous blue water, and the scary steep cliff walls that drop right into the water."

"That's easy to understand. There are very few places on earth that have lakes this color and deep. It's the mineral content, did you know that?"

"No, I didn't."

He felt the conversation after dinner had gone well. She now knew the plan, and like it or not, was ready to embark on the next stage of their journey. They cleaned up their few dinner implements and decided to go to bed early. Rashid wanted to get a head start on the day. He hoped the drying carp would not attract any wild animals to their site.

He lay on his bedroll and wondered what he looked like. He had not shaved in days, and his beard was coming in thick and dark. He imagined he was going to blend in nicely with the nomadic men. He made a mental note to warn Kendall in the morning to wear the full blue *burqa* robe still worn by many of the Afghan women in the north. He was so glad that Jangi's wife had pressed one on them before they left.

As he began to drift off to sleep he was completely unaware of the convoy of military vehicles slowly proceeding into the Band-e-Amir Lake area.

# CHAPTER THIRTY-SEVEN

After an extra day in Tel Aviv to secure the necessary approvals and acquire the proper documentation, the Orion plane was readied for the journey back to Seattle. It would make one stopover for refueling, and then land in Seattle early evening. The flight was uneventful, except for the eclectic mix of passengers. There had never been such a diverse group of people on the Orion plane before. The most amazing part was that it all seemed so normal now for Paul Fields and Glenn Carson. They couldn't have cared less who was on board the return flight. They were so relieved to be free of their Afghanistan adventure and to be heading back to the U.S., that flexibility had somehow become the norm for them.

Fields was wondering if he would ever be able to bark orders and make demands again. He had personally experienced the effects of too much power placed in one man's hands. The fact that Mujtaba Shazeb came to rule because of a power grab only added to the tyrannical nature of his rule.

Once the flight passed into U.S. airspace, the Orion executives let out a sigh of relief. They were safe now. The plane's initial leg of the journey took it to Andrews Air Force Base in Washington, DC, where the Immigration and Customs Enforcement, or ICE, officer, FBI agents, and sour-faced State Department official took Maysah Siddra off the plane. The plan was to speak with her for a couple more days in DC, until all necessary paperwork, approvals, and living details were attended to before her final move to Seattle.

Two mysterious and grim-faced officials came on board during the refueling at Andrews Air Force Base. They urged Fields and Carson to disembark for additional questioning in DC. The Orion executives flatly declined the "invitation" and in no uncertain terms made their wishes known. They were going back to Seattle to be re-united with their families. If the government wished to speak with them further, they would happily make themselves available in Seattle. The men had figured on that response all along. But now they had secured the continued cooperation of the executives and should have easy access to them in the days to come.

After a quick check on Carson's well-being, and his insistence that he was fine and they should depart, the plane was back in the air heading due west. Mickey looked around. The only ones left on board were Fields, Carson and his wife, the plane's crew, and the Orion security team. They landed to much fanfare at Boeing field, where the homecoming had been big news all day. Carson was visibly worn out and was quickly whisked away by his wife and a security detail.

Fields stayed ten minutes longer to give a general statement and answer a few questions from the press. He promised the media that he would make himself available for a lengthy interview once he had settled into his old routine. He was impatient to see his wife and kids and opted for one of the company helicopters, which was standing by to deliver him to his secure compound. *Thank God for Mickey*, he thought. *That man can make anything happen.* After only five minutes, the helicopter touched down on the rooftop pad of his private complex. He had a brief moment of fear when his mind took him back to the rescue off the rooftop of the AIDC building in Afghanistan.

As the rotor blades slowed to a stop, the rooftop door opened, and his three children burst out and sprinted towards their father. He ran forward and sank to his knees, so he could gather up all of them in one big bear hug. They squealed with delight and alternately asked him if he was okay and told him how much they had missed him. He knew the stress on them had been tremendous. Each day of his captivity, they had taken their cues from their mother's demeanor, and had watched her alternate from affected cheerfulness and denial to fear and despair. When they came down for breakfast a few days ago to find their mother humming to the beat of a fast-paced Jamaican song, they brightened right up. After telling them the good news of their father's rescue, she allowed them a day off from chores and summer studies to celebrate their father's release. When he sauntered into the brightly-lit kitchen where his wife was overseeing the staff in the preparation of the evening meal, he thought she had never looked more appealing. She was dressed in a casual but elegant manner, with taupe-colored slacks and a cream-colored silk blouse. The fine gold jewelry bracelet and matching necklace were chic and understated. The couple hugged for five minutes, neither wanting to let go. Fields couldn't get enough of the feel of her soft body against his. He didn't want to release her as he continued to stroke her long blonde hair. He reveled in the oh-so-familiar, sensual perfume and scent of her freshly washed hair. He looked at her in a new way. In the past, he had never appreciated her like he did in this instance. He vowed that he would never take her for granted again.

That night, sitting around the formal dining room table overlooking Lake Washington was memorable. It was all so civilized, comfortable, and ordinary. He loved every minute of it. There was no reason to fear anything. He couldn't even remember the meal, because he was too aware of the happy, festive mood of the whole household, and the normalcy of being surrounded by his family and the things that meant the most to him. The children beamed at the joyous occasion and had a hard time getting to sleep that night. Sometime in the middle of the night, Fields woke up to find his six year old on his side of the bed ... staring intently at him. He reached his arm out and stroked the little chin.

"What's wrong, buddy, can't sleep?"

The child solemnly declared that he just wanted to make sure his father hadn't gone away again. The CEO wanted to cry at the outrageous emotional upheaval that had been thrust upon his family through no fault of theirs. He scooped up the toe-headed youngster and nestled him next to his chest. He reached behind him for his wife, and she rolled over to cuddle him. It had been a long time since he had felt secure in the loving arms of his family.

***********

Paul Fields jumped out of bed the next morning at the crack of dawn and announced that he was going into the office. His wife was disappointed but not surprised. The family had been seeing a grief counselor while he was gone, and this was something the wife had been warned about. Nevertheless, she made one attempt to get him to stay home.

"But Honey, we haven't had any time with you. We want to spend the day with you. We want you all to ourselves."

He climbed over his sleeping son and got back into bed and kissed the top of her tousled head. "And I would like nothing more than to stay at home with all of you. But I need to go over some emails and talk to my data security guru."

"Oh, you mean Daniel."

"Very good! You met him at the office Christmas Party. I can't believe you remember him."

"Well, I met him this year ... six months ago. He was so unusual that I could hardly forget him."

Fields gave a laugh. "Why was he so memorable?"

"Well, I remember listening to him talk about how important data security was to the very survival of the company. He was so passionate about it. It made me want to go to Orion the next day and help him out."

He smiled at the thought and gave her a hug. "Oh, Darling, I missed you so much."

Her tone sobered and she whispered, "Paul, was it awful?"

He got a faraway look in his eyes and said, "Well, it wasn't a five-star resort."

"But did they mistreat you?"

He frowned. "That's a matter of perspective. They didn't do anything physical to me, but they were plenty brutal to others."

She just couldn't hold back any longer. "Was there really a woman with you and Glenn?"

He looked miserable and nodded. "Yes. Kendall Radcliffe. That's why I need to go into the office."

"What happened to her?"

Fields was lying on his side, his face very close to his wife's. He stroked the side of her face. "I don't know. There was so much commotion around getting Glenn and his medical paraphernalia into the helicopter, that she was last in line to board. We were about to come under fire, and the helicopter was forced to take off ... " His voice trailed off into a whisper, "... without her."

"That's awful! You must have felt terrible leaving her behind."

"That would be an understatement. I was enraged."

"So, she's somewhere in Afghanistan?"

He looked like he was going to cry. "I don't even know if she's alive. The building was blown up seconds after we took off. How could she possibly have survived that?"

She cupped his face with her hands. "I'm serious! What can I do to help?"

"You can continue being the light of my life, and forgive me for not putting you and the family first. I love you, and I promise that I'll never make that mistake again."

With that, he gave her a warm, slow kiss and then rolled over his sleeping son to head into the shower. He turned on the television in his huge bathroom and luxuriated in the heated floor, as he padded across the tile and stepped into the oversized shower stall.

He purposely arrived at the office before any of his executive staff. He wanted to avoid any drama. He planned to be up to his elbows in paperwork and on the phone when they started trickling in. In the past, he had insisted on driving himself to work. The independence and freedom at the wheel had been too much of a luxury to give up. Plus, he loved the feel of driving the Bugatti Veyron. It made him feel powerful and omnipotent.

But this morning, a security detail was present in the compound when he exited the front door. They insisted on driving him to the office. He was fine with that, and made a mental note that he would be selling the Bugatti. He was no longer enamored with that car, and in fact, it made him feel guilty, just knowing it was in the nearby underground parking garage. He was a family man whose precious wife and children were more important than even his business. He would now act like it, starting with divesting himself of that ridiculous vehicle.

He actually whistled as he walked into his spacious office overlooking Lake Union and flipped on the light switch. He felt his adrenalin pumping when he methodically walked around turning on his various computers and printers.

His staff hadn't expected him in the office for a couple days. Upon their arrival, they were shocked to see their boss hard at work. He looked happy and determined, but always with his headset on as if he was on the phone. They tiptoed by his office as they went about their daily duties, curiously and sheepishly peering into his fishbowl-like office ... *probably to see if I'd become unhinged during my impromptu adventure*, he told himself. Every once in a while, he would see one of them and wave a greeting. They looked relieved that he didn't appear to have grown horns or an extra head during his absence.

He finally reached Daniel mid-morning. The young man was ecstatic that his boss was home and anxious to fill him in on what *Prophecy* had learned. Fields made a mental note to tell his wife about *Prophecy*. He was tired of keeping that secret. His wife would know what he should do about it. He smiled, and moved her photo closer to him on his desktop.

Fields listened carefully as Daniel told him that he had found General Omar and staff's email paths fairly quickly; that they didn't have any real evidence of sabotage or conspiracy to assassinate President Shazeb. Omar, ever the opportunist, had simply made a power grab in the ensuing chaos following the death of President Shazeb and the destruction of the government building in Kabul. In the absence of government control, Omar became the voice of reason, calming the citizens and assuring them he was in control and restoring order to Afghanistan.

Further, Daniel could tell from the tone of the emails that Omar had never cared for Rashid and jumped at the opportunity to lay the blame at his feet and to basically discredit him in whatever way he could. The emails confirmed that the bodies in the burned-out palace were part of the debris. For days now, the grounds had been raked for bones and other evidence of human remains. Omar had no intention of conducting a thorough examination and analysis of the scene, other than to confirm that the deceased parties were, in fact, the Shazeb family. That would put the general in the clear to assume the leadership mantle over Afghanistan, with no concern for a sudden appearance of one of the male family members.

Once the smoke had cleared from the palace, within twenty-four hours of the fire, the general had given the order for the physician to identify the bodies and then place the president's remains in a separate coffin to be buried within days. It had been easy to identify the president from the clothing found after the fire. It was clear from Omar's emails with the physician that no mention was to be made of the huge bullet hole entering his skull in front and exiting out the back.

The rest of the family's remains would be placed together in several coffins containing a mixture of the fragments. The deceased security detail and any staff who had been at the palace would be buried together in the nearby military gravesite. The recovery was to be swift and not painstaking. Expedience was the order of the day, so the Afghan people could mourn and move on.

The late President Shazeb would have the full military honor of a flag-draped coffin as it proceeded through Kabul for mourners to see and put to rest. The processional route would end at the outcrop overlooking Kabul's diplomatic enclave known as "*Swimming Pool Hill.*"

Daniel did some follow-up research and discovered that the pool was built by the Soviet military in the 1980s. The large Olympic-sized pool was constructed of concrete that included a concrete diving board. It was never used as a pool, and never contained water. The hill was so steep that no one knew how to get the water up the hill. Instead, it was used by the Soviet army as a lookout. In the 1990s, the Taliban used it against "criminals." The blindfolded wrongdoer was taken to the highest diving board and given a push, where he fell onto the hard concrete surface below. If the perceived lawbreaker survived, he was deemed innocent and could live. Apparently, as evidenced by the stains on the concrete floor, few survived.

Fields was fascinated at the historical reference and almost wished he had been able to tour Kabul while he was there. He shuddered and blinked when his name was called.

"Paul, are you still there?"

"Yes, Daniel. What have you learned about Kendall ... and, of course, Rashid?"

"They are front page news every day. General Omar is keeping them in the news to both warn people about their diabolical natures and offer a reward to kill them and notify the military."

"Interesting. He wants them dead?"

"Yes. Sick, isn't it? Obviously, he wants to bury the truth for good."

"That's right! The only remaining people alive in Afghanistan who have knowledge of the events at the palace that night are Kendall and Rashid. But how ironic, as it also includes me. General Omar just doesn't know it."

"But why does he need them dead?"

"My guess is for two reasons. So he doesn't have to compete with Rashid, and to obviate the need for further investigation."

"Ruthless bastard!"

"To put it mildly, Daniel."

"How is she ever going to survive if everyone thinks she's behind the assassination and bombing?"

Fields sighed. "I just wish we knew if she was still alive!"

Daniel brightened. "We do know that, and she is."

The Orion CEO stood up, he was so excited. He stammered, "Why, er … How do you know that?" He sank back down into his plush executive chair.

"Because the Afghan news reported that Rashid and a woman were seen in a town by the name of Bamiyan. They were spotted at some caves—"

"Yes, yes, I know those! That's where the world famous Buddhist statues are that the Taliban desecrated. Go on … what happened at the caves?" Fields voice was intense as he prompted Daniel for more information.

"The officials claim the two set off a bomb disrupting a local event and causing a boy's death. Needless to say, the Afghan people are looking for blood now. They also want those two dead now."

"But how were they identified in Bamiyan?"

"They were living in a cave, and people around them noticed they were different, and that they spoke English."

"So, were they caught?"

"So far, no. They escaped a few minutes ahead of the military police and have not been seen since. Paul, they seem to be staying a step ahead of the authorities, but just barely. And how?"

"That's easy! From what I saw of Rashid, he's intelligent and quick witted. He can also take care of himself. The man would make a perfect CIA operative or Navy Seal. He has the ability to blend in. My guess is that's what's keeping them alive. As far as Kendall, do we know for sure that it's her?"

"No, Paul, but it's got to be her. If they were speaking English, it's her. I just can't believe she survived the bombing of the Afghan government building."

"I wonder what the Bamiyan bombing thing is, and who got killed? Rashid wouldn't go around arbitrarily setting off bombs and killing children. There has to be another explanation."

"So, where do we go from here?"

"Daniel, can you bring up a map of the Bamiyan area for both of us to see? Let's connect remotely. Oh, and don't even think about data streaming my computer with *Proph*. Ha!"

Daniel thought, *Hmm! Too late … already done.* He expertly input the various codes, and finally the computers were linked to the same site. They were both seeing identical images but on their own laptops.

Fields studied the map and frowned. "Shit! Bamiyan is in the center of the country! They're going further into Afghanistan when they need to be getting out! They could head in any direction, including across Shibar Pass, which is probably the way they came. But no way would they take that back into Kabul without running into troops."

"There's Herat to the West towards Iran. Hmm. That's unlikely too, as Iran would love to get its hands on a young American with no passport."

"Right. The Israelis told me there was bombing all day along the eastward route from Kabul to the Khyber Pass and into Pakistan. General Omar blamed it on Rashid and Kendall, but I don't know why that area would be bombed."

"Okay, so we know they wouldn't be heading west or east. They could go south to Kandahar, but there's some pretty treacherous-looking unpaved roads between Bamiyan and Kandahar."

Fields finally offered a theory. "I think they're headed north to Mazar-e-Sharif, near the border with Uzbekistan. It totally makes sense. But they would need to stay off the main roads and highways."

Daniel jumped in, "So they lay low for a while at some place that has water nearby."

The excited CEO jumped up and shouted, "That's it! Oh my God, I know where they are!"

The young techie squinted at his screen, wondering what the boss was seeing that he wasn't. "Where?"

"They're at the Band-e-Amir Lakes! That place has six lakes and lots of camping. It's part of a National Park."

"So, it's good?"

"Well, maybe not. If we can figure it out, surely that pointy-headed General Omar can too, especially after they were spotted in Bamiyan."

"What happens if they are seen at those Lakes?"

Fields shook his head. "That would not be good. It looks like there's only one road in and out. Otherwise, it's over the mountain pass on foot."

"How long would it take them to get to Mazar-e-Sharif?"

"Probably more than a week. And by that time, General Omar would've sent up helicopters, and they'd be spotted. Damn! This is not good."

"What do we do, Paul?"

"You get back to monitoring Omar and the military's activities. It sounds like Kendall and Rashid will get cornered. Since they're headline news in Afghanistan, we should be able to get up-to-date reports on them. I'll call some of my friends in DC and make sure they know that Kendall is alive, and that both she and Rashid need rescuing."

Daniel didn't dare let on that he knew who that person was and their connection with Fields. The call was ended and the link-up terminated. Next, Fields picked up the phone to dial his frat brother, Frank Reynolds, at the NSA.

***********

Mossad leader Benjamin Zimmerman was pacing his office as he watched the scene unfold over the satellite image. He saw the movement of Afghanistan troops into the Band-e-Amir Lakes and visibly calmed down. He had thought for sure that idiot, General Omar, was going to lose track of Rashid and the girl. But fortunately, Rashid still had the satellite phone with him. Even though it was deactivated, the Mossad was still able to follow their path because of a built-in electronic tracking device. The Mossad didn't always tell its young agents everything they needed to know ... particularly when it involved spying on their own. So, the Mossad had been able to track Rashid from Kabul over the Shibar Pass to Bamiyan and then on to the Band-e-Amir Lakes.

When it looked like General Omar had lost the trail, the Mossad sent the hapless Afghan leader an anonymous, untraceable email, pointing the Afghan troops into the Band-e-Amir Lakes. From a look at the satellite view, the message had been received.

Now Zimmerman need only wait for confirmation through the media of the deaths, since they would never be allowed to survive more than an hour after capture. His blood still boiled at the thought that Rashid had probably taken Shazeb's drug money. Yes, it would be satisfying to know when the two were dead. The *coupe de gras* would be that Afghanistan, and the rest of the world, would never know that it was Israel that had bombed the palace, the government building, and the farms and trucks on the northeastern roadway into Pakistan. The secret would die with Rashid and Kendall.

# CHAPTER THIRTY-EIGHT

Rashid awoke early to an uneasy feeling in the pit of his stomach. He unfastened the tent ties and scrambled out into the clear morning sun. The pristine, undisturbed lake waters lay before him, and yet he couldn't enjoy them. He looked around for the source of his discomfort, and everything seemed normal. He walked over to the drying carp and it remained undisturbed from the night before. He saw a cloud of dust in the distance, toward the visitor area, and rummaged around for his binoculars.

Peering through the lens, he froze. Right in front of the little hotel and visitor center were ten military vehicles with men walking about readying themselves for the day.

Rashid flew into action. He ran over to the tent and knelt down. "Kendall, get up quick! The military's here. Put on the blue robes with the head covering. Help me unload the rest of the jeep. I have to get rid of it now."

Without a word, she willingly did as he said, stopping only long enough to find a large boulder to pee behind, and stuff a quick bite of dried fruit and nuts into her mouth. The jeep was unloaded in ten minutes. He made a fire for her and told her to sit next to it, with her back to the dusty road. Before he left, he handed her a stiff branch with coarse needles on it and instructed her to wipe away any signs of the jeep's tire tracks.

He took off in the jeep away from their campsite, driving across the open terrain. He was very careful of the landmines that dotted the land. A large rise loomed ahead. He drove about a mile around to the back side of it and then put the jeep in low gear and climbed as far as he could up the steep slope. The jeep jostled and bucked over the dried weeds and loose rocks. He was able to go about a quarter of a mile up the side of the incline and finally stopped. He was now on the back side of the cliff from where Kendall and the lakes were.

He couldn't afford to blow up the jeep now, as it would cause an explosion and attract attention. He shut the engine down and jumped out. After giving the jeep a once-over to make sure they had removed their belongings, he put the vehicle in neutral and pushed it off the cliff face. It landed on the rock-strewn floor below with a huge crash of twisted metal, and sent up a dust cloud that quickly dispersed.

Rashid made his way down the steep hillside and surveyed the wreckage. He gathered up nearby branches and threw them onto the pieces of the twisted vehicle frame. Anyone venturing past would now think it had lain there for some time, maybe even years. One would need to get fairly close to even identify it as an old jeep. Because of the constant wars over the past forty years, old, rusted, broken-down jeeps were not an uncommon site. Rashid banked on that being the case.

As he headed back the way he came, he missed the bits of aluminum alloy and polymers scattered about that used to be his satellite phone, courtesy of the Mossad. It had been stowed far into the wheel well to escape the notice from any surprise inspection.

He continued on his way toward the campsite and used a scraggly branch to wipe away the faint tire tracks. One good dust storm would eliminate the tracks, but he didn't want to take any chances. It took him longer to walk back, as he needed to be extra careful to avoid the landmines. Finally, he was within half a mile of the campsite when he saw the camel train off to the right behind a rise in the distance. He changed course and walked toward it.

In the meantime, ten of Omar's troops headed to the far end of the lake where Rashid and Kendall's campsite was, and ten worked their way from the visitor area. They planned to meet in the middle and keep in contact by radio transmission.

Kendall was terrified as the approaching jeeps made themselves heard over the rough, unpaved roadway. As she quickly scanned their campsite, her stomach lurched when she saw how scattered and messy their site was. A hasty, dusty, tarp had been haphazardly thrown over some of their more expensive items in an effort to hide their distinctive western or more modernized things. Making matters worse, she thought, was that she was in bare feet ... not having had time to locate the *paizar* or flat shoes worn by Afghan women, which the female doctor Maysah Siddra had been so kind to provide her with.

The military men got out at the end of the roadway seventy-five feet from her and walked about, pointing and gesturing over the lake and land. They did not approach her or say anything to her. She held her breath, and a small Afghan Snow Finch landed on a nearby tree branch overlooking the lake. She focused on the little bird and recalled that Rashid had pointed it out the day before as being a species exclusive to Afghanistan. She noticed right away that it was making the sharp *tsi* alarm tone rather than the usual *zig-zig* sound, as Rashid had shown her. She thought, wryly, that was particularly fitting under the circumstances, but it didn't do anything to assuage her immediate fears.

As the soldiers looked around their sloppy campsite, she soon realized they were regarding it with derision and contempt. They had chalked this family up to being poor, unfortunate souls who had little by way of possessions. They most likely deserved their lot in life because of the careless way they treated their belongings. One soldier made a loud comment and gestured toward Kendall sitting rigidly around the fire, her robes only just covering her bare feet. The others laughed and then walked to their vehicles and drove away to the next camp site.

What she didn't realize was that the sloppiness of the campsite, coupled with her rigid lack of curiosity toward the soldiers, actually saved her. They were so disgusted at the careless scene, they wanted to be away from it lest they too succumbed to a dull and poverty-stricken life, with next-to-nothing to their names. As they drove away, they were glad of their own lives and the meager possessions they had. In their eyes, at least they had something by way of a small house or a few children.

Rashid had made his way to the camel train and saw that the people were a large, extended, closely knit family of *Kuchi* nomads who had made the Band-e-Amir Lakes their home for a few weeks. Their sheep, goats, and camels were grazing around the nearby slopes under the watchful eyes of the *Kuchi* tribes' young men. Sauntering up, he approached an elder overseeing a line of kneeling Arabian *dromedary,* or single-humped camels, contentedly chewing their cud in the mid-morning sun.

The older man nodded and voiced a *Pashtun* greeting. He quickly sized up a very dirty and tired—and slightly rank—Rashid as most likely a military deserter. He had a look of strength and vigor, and was obviously well-fed. He carried himself like a leader and seemed to be independent and strong-willed. The elder was curious what the young man wanted, and being no fan of the late President Shazeb or the military, had no bone to pick with him, *per se.*

Rashid pointed towards the camels and inquired about purchasing an older—maybe twenty-five-year-old—camel. The *Kuchi* elder nodded and was pleased with his first impression. This poor young man didn't have much money and could not afford one of the prized younger camels.

The wizened man figured he wouldn't get much *Afghani* from this guy. He shrewdly moved over to a thirty-five-year old camel that looked as if it wouldn't last the day, and indicated he would sell this one for a very fair price. Rashid eyed the soft, small hump and thinning quarters and asked the wrinkled man to have it stand. The elder complied. The young man quickly realized the camel's breast pad, which would bear the most weight, was weak and the girth unsteady. Rashid felt a flash of anger at the insult at being offered such a broken-down animal. But he held his annoyance in check and vehemently shook his head.

They moved on to an average but sturdy-looking male camel. "This camel's name is Babar. He is a younger, strong camel. I will sell him to you for a quarter million *Afghani*." The old guy doubted the younger man even had that much *Afghani*.

Rashid was pleasantly surprised, but knew that was all he had on him ... at this very moment. He feigned shock. "But that's all I have. I need to buy rope and padding."

The old man nodded, "And you also need a saddle and permanganate for any wounds."

Rashid's face fell, as he realized he may just have to buy the old rickety camel. But the shriveled old man took pity at the crestfallen look on Rashid's face, and agreed to the purchase price of a quarter million *Afghani* or approximately $5,000, which would include two ropes, three old pads, and the medicine he would need, along with surgical scissors and a knife.

Since Rashid needed a saddle, the older man helped him construct a crude but functional four-stick camel saddle, the kind often used in Kenya and Somalia. After the three pads were placed over Babar's back, two pairs of sticks were crossed over the withers on one end and the breast plate on the other. The sticks were held into place with a rope that passed under Babar's belly. Now, Rashid would be able to sling his two large water skins on either side of the animal. The saddle would also help balance the load.

Rashid dug *Afghani* out his pockets. It was almost comical the way *Afghani* were popping out of every nook and cranny on Rashid's clothing. It also gave the impression this was all the money he had in the world. The old man went away satisfied but feeling slightly guilty that he had just taken all of the younger man's *Afghani*.

An hour later, Kendall looked up to see Rashid, dressed in the same traditional nomadic robes with a *Kufi* white hat perched on his head, leading a camel carefully over the rocky landscape. Using a stick to control the camel, Rashid looked comfortable maneuvering the animal. Kendall laughed when she was told its name was "Babar."

They quickly loaded all of their supplies and headed out in the same direction of the jeep remains. Kendall filled Rashid in on the soldiers' coming around. He was nervous, and felt they would be back at the campsite if anyone mentioned that a jeep had been parked there for the past couple of days.

As they walked somewhat close to the remnants of the jeep, Rashid indicated the heap of metal off to the right. Kendall could tell he was struggling with having to part with the vehicle. It had been with him for over ten years and, just like that, he had smashed it to pieces. He averted his eyes and trained them on their route up into the Hindu Kush Mountains.

They walked for two hours and were finally far enough away that Rashid felt they could stop for a break and a decent meal. They stopped near a stream and washed the dirt and grime from their hands and faces. Babar began to drink an enormous amount of water. Kendall fretted. "He's going to get sick! He's drinking too much at a time."

Rashid laughed. "He's fine! Camels can drink a hundred and fifty liters, or about thirty-nine gallons of water at a time."

"My God! We'd better stay close to water."

"It doesn't work that way. He's just storing it. He doesn't really sweat. When he exhales, the vapor is reabsorbed into his body, conserving water."

Kendall was feeling cranky. "Whatever! I'm starved! What are we going to eat?"

Rashid looked around and quickly identified some wild, bleached rhubarb, mulberries, and mushrooms. He spied a nearby *camelthorn* bush. He quickly and expertly scraped the dried, crunchy sap. When he offered Kendall some, she was a little hesitant. "What is it?"

He grinned. "It's from the Old Testament. It's called *Hedysarum* or manna."

She nodded and took a bite. It was sweet and tasted of nuts and brown sugar with a tinge of honey and maple syrup. She thought it was delicious and helped collect more to store in one of the few containers they had. As they gathered up their things to forge on for another two hours before making camp for the night, Kendall looked over to see Rashid struggling to get Babar to kneel. The camel did not want to kneel and was prancing about.

Even Kendall understood the situation. With hands on hips, she declared, "Rashid, I think he has to pee."

Rashid let go of Babar's rope and let him wander a few feet away. Back legs spread, the camel began to pee. Kendall was shocked. "Oh my God! It's as thick as syrup! That's disgusting!"

After a minute, when the animal was still peeing, Rashid laughed, "Yeah, and I don't think he's done yet. Pay attention. I think you'll learn something." They let the camel walk around and then it produced a good-sized hill of dung. Rashid got one of his many cloth bags out and walked over to the dung, picking up each individual piece. He looked at the horror on Kendall's face and laughed.

"If it helps any, we're not having this for dinner."

"Then I'm almost afraid to ask what we're going to use it for?"

"To make our fire tonight. It's an excellent fuel source and doesn't need to be dried out. It's ready to go."

"Fine, but please make sure you wash your hands in the stream when you're through."

Rashid chuckled. He was able to get Babar to kneel right away and load their things. They walked for another couple hours with Rashid in front—always on the lookout for landmines—and Kendall following using the same path. Every so often they would stop, so Rashid could use his binoculars to survey the landscape to see if they were being followed. He relaxed visibly when they found an isolated spot for their first night of camping. It was behind a small hill, and anyone walking by could easily miss them. He felt relieved and safe for the evening.

***********

The captain of the troops at the Band-e-Amir Lakes, Lutfi Jabar, was irritated. Had they been sent on a fool's errand? The entire area along both sides of the six travertine lakes had been canvassed. They had an enlarged picture of Kendall from her driver's license photo. The image was so deteriorated that no one would ever recognize her. But Rashid's picture was clear and bright. There was no mistaking the rugged good looks of his chiseled jaw, dark hair, and piercing brown eyes. The third picture was of a jeep similar to Rashid's.

The photos were shown to everyone they came in contact with, but no one seemed to recognize the duo or the jeep. Several people remembered seeing a similar jeep, but didn't pay attention to which way it went. It didn't help when some eye witnesses recounted seeing it heading west and then others pointed toward the east.

It was now almost dark, and the troops needed to decide on their orders for morning. Captain Jabar watched as a scraggly-looking old man got out of a small, homemade boat that did not look at all to be seaworthy. The older man had done well fishing, and raised up a string of milk fish to show the two young boys who scampered up to his boat. The young boys got in and were about to shove off for the lake, so they could row over to their campsite.

The captain pointed to them and asked if the pictures had been shown to the older man. The troops looked at each other, seemed confused, and finally shook their heads. Grabbing the photos, he yelled for the man and the two boys to stop. He marched up to them and demanded to know if they had seen the two people or the jeep. The boys were afraid of the brusque military man and said nothing, lowering their eyes in submission. The elder man handed back the photo of Kendall and quickly shook his head.

He then studied Rashid's picture and compared it with the jeep, and a slow smile spread across his face revealing several missing front teeth. He had seen Rashid and the jeep. Jabar was excited and peppered him with questions. Exactly where had he seen Rashid and the jeep, and on what day? The older man thought back and recounted it was two days ago at the last spot along the furthest eastward lake. He told the story of his missing grandchild who had wandered off in the middle of the night. The elder had gone to Rashid's tent and asked him to help in the search. The man definitely remembered the jeep, because he had admired it and wished he had one too. The next day, the man and his extended family moved their camp closer to the visitor area concession shacks and had not seen Rashid or the jeep again.

The weary but excited military leader gathered up his troop and asked who had been to the eastern most side of the lakes. Those soldiers recalled only that the last spot was extremely messy ... with no jeep or man in sight. They remembered the woman dressed in a traditional robe sitting next to the fire. She didn't speak to them or even turn their way as they inspected the campsite. They thought there was something wrong with her, and that maybe she was deaf ... or afraid of her husband.

The captain was discouraged but would not give up. He had not gotten all of those promotions by believing everything he heard. His gut told him they were on the right track. Maybe Rashid and Kendall had moved on from that campsite. But where would they have gone? Surely, they would have run into the troops heading into the National Park. He vowed that at dawn's light the troops would head over to that last spot and give it a thorough inspection. He sighed as he consulted his watch. The men moved to the *chaikhana* next to the hotel they had commandeered for the night. The handful of rooms, though occupied, was quickly emptied of their guests. The men would sleep several to a room, rolling out mats and blankets for the night.

While the men ate a robust evening meal of goat's brains and watched the television on the wall, their leader phoned General Omar and reported the promising lead. The general made his wishes known. Nothing but complete success—the deaths of Rashid and Kendall—would satisfy the general. He ranted into the phone that he hoped Captain Jabar was successful on his mission the next day. Then he issued an underlying threat that the lower-ranking officer would certainly feel the effects of any failure, as it would not do to reveal any incompetence or weakness to his men ... or to General Omar.

The captain was mildly fearful at the outrageous implied threat, but more enraged with the cat-and-mouse game he seemed to be playing with Rashid. He vowed to teach the young man a lesson when he caught up with him. As he hung up the phone, he visualized the moment of capture, and how he would make Rashid watch as he degraded and humiliated Kendall and then turned her over to his troops for their enjoyment. Once she was shamed and fully punished, then they would show mercy and cut off her head. He smiled, thinking how the young soldiers always clamored to be the one to wield the *scimitar* or backsword to do the final deed, and how they lay bets on whether it would be done in a single stroke. Maybe this time he would do it himself.

Two troops were posted at the entrance to the Band-e-Amir Lakes. In the morning, the remaining troops made their way to the last campsite at the eastern most lake. The site was now vacant. As Jabar walked around the uneven ground, something bothered him about the site. But he couldn't place the source of his disquiet. He peered into the abandoned fire and stirred the long-dead embers with a stick. Nothing out of the ordinary jumped out at him. He sent the men out fifty yards and then one hundred yards to inspect the surrounding area. After a couple of hours, the men reassembled at the campsite.

The lakeside campsite was isolated and would have been perfect for Rashid, the military leader thought. They couldn't have just disappeared. Something kept drawing the captain's eyes toward the north ridge. But there was no way the fleeing couple could have gone far in the jeep. Nevertheless, the nagging thought wouldn't go away.

Finally, it hit him. The place was too clean. It looked like it had been swept of all traces of occupancy. Not even footprints could be detected when they first arrived on the scene. Jabar surmised that perhaps the messy nature of the reported campsite from the day before was because whoever was staying there was preparing to flee. Armed with that thought, three quarters of the men were sent north to walk for two hours and see if they could find any evidence of the trail of the would-be criminals.

The captain was about to shout a warning to look out for any unexploded mines, but then, in his currently bad-tempered state, he decided he didn't want or need any soldiers who still had to be told to look out for the obvious signs of an active minefield. He shrugged his shoulders and sat down at one of the boulders around the campfire. His troops kept in touch every thirty minutes.

It had now been forty-five minutes since his lieutenant had checked in. Captain Jabar was beside himself. He had given explicit instructions on the frequency of checking in. The only logical conclusion he could think of was that they had either found something related to Rashid or were all dead. Jabar was just angry enough to wish for the latter, except that he would have a lot of explaining to do and would most likely find himself at the wrong end of a *scimitar* once he reported the unfortunate mishap to General Omar.

The radio crackled, and a voice cut in and out. The young lieutenant had obviously come upon something and, in his excitement was not speaking clearly into the radio. In his nervousness, he was alternately pushing and releasing the button.

The captain screamed at him and vowed to order a lashing for the lieutenant in the evening. The young officer calmed down and relayed the message that they had stumbled on a jeep that had gone off a nearby cliff. It made no sense that the jeep had even been up there. The only assumption one could make was that it had purposely been driven off the cliff in order to hide its presence.

Captain Jabar ordered the men to gather any evidence from the jeep. He and the remaining troops would drive out to meet them. They would rendezvous in about twenty minutes. Their military vehicles were sturdy and could withstand the rocky terrain. Five vehicles took off in the direction of the earlier troops.

Jabar insisted on driving his own vehicle. He sped off way ahead of the others. In his haste, he missed the unexploded ordnance on his right side and tripped it with his front tire. The vehicle went airborne and flipped onto its front, crushing the windshield and killing the leader.

# CHAPTER THIRTY-NINE

"Reynolds."

"Frank, this is Paul Fields."

"Paul, you're back! Are you okay?"

"Yes. I'm fine. Thank you for asking."

"How's Carson?"

"He's still recovering but should be okay to return to work in about ten days."

"Thank God. I only wish I could have been the one to use *Prophecy* and locate you. I had it narrowed down to Afghanistan, though."

"That's okay, Frank. I'm hoping you can use *Proph* now and we can save our female employee who got left behind."

"Geez, Paul, how the hell did that happen? And who is she, this Kendall Radcliffe lady?"

"Kendall is the director of operations at Orion. She was on a business trip and happened to be staying at the same hotel as Carson and me. Her luggage got mixed up with ours, so we invited her to fly back with us. The plane got hijacked to Afghanistan, and the rest is history."

"But how come she wasn't on the rescue flight?"

Fields was beginning to hate this speech. He had told it umpteen times now, and it wasn't getting any easier. "It took time to get Carson and his medical paraphernalia and doctor on board. Kendall was almost the last to board. Suddenly, troops were moving onto the rooftop, and it looked like we were going to take fire. What can I say? The damn helicopter pilot took off with me half hanging out the door." Now he'd resorted to embellishing. His stomach was decidedly queasy.

"But, didn't that government building get blown up? She must have died."

"No, Frank, that's why I'm calling. I don't trust anyone but you to get to the bottom of it. I have confirmation that she and her Afghan companion, Rashid Sharif, are alive and on the run."

Reynolds gasped and offered, "From what I hear, General Omar is as crazy as President Shazeb and his boys. If they did indeed make it off the rooftop, they'll be hunted like animals. Good God, it's been a week since you were rescued! If they're still alive, they must be living in a hole."

"Have you been listening to any of the Afghanistan news?"

"Only the first few days. I've been more interested in what happened with you and Carson and the Israelis."

"Well, the news is that they were spotted in the Bamiyan Valley where they were blamed for a bomb that killed a child. I believe they are now at the Band-e-Amir Lakes. I looked at the map, and that's the only place off the main roadways that's not too remote. But if it's true, that would be bad."

"Why?"

"Because they would be cornered at the lakes. To escape, they would need to go up into the mountains on foot, if they managed to avoid the troops."

"I see. So you want me to monitor General Omar and the Afghan government and military communications?"

"Yes. Find out what their plans are. Call me every day and let me know what the word is about Kendall and Rashid's whereabouts."

"Paul, who is this Rashid guy? Is he a good guy?"

"It would seem. He masterminded our escape ... at great risk to himself, I might add."

"Since the Afghan army is hunting him, I would imagine he has quite a price on his head."

"Among other things. Frank, we need to locate them and arrange for a rescue."

"Gotcha! I'll ratchet up the eyes and ears and alert one of my trusted military advisors who can set this in motion." Reynolds hesitated, then went for it. "Paul, why were you all kidnapped in the first place?"

The Orion CEO barely paused. "Beats the hell out of me! Probably because we were U.S. assets and they could get a large bounty for us?"

"Correct me if I'm wrong, but they never made a ransom demand, right?"

"I'm not sure. But I think that's true."

"Well, then why did they keep you so long?"

"I don't know, Frank. For Shazeb's perverse humor, I suppose. Who knows how that man thought."

"Did you meet his boys?"

"Oh yes. What a scary duo. I stayed out of their way and made myself invisible."

"One last question?"

"Yeah, but I feel like I'm at the Inquisition."

"Sorry, Paul, but I'm just so curious. Why haven't you told the Israelis about your theories?"

"I don't trust them, Frank. There was something very underhanded going on when I was on the ship and then in Tel Aviv. They asked pointed, ridiculous questions about Kendall and Rashid. If I didn't know any better, I'd say they were trying to pin all the bombings and probably even the kidnapping on those two."

"But why?"

"That's the million-dollar question. I'll let you figure it out. You're in the spy business. I have a company to run." Fields looked at his watch and stood up. "In fact, I have my first meeting with a very nervous board of directors who probably think I've gone around the proverbial bend after what I've been through. So, I have a lot of handshaking and ass-kissing to do in the next hour. Call me if you hear anything."

Frank chuckled, greatly relieved that his friend seemed none the worse for wear. He hung up and promptly notified his team of *Prophecy* experts, Alex and Ping, of an urgent meeting and then sat back to await them.

After an exhausting catered lunch with his immediate staff where he kept insisting that he was fine, Fields escaped into his office for some quiet time. Mid-afternoon, he got a call from Daniel at the datacenter complex. "What's up, Daniel?"

"You're not going to believe this! The goddamn Mossad Director Zimmerman sent an anonymous email to Omar telling him where Kendall and the other guy were."

Frank sat back in his chair, stunned into silence. He whispered, "But why would they do that?"

Daniel was disgusted at the people who funded his education and who he had—under the table—granted access to *Prophecy*. *Damn, this was a mess now,* he thought. His "friends" were fast becoming his "enemies," risking the lives of the very people he'd like to be friends with.

"What are we going to do, Paul?"

Something was nagging at the CEO. "Daniel, how were the Israelis able to track Rashid and Kendall when the Afghans haven't been able to?"

"I don't know. Maybe with a satellite image or use of a drone. Everyone's got them now." Daniel was sweating, hoping there would be no comments about the prospect of the Mossad's having access to *Prophecy*. That was his little secret.

Fields nodded. "Yeah, that must be it. But the Afghans have drones too."

"It's clear there's more going on than we know, particularly with this Rashid guy. It's just so awful that Kendall has been caught in the middle of it."

The Orion CEO stroked his chin while he thought long and hard. Daniel patiently waited. He could almost hear the whirring of Fields' brain through the telephone wires. "I told myself that from now on we would only use *Prophecy* for good, and I mean to do that ...." His voice trailed off, while Daniel's mind imagined all sorts of odd scenarios. Finally, Fields continued, "Do you think you could disable or sabotage the Israeli military communication network?"

"Well, I can certainly cause a disruption for a day. But are you asking me to render the system inoperable, as in permanently?"

Fields was emphatic. "Yes. That's exactly what I'm asking. They would need to rebuild their systems from the ground up. Can you do it?"

Daniel was going to have to think about this. He could do it so as to avoid detection, but the Mossad was smart. It might figure things out and cut him off financially forever, not to mention exact some kind of revenge. He could basically lose the very lifeline that had brought him peace of mind through financial security. His offshore bank accounts were fat and growing, but he had planned on more. His decision boiled down to money over friendship. *What am I going to do?* he asked himself.

"Hello? Are you still there? Is that technologically impossible without being traced back to the source? What's the problem, Daniel?"

"I, uh, I just don't want to put the company in jeopardy. If it was traced back to an Orion act, that would be disastrous."

"To say the least. So, how do we do it?"

"I need to use a computer and a network that is not linked to me or Orion. In fact, it would need to involve cloned computers and proxy servers."

"Can you do it?"

"Yes, but it will take some time and should be done from outside the U.S."

"Fine. Leave tonight for somewhere like Mexico or eastern Canada."

"I was thinking Toronto would be perfect. I'll find some seedy motel that has a wireless network and doesn't require credit cards."

"Daniel, I can't caution you enough about the importance of not getting caught or leaving any type of trail back to Orion."

"I understand and will double check everything."

"Leave your traceable cell phone and company laptop home."

"Absolutely. I know just where to find a working laptop that has been wiped clean."

"Good. Just make sure you use cash for the purchase."

"Yep."

"Okay. Good luck, and only call me if there's an emergency."

"Will do. Bye."

Daniel hung up the phone and sat back, realizing that the decision had been made for him. He was committed and would now set out to destroy the Israeli military communication network.

***********

In Afghanistan, General Omar had received the news that his captain leading troops in the search at Band-e-Amir Lakes had driven over a landmine. He was furious at the stupidity of a high-ranking officer, particularly one he had personally trained. He sent a helicopter to retrieve the body and bring his replacement. He urged the new leader to use the military's new drones and reminded him to report back on any discoveries.

The new officer, Captain Qadi, was young and anxious to please. He could already taste the blood, and he hoped to be the one to capture and kill the scoundrels on the run. He knew a little bit about Rashid, as they had worked together on a few projects. He'd never cared for Rashid, finding him to be calm, reasonable, assured, and therefore weak. The young captain respected and admired fear and tough talk, followed by brutal action. His swagger was noticeable, and he assured General Omar that he would have the quarry by the end of two days. The latter chuckled at the bravado and waited with bated breath for the sheer entertainment value of the soon-to-be bloodbath. He figured the captain would either be true to his word or die trying.

Four hours later, as the sun was beginning to set, the military helicopter dropped down onto the rugged terrain north of the Band-e-Amir Lakes. The ground had been carefully swept and cleared of all landmines. Captain Jabar's remains were loaded onto the helicopter, and supplies were dropped off for the weary men. They had been on the road for over a week now and had been patrolling the main roads and highways around Kabul, Bamiyan, and now the Band-e-Amir Lakes. Their jobs were about to get tougher: Captain Qadi was informed the fleeing duo had now gone off road; they looked to have made a run for it into the mountains to the north.

Qadi instructed the troops to create a camp right there near the jeep carcass. In the morning, he would survey the scene and decide on their course. He sent two troops in a vehicle to the front of the National Park to relieve the ones currently posted.

Behind Qadi's back, the men grumbled at having to sleep on the hard rocky ground and eat foreign-purchased military rations. At least this time they had the Soviet MREs or meals-ready-to-eat, that included biscuits, meat preserves, and dried fruits. They were not particularly fond of the eggplant caviar. All of last week, the troops ate Chinese MREs, which, in their eyes, was barely edible with the compressed food, pickled mustard tuber, and red bean mooncake. The most distasteful part of the latter MREs was that water could be added to the dried compressed biscuit to form porridge for the morning meal.

They were all anxious to catch Rashid and Kendall, and were beginning to project their anger toward them just for the inconvenience of the past week. Yes, they would make those two pay.

In the morning, the very stiff men awoke to a sudden but light sandstorm. They seemed to be in the eye of the storm as it raged about them. They quickly covered their vehicles from the offending abrasive elements and sat out the storm.

Captain Qadi was beside himself with fury, knowing the ground around the jeep remnants would be altered. It hadn't even occurred to him yet that any trail left by the pair on the run would also be obliterated.

Finally, in the early afternoon, the dust storm abated, and the entire troop walked the short distance to the twisted jeep. Qadi slowly surveyed the scene, took out his picture of the jeep, and pronounced it to be Rashid's vehicle ... the one that had carried the American prisoners away from the palace more than a week before.

As he looked for signs of personal items, he noticed the jeep had basically been picked clean of its contents. Even the tire iron and loose tools one always carried with them seemed to have been removed. The soldiers had not reported finding any effects, and therefore nothing had been blown away by the storm. That meant the duo had not simply walked into the mountains. He surmised they had either stolen or purchased some kind of animal—a horse, donkey, or maybe even a camel. The animal was used to carry their supplies. The semi-intelligent captain realized it couldn't be a donkey. His troops had seen the possessions at the campsite of the lady sitting by the fire. They reported a pile of belongings, including tools, cooking utensils, fishing gear, and clothing. A donkey would not have sufficed.

As he explained this to his men, one of the soldiers offered that a camel caravan had been spotted in the distance to the west, just past where they left the Band-e-Amir Lakes. The captain's gut told him that was key. Somehow the fleeing pair had acquired a camel for transporting their things. He ordered the troops to follow him to the caravan. The men carefully drove in single file to the camel train, pointing out various unexploded landmines as they drove past the offending ordnance at a safe distance.

When they arrived, they could see the caravan was packed up and ready to head out. The captain had good instincts and knew who to approach when the truth needed to come out. He was familiar with these *Kuchi* nomads. There was no love lost between the Afghan military and these independent tribes. He surveyed the scene and realized that he and his men were outnumbered. That meant he needed to be tough and brutal in order to quickly command their fear and cooperation.

The *Kuchi* men tried to ignore the troops and continued tying down their loads. The women hid their faces and moved away from the soldiers as they walked about. Qadi approached a young boy, dropped to his knees, and patted the youngster on the head. He then grabbed his arm in a firm way and asked him if any camels had been sold in the past two days. The young boy had no experience with soldiers, yet knew there was something scary about them. He saw the reaction of the men of his tribe. The boy was frozen with fear and just wanted the armed men to go away. He solemnly looked into the stern soldier's eyes, nodded and pointed to an elderly man down the line. The captain stood up, and as soon as he turned his eyes toward the elderly man, the boy scampered away.

As the troops approached the elderly man, he shuffled away toward the kneeling camels onto which he was loading supplies. Qadi yelled for him to stop. All eyes turned to the scene, as this was one of the elders of the tribe. The other men of the tribe approached as if providing backup. They were all armed and ready to defend their honor if need be. The elderly man was treated with the utmost respect by his clan, and they were afraid at the tenor of the captain's voice.

With slow, purposeful steps, Captain Qadi approached the old man and asked if any camels had been sold or traded recently. The elder's eyes gleamed with pride and honor ... and hatred for this military leader. He shook his head and indicated in the negative. Without warning, the young captain whipped out his sidearm and shot the elder between the eyes.

No one moved, not the tribesmen nor the soldiers. The captain re-holstered his gun on his hip and walked a ways out so that he could see and address the entire tribe.

Speaking Dari, he yelled, "I want to know *now* where the two people went who bought a camel." He paused, turning to look right and left, and then continued emphatically, "... or I will start killing one man after another until I get an answer!"

Another elder stepped up to the captain. "Two people did not buy a camel, Sir."

Qadi swung his head toward the elder. "What do you mean?" he demanded.

"A young man traveling alone bought a camel for a quarter million *Afghani*."

The captain thought quickly and realized the camel must have been purchased while the woman was left by the fire. Rashid had probably already smashed the jeep by then. He stared hard at the elder, who held his ground.

"Which way did the man go?" Qadi realized that was a stupid question. Of course, Rashid went back to the campsite to load his things.

The military officer spied the same young boy peering around his mother's robes. He strode over and pulled the boy away from his mother. She was terrified and looked to the captain for mercy. He smiled at the boy and again knelt down. "Well, my little soldier, did you see the man and his camel after he went away?"

The boy slowly nodded and somberly pointed north toward the mountain range. He was rewarded with a pat on the head and given a piece of the hard candy *lur* from the captain's pocket. The young boy did not want the candy, having just seen his beloved great grandfather killed, but he didn't dare refuse it. He took it out of fear and ran back to his mother, hiding his face in her robes.

The captain wished them a safe journey, and the troops retraced their path to the route heading into the back side of the Band-e-Amir Lakes. The soldiers reorganized when Qadi ordered half of them to pack their gear and head into the mountains to follow Rashid and Kendall. He figured they had at least two hours of daylight before they needed to make camp for the night.

There were just enough troops remaining for each man to drive a vehicle back to the Band-e-Amir tourist area, where they were fortunate to spend the night at the hotel and eat a decent meal at the *chaikhana*.

Captain Qadi made a call to General Omar's headquarters and was pleased when the general praised him for such quick work in locating Rashid's jeep and figuring out the direction and mode of transport. If the young officer kept this up, he would be receiving another promotion in no time.

Omar was in a great mood, and thought for the first time that it just might be possible that Rashid and Kendall would be dead by nightfall the next day. He had a celebratory drink ... or two ... and staggered to his newly renovated and enlarged opulent bedroom at the military base. It would take time to rebuild the palace, which was currently still undergoing razing and bulldozing to remove the offending charred ruins of the building.

***********

It was morning, and Daniel Blumfeld sat in his room at an out-of-the-way bed-and-breakfast guest house on the outskirts of Toronto. It had been a long trip from SeaTac Airport to Toronto on this one-way ticket. He used the one false passport and driver's license he had reserved for emergency purposes. Carrying thousands of Canadian and U.S. dollars, he paid cash for everything.

He made a deal with a used-car lot in a Toronto suburb to rent a broken-down but generally reliable car for several days. The amount he paid for the automobile was more than the car was worth. But the agreement was that the proprietor of the used car lot wouldn't ask questions and accepted cash. As the owner figured, if the mysterious guy never came back, he would file a stolen-car report and collect on the insurance.

Blumfeld made sure to throw in plenty of Canadian gestures and phrases complete with a smattering of French. On the long journey east, he memorized Canadian phrases and speech patterns, like "bunny hug" for "hoodies," "whitener" for "non-dairy creamer," referring to America as "The States," "canteen" for a "small cafeteria," "tea towel" for a "dish towel," "shinny" for "hockey," "vico" for "chocolate milk," a "mickey" for a thirteen-ounce size, "loonie" for a Canadian dollar coin, and "toonie" for a two-dollar coin. The latter terms had come in handy, and he was using them constantly. Drinking *vico* was his new favorite, and he was always looking for the nearest *canteen*. He tried not to stand out, though, and simply blended in with his environment, speaking only when necessary.

He located a seedy-looking shop that sold used but working laptops and purchased several with cash, making sure they came with the correct network cables and multiple built-in ports. He assembled everything he needed and set up his operation in his room, planning to complete his mission and depart within twenty-four hours.

Daniel ate, slept a few hours, and then returned to his passion of tinkering with computers. He loved the thought that they could be invisible and untraceable. For the first time in his life he was at the top of the heap. He alone was working on this important project. He was the master and the boss on this assignment. He worked carefully and diligently as he built his anonymous barriers to impede any attempt to trace the source. False paths were established to send any Israeli technical investigator on a wild-goose chase. The account information was imaginative and in no way connected with Orion or himself. He refrained from using any cleverly hidden messages that contained cryptic clues that might lead back to him. This was serious business, and he could not afford any mistakes.

Finally, midway through the following day, his mission was complete. He checked and rechecked his steps. The moment had come. He activated the sequential key strokes and waited for the confirmation. Success! Daniel was pleased.

He packed up his things, being careful to wipe the hard drives and remove them for physical destruction. The laptops and accessories were dropped into a nearby Goodwill bin and wiped down of any trace evidence. The car was returned to the dealer a day early. The tired and noticeably boozed-up proprietor remembered nothing about him and merely accepted the keys and waved him off. He took a train from Toronto to Niagara Falls, where he transferred to a bus bound for Rochester International Airport. He flew from Rochester to DC and arrived back in Seattle.

Daniel spent the night at a hotel in Seattle. He planned to meet with the Orion CEO in the morning. Fields had made sure that Daniel's hotel reservation in Seattle began a day earlier. Mickey checked in for him, providing a copy of Daniel's driver's license and credit card with the explanation that he was stuck in an executive meeting and would want to go straight to his room later. The hotel was used to the quirky demands of these high-tech company visitors and business associates. If contacted, the hotel would never remember the check-in sequence of events. It was all very ordinary and low key.

The exhausted traveler lay back on his bed overlooking Puget Sound to the west. The lights of the superferry *MV Puyallup* twinkled as it glided into the Seattle port. Daniel was exhausted and exhilarated. He ordered dinner and turned on the television to hear a breaking news report off the international wires.

# CHAPTER FORTY

Rashid and Kendall had been slowly climbing northward and camping for two days now. The journey had been relatively smooth, with enough to eat along the way and plenty of fresh spring water for them and their camel. It was midday, and they came out of a sub-alpine grove of poplar trees onto a steppe, or prairie of grassland dotted here and there with shrubs. They could see grazing sheep in the distance and a nomadic tribe of valley inhabitants encamped off to the side.

Kendall could sense Rashid's hesitation. "What's the problem, Rashid? Do we need to avoid these people?"

He shielded his eyes from the sun and frowned. "That's not the problem. We've been keeping close to the tree line, using whatever we could as cover. But if we venture out into the open land here, we no longer have any protection or cover. If we go down there, we are basically joining the tribe. We have to blend in when we're around them. They'll provide us with the perfect cover. Also we can travel further on a route that's more passable and direct if we stay out in the open."

He turned to his right and pointed to the barren peak of the closest mountain. "We either walk over several mountain peaks or opt for the somewhat open valleys. The mountains are easily traveled, but don't have a lot of trees, plus we'd run into wildlife."

Her eyes widened, "Such as ...?"

He laughed at her concern. "Oh the usual—a Siberian ibex or *markhor*, which is a wild goat. There are some brown and black bears and grey wolves." He refrained from mentioning the spotted snow leopard that lived in the higher peaks in the summer. If he told Kendall those secretive carnivores actually stalked their prey, she'd probably never have a moment's peace the rest of the way to Mazar-e-Sharif, not that she was having a lot of restful nights as it was. But he also knew it preyed on livestock when the food up high was not plentiful. Therefore, he reasoned, that damn killing machine could get them either way.

"Are you worried about helicopters spotting us out here in the open?"

"Exactly. We have yet to see one, but that just means Omar is two steps behind us. By now, if they stumbled on the jeep, they'll know which way we're heading." He surveyed the sky in all directions. "I'm just about positive that we'll see a helicopter or two today. Otherwise, the general really is an idiot."

Kendall was immediately alarmed. "Wow! We either get eaten by wildlife or beheaded by Afghan troops. What a choice."

Rashid hesitated and then decided that he may as well tell her the rest. "Uh, Kendall, that's not all. There's something else you need to know."

"Wonderful! Now what: The meadow has poisonous snakes?"

"Well, no, but there are some other insects you need to avoid. But that wasn't what I was referring to."

"Tell me," she begged.

"Afghanistan is a multi-cultural society. The nomadic tribes that wander these mountain ranges are all from different ethnic groups. Some might like us and others not. Various languages are spoken, and I may not be able to communicate with all of them. We're going to have to go with the flow. If it looks like they aren't friendly, we'll move along very quickly. Another thing is that they'll assume we're married. In fact, anyone who crosses our path will assume that."

"I already figured that."

"Well, you'll need to behave like a tribal woman. Keep your head and eyes down and stay behind me. Do not look about with curiosity. I've seen you do that." He wagged his finger at her and continued. "That would be an open invitation for trouble."

"I'll be a dutiful wife, Rashid." She rolled her eyes.

"If you're not my wife, then you'd be my sister, in which case I'd find myself negotiating a marriage contract within an hour of our arrival. So, don't think the marriage scenario is the worst that can happen." He stroked his chin and with a twinkle in his eye, and said, "Come to think of it, I wouldn't mind having a horse."

She glared at him but decided to shut up. This whole conversation was surreal.

Rashid moved forward, holding tightly to the camel's lead, and Kendall dutifully followed. As they made their way down onto the pasture land of the steppe, she could see the sheep looked way different from the ones she had seen every year at the local Washington State Fair in Puyallup. When they got within a hundred yards of the animals, she couldn't stand it anymore and pointed to the woolly creatures. "Rashid, what kind of sheep are those?"

He found her wonderment and curiosity funny and yet maddeningly exasperating. She obviously wasn't going to let it go until she had an answer. But he was also pleased that she cared to learn something, which showed her intelligence and ability to quickly grasp new concepts.

Rashid stopped and yelled, "They're called fat-tailed sheep. See their large tails?"

She yelled back. "I can see that. But the whole back end is larger than the ones I've seen."

"They're bigger and hardier to withstand the desert life."

"What's the deal with their tail?"

"It stores *allyah* or fat, as you know it. The fat's used for cooking, but not as much now as in ancient times when that's all they had. Now, there are other oils and fats."

Kendall's eyes wrinkled as she peered to get a closer look. "Is the wool the same as in the U.S.?"

"No. As a matter of fact, here it's coarser and has colored fibers. It's apparently of limited commercial value. The wool is primarily used for rug-making and blankets."

She nodded in wonderment at the strange-looking beasts.

He patiently waited for any more questions. When none were forthcoming, he said, "Can we move on now?"

"Sorry, yeah."

As they approached the tribal camp, an elder came out to greet them. Rashid was relieved to get a warm smile from the man. They were invited to stay for a meal and camp if they wished. Babar was unloaded and joined the other camels. Kendall had already bonded with the beast and worried about his treatment by the other camels or that he might pick up a disease. Rashid was more concerned that he wouldn't be able to tell him apart, but soon saw the distinctive markings that Babar bore on his front legs.

Rashid was able to converse a little with the men of the tribe. He quickly learned they were *Pashtun* nomads and part of the overall *Kuchi* nomad tribe. So long as Rashid was not a local *Hazara,* he was in good stead with this transhumant group. He knew the *Hazara* people didn't care for the nomads that grazed on the lands. The former claimed the exclusive rights over the ancient lands of their ancestors. These poor nomads were just trying to eke out a living however they could. But the *Hazaras* did have a point, that overgrazing and erosion was occurring solely because of the nomadic tribes.

Kendall was led to a covered area with the other women. They nodded shyly to her, and one woman grabbed her hand and led her to a rug where the women were eating and having their tea. She found the savory mutton stew with wild vegetables and *naan* bread delicious. She couldn't understand anything the women said so just sat there nodding and smiling. The women were curious about her. Though she dressed somewhat like them, she had the air of a foreigner. They decided amongst themselves that she had been acquired for Rashid in some sort of tribal exchange. They thought she was exotic and probably from Iran or maybe even India, though her skin looked more tan than permanently dark.

When the meal was over, the women went out to tend the sheep. They laughingly pulled Kendall with them. Rashid looked over to see her walking with the other women. He was amazed that she just blended right in.

He had joined the men as they were finishing their meal and green tea. He ate quickly of the fare that was offered. A few of the men left to tend the goats and sheep. He walked over to the large roped-off area with them. The men lined the goats up for milking. Rashid watched closely and joined in. As the men picked up the pace, they joked and cajoled each other to finish first.

Suddenly, there was a roar overhead, and two helicopters swooped low. The men looked up and shrugged their shoulders. Affecting curiosity, Rashid inquired about the helicopters. The men stated they had come by four days in a row now, usually just once, and then weren't seen again until the next day. They seemed to be looking for something, but the men didn't possess any further details.

In the meantime, Kendall was out in the field with the sheep and the other women. She had hold of a stick like the other women, and they were herding the sheep a little farther out. She blanched when she saw and heard the whir of the rotor blades overhead but kept her head down and appeared focused on running after a lamb that had been spooked by the loud noise and creeping dark shadows.

The two stayed another hour and then indicated they needed to push further north to meet up with the rest of their tribe. It took them another thirty minutes to get their supplies loaded onto Babar. As they set off for the north, Rashid and Kendall said their goodbyes and waved at the people.

They headed north for the cover of a grove of willow trees their new friends advised them was about eight miles ahead. Rashid figured if they moved rapidly, they could get there before nightfall. It would be a perfect place to set up their camp for the night and provide shelter from prying eyes from above. He also felt optimistic with the addition of Babar, and that they were traveling in local costume.

Perhaps he was feeling a little too sanguine, given the precarious journey they had embarked on and the perils that would soon befall them.

They were exhausted and dirty when they made camp that night. The stream was a little farther away from their campsite than Rashid had wished. At least they were protected by the willows. Kendall bathed first and changed into a pair of jeans and thick muslin shirt with the usual robes over the top. She washed out her dirty clothes and hung them on a lower branch under one of the willows. Rashid made camp and had dinner ready when she returned. While she ate and drank her tea, he bathed in the stream and washed out his clothes.

An hour later, he joined her for the last remnants of the smoldering campfire. She asked him about the goats and wished she could have watched or helped them. Rashid vigorously shook his head. "That would never be allowed. In this tribe—they told me—only men can milk goats."

She was incredulous. "What? Why?"

"It's part of the culture that's been handed down for centuries. And anyway, I don't think you want to know why. It has something to do with cleanliness and the way women are viewed."

Kendall sniffed. "I hope you don't subscribe to those beliefs."

"Did I say that I did? Have I not been defending you and treating you as an equal whenever we're alone? Do you see me handling you roughly and without respect?"

She shook her head, feeling guilty at projecting her anger at him. "No. As a matter of fact, you've been completely wonderful. But I get so mad at the ignorance of this country."

"Kendall, that's not fair. It's a combination of a tribal culture, a mix of so many different ethnic groups, and decades of war. It's just different from your world. That's all."

"Would you ever consider living in the U.S.?"

He was thoughtful for a few minutes. "I suppose it's like living in England, where I went to the University."

"Somewhat, but things are not so close together."

He laughed. "I can't even imagine what you mean."

She didn't want to get into another debate with him, so she changed the subject. "Tell me about Hindu Kush. What does that mean?"

"Everyone has their own explanation for the name. One of the most popular stories is that the word '*Kush*' means death. The name came from the days when Indian slaves died in the mountains here during their transport to Central Asia. Another story is that a medieval traveler called it 'Hindu Killer' because the inhabitants of the mountain region were enemies of the Indians who lived on the plains below."

"Are all the Afghan mountain ranges pretty much like what we've seen so far?"

He shook his head. "Not at all. In fact, I wish you could see the mountain range due north of Kabul. The glaciers are more visible, the peaks higher, and the temperature varies greatly from night to day." Looking into the darkening skies, he took her there with his vivid account. "It's called an ablated snow hummock, or *penitentes*. They're quite magical the first time you see them. It's a formation of the snow that's a few feet high, sort of like an ice stalagmite. It's caused from the bright sunlight and quick evaporation and then rapid decrease of temperature at night. It gives you an illusion of a kneeling figure. The whole floor is covered with them. They really stand out in the early morning light."

"Sounds breathtaking! I'd love to see them."

"And so you shall some time. But not on this trip."

She nodded solemnly. "Yep."

The first thing Rashid noticed when they got up the next morning was how quiet the campsite and surrounding area was. He was instantly on alert. Something wasn't right. He looked around, but all seemed quiet. Just to be on the safe side, he took out his nearby semi-automatic rifle, made sure it was loaded with a full magazine of bullets in the clip, and leaned it up against the nearest tree for quick access.

When Kendall stepped out of the tent a few minutes later, she saw the rifle and quickly looked to Rashid. "What's that for?" she demanded.

He tried to appear casual. "I just want to be ready."

"You're scaring me. Do you think there are troops nearby?"

He shrugged. "I don't know, but let's get going."

"Okay. I'm going to wash my face at the stream and brush my teeth. Is that okay?"

He wasn't happy that she'd be that far away, but didn't want to alarm her. "Fine, but make it quick. I'm anxious to get going this morning. In fact, do you mind if we skip a fire and sort of eat on the run?"

"You mean, no tea this morning? Well, okay, if you think it's necessary."

He gave her an intense look. "I do, Kendall. I, uh, just want to get out of here as soon as possible."

"All right, give me five minutes."

With that, she grabbed up her few personal items and ran down the path for the stream. She was reveling in the cold, crisp mountain spring water as it splashed over her face. She felt quite refreshed, and hurriedly brushed her teeth. As she shoved the face cloth and toothbrush into her small sack, she thought she heard voices. When she lifted her head to concentrate on the muffled sounds, she realized with horror those were the unmistakable sounds of angry voices ... at the campsite.

She carefully made her way toward the campsite, looking around for any soldiers. She stealthily moved over the rocky ground, making sure not to step on a stick and make her presence known. As she approached three large poplar trees growing together at the edge of the campsite, she peered through their leaves. Three soldiers with their backs to Kendall were about seventy-five yards away on the other edge of the campsite.

One of them moved, and Kendall sucked in her breath. The three soldiers had their weapons trained on Rashid, who was on his knees facing them with his hands behind his head. They were clearly about to shoot him, but were demanding to know where Kendall was.

She quickly looked for Rashid's weapon and saw it in the same spot as when she had left. She laid her things down, and in a crouched position quietly covered the ten feet to the weapon and swung it into her arms. Using the cover of bushes and boulders all around her, she returned to the hidden place behind the poplar trees. The weapon felt heavy in her arms, and she knew she needed help steadying it, especially if she was to get off three shots.

She brought the barrel up and rested it on one of the low branches of the tree. She looked through the scope and lined up the farthest soldier between the crosshairs. Even if she got off one shot, the other soldiers would shoot Rashid. She refocused her attention on the area immediately surrounding the soldiers and caught sight of Babar munching on some vegetation off to the left of the men. Kendall reached down and grabbed a small rock and then re-sighted the soldier in the crosshairs, being careful to stand with feet wide apart and her weight forward to absorb the repercussion. She disengaged the safety button and then, without taking her eye from the gun sight, threw the rock toward Babar as hard as she could. It landed at his feet, and he gave a moaning bleat. The three soldiers instantly reacted and looked over at him, retraining their weapons toward Babar.

Kendall got off three quick shots, hitting each soldier in the back of the head, dropping them where they stood. They were precision hits, and both Kendall and Rashid were amazed. With the blast from the first gunshot, Rashid had dropped the rest of the way to the ground, unsure of who was actually shooting. He scrambled to his feet and checked to ensure the soldiers were dead.

Kendall was momentarily stunned from the roar of the semi-automatic weapon. Her shoulder was bruised and battered from the recoil action. But her adrenalin was pumping, and she simply ignored the pain in her ears and shoulder. She re-engaged the safety mechanism and ran over to Rashid. Overcome with unbelievable relief, he gave her an impromptu hug and kissed the side of her head. Grabbing onto her arms, he pushed away from her and searched her face. "Now you see why you practiced so much? Good shooting!"

Kendall's eyes were still wide from the shock. "I didn't have time to be scared. It was them or us. I chose life."

He nodded, and she continued. "Wasn't Babar wonderful?"

Rashid laughed. "Let's get going! We need to hide the bodies. The good thing is that we now have three additional weapons and more supplies."

They quickly ran around gathering the items and loading everything onto Babar. They dragged the soldiers' bodies and pushed them under some brush.

Rashid figured they wouldn't be discovered until the smell of their decaying bodies gave them away in a few days. They hastily cleaned up the campsite, using branches to hide their presence. The ashes from their fire were scattered about. Rashid wrestled with whether to take the troops' radios but knew they contained radio frequency or tracking chips. He was fairly certain how to remove the chips. But if he made a mistake, it would lead the others to them. He made a quick decision to remove the chips, destroy them, smash the radios, and leave all of it behind with the remains.

The fleeing duo was finally on the move and proceeded higher into the mountains. Rashid made the critical decision to move away from the river and streams. It was too easy to track them. They filled all of their water skins, including those taken from the soldiers.

As they worked their way higher into the rocky mountains of the Hindu Kush range, there were fewer trees and more outcrops and rock faces. Rashid had miscalculated the need for trees. On the higher slopes, it was easy to spot approaching aircraft from afar and to find shelter in a cave or under a rocky ledge. Even Babar was able to keep out of sight whenever the helicopters and planes flew overhead.

They stopped only briefly for small breaks to get something to drink and a quick bite. Otherwise, they made good time. Rashid felt they were able to trek some ten miles toward Mazar-e-Sharif. In the early evening, as they looked for a somewhat spacious cave that could accommodate a dromedary and hide a campfire in the dark, he scanned the horizon. All day, they had seen various aircraft circling the area way off to the east. Rashid was relieved they had gone in a northwesterly direction. Their trail had apparently been lost, and General Omar's troops were no longer on their heels.

They found a perfect cave where they made camp for the night. They weren't even going to need the tent. Rashid made a large fire, and they were soon sipping hot green tea. Kendall had never wanted anything more in her life, having gone all day without any warm beverage. The taste of that hot drink calmed her nerves and helped her relax. She knew there'd be no bathing tonight and probably tomorrow too, but she was thankful most of their water skins were full and that no one was breathing down their necks.

In the morning they had a quick campfire for hot tea and then gathered their belongings. Rashid was taking stock of the weapons and handed Kendall an MK25 P226 semi-automatic handgun. She stared at it, and raised her eyebrows. He waggled the gun at her and urged her, "Go on, take it! You should've had this on you the moment we left the lakes. Now, you'll feel safer."

"Is it loaded?"

"Check it! You know the drill. When someone hands you a gun, you should always check its status."

She turned away, slid the chamber open and verified there was no round in the firing position, ejected the magazine, and saw that it was fully loaded. After shoving it back into position and making sure the safety was engaged, he showed her how to clip it to her waist. He then pulled out a knife and sheath that had come from one of the dead soldiers, and strapped it to Kendall's leg. "There, you are ready for war now."

She frowned. "Not funny! I hope I never have to shoot a gun again. My shoulder still hurts."

Rashid chuckled. "Yeah, well, as long as we're prepared, then you know we won't need them."

They continued their way north and were happy to run across a small stream at midday. As they sat down next to a rocky outcrop for a brief meal, Rashid went around the corner and behind a cluster of trees. Kendall was sitting on a fallen log with her back to the rocky projection. She had her hands at her waist, undoing the P226. All of a sudden she heard a strange chuffing sound followed by a breathy snort overhead. Babar, who was grazing nearby, let out a long moan and loped off in the direction of Rashid.

Kendall stood up and slowly turned around, and there, overhead, not ten feet away, was a full-sized male snow leopard. As it crouched in a position from which to spring at her, she hastily and awkwardly grabbed for the handgun. The snarling animal leapt off the ledge right at her. The last thing she remembered was a whirl of spots descending toward her, beady green eyes locked onto hers and, at the last moment, hot breath on her neck.

# CHAPTER FORTY-ONE

Captain Qadi scanned the horizon and yelled into the radio. He had received routine status reports of no sightings from several troops that had split off. But one of the groups that tracked the most obvious route had been unresponsive. He couldn't imagine it had been taken out. Rashid wasn't that good, he reasoned. Worse, the tracking chips in the missing troops' radios were silent. Qadi was uneasy as he processed this mystery. Finally, he ordered several troops to backtrack to the last trail of the missing soldiers.

Making matters worse, the search helicopters and drones had come up empty. They had covered the region between Band-e-Amir and the northern border with no sightings. Rashid and Kendall could be dead, Qadi told himself, but then thought bitterly that he didn't have that kind of luck. General Omar was anxious and pissed that his young swaggering captain had not located the criminals. The leader decided to hold his tongue for now and refrain from threatening the captain for another day. Instead, he urged him on and offered more ground troops.

Qadi accepted the extra troops and specified they be sent to the western part of the Sar-i Pul Province in case the couple on the run were headed to the western border with Turkmenistan. The captain specifically wanted troops to scour the cities of Sar-i Pul, Maymana, and Shibirghan. The last one had a direct route and was closest to Mazar-e-Sharif. The general pointed out that the troops would be spread all over the northwestern area of Afghanistan. There was no concentration of troops at any one location. He knew that was not a good idea, particularly if they were up against a worthy opponent like Rashid. That man was known to be patient and would use stealth and intelligence to best his adversary.

The general sighed at the seemingly unorganized nature of the search and bitterly blamed President Shazeb for not investing in the infrared equipment that would have been of enormous help to the air search crews. But the former president was too busy diverting natural gas revenues into his own pockets and seeing to his personal business interests. Besides, he had always told Omar there were no other countries at their doorstep. Afghanistan had finally been left to its own devices. It didn't need to waste money on electronic toys it had no use for. The only unruly citizens were the independent nomads who only cared about their immediate families and the nomads' very survival.

The Afghan troops had been run ragged for over a week now, and didn't seem to be much help. The pair on the run were either blending in well with the local tribes they ran across, or they were handling the mountain trek by themselves with no problem.

When Omar received word of the missing soldiers, he refused to believe they were taken out by Rashid. He told himself the guy was dragging behind him a slow animal and a silly female who would be of no help. It wasn't like they were an experienced combat team. There also had to be a rational explanation for why the radios were not working. He advised the young captain not to worry, and offered the theory that the troops probably fell in the water and got their radios wet and were simply unable to communicate. Omar was not going to be made a fool of. Therefore, he refused to even ponder the untimely demise of his soldiers. That they would have been ambushed was unthinkable.

***********

Mossad leader Benjamin Zimmerman was incensed when he got the word that Israel's satellite had been destroyed by an unknown saboteur that had brilliantly built an army of clones using proxy servers all over the world that were impossible to trace back to a single source. Israel's best computer experts would do the painstaking investigation to reverse engineer the act, but it would take days, if not weeks.

This time Zimmerman knew it couldn't have been Rashid. He was on the run or dead, and he certainly didn't have any computers at his disposal. The older man wouldn't even try to blame the young man. Everyone within the tight Mossad agency knew this act of sabotage took a special kind of skill that very few possessed. Even their own computer science specialist, Shane Menard, wasn't capable of this magnitude of electronic destruction. No, it would have to be the act of someone who despised Israel, he told himself.

Frankly, the only person he could think of who might have the know-how was the young protégée in Seattle, Washington, Daniel Blumfeld. But that thought was absurd, because he was one of their own. He would have no reason to burn them. He was paid handsomely by Israel. So far, he had always done what was asked of him. Still, the young man might have an idea who could've done this.

For his own edification, using *Prophecy* Zimmerman checked on Blumfeld's cell phone pings. He was relieved to see the device's history pinged on the same location in Seattle for the past couple days. It only showed a movement from the Orion Datacenter location to Seattle, where he must be in meetings. That was all ordinary and normal in the Mossad leader's eyes. He felt guilty for even allowing himself a momentary look at Daniel as the possible saboteur.

The puzzling part was the whole Afghanistan plan of the demise of President Shazeb and the rescue by the Israeli military. The timing was too close to the sabotage. Was it coincidental? The Mossad leader didn't think so. But what was the reason then? Walking through it logically, the result was that Israel's communication was knocked out for a few days. Other satellites were this very minute being brought online to service the communication network. The rerouting was being programmed now but would take at least another day and a half.

So, what was so important that the communications needed to go dark for a couple days? Who needed a few days? That was easy. Rashid did. Zimmerman threw his notebook across the room. *Back to that man again*, he raged. It was like the young man was taunting him from afar. The Mossad leader was not about to take the blame for the sabotage by any of his underlings, particularly those he, personally, had brought into the agency. No. He would lay low and offer the usual sacrificial lamb: Iran or Palestine. He would bolster that with the theory that they were jealous of Israel's recent high-profile rescue.

As he calmed down and returned to his desk, he decided that any investigation would be cursory at best. If it did relate to Rashid, then he didn't want to know about it or, rather, he didn't want the Israeli leadership to find out about it. Right now, they were more concerned about the incredible waste of money as a result of the satellite destruction.

Zimmerman was exhausted. His job was currently more stressful than he'd ever experienced. It just didn't seem worth it any more. But he was at least ten years from retiring. Maybe he'd ask for a transfer to a country where nothing ever happened. He sighed and turned his attention to his monitor, where a list of invoices needed approval.

***********

Fields was ecstatic when he heard the headlines upon waking. Now, he just hoped that Daniel's path was untraceable. But knowing the brilliant computer science whiz as he did, he had faith their secret would be safe. He and Daniel had not spoken since the latter returned from Toronto. That meant there were no unforeseen issues, and their plans had gone off without a hitch.

After spending the night in Seattle and meeting with Mickey, Daniel had returned to the Orion datacenter plant. His drive back to the plant had been pleasurable. He replayed the events in Toronto in his mind and looked for any weaknesses or mistakes he might have made. None came to mind. In fact, the scene where he returned the used car was the *coup de gras*. The guy was so focused on his phone call, that he took the keys and waved Daniel away. He didn't even stop to ask where Daniel was going, offer him a ride or to summon a taxi, or watch as he walked the two blocks to the nearest bus stop.

Once he was home, just to be on the safe side, Daniel burned his fake passport and driver's license. It had come in very handy, and he decided to get himself another set real soon. One must always have an extra set of IDs in the event of an emergency, he told himself. You never know when your real name might become obsolete ... or a liability. He chuckled to himself.

The world was talking about the Israeli satellite having been sabotaged. Concerned countries were worried they were next. Business was good for computer science experts and consultants. Companies performed audits and checks of their networks to ensure there were no unauthorized eyes.

NSA Agent Frank Reynolds was curious about *Prophecy*. Would it weather the intense scrutiny of internal systems? He was both fearful and in awe of the seemingly invisible eyes. There was no change in his team's ability to covertly monitor others via *Prophecy*. His team still wasn't getting much from Israel. It was like it had put up a shield. At first Frank thought it was due to the destruction of the satellite, but as it continued, he realized *Prophecy* was being shut out of Israel's intelligence data and communications.

Reynolds phoned Fields at his preferred time. It was noon in DC and early morning in Seattle. Most of the government minions were out and about midday. He could go anywhere or do anything and not be noticed. If he stayed at his desk, which was precisely where he was at this moment. Not only did he have privacy, but anyone passing by would think he was hard at work. In fact, he was hard at work. It just wasn't the government's business, he rationalized.

Fields answered on the first ring. He always knew when his frat buddy was calling. "Frank, how's it going? Did you see the news?"

"Yes. It's a bit coincidental, don't you think?"

"How so?"

"Well, the timing of it, just a few days after the rescue. Don't you think that's odd?"

"Sorry, Frank, I deal in definites, not odds. That's your field, so to speak."

"Paul, I'm serious. What does Israel know that it doesn't want the rest of the world to know? And who knows about it and didn't like it?"

"Geez, Frank, you sound paranoid. Well, the only thing I can tell you is that I happen to know that Israel knows that Kendall and Rashid are alive. Are you ready for this?" He paused for effect. "Israel sent an anonymous email to General Omar, telling them exactly where they could find the pair."

Frank Reynolds' mind was shocked into silence. "But how? And why?"

"Rashid must have known something about Israel that it didn't want made public. It must be in Israel's best interest to see Rashid dead. Kendall's probably nothing more than collateral damage."

There was continued silence on the other end of the line. "Frank, are you there, buddy?"

Reynolds was getting an idea of what had transpired, and it was scaring the hell out of him. If all of this was true, then how come his friend, Paul Fields, knew all of this? Furthermore, Fields must also know about the destruction of the satellite. In fact, what part, if any, did he play in it? At this point, did Reynolds even want to know the truth? How had his friend and frat brother gone from being a CEO to playing God, using his incredibly illegal but brilliant *Prophecy*?

"Frank, you're scaring me! What's going on?"

"Oh. Sorry, Paul. I'm just connecting the dots. If what you say is true, first, how do you know this?"

"*Proph*. How else?"

"But I have *Prophecy* too. I don't ever get anything from Israel any more. It all seems so gray and mundane. I feel like the blinds are down for me."

"Well, you don't have my, uh, expertise."

"What the hell does that mean? Do you have some newer version that I don't?"

"Not at all. But you, my good friend, don't have my technical expert who, incidentally, developed the tool. He has had to do some maneuvering to get past the Mossad's technical shields. He knows *Proph* backwards and forwards and can apparently modify it at will to blast through any new technical obstacle."

"There's got to be more than that."

"Frank, do you really want to know everything I know? Wouldn't it be better if you stayed in the dark for some of the details?"

"Tell me, and then I'll decide."

"Ha, ha! Okay! But don't blame me if you find yourself knowing too much and it gets the best of you. You know that by now, you'll never be able to pass another internal polygraph test?"

"Piece of cake, Paul. They aren't that difficult. One just needs to know how it's done and then practice. I've taken several mock tests and had no problem passing them."

Reynolds was still freaked. The bizarre conversation was not making it better. "Back to the issue, Paul. What do I need to know about your techie guy?"

Fields thought quickly. He had to protect himself and Daniel. There was no reason to give his buddy all the background. How ironic. Even Fields didn't know the extent of Blumfeld's involvement with the Mossad. He decided to throw his buddy a bone. "He's Jewish, you know."

"So what?"

"So, he's always been interested in the Israeli network infrastructure. He's studied it, knows how technically astute their experts are, and used it as his guinea pig, if you will." *Good one, Paul,* he told himself.

"Is that all? That's not so exciting or earth shattering."

"I told you so."

"One more question, Paul."

"Uh-huh?"

"Did Orion have anything to do with taking down the Israeli satellite?"

"Orion? Absolutely not! We are not in the spy business, Frank. How many times do I have to tell you that?" He held his breath, waiting for the obvious follow-up question: Did Daniel, working on his own, have anything to do with the sabotage? But it never came. Reynolds was outmaneuvered. He was too much of a thinker and computer guy and simply not quick enough to process the information. That's why he was an analysis agent and not a field agent.

Fields took the opportune brief pause to change the subject. "Frank, I have one last question."

"What?"

"Have you located Kendall and Rashid? Are they okay? Where are they headed? What are you hearing from the Afghanistan military?"

These were all inconsequential questions that Fields already had the answers to. But he wanted to end the line of inquiry about Daniel. If Reynolds stopped and thought about it, he would realize this. The poor guy wasn't too savvy, that's for sure, Fields thought.

"We've traced them into the Hindu Kush Mountains where they are currently in the wind."

Fields played along. "Are they on foot?"

"Yes, apparently with a camel carrying their things."

For some perverse reason Paul found that scenario almost comical. "So, what is the Afghan military doing? Are they that incompetent that they can't locate them?"

"Actually, Paul, it's kind of humorous. They keep losing their captains and having to reorganize."

"Really?"

"Uh-huh. The last one in the Band-e-Amir area drove over a landmine and blew himself up. That bought Rashid and Kendall almost half a day."

"Incredible! So, any theories on where they're headed?"

"Either north to Mazar-e-Sharif or west toward Turkmenistan. Mazar-e-Sharif is too obvious, but it's a larger city and they could more easily blend in. But it will have a huge military presence. Also, it's the closest. I think it's a toss-up and depends on what happens with the troops. If the two want to lose the soldiers, they should head west. So what if it takes them another three days?"

"Well, if by then the soldiers haven't found them, they'll know the two headed west."

"Okay. Keep looking, Frank. Let me know if you learn anything new."

"I always do, Paul. Later."

***********

Doctor Maysah Siddra spent forty-eight hours in DC, where she was grilled for hours every day. Finally, the U.S. State Department, CIA, Secret Service, FBI, NSA, and Homeland Security lost interest in keeping her any further. By the time of her release, they had employed the latest in biometric data monitoring. Every part of her body that was unique—like her palm print, facial features, eyes, blood, DNA, et cetera—was taken and input into the intelligence database. She was then shipped off to Seattle, where ICE kept her for another two days while it finished the paperwork for an extended stay in Seattle under the mentorship of Paul Fields.

She certainly didn't qualify for an I-9 immigration status, since she wouldn't technically be an employee of Orion. It had no reason to hire a medical doctor, albeit one who wasn't licensed in the U.S. Immigration Enforcement gave her a temporary visa allowing her to work toward full U.S. citizenship, if that's what she chose.

Finally, she was approved to be released into Mickey's custody with the strict instructions that she was to report in to Immigration on a weekly basis to see how she was progressing toward citizenship and being assimilated into local life.

Mickey was happy to finally get some alone time with her. He liked to know his team and those around him. He was going out on quite a limb for her, and he hoped she would at least be pleasant and grateful. On the flight from Tel Aviv to DC, she hadn't made eye contact with anyone. He was fearful she was going to be cold and unfeeling and, worse, demanding. While his boss was funding this "project," Mickey was doing the legwork.

The condominium at Lake Union was ready. Since Fields had purchased the building's model home that was fully furnished—including two flat screen televisions—he and Mickey decided it would be prudent to buy all the furnishings too. That made the housing details very easy. The deal was closed within days, and Mickey had the keys the day before Maysah Siddra was released from the Seattle ICE office. He took a couple of his security staff and went grocery shopping to stock her refrigerator and purchase cleaning supplies, including a vacuum cleaner. He had her utilities and cable connected. In the process, he learned a lot about international foods, and was pleased with himself for discovering Trader Joe's. He thought Maysah would be relieved to see a few food items she recognized, like fresh hummus, *naan*, and organic dried fruits.

He was finally given the go-ahead to pick up Maysah from Immigration one afternoon. He took one of his female admins with him, so the Afghan doctor would not feel uneasy alone in his presence. As they walked into the sparse, dingy office of Immigration, Mickey looked around and couldn't help but compare these offices with the incredible condo that was being provided to Dr. Siddra for her stay in Seattle. She might live there for a month, or she might be there for years; it all depended on her and how she adapted to her new life. He fervently hoped she would like living in Seattle and becoming comfortable with her new mentors. Everything hung in the balance. She could choose to make the transition difficult by refusing to work with them or try to go off on her own and sabotage their efforts. Worry lines were etched on Mickey's forehead when the inside door opened and she walked out. She raised her eyes and looked directly into his. He swallowed hard.

# CHAPTER FORTY-TWO

It all happened in a flash. Babar raced past Rashid, who called after him. Then the loud sound of the discharge of a weapon rang out. Rashid knew it was Kendall, and momentarily thought she had shot herself. But that didn't make sense, since Babar had been on the run before the shot. Rashid ran back to the midday camp spot, and to his amazement and horror there lay Kendall flat on her back with a dead spotted snow leopard atop her. The magnificent creature's paw was casually draped across Kendall's face. Neither one was moving.

As Rashid ran over to her, he could see a trail of blood flowing down Kendall's neck. Suddenly her eyes flew open and she looked into his eyes. "Am I alive?"

He laughed out of sheer relief and began examining her for injuries. He quickly realized the blood trail down her neck was from the animal. She had shot it in the neck.

She stated matter-of-factly, "Would you please get this stinky thing off me?"

Rashid grabbed hold of the two front legs and swung the leopard off her. He then knelt down and ran his hands deftly over her limbs, checking for broken bones, puncture wounds, or deep scratches. She sat up and brushed his hands aside. "I'm fine!" And then she looked over at the dead animal at their feet. "But this guy isn't! Wow! He's beautiful."

Babar was still bellowing a hundred yards away. Rashid went to retrieve him. As they approached the camp site, Babar shied away and threatened to run again. Rashid finally tied him to a tree just out of sight of the camp.

Rashid expertly skinned the animal and laid out the pelt to dry. Kendall watched with interest when he pulled out a sack of rock salt and began pressing it onto the flesh side of the hide. "So that's why you were carrying all that salt."

Rashid nodded. "When you go up into the mountains around here, you have to be prepared. This is a beautiful hide. If we don't dry it correctly, it'll spoil and rot." He hung the hide at an angle in the hot sun and then set about to cut the meat into long strips. Just as he had done with the carp from the Band-e-Amir

Lake, he followed the same process and within two hours had strips of meat hanging on every available string he had.

"Are we going to make camp here?"

Rashid frowned, looked up at the sun, and shook his head. "We can't. We need to move away from the gut pile. It's going to bring every jackal around. We're probably already surrounded."

Kendall looked around nervously. "Do you think the leopard was stalking us?"

"I'm afraid so. And that was my mistake. I saw the telltale signs of fresh scat. I just assumed it was tracking another animal. Snow leopards are stealthy and usually hide. That this one came out in the open for us to see, is a little unusual. Maybe its den is close by, or it had a kill it was working on and saw us as a threat. Anyway, you see that Babar is still going nuts. He can smell the gut pile. We need to travel another hour to get away from the fresh blood here."

They had a quick drink of tea and ate some fresh meat. It didn't taste too bad, Kendall thought. But the idea of eating any raw meat had her stomach roiling in protest. Finally, they packed up their things. Babar was very unhappy and skittish as they loaded the strings of meat over his back.

They climbed higher up the mountain and came to a clearing that broke into a wide meadow. They made camp on the edge of the trees, and this time had to set up the tent. Rashid showed Kendall how to collect fresh, wild vegetables and herbs. He cooked up some of the meat and added the vegetables. The evening meal was fresh and delicious. Kendall thought the leopard meat tasted like pork loin.

When they climbed into the tent at the end of the day, they realized they could hear the rush of a waterfall not too far away. Rashid promised her they would search it out in the morning and she could bathe. She had only flung some water on her arms and neck to get the leopard blood off her. She was sure she was beginning to smell rank.

In the early morning, they searched out the source of the running water, and Kendall was delighted to see a gentle waterfall cascading away from a rock cliff and into a perfect-sized pool. The area was surrounded by trees, and it offered as much privacy as she wanted. Before Rashid could change his mind, she grabbed up her things and promised him she would be back within thirty minutes. He smiled and decided they would take their time this morning.

The ideal setting for the waterfall had not escaped his notice. He fully intended to wash a few layers of grime off as well.

She was just finishing her third cup of green tea for the morning when Rashid strolled up looking clean and smelling of pomegranates. He surveyed the campsite, deciding what to do first.

They were soon on their way north and made good time, staying at the tree line or taking breaks in various caves they ran across. The search helicopters continued running from the Band-e-Amir Lakes up north to Mazar-e-Sharif. They stayed well to the east of where Rashid and Kendall were traveling. The two were surprised to see additional helicopters to the west of them as well on this day. Obviously, Omar was concerned the duo were possibly headed west for Iran or Turkmenistan.

Just after leaving the Band-e-Amir Lakes, Rashid had toyed with the idea of heading west or stopping at some of the small cities on the way north, like Sar-e Pol. But with the concentration of helicopters roaming the mountainside on both east and west of the route that would lead them to Mazar-e-Sharif, he decided to go the entire way without stopping at any of the little cities and towns along the route. They had done fairly well so far on their own, except for the unfortunate incident with the soldiers the day before. If they just remained on alert and stayed on course through the back trails and maybe even off the beaten path, they should make it to Mazar-e-Sharif without any further interruptions.

The sky was particularly blue this summer day, and it had been quiet as they trudged along on the last leg of their journey before they made camp for the night. They came upon a beautiful meadow dotted with funny-looking round huts. There were a hundred goats and sheep grazing on the pasture land.

Kendall was amazed at the huts. "What are those houses?"

"It's called a *kherga* in Afghanistan. I think you know them as *yurts*."

"Oh, I've heard of those. How did they get them so round?"

"They use steam to bend the wood into sort of a crown, and then put up ribs of bent wood around the structure."

"But how does the roof stay up?"

"There is a tension band stretched from the roof to the walls. That keeps the walls in place. The last step is a cover around the structure, providing insulation and keeping the elements out."

"Are they mobile?"

"Yes. They can easily be taken down and moved to a new location."

"Are these people more *Kuchi* nomads?"

"Nope. It looks like they are *Kyrgyz* nomads."

"Wow! How can you tell the difference between this group and the *Kuchi* nomads?"

"I know that *Kyrgyz* nomads live in the northern regions up high, and they live in yurts. This tribe is a little different, though."

"How?"

"Most of the *Kyrgyz* tribes live and move around in the far north of Afghanistan in the Pamir mountain range. I think there's snow there most of the year. This tribe must be here because they're looking for better pasture and meadows. When you find them this far west, they were usually forced to seek better living grounds. It could be their stock did not do so well during the last winter."

"How long will they stay here?"

"They move three to four times a year."

"How do they make money? They must need wheat or some sort of flour for baking."

"They make their living from trading their livestock with various traveling merchants. All the basic things like salt, sugar, flour, and medicines are bought with the money they bring in from their animals."

Kendall was impressed with the active life teeming all around the meadow. Children were helping the men with the animals, the women with the cooking and sewing. But the scene before her was noticeably out of touch with time. She shook her head. "They don't have electricity, do they?"

"No, they don't."

"I can't imagine living like this. How do the children survive to adulthood?"

Rashid looked grim. "Most don't. Half of them die at birth. And while most of the adults look weathered and old, almost all of them are barely forty. Most don't live past the age of forty. It's a difficult life, Kendall."

"I don't see why they'd want to live up here when they could move to the lowlands like Bamiyan, and live like Jangi? They could have both livestock and a crop or two."

"They are living a traditional life mostly untouched by time. They are a proud people and choose to live that way. I heard a story about a doctor who came across a *Kyrgyz* tribe. The doctor offered to vaccinate the children, but the adults were wary. Finally, they agreed that if the doctor paid each family, they would comply. The doctor went away without inoculating the children."

"That's very sad. It seems so lonely and isolated up here."

"It is! This place is pretty much at the top of the world. In fact, we couldn't travel this route if it was any other time of the year. One month either way, and we'd see snow. We are so fortunate that it's summer."

"Maybe, but this hasn't exactly been a vacation. I feel like it's been one long trauma for months. Geez! I'm living under constant stress."

"Calm down! Just be glad you don't have to live like these people. We are only a day out of Mazar-e-Sharif. We'll be there and will make our connections and escape to safety."

"Hey, I'm entitled to be angry at being forcibly taken to Afghanistan where I watched people murdered or could hear them being tortured every night!" And then dripping with sarcasm, she added, "Though the past few months has done wonders to enrich my cultural experience!"

Rashid was patient with her fit of temper and quietly responded, "And on behalf of my country, I apologize. But please don't blame me. I'm doing all I can to keep you alive. We're almost there. We could be free in three days." He paused and then continued in a grave tone, "One more thing, Kendall. You may have lost your freedom for a few months, but I've lost my country. I lost my family when I was young, and now my way of life has been completely altered. I'm being blamed for things I didn't do, and people want me dead. If I actually survive, I'll be forced to assume a new identity and live in a foreign country. These are not things I would have wished for."

He let her stew a few minutes longer and then got out his binoculars to give the tribe a once-over from afar to gauge its temperament. After a few minutes, Kendall visibly relaxed and was mortified at her outburst. She knew that Rashid hadn't deserved her anger. She was just projecting her frustration onto him, because he was the closest target ... hell, the only target. She asked to use the binoculars too. Peering intently at the busy activity in the meadow, she said, "Are we going to pass them by or stop?"

"Well, they look friendly enough. We could use some bread or flour. We have lots of leopard meat and the hide. We can trade a lot for that hide."

They made their way across the meadow and encountered a very surprised tribe of people who could not fathom why a young couple and a camel would be traveling across the high mountain range. It looked like it was going to be awkward at first, as the men of the tribe gathered around them. But one of them spied the leopard pelt drying on Babar's right side and exclaimed at how beautiful it was and rare to even see a snow leopard let alone get close enough to kill it. Rashid decided it would be prudent to share the meat. But first, one of the young boys who was comfortable around camels unloaded Babar and led him over to the other camels.

Rashid offered dried meat and fish to the elders. That broke the ice. The *Kyrgyz* people were about to start their evening meal. With the unexpected guests, the evening was turned into a festivity of sorts. Many dishes suddenly appeared before the weary travelers, including the leopard and carp. The entire camp sat on the floor inside the largest *yurt,* with the elders sitting closest to the fire. Kendall was able to stay near Rashid.

The tribe's people wanted to know where they came from. Rashid detested telling lies. He spoke of his long-deceased family as if they had recently passed. He talked about having lived on a farm. Kendall then noticed he incorporated some of Jangi's farm details into his story.

She would be glad when they were no longer the object of curiosity and she would have the comfort of knowing she was in a safe environment. Even now, as she looked around her, she caught the eye of a wizened old woman. The elder practically gave her the "evil eye." Her piercing look felt like daggers in Kendall's heart. She wanted to run away. At the very least, she didn't want to stay. She actually felt like her life might be in danger from this old, frail woman if she stayed the night.

The children wanted to hear the story of how they acquired the leopard. Rashid was a natural with children. He made the unusual encounter into a thrilling story. While their little eyes were round with amazement at what Kendall had done, they giggled and laughed at the image of Babar running past him when he was otherwise disposed.

Everyone exclaimed at how delicious the leopard meat was and beamed at Rashid. The two travelers could not get enough of the fresh warm flat bread. They immediately made a trade for enough *naan* to last them the rest of the way to Mazar-e-Sharif in exchange for their dried fish and some salt.

When Rashid suggested that he needed to set up his tent, there was a murmur among the tribe. The elders confabbed, and Rashid thought they were discussing the best place for his tent. After some time, the elders nodded in agreement, and one went to Rashid and motioned for him to follow.

The *yurts* were laid out in a pattern at fairly close proximity to the next. There was a yurt a little further away from the rest, almost as if the residents were being shunned. The placement was by design. The elder explained that the young couple who had lived in that yurt were recently deceased. The yurt was being cleansed of all evil before another tribesman took possession of it. Because Rashid and Kendall were not part of their tribe, they were assured that any existing evil would not be extended to them. Kendall demanded to know what the story was behind the deceased couple.

Rashid politely asked for the facts about the young couple and then relayed it to Kendall. The young wife had given birth to a daughter. The husband was headstrong and insisted all the way through the pregnancy that she would have a son. He apparently believed that by proclaiming the baby to be a son, it would, in fact, be one. When the daughter was born, the husband was so angry, that he killed his wife and newborn daughter. The tribal elders met and realized that if their tribe were to survive, this behavior would not be allowed. The husband, now a widower, was told he would either be banned and must immediately leave the tribe, or he should restore honor to his household by ending his own life. He chose the latter, and slit his own throat.

Rashid asked Kendall if she was concerned at sleeping in the abandoned *yurt,* given the circumstances. "Not at all," she said. If it meant they didn't have to set up the tent and basically had protection from the elements, she was fine with it. But she did express concern about the old woman with the piercing eyes.

Rashid laughed and told her the woman was telling everyone that this young traveling couple hadn't borne children because they were living a carefree existence and hadn't cemented any roots yet. She had several suggestions of various tribal remedies, and Kendall just rolled her eyes at Rashid. He didn't dare tell her the old woman laid the entire blame for not having any children directly at Kendall's feet. Her spirit was apparently too independent.

In the morning they said their goodbyes and once again headed north. There were several well-worn trails leading to the nearest city on the way to Mazar-e-Sharif. Rashid was thankful the elders had pointed them out, as he intended to avoid them. There was one trail in particular that they were advised at the last minute to avoid. It was treacherous and rocky, but almost entirely within the tree line. Naturally, that was the trail Rashid chose.

The elder he was speaking with had already realized that Kendall was not just foreign, but probably from the West. He decided to be prudent and keep this information to himself. No reason to alarm the tribe or cause speculation and gossip. He even doubted the young couple was married. In fact, they almost seemed to be on the run. The elder was curious but had seen it many times with people who had wandered into his camp. He could tell the travelers looked down on his nomadic lifestyle, just like Kendall did. But he could see misery, worry, and conflict in the travelers' faces. Just who was the unfortunate one here, he thought? He offered a prayer for his noble and hard-working tribe and was thankful for the tribe's simple, traditional ways.

As Rashid and Kendall prepared to head out, the elder grabbed Rashid's hand in a final brotherly way, knowing he would never see him again. As he gazed into Rashid's eyes, the latter knew immediately that this wise old man had not been fooled. But the old man saw goodness in the young couple, and believed they were not bad people. There must be a good reason for their being on the run, he told himself. It wasn't his business to inquire further. That's when Rashid was quietly advised of the alternate trail. With that final benevolent and compassionate gesture, Rashid unfastened the spotted leopard hide and presented it to the elder as a token of respect. The old man was sad to send these two young people off into the wilderness. They would've made fine additions to his tribe.

Kendall, Rashid, and Babar trudged along the difficult terrain for hours with barely a stop for some water and food. Now that Kendall knew she was within a day of Mazar-e-Sharif, she kept pushing them onwards. They were finally forced to stop when she twisted her ankle. It was clear they needed a long break.

The only blessing about the treacherous path they chose was that it paralleled a river. As Kendall, with her shoes and socks off, sat on a rock at the edge of the river soaking her aching feet and painful ankle, she noticed all the fish and pointed excitedly, "Look, Rashid. There's tons of fish. What are they?"

He peered into the river and said, "That's brown trout. They live in the alpine region waterways. They're really good eating. Do you mind if I catch a few, so we can have fresh fish tonight?"

"No. Good idea."

She watched as he made a makeshift net out of material and a small sturdy piece of wood. He caught two fish on the first scoop. He dipped his improvised net one more time. As Kendall watched him skillfully gut and clean the fish, she was already salivating at the prospect of fresh fish for the evening meal. She was so tired of the dried fruit and dried fish and meat. Anything fresh was of great relief.

They packed up their belongings once again and set off on the nasty trail. This time they moved at a slower pace. The path seemed to get even more difficult. Kendall was about to grumble at the horrible choice Rashid had picked. She knew the elder had pointed out several more passable trails and was thoroughly irritated that Rashid chose this nasty, rocky terrain. Much of the time they were single file, with Rashid in front and Babar in the middle. She was tired of looking at Babar's ass all day. The way he walked, by swinging from side to side, made her dizzy if she focused too much. She decided to be prudent and concentrate on her feet for a while.

Suddenly they heard a whirring close by. Rashid pulled them all under a thick pine tree and they waited. Babar was not happy at being pushed against a tree trunk, with Kendall and Rashid pressed against his neck. A helicopter was flying overhead, but a little to the east. The fleeing pair stood little chance of being seen, so long as they were quiet and stayed put. Rashid was worried about Babar's twenty-inch tail. It kept flicking from side to side.

Kendall's eyes got wide as she realized this was the closest they had gotten to a search helicopter. She tried to crane her neck to see the helicopter, but Rashid pulled her up against his chest and hissed in her ear. "Kendall, stop it! Do I need to remind you that these guys fully intend to shoot us on sight?"

"Well, they're going to have to get a lot closer in order to shoot us."

He was annoyed that she would even think of arguing with him. He squeezed her arm and responded, "They don't have to shoot us! They would spot our movement and bomb us to hell! Is that what you want?"

She got the message and stopped squirming. They must not have been spotted, because the aircraft's presence seemed to be merely a fly-by. It buzzed by them and continued on its way.

Rashid was disappointed they had not made very good progress today. The going was rough, and he had been warned. But still, it was aggravating that their efforts seemed to have been wasted. That night they camped at a rocky outcrop that included a cave. Their campsite overlooked a lush, green steppe. Herds of yaks and ibex roamed the nearby rocks and grazing grounds below. They even saw a few funny-looking long-haired sheep.

Kendall pointed their way. "What are those goat-like things with the large corkscrew horns?"

"Those are *markhor*. The name means something like snake killer. Local superstition has it that the *markhor* can kill a snake and eat it. And then when the cud is being chewed, a foamy stuff comes out of its mouth and falls on the ground. The substance dries and then the local people pick it up and use it on snakebites to extract the poison."

"Gross." She squinted as she peered through the binoculars at the strange-looking goat creature. "It looks like the males and females both have horns."

"Exactly. Except the females have a reddish coat and are smaller and have no mane."

"If you noticed, we're out of the high country now. We've been traveling all day in a scrub forest of mostly junipers, pines, and oak trees. That's why we're seeing different wildlife than before."

"Yeah, I had noticed that. We seem to have lost a lot of elevation today. That's a good thing. We're closer to Mazar-e-Sharif, right?"

"Yes, but we didn't go that far today. It will take us all day tomorrow to get there. We'll have to be extra careful and stay out of plain sight."

She nodded. As they settled in to their camp for the night, Rashid spotted a different kind of manna growing nearby. "Come, look, Kendall. We can eat this." Spying the strange-looking lump of cream-colored stuff with something that looked like nuts on the inside, she wrinkled her nose. "What is it?"

"It's called *shir khesht*. It means 'dried milk.'" He picked up a chunk of the stuff and handed it to Kendall, urging her to eat it.

She slowly put it in her mouth and savored all the different textures and tastes. "Weird! It's kind of gummy and sweet and it melts in your mouth. It has a menthol sensation. And I taste some honey or lemon."

"Exactly. It's apparently supposed to have medicinal qualities."

Kendall thoroughly enjoyed watching the wildlife around them. But they kept their guns at the ready just in case one of the curious jackals or caracals caught their scent. Rashid began the mental preparation for their re-emergence into civilization. "Kendall, you need to dress differently tomorrow. Since we may make Mazar-e-Sharif by nightfall, you should go back to wearing the robes and cover your head completely."

She frowned. During the mountain trek, she had gotten away with loose flowing clothing and a scarf. It suddenly occurred to her that none of the nomadic tribal women they had encountered so far wore the traditional full robes.

Rashid watched her facial expressions as she processed the new information. He put up his hands. "I don't want to hear it. It's for your own good, and will keep us safe and away from scrutiny."

"I get it!" she said, thoroughly irritated at the reproving, but much-earned tone in his voice. She was quiet the rest of the evening as she anticipated their last day on the road. It hadn't been as bad as she'd expected. Taking stock of their encounters along the way, she had to admit that it had not been dull. Though they were on the run, and some of the time had been downright terrifying, she had felt safe around Rashid, and was deeply indebted to him for her safe travels so far. She would miss him and wondered what would become of him. He didn't belong in her world, and yet he had nothing he could call his own to go to. She felt her spirits plummeting at the thought of his future.

Rashid sensed her somber mood and sought to lift her spirits. "Kendall, did you know there is skiing in the lower mountains just above Bamiyan?"

She clapped her hands and laughed. "No way! Too funny. Tell me more."

"Well, it's in the *Koh-e-Baba* mountain range. People stay in rented huts or go on day trips. You can arrange alpine trips across the tops of some of the lower ranges. You can also ski right to the Band-e-Amir Lakes, which are frozen during the winter."

"Wow! I would love to see that."

"The only ski shop and snow guides in the entire country are in Bamiyan."

"Amazing! That's the only place in Afghanistan where you can ski?"

"Yeah, weird isn't it, given the mountainous quality of Afghanistan? Actually, there is skiing just northeast of Afghanistan in the Wakhan corridor. But that land is really between Pakistan, Tajikistan, and China. Up that high, you're in glacier country. But it's still good cross-country skiing, so I've heard."

Kendall was very interested in the conversation and relaxed visibly. But she was not aware of her surroundings, having lost herself in the tales of local legends and mountaineering activities. As she listened enthralled at a particularly gripping story, she felt a slight movement on her shoulder and absentmindedly reached back to scratch the tickling sensation.

Rashid's eyes fixed on her face. In a matter-of-fact but unnatural tone, he said, "Kendall, do not move at all." She instantly felt fear and a prickling sensation at her shoulder. His eyes locked onto hers, willing her to remain calm and still. He slowly rose and leaned toward her.

# CHAPTER FORTY-THREE

It was late in the day when Captain Qadi got the news that the three missing soldiers had been found literally in the jaws of a pack of jackals that had smelled their rotting corpses and dragged them out from under the bushes. As the grisly scene was described to the captain, the dead soldiers were each killed with a single shot to the back of the head. The young soldier on site gave his opinion that the scene didn't make sense. The deceased had to have been lined up, yet ambushed. After the first shot, the other two should've moved. Therefore, he reasoned, the shooter was an expert marksman who got off three precision shots that accurately hit its mark each time.

The captain replayed the scene in his head. For the soldiers to have been lined up, they must have captured one of the fleeing pair. If both had been captured, the soldiers would've surrounded them. So, as Qadi reasoned, while one person was captured, the other must have snuck up behind the soldiers and shot all three, sniper style.

Up until now, General Omar and his troops had never given Kendall any credit for intelligence or the ability to shoot. But Captain Qadi came to the slow realization that Kendall had to have been the shooter. If she had been captured alone, the troops would've been less disciplined and certainly would not have been standing in firing squad formation. If Rashid had been cornered, the troops most certainly would've been on the highest alert and conducted themselves as such.

The captain sighed and picked up the phone to alert General Omar. The older man was enraged. He demanded to know how this could've happened. He was prepared to have Qadi removed from his position and severely punished as an example of the consequences of incompetence, for the rest of the troops. But when the captain relayed how Kendall was the shooter—and a sharpshooter at that—the general realized they had underestimated her. The search teams were badly misinformed and did not have all the relevant information. He now had to factor that in to their current plans and adjust the mission going forward. The young Captain Qadi was praised for getting to the bottom of this shocking news item.

A communiqué went out to all Afghanistan military and the public that Kendall was a deadly killer and should be treated as a high-caliber criminal. General Omar figured that either Kendall learned everything from Rashid or, more likely, was part of the kidnap scenario to get herself into Afghanistan. He advised the troops that she was most likely a CIA operative and was to be taken alive at all cost. Any soldier caught killing her would be severely punished. A separate bounty was now issued for Kendall. Her status had been raised in the eyes of the Afghan military.

General Omar's eyes gleamed at the prospect of personally meting out the punishment to Kendall when she was caught. First, she would be interrogated and tortured to within an inch of her life, and then she would be allowed to recover somewhat, all while she was being abused on a nightly basis. Then she would be shot and finally beheaded. He was salivating at the vision in his head.

The military leader decided that Rashid was a dupe who had fallen for Kendall—the temptress—and would simply be killed as soon as he was found. The young man fleeing for his life was no longer of use or interest to Omar. Rashid's stock had sunk; he was not being given credit for any of the current mess of the last couple weeks, other than to comply with the instructions from others. Kendall was really the mastermind behind all of it. After all, she wasn't an Afghanistan citizen. Whatever her original mission was, Omar thought, Rashid had become bedazzled with her charm and lost his head in the process, allowing such horrible things to happen to the now-deceased president and his family.

General Omar felt better and more confident now that he knew the truth and the mission was refocused. His intense hatred was now directed tenfold at Kendall.

***********

Mickey cajoled his sister, Caitlin, into staying in Maysah Siddra's condo with her for the first month. He had to promise all sorts of things to get her to put her own life on hold for a little while. But it wasn't like she had a job or place of her own yet. She had just finished her Master's program at the nearby University of Washington, was staying with Mickey, and hadn't decided if she was going to get a full-time job or go abroad for a year. Her brother desperately needed her help, and he knew he could trust her to look after Dr. Siddra and be a sort of companion for a little while. Once the pretty young doctor was comfortable moving about the city, improving her English, and maybe even getting a driver's license, then the pressure would be off Caitlin and she could resume her normal routine. She had finally relented and actually looked forward to this high-style living for a bit.

Caitlin was waiting at the condo when Mickey arrived with Maysah Siddra and the Orion admin. She was amazed to see all three chattering animatedly. The doctor looked happy to be free of the constraints of her former Afghanistan society. She was relaxed and peered around with curiosity and wonder. The unit was spacious and looked out over Lake Union. As she walked over to the dramatic floor-to-ceiling picture window in the living room, a De Havilland DHC-3 Otter floatplane glided down onto the choppy lake waters. Maysah was delighted and exclaimed at being able to witness the landing right there in her own living room.

Mickey was relieved and happy this "project" appeared to have been a good decision. The four went to dinner at the rotating restaurant atop the Space Needle, which was only two miles down the road. The doctor was overwhelmed at the warm reception she had received so far. Her new temporary, but maybe long-term, residence, was more than she ever expected. She beamed all the way through dinner as the others pointed out various sights five hundred feet below and off in the distance. The views of Mount Rainier and the Cascade and Olympic ranges were just enough like home to be of great comfort. She knew she had found her new home and would be happy here.

In the morning, the young Afghan doctor was anxious to get started on her new life. She asked to see Paul Fields, so she could personally thank him for all he had done. Caitlin had planned a quiet day to help Maysah acclimate to the city and maybe have a few English lessons. She was fine with the request and worked out the timing with Mickey. He met the two at the Orion building housing the Executive Offices and escorted them to Paul Fields' private reception area. As they looked out the five-story building on the southeast end of Lake Union, Maysah realized she could see this very building from her living room on the west end of the lake.

Fields came out and greeted them. After handshakes and hugs, he ushered them into his private conference room. He asked Mickey to join them. Dr. Siddra was awed at the magnificence of the huge conference room. There were twenty-four plush leather ergonomic chairs around the table. The little group huddled around one end. There was an elevated podium at one end, along with several big screens around the room and a kitchenette off to the side. Even Caitlin was a little more than impressed and intimidated at the high-tech nature of the meeting room. As she looked around, she suspected there was every type of electronic monitoring device that money could buy for this special room. She hoped they weren't bothering the busy CEO too much. With a company like this, and after what he had been through, she supposed he was frantically trying to catch up and yet get his life back to normal as quickly as possible.

Fields' eyes were warm as they settled on Dr. Siddra, sitting to his right. He was in his usual position at one end of the formidable conference table. He reached over and patted Maysah's hand. "May I call you Maysah?"

She nodded, "Oh, yes, Mr. Fields."

"And you should call me Paul." He looked over to Caitlin, "And you too, Caitlin. I can't thank you and Mickey enough for all the work you've done so far and will be doing in the next few months." He turned his attention back to his new protégée and was encouraged by the young doctor's friendly and open expression. He leaned toward her. "Was there something you needed or wanted to ask me?"

She nodded and replied slowly and in a formal tone, "Yes. I'm wondering about the young woman that I looked after in Afghanistan. She and Rashid did not make it onto the military plane." She stopped and was obviously searching for the right words.

Fields jumped in. "You mean the helicopter. That's right. They got left behind. That was terrible."

She cut in anxiously, "Do you know where they are? Are they still alive?"

The CEO exchanged a quick glance with Mickey. "We believe they're alive, which is a miracle unto itself, since the building we were all standing on was bombed seconds after we left. Based on news reports out of Afghanistan, they've been spotted in several places. We're not sure where they are headed—maybe north or west." And then his eyes brightened and he grabbed one of her hands. "Maysah, is there anything you might know that would help us find them or know where they're headed?"

She eagerly nodded. "Yes. I know exactly where Rashid is."

Paul Fields and his Head of Security looked at each other, stunned at the revelation. At the same time, they both said, "Where?"

She looked around and frowned. "I need a computer, so I can access my email account."

Mickey quickly left to find an available laptop. Fields' mind raced at the thought that they just might be able to locate Kendall and Rashid in the very near future. He was anxious to ask more questions, but knew he needed to wait for Mickey to return. As soon as the latter walked through the door with the laptop and necessary accessories, Fields urged Maysah for more information. "How do you know where he is?"

"He has an electronic chip in his lower back. I did it myself for the whole Shazeb family at the order of President Shazeb. He was worried his family would be kidnapped, and was paranoid they wouldn't be found. So, he had me insert the chips about two years ago. I have Rashid's coordinates saved in a file on my email account. I used one of those free email accounts that was not affiliated with any of the Afghanistan software or servers."

"Weren't you afraid of getting caught by President Shazeb?"

"I was caught by Saaqib during one of his crazy audits. Rashid happened to speak to him first and convinced him this was a good idea to ensure the data would never be lost. He even talked him into using the story that if his father—the president—ever found out, he should say it was his idea for security reasons. That his father would think he was brilliant." With eyes wide, she looked at Fields and Mickey, "As far as I know, Saaqib never said anything to anyone else."

The laptop was booted up, and they crowded around the young doctor as she worked her way through the commands ... sometimes needing help with the characters or key strokes of the unfamiliar keyboard. Finally, she opened her free email account, and found the folder. There was one email that contained the coordinating numbers and a barcode image after each name. The CEO quickly called his admin and asked her to bring him a barcode reader and a handheld GPS. Both were commonplace these days.

Mickey couldn't help himself. "I get the paranoia mentality of President Shazeb, and it's quite the norm in the U.S. now to be chipped at birth. But why would Rashid have been included? He wasn't one of the members of the family."

"Because the president had virtually raised him, trusted him, and counted on him to keep the boys—his peers—in line. You just don't realize how much the boys hated each other and how much the president relied on Rashid. The competition for their father's love and admiration was huge, especially since the president was so obvious in his preference for the younger son. If it weren't for the lack of a blood tie, my guess is that Rashid would have been the chosen successor."

Mickey shook his head and sighed. "I guess I'll just never understand it."

After another fifteen minutes and a much-needed coffee break, the laptop was connected to the closest big screen. The peripheral devices were plugged in, and soon they were inputting the coordinates. Just to be on the safe side and away from prying eyes, Mickey rose and closed the blinds at the main window along the interior hallway.

As the image appeared on the big screen, they watched the satellite view come into focus and zero in on a point just outside of Mazar-e-Sharif. Fields, Mickey, and Caitlin let out a whoop of joy. They couldn't believe it was that easy. Fields was the most technical savvy of the group and took over at the laptop. He continued to refocus the image to bring it closer into view. When he got to a point where the land was visible around the bolded dot, Maysah confirmed the larger dot was Rashid. The smaller dot next to him was another person ... most likely Kendall.

Fields took the image a little further out and was able to tell they were near a meadow, with scrub brush and rock faces all around them. He was anxious when he saw lots of dots to the east and west. The fleeing couple seemed to be surrounded by other people. He assumed the people were soldiers. He pointed at the other dots and looked at Maysah for confirmation, saying, "Soldiers?"

She shook her head. "No. The dots are concentrated in bunches and are actually miles away from Rashid. My guess is that these are various nomadic tribes. If you look at their locations, they all seem to be in pasture lands, and are evenly spread out." He nodded. Then she frowned and pointed to several tiny clusters of dots. "Those are soldiers. You can tell they're on the move. This group over here is walking single file. See? The dots are all in a line. They must be on a trail."

It was a little unnerving knowing the duo was surrounded by troops, but the good news was that none were within five miles of them on any side. Fields was frustrated that he didn't know the landmarks or cities around the area. He turned to the doctor, "Where are they headed?"

"It looks like Mazar-e-Sharif. That's close to the Uzbekistan border. They must be hoping to cross there."

Fields was torn. He needed the help of the U.S. government now, but couldn't tell them how he knew this information. The authorities would surely come and get Maysah as a material witness. He didn't want to lose her. Not after all the work he and his staff had done. He also didn't want Mickey and Maysah sitting there when he called his frat buddy, Frank Reynolds, at the NSA. Mickey didn't know about *Prophecy*, Frank Reynolds, or Daniel Blumfeld's involvement.

He sat back as his mind raced to figure out in what direction he should go first, and who should be privy to the information. Finally, he casually asked Maysah if there was anything else he needed to know. She shook her head, and he thanked her profusely for the information. He assured her that he had government contacts and hoped to arrange for a rescue in the next twenty-four hours, thanks to her. The doctor was happy she could assist. Fields nodded at Mickey, and the latter rose and showed the women out. They were given strict instructions that they were to stay close to Caitlin's cell phone and not venture out of the city for the next couple days. If they were needed, they should come back to the Orion offices at once. Fields knew he might need the doctor to point out various landmarks.

Then he told Mickey that he was going to make a few phone calls, and as soon as he needed his head of security's help, he would call him. Mickey nodded and returned to his office. Sometimes, especially since his boss's return, he felt that his superior was holding out on him ... almost like he was harboring a secret. He couldn't quite put his finger on it, but sensed that he wasn't being told everything and didn't have all the facts. He knew the CEO had a wide range of friends, mostly in the upper echelon of society. Mickey figured a senator or two would be contacted with cryptic information on how to locate the missing American citizen and her companion. He just didn't understand why the need for privacy or the unmistakable feeling that behind-the-scene maneuverings were in the works. In fact, the more he thought about it, he had the distinct feeling it involved something highly illegal. He told himself that he didn't want to know if his boss was up to something illicit. That at the end of the day, if it brought Kendall back safe and sound, then he certainly wouldn't ask questions. He patiently waited in his office to be summoned by Fields.

The first person the CEO called was Daniel. The latter was very happy to hear they were able to pinpoint Kendall's location in Afghanistan. Fields urged him to check and re-check the Orion network to ensure the Israelis couldn't stream the new data. This would be very bad for the pair on the run. After he had shored up the Orion system, Daniel was then to specifically watch the Israelis and Afghanistan for any new revelation of sightings and strategic military plans ... most likely focused on Mazar-e-Sharif. They rang off, and then the technical wunderkind set about building two more levels of sophisticated electronic shields to block any possible snooping by Israel ... or any other entity, for that matter.

After hanging up with Blumfeld, Fields phoned Frank Reynolds at the NSA. It was the end of his day, and he was winding down and about to meet some buddies at the local pub for beer and pizza. He scowled when he saw the caller I.D. display. He was exhausted from the activities of the last couple months, and he really needed some down time to kick back and relax. He was happy that his frat buddy was okay, but all of this sneaking around from his own co-workers and bosses was fraying his nerves. He looked at the flashing phone line again, sighed, and picked up his headset, telling himself that it was only a call for a status report. Since he didn't have anything new to report and nothing had changed since the last conversation, this call would be quick.

Before Reynolds could even say hello, a stressed and hyper Fields yelled out, "Frank, I know where they are!"

The NSA Agent was instantly energized. "What? How?"

"Never mind how. They're just outside of Mazar-e-Sharif. Do you think you can pull some strings and have a helicopter and a seal team or two swoop in there and collect the two?"

"I can buy time with an anonymous source angle. But I'll have to provide more precise information as to their location." There was no response from Fields, who was madly processing the request and deciding the best course of action. "Paul, you there?"

"Yes. I've come in to some knowledge about Rashid. He has a tracking chip implant. You can locate him via GPS."

"No shit! Awesome! Give me the information, so I can see it for myself." His dinner plans now long forgotten, Frank used the tricked-out electronic devices in his computer to download the image and coordinates from Fields, who sent the information via scrambled code. Within five minutes, the NSA agent could see the large dot representing Rashid. He was beside himself. "Paul, that's, that's so incredible!"

"I know. I'm pretty stoked too! What can you do with it? I mean, I can call some Senators, but that's several layers from where we need to be. Can you get this to the right people without revealing anything about me or Orion?"

"Now that I have the chip info, damn right I can. In fact, I'd be a fool to mention your name. I'm going to be a hero!"

Fields was a little alarmed but chuckled. "Now, Frank, don't get ahead of yourself. You're going to be pumped for information, so be prepared for an explanation that reveals nothing."

"No problem! I already know how I'm going to handle it."

The CEO was suspicious. "How?"

"Paul, that's classified! The U.S. intelligence community is not without its own electronic toys. We've come a long way in the last few years. I can actually locate Kendall now, so long as I'm within ten miles of her location."

"Oh my God, really? Why weren't you doing that before?"

"Obvious, Paul! I didn't know the exact area where she was. I've seen the map of Mazar-e-Sharif. It's not that large of a city. It might be the fourth largest city in Afghanistan, but there are less than half a million people. From the look of their current location, they should reach the city tomorrow. The city is known for the religious shrine called the "Blue Mosque." So, tomorrow morning when I get into the office, it'll be their evening. They should have found a place to hunker down for the night. I'll zero in on them then. Let's just hope nothing happens in the next fifteen hours. Paul, I'm going to call my military contacts right now and at least get some troops in to the old Uzbekistan base."

"Perfect!"

"Well, not really. It'll be tricky at best, since the U.S. pulled all its troops out years ago. The political relationship is stable and friendly. But remember they threw us out of the country. I'm hoping the Uzbeks will allow us to use the old base for a one-time military emergency. If we set the ball in motion now, we just might have approval within a day or two."

"It's too bad we can't do what the Israelis did and come in from the Arabian Sea."

"No way will that work. We'd have to take out the Afghan government computer network which has just come back on line. They're on high alert. We'd have to go in there with guns blazing. We'd end up blowing things up and shooting people ... all for one hostage? I don't think so, Paul. It's got to be from the north."

"Whatever! Make your phone calls. Later!"

They rang off and Fields felt jittery from all the events of the day. He didn't usually drink during the day, but pulled out his rare bottle of *Loch Dhu* single malt black Scotch Whiskey. He poured himself a glass and then swung his chair around to savor the distinct aromas and complex flavors while he looked out the window across Lake Union. He was delighted at the spectacle of a forty-foot *Bermuda sloop* heading away from the west side marina. Fields picked up his binoculars and watched spellbound as the captain furiously worked the rigging to set the mainsail.

The contented CEO could just feel that Kendall would be rescued within days. The anticipation was killing him, but the immense satisfaction that would come from knowing his part in the successful extraction was ten times greater than any business deal he had ever fought over and won.

The cloudy gray summer day did nothing to dampen his spirits.

As North America slept and Afghanistan awoke, there was a sudden imperceptible change in the dynamics of the single-minded pursuit. The bolded dot representing the whereabouts of Rashid Sharif flickered and went dark.

# CHAPTER FORTY-FOUR

Out of the corner of her eye, Kendall caught the first glance at a large hairy looking thing on her shoulder. The creature's two lateral *chelicerae* were in a chomping motion. She felt a huge scream bubble up to the surface when Rashid calmly flicked it off her shoulder. The twitching thing landed to the side of her, stunned. As she quickly turned her head to look, she about fainted at the sight of the whole body. The bizarre-looking arachnid was over six inches long. Rashid grabbed the closest rock and smashed it on top of the hideous thing. He peered over at Kendall, as she wasn't making a sound.

"Wha-wha-what was that?" she stuttered.

"A camel spider. It's really not as bad as it looks. Yeah, the bite will hurt, but it's not poisonous."

Her eyes were wide with fear. "That thing is a spider?"

"Uh-huh. It's actually more like a scorpion. But it's in the spider family. It can run ten miles an hour. Isn't that incredible?"

"You're not helping, Rashid. I'm never going to sleep tonight."

"Well, if it makes you feel any better, if there's another around here, it will eat all the insects and rodents. We'll be safer. It even eats small birds."

"Wonderful! I'm glad I don't have a baby."

"Oh, it's not that bad. No one's ever died from a camel spider bite. It just looks particularly scary."

In fact, she slept soundly that night. Rashid didn't have the heart to tell her that things could get very hairy for them in the next twenty-four hours. They were either going to find their way out of Afghanistan via Mazar-e-Sharif, or they'd end up dead. His heart was heavy as he worried about the next couple days. At least Kendall would be able to blend right in by using her full-length *chador*. It would be hot and annoying, and he was sure he would hear about it from an irritated Kendall. But if it kept her safe it was well worth it.

In the morning, they took quick baths in the nearby stream. Rashid figured this would be the last chance to wash up before they fled Afghanistan for good.

They loaded their possessions onto Babar for the last time and trudged off in a northerly direction. Kendall couldn't understand why she felt so apprehensive and maybe even a little sad. She should be excited that their journey was coming to an end, but for some unknown reason that she could think of, she wasn't.

They stopped for an hour at midday, and Rashid pointed out a family of *caracal* a few hundred yards away. The Persian lynx mother and her babies were a beautiful reddish brown color. The two white spots above each eye were very dramatic. But Kendall finally had enough of witnessing the brutality of nature when the mother *caracal* took off after a fawn and quickly returned with the dead baby in her mouth ... legs dangling like small sticks.

Kendall urged them on and didn't utter a complaint as her heavy garment twisted about her legs. As they approached the outskirts of Mazar-e-Sharif, Rashid took a look through the binoculars. He frowned and muttered to himself.

"Rashid, what's wrong? Are there soldiers?"

"Yeah, everywhere. We're going to have to enter through a side route."

He wasn't totally familiar with the layout of the city, and hated not being prepared for the awaiting troops. Fortunately, there was a celebration going on. The city held a festive atmosphere, with more people on the street than usual. Suddenly there was a commotion on the east side of the city. There was a particularly heated and physical game of *buzkashi* going on. It had turned violent, and a fight had broken out between the players and the spectators. The soldiers, always looking for an excuse for physical gamesmanship, saw this as an opportunity to let off a little steam and break a few bones in the process. They would teach these locals how to behave and to respect the law.

This unexpected diversion allowed Rashid and Kendall to slip into the city at dusk from the west side. They walked a few blocks and came upon a crumbling mud-brick structure with seven-foot-high walls and no roof or door. It had obviously been abandoned some time ago, and was in a complete state of disrepair. Rashid ushered Kendall and Babar into the interior of the structure, which was separated into several rooms. As he unloaded their things from Babar, a wizened old man with white-gray hair and a long beard appeared in the doorway. Rashid rapidly engaged him in a discussion in *Dari* ... the most common language spoken in Mazar-e-Sharif. He managed to convince the man that he and his young wife had just arrived from Herat. They had no money and were going to be looking for work the next day.

Rashid knew that Babar was very valuable. He pointed out that Babar was their only asset. He asked the elder if he could exchange a week's stay for Babar. The old man couldn't believe his fortune. He agreed, and not only let them stay there, but brought them a hot meal. Kendall felt sick to her stomach when Babar was led away. She'd become very fond of him. Even the funny noises he made. She'd miss him.

Rashid could see the expression on her face. "Kendall, he'll be fine. He basically saved our lives. The *chowkider* thinks we're the most foolish young people he's met in a long time. I'm sure he feels guilty that he's taken advantage of us."

"What did you call him?"

"He's a *chowkider* ... a caretaker. Apparently, he checks on this place every day for precisely the reason we're here. A lot of people try to move in here." He grinned, "Well, we just rented it for a week."

In the morning, the two rose early. Rashid knew of an Internet café where they could use a computer. He wanted to check the news and look for the best way to exit the country. He was feeling relieved they didn't have Babar with them any longer. The soldiers were most likely looking for two people and a camel. Now, with Kendall fully covered, she could walk freely around the city. He was the one who needed to stay out of sight.

He was very glad he remembered the computer chip that had been inserted in his back just under the skin a few years ago. It had taken some convincing for Kendall to agree to remove it yesterday morning. But there wasn't much blood, and the deed was done. He took a rock and smashed it. He didn't think the records could be recovered from the Afghan government's computers, and even if they were, the late President Shazeb had not exactly been communicative about his paranoia that his family might be kidnapped.

Kendall and Rashid walked through the open market. At one stall, Kendall asked if they could stop and buy some fresh fruit. They walked a few streets further and encountered the Internet café. They weren't sure how helpful it would be, but both got on separate terminals, with Rashid helping Kendall maneuver through the Afghan keyboard. He kept looking around and was very worried the soldiers would check the café. They agreed to stay for only twenty minutes so as not to raise any suspicions. Kendall didn't know who to send a message to that could help them here. She took a chance and sent an email to the only person who might possibly understand what she was going through ... Paul Fields. She knew he had an admin who monitored his emails. She hoped there wouldn't be too much of a delay. She made it short and to the point.

Paul, Need help. In Mazar-e-Sharif with R. K

When she looked up, the proprietor was staring intently at her. Of course, he couldn't see her eyes or face under her full head cover. She nudged Rashid's elbow and hissed that the café owner appeared to be monitoring their emails and maybe even keystrokes. By now, the shopkeeper was interested in both of them. As he picked up the phone, Rashid jumped up and ran to the front desk. He grabbed the receiver from the man and yanked the phone line right out of the wall. The proprietor backed up against the wall, terrified he was about to be shot. With that, Rashid and Kendall burst out of the café and zigzagged their way back to the mosque ruins.

While Kendall would be fine, he knew he had to change his appearance. He had Kendall cut his beard as close to his face as possible. The only implement he had was an old, crude, rusty, dull scissor. Under his breath, he said a little prayer for steady hands for Kendall. Afterwards, he changed his clothes to the pajama-like garment and wore the *Kufi* on his head and sandals on his feet. Kendall scrutinized his new look and decided he would escape notice.

When the *chowkider* came by to check on them, he sensed they were in trouble. He was a kindly soul, and Rashid was afraid the old man would be severely punished or even killed if he was caught helping them. Rashid took a chance and explained their predicament in somewhat cryptic terms. He said they needed a way into Uzbekistan and didn't have the proper documentation. The caretaker, a romantic, decided this young couple had run away to marry, and were hiding from their families. He remembered the days long ago when he was in love and forbidden from marrying a girl from the wrong tribe. His heart was broken and though he vowed to make it happen, her family moved away and he never saw her again. Just remembering that heartbreak brought tears to his eyes. He was determined to help this poor young couple. He even thought that maybe they hadn't married yet. How scandalous, he thought, but terribly romantic.

He told Rashid that he knew of a "safe house" where they could arrange travel into Uzbekistan ... probably via the upgraded rail system. He assured them he would go at once and speak with the owner.

Kendall fretted the whole time he was gone. She paced the dirty floor of one room after another. Finally, she stopped in front of Rashid. "I don't see why we couldn't just walk across the border during night time."

He laughed and sadly shook his head. "First, there's no cover or place to hide. The land from here to the border—some thirty-five miles—is completely flat. It's a steppe ... a grass-covered plain. That's a long way out in the open. Even Omar's troops know we wouldn't be that foolish.

The *chowkider* was back within an hour. He had a wide grin on his face. He explained the arrangement, and they walked to within fifty yards of the normal-looking inauspicious mud-brick house. Rashid insisted on leaving Kendall at the market to watch from afar while he checked things out in the "safe house."

The two men disappeared inside the little house while Kendall casually perused the display items at a tourist kiosk just down the way. As she gently stroked a lovely polished lapis necklace, there was a huge blast that knocked her flat.

She scrambled to her feet and turned to look at the little house down the road. It was gone. All that remained was dust and debris that settled all around them. She suddenly realized that someone was screaming. It was her! People rushed to her and asked if she was okay. She had no idea what they were saying. She was scared and alone now. She pushed the well-meaning arms away and ran for her life. In the frantic chaos and aftermath of the explosion, no one noticed the woman running down the street and into the noble shrine and famous *Blue Mosque*.

She didn't even know how she got there. She seemed to have been propelled in that direction. As she approached the famed *Blue Mosque* in the center of the city, Kendall noticed there was a crowd of women in the courtyard. She realized she could easily blend in. So, she joined the throngs of females. She didn't know it was Wednesday ... ladies day at the *Blue Mosque*. There were many groups of women huddled around picnic lunches. Kendall sat on a stone bench and stared at the hundreds of white pigeons and the beautiful blue mosaic tiles that comprised the mosque's exterior.

Her mind was racing, but most of all, she was in shock. Rashid was dead. Her Rashid, who she had grown close to and literally depended on for her very survival. What was she going to do? She was too afraid to go back to the old mosque where their possessions were. But she had no choice. She knew that Rashid had money in the bags. If she could at least locate some of his *Afghani*, she would be able to buy food and maybe even go to a hotel. She no longer cared if she was caught. She was tired of running, sickened by all the death and brutality, and, most of all, heartsick that Rashid was gone. She sat on the bench by herself for an hour.

She sobbed uncontrollably. Finally, there were no more tears. There was movement all around her. The women were leaving *en masse*, and men were entering the courtyard. She looked around, and no one paid attention to her. She got up and realized she was extremely hot and parched. She slowly and cautiously shuffled her way back to the mosque ruins. She circled it three times before she had the courage to go inside. Even then, her movements were tentative as she poked her head inside the familiar dingy walls.

Kendall swiftly made her way to their belongings, and she rummaged through Rashid's things, trying to remember where he stashed his *Afghani*. She found it in several pockets and quickly stuffed it into her pockets. She had a flat purse-like muslin pouch strapped onto her front. It easily fit behind the cumbersome robes. She stuffed as much *Afghani* as she could into the small bag. Lastly, she took one of their travel bags and filled it with a few items of clothing, some food, a knife, and the handgun and extra ammunition. She slung one of the water bags over her shoulder and, carrying a blanket, headed to the opening of the mosque.

Her head was clearer now that she'd been forced to focus on her task at hand and organize their belongings into what could be taken and what would be left behind. As she reached the doorway, she stepped out into the bright sun. Something metallic reflected in her eye and temporarily blinded her. She blinked and dropped her goods.

She was surrounded by at least ten soldiers ... each with his automatic weapon trained on her.

# CHAPTER FORTY-FIVE

NSA Agent Frank Reynolds was shocked when he checked on the coordinates signaling Rashid's position upon his arrival at the office first thing in the morning. There was no tell-tale sign of the young Afghan on the GPS indicator. He rebooted his system several times. It simply didn't make sense. It wasn't the worst thing that could happen, but it was frustrating. He called Fields' office number and left a voice mail. He expected the call back in a few hours. In the meantime, he got busy and made a few calls to his contacts at the State Department and the U.S. Navy. He had started the ball rolling last night, but it was so late in the day yesterday when he made the initial phone calls, that most of his calls had gone to voice mail.

He had one other trick up his sleeve ... facial recognition using the latest in thermal imaging via satellite. Using a picture of Kendall Radcliffe, he set the coordinates as the area around Mazar-e-Sharif. Once the satellite found her, he could manipulate the picture to see the surrounding area and people. As the satellite scanned the faces around the city, he went to get some coffee and a danish. When he returned an hour later, his phone was blinking.

***********

Paul Fields was in the office particularly early on Wednesday. He was anxious to do something with the information Maysah Siddra had shown them. He booted up his computer and quickly programmed in the scan for Rashid. He, too, was taken aback when the results came back with no data matching the criteria. He wondered what the hell Reynolds had done. He even imagined that the U.S. accidentally bombed Rashid and Kendall instead of rescuing them.

As he was sitting in front of his terminal, his admin hurried in. He looked up at the sudden motion in his doorway.

"Mr. Fields, Uh, Paul. You've received an email from Kendall Radcliffe's personal email account."

He was stunned at first, trying to comprehend what the stuttering girl was saying. "What? From her personal account? Hmm, strange." Then he realized that of course any communication would not come from within the Orion network. If Kendall managed to find a computer, she'd have to use a personal account from one of those free services.

He jumped out of the chair and was by the admin's side in two seconds. He grabbed the printed document from her hand in such a violent way that it sent her scurrying out of his office in fear. The CEO scanned the cryptic message and was relieved they had made it to Mazar-e-Sharif. They were so close to the Uzbekistan border now. He just knew it was all going to work out fine. Now, if his frat buddy, Frank, could just set the rescue details in motion, they might actually get out alive.

There was a nagging doubt that the message was a hoax. He immediately called Daniel, who walked him through the IP address within the header details at the top of the printed email message. Daniel checked on the sender information and confirmed that it had originated from Mazar-e-Sharif. Fields was relieved. The message had to be authentic. He was in the middle of congratulating himself when the computer whiz kid interrupted him.

"Paul, there's bad news. It looks like Rashid is dead. He went into a building known for arranging back door exits from Afghanistan. While there, the building was blown up."

"Shit! I can't believe it! He made it this far only to lose on the last lap?"

"That's not all."

The CEO gulped his coffee and instantly burned his throat. "Damn! What else? Where's Kendall? Is she still alive?" He was sitting down now, expecting the worst.

"She escaped the initial blast but was found by the soldiers later in the day. She's been taken to a military site on the outskirts of Mazar-e-Sharif. General Omar will be flown there in the morning and will decide her fate then."

"Oh, God. I don't know what would be worse. Being blown up in that building, like Rashid, or having General Omar decide your fate." Fields paused, thinking back to the days when he saw the general on a daily basis. "Daniel, I can't begin to describe him. He's a thug. Scary, brutal, and sadistic. He thirsts for revenge and revels in the punishment. I can't even imagine what he will do to her."

"Well, it's nighttime there now, so we have about twenty hours to make something happen."

"Thanks, Daniel. Keep me posted."

Fields sat back in his chair and again was thankful for *Prophecy*. It had allowed Daniel to keep tabs on the Afghanistan military. Without that, they would never have known what happened to Rashid, and that Kendall had been caught and where they were holding her. He would never feel guilty again for masterminding the wonder tool, he told himself. And then that little voice in his head followed it up with, *"So long as it's only used for good."*

His phone rang. It was Frank Reynolds, who didn't even wait for the CEO to announce himself. He blurted out, "That guy—Rashid Sharif—is dead! His embedded chip no longer works. If they blew him up, maybe that's why it isn't pinging anymore."

"Who the fuck cares why it doesn't work, Frank?" Fields felt like Reynolds was stalling. "Is that the only reason you called me ... to tell me that he was dead?"

The NSA Agent affected a more normal tone. "Of course, not, Paul. I-uh. Oh shit! Your girl's been captured!"

"Uh-huh."

"What? You already know this, Paul?"

"I've got the same resources as you, Frank, remember?"

"Well, yes, but I thought you only used it for company business, not to gather military intelligence? That's my job!"

"Desperate times, Frank!" There was a pause while both men calmed down. Fields, having more of a vested interest, spoke first. "Frank, talk to me! What's being done to help Kendall?"

"I've engaged the right people and am waiting for word that a plan is being finalized as we speak."

"Okay, good! But you know it's nighttime in Afghanistan? That bastard, Omar, will have her tortured and killed by the end of the day tomorrow. You know he will!"

"We're watching now, Paul. We can see her. She's fine so far."

"You can see her? How?"

"That's classified, Paul. Just trust me!"

The CEO was incredulous. "After all that we've exchanged over the years, you won't tell me?"

"Not over the phone, Paul."

*Geez,* Fields thought. This spying has gotten way out of hand. Since they routinely spied on whoever they wanted to whenever, now they were paranoid that they, in turn, were being listened to and their communications monitored. He was back to despising *Prophecy*.

Reynolds was pleading with him. "Paul, please trust me that everything that can be done is being done. This whole thing should be resolved within forty-eight hours."

"Yeah, if she survives. Those bastards! I can't believe they killed Rashid! He was a decent man and didn't deserve this. He saved our lives and took a big risk."

"I know, Paul. Just hang on another day, and hopefully we'll have some good news."

"I'm holding you to that, Frank! Later!"

After hanging up, Frank Reynolds felt sick to his stomach. He hadn't the heart to tell his frat buddy that his military contacts flatly refused to send in a rescue team. The final word was that she wasn't a high-enough-value asset to the U.S. to risk the ensuing international incident that would surely result from an unauthorized incursion into Afghanistan's airspace, not to mention Uzbekistan, whose military base would need to be used to stage the mission. With a heavy heart, the NSA Agent turned off his office light and headed home for a good stiff drink ... or two.

# CHAPTER FORTY-SIX

KENDALL LAY ON THE HARD stone floor at the 209th Corp of the Afghan National Army base. It was cold last night, and she couldn't sleep. She knew it was all going to be over soon, one way or another. She didn't much care either way. Rashid was gone now, and maybe she'd be joining him soon. She regretted that they never got to take their relationship to the next level. He was always so focused on the next step in his plan. He never allowed himself to stop and relax or enjoy his surroundings. She allowed that he seemed to have enjoyed the fishing and the evenings around the campfire. Looking back on the long trip, she wished she could have enjoyed it more too. But the constant threat of capture, the savagery of the desert lands, unfamiliar animals, and the sad people with their throwback lives was a constant source of stress that had ultimately gotten the best of her.

She wished she could have introduced Rashid to her world. Her Seattle ... where she skied in the winter and boated in the summer. She never missed Opening Day of boating season the first Saturday in May. This year she had gotten to join the procession of boats through the Montlake Cut that joined Lake Union to Lake Washington. She had been on her friend's sailboat. It was thrilling as they sailed east under the Montlake Bridge. They had to stay exactly in the middle of the channel, because their masthead just barely cleared the bridge structure overhead. The thousands of spectators who lined the shore on both sides and along the bridge above them cheered and roared as the famed University of Washington rowing teams led the way.

Kendall told herself that Rashid would never have liked it. There were too many people and too much frivolity. Life had been so serious to him, and he probably would have hated all the water. Salt water and fresh water everywhere. She felt worse, and realized it was because she was already thinking of him in the past tense. The other important person in her life, her dear mother, had also apparently died while she was away. Yes, people were dying all around her, including the innocent smiling boy, Poya. And the one she thought was the love of her life, Jeremy, who she was prepared to spend the rest of her life with, had turned his back on her in the name of money ... and his mother. Just like that, it was all gone.

She hoped the end would be quick, like Rashid's. But she resolved to go down fighting. They wouldn't take her spirit. She said a quick prayer for her mother and Rashid, but dismissed the memory of Jeremy Levy as nothing more than an aberration in her life.

In the cold morning light, the soldiers actually let her have a bathroom to herself, where she was allowed to take a shower. They provided her with clean women's attire—robes and head scarf—and said something about dying before Allah and the need to be cleansed in body and spirit. She was grateful for the shower and felt like a new person. They brought her a bit of food, and she could hardly choke it down.

General Omar arrived mid-morning and came right over to see her. His eyes glinted with cruelty and something she couldn't identify. But it caused her to back away from him. He made her stand in the middle of the courtyard while he walked around her. Weapons were pointed at her from every angle. She wondered if she would be shot right there in the military compound.

She'd been standing in the hot sun for an hour with nothing to drink when there began a slow rumbling sound. Everyone looked around and then at General Omar. Thinking they were about to be overrun, he ordered everyone to secure the doors. As the thundering grew louder and the ground began to shake, it was clear this was an earthquake. It was a sizable temblor with the epicenter just outside Mazar-e-Sharif. Because it was shallow, the ground shook more violently than usual. One of the mud-brick walls of the military base gave way.

Kendall was standing in the most perfect place in the center of the courtyard. The heavy stone walls came down on top of the soldiers. Dust and debris swirled everywhere. Omar, who was very superstitious, was sure that Allah was angry that Kendall was still alive. But right now, he needed his troops to regroup and take stock of the casualties. He knew that the citizens would need his help in rescuing trapped citizens, clearing water lines, and moving the injured to the local hospital.

He grabbed Kendall and roughly pushed her into the closest cell. The ground continued to shake, and she couldn't believe she was now going to die in an earthquake. The irony didn't escape her. As she fell onto the hard ground, she watched curiously as the soldiers ran about. Most of them left the compound and headed out to the *Blue Mosque* first to see how bad the damage was. Some of the structure was first built around the twelfth century and was destroyed and refurbished many times over the years due to earthquakes, battles, and expansion at the sacred site.

Suddenly the lights went off. The power grid had been compromised ... again. As the ground took its last shake, Kendall could feel the outside wall on which she was leaning, giving way. She quickly scrambled to the interior wall just as the outer wall crumbled down onto the spot where she had been sitting. She couldn't believe her luck. She was now looking at daylight and people scurrying all around her. There was chaos, shouting, and wailing. No one paid attention to the lone figure in the dark cell.

She made her way to the park at the *Blue Mosque*. Hundreds of people had gathered there for safety in the wide-open space yet within the confines of the compound. Kendall could not believe it when the *muezzin* assigned to call the faithful to the *Zuhr*—or early afternoon prayer—began their unisoned chant from the four corner minarets of the *Shrine of Hazarat Ali* or the *Blue Mosque*. Since they obviously did not have the benefit of audio amplification, they yelled out in their own voices which carried over the carnage below them. The melodious chanting was strained but beautiful over the din of the chaos. Everywhere, people stopped to pray right where they were. It brought tears to Kendall's eyes, knowing that even with the pain and uncertainty the city's residents were feeling, they were pausing in their misery to give thanks and praise to their God.

She huddled in the mass of people and became part of the homeless seeking shelter. General Omar forgot all about her for hours. He managed to receive word that the United Nations and the nearby countries were gearing up to send charter flights bringing supplies and emergency provisions. By early evening, those flights began to land at the badly damaged Mazar-e-Sharif Airport.

By evening, General Omar remembered Kendall and went back to the Afghan National Army Base. He was sickened at the sight of the crumbled wall and the empty cell. Kendall was nowhere to be found. But he wasn't too worried, as there was no place for her to go. He figured that once order was restored, she would stand out from the locals. Still, it irritated the hell out of him. As if he didn't have enough to worry about!

The relief missions by air and overland by transport trucks came and went all evening long. The trains were no longer running because of the damage to the rails. Border crossing was not as strict, to let supplies in and people traveling to their relatives in the neighboring countries out.

In the midst of the airport landings, a sturdy-looking C-130 Hercules landed and taxied to a corner of the rough and broken tarmac. Once the rear cargo hold was opened, pallets of supplies were rolled out to the huge opening and lowered to the ground via hydraulic lift. The supplies were loaded onto trucks, and the troops transporting the goods drove into the city to begin distributing the much needed water, food, and blankets.

When Kendall caught sight of the U.N. armbands and helmets, she made her way to the crowd of people pressing forward for a handout. As soon as she heard English being spoken, she ran up to the female volunteer and pulled on her sleeve. "Hello, Miss. My name is Kendall Radcliffe. I was kidnapped and taken prisoner with Paul Fields and Glenn Carson months ago. They were rescued, and I got left behind. Please help me! I've just escaped from the soldiers."

The young English-speaking soldier was taken aback. She looked around and saw that no one was watching, and quickly motioned Kendall to climb into the cab of the truck up front and hunker down on the floor boards. The young soldier took off her helmet with the U.N. insignia and handed it to her. Then went right back to distributing water. When the truck was empty of supplies, the driver and young female soldier closed the doors, climbed into the cab, and began to drive away. They had no idea where the young woman went, and thought she might have disappeared into the crowd of people. The female soldier even speculated that she had imagined the whole bizarre encounter.

They had gotten about half-way back to the airport when their truck was suddenly overtaken by Afghan troops. The angry-looking general who marched up to their truck demanded they open the back door. They exchanged looks and got out to accommodate the general's wishes. His troops climbed up into the back of the truck, inspected the interior, and then jumped out. The general opened the driver's door and looked into the cab. There was nothing suspicious there, so he allowed them to drive on.

As soon as the soldier and her driver reached the C-130, they scanned the surrounding area and then looked behind the seats of the truck. They hadn't told Kendall to hide there, but somehow she knew to move from the floorboard in the front seat to the small area behind the bench seat. They couldn't believe she had wedged her body sidewise so as to fit in the narrow pocket of space. While one helped her out of the cab, the other one yanked her head scarf off. She walked between them and up the ramp into the C-130.

They were on their way within thirty minutes, just biding their time awaiting clearance to take off. There were extra clothes on board, and Kendall swiftly changed out of the Afghan women's clothes and into jeans and a t-shirt, with a baseball cap shoved on her head.

Finally, they were cleared for takeoff. As they taxied down the runway, Kendall held her breath, and slowly let it out when the plane went airborne. On the short flight to the Uzbekistan base, Kendall explained her situation and how she came to be in Mazar-e-Sharif. The C-130 crew radioed back to base with the news that they had an extra person on the return flight. That became a problem when they landed. The manifest showed ten people outbound, yet they returned with eleven.

The Uzbek officer at the base was thoroughly irritated. It had been a long and trying day as several nations requested use of their base to assemble and distribute relief supplies into Mazar-e-Sharif. Complicating things was that Kendall had no paperwork with her. The base officer had no idea what to do. He was too busy to deal with this issue. The head of the U.N. mission—who just happened to be an American—quickly sized up the situation and kindly suggested that in the stress and chaos of the flight out, she got overlooked somehow. He offered that she couldn't possibly have come from Mazar-e-Sharif on her own. She was dressed in western garb and would never have been allowed to look like that there. The Uzbek officer agreed. The U.N. leader apologized profusely for having incorrect numbers and improper documentation, but offered that this is what happens during emergencies. Protocol and organization were the first casualties.

They all laughed, and the U.N. team was allowed to proceed. Within an hour, Kendall flew out on a helicopter that rendezvoused with a carrier in the Gulf of Oman. When she landed on the American ship, she stepped off onto the carrier's deck and sank to her knees in sheer relief. She was safe. Her journey was over, and she was going home.

The commander, who had a couple hours' warning, had advised Washington, DC by the time she arrived on board the carrier. Because she had no documentation on her, there was a flurry of passport photos and driver's license pictures sent electronically to and from the ship.

Frank Reynolds got the news through internal channels at the end of his day. He quickly called Fields. The latter knew that time was running out. He was beginning to despair that they wouldn't be able to rescue Kendall. His Caller I.D. showed Reynolds' number. He fumbled to pick up the receiver. He barked into the phone, "It's about time! What've you heard?"

There was a pause and then Reynolds announced, "She's safe! She's on her way home."

"Oh thank God. How? What happened?"

"I don't have all the details, and I'm not sure how much will be made public. All I can tell you is that she was secreted out of Mazar-e-Sharif during the aftermath of the earthquake that hit today. There was some maneuvering to get her into Uzbekistan. The U.S. doesn't want to start an international incident, so it's downplaying the Uzbek's role.

Basically it's going to be chalked up to serendipity and taking advantage of the fog of disaster."

"Frank, I can't thank you enough for your support during all of this. I don't know about you, but I'm going home to celebrate, as soon as I make a few phone calls. Was there any word on Rashid?"

"Unfortunately, no. She was alone when she was found, and left Afghanistan alone."

"Damn! How sad."

"Yeah."

Fields hung up and promptly called Daniel and Mickey. He told them he would compose a company-wide email that would be sent sometime the next day, as soon as the U.S. government provided its version of events to the public. Mickey rolled his eyes and chuckled.

The Orion CEO asked Mickey to take care of readying Kendall's home for occupancy by airing out the place, adding fresh flowers, restocking the refrigerator, and collecting her mail from her neighbor. He was proud of the company for making sure she had plenty of money in her bank account for the automatic payments made every month. He hoped she wouldn't mind that after the FBI was through going over her mail, Mickey had opened all of the mail that looked like bills and made sure her accounts were kept current.

# CHAPTER FORTY-SEVEN

KENDALL HAD BEEN BACK IN Seattle for a month now. Her employer, Orion Premier Net Services, took care of all the details of her homecoming. She was overwhelmed by the kindness and security the company provided. To get the press off her back, Orion's media firm arranged for a one-time interview with both Paul Fields and Kendall Radcliffe. Glenn Carson's wife was so traumatized by the event that she talked him into taking a year's sabbatical. He and his family had taken sanctuary at their secure compound in the San Juan Islands. Everyone doubted he would ever rejoin the company.

During Kendall's post-Afghanistan month-long leave while she was settling back into her normal life, she buried her mother and took care of the estate details. She also reacquainted herself with her old friends. But Fields and Mickey felt she should know the truth, and explained in detail the unwarranted suspicions that had been raised about her. She understood why, but was still stunned and saddened that her friends at work had so readily believed the lies and written her off. She was grateful to Daniel for his tireless work, but she didn't really understand the technical nature of it.

Her neighbor, Heather Jacobs, had been wonderful and checked on her daily to make sure she was not sinking into depression over all the trauma she had suffered.

The news reports were more than she could ask for. They painted a picture of a strong and determined young lady who had fought her way out of an untenable situation. They painted her as a hero. Naturally, her old boyfriend, Jeremy Levy, decided this would be good for his and the family's savings and loan association's image if they were together. He attempted to repair the split, but quickly found out that wasn't going to happen. Kendall could barely look at him when he came to her door unexpectedly one afternoon. Too much time had passed since the breakup. She had lived a lifetime since then. She'd moved on emotionally and spiritually. She saw him for exactly the person he was: a charismatic, one-dimensional, weak mama's boy who would never know the closeness and intimacy of two soul mates.

She thought of Rashid often. Mainly, how much she missed him, and torturing herself with the what-if scenarios.

Finally, it was time to go back to work. The State Department was at last leaving her alone. With the help of Orion's outside legal team, she had submitted to several interviews and answered every possible question. The investigation was coming to an end. There was not much word out of Afghanistan other than that General Omar had appointed himself president, and a new palace was being built for him and his family. While he was disappointed that he hadn't gotten to mete out the punishment to Rashid and Kendall in the way he would've liked, there were constantly new recruits to pick on and citizens to discipline. He was happy with his new position and didn't much care to talk about the last six months.

***********

Kendall had been back in the office a few days when she received a phone call from Paul Fields. She still winced whenever she heard his name or voice. It would forever be etched into her head and heart as a harrowing time and experience that would follow her the rest of her life. She tentatively picked up the receiver. "Paul, how are you?"

"I'm fine, Kendall, and I'm so glad you are back to work. Nothing like a normal routine to get back into the swing of things." There was an uncomfortable pause, and then he continued. "Would you please come over to my office for lunch? I've decided to start a foundation to help homeless children around the world. I want you to head it."

That came as a surprise. She didn't know what to say. "Wow, that's a wonderful plan. I'm not sure that I'm qualified to run a foundation, but it certainly sounds interesting."

"Good! Then, I'll see you in my office in an hour."

Her spirits lifted at the news. She couldn't think of a better use for his billions. It would also make her feel good every day, knowing she was helping distressed children all over the world. Somehow, she was going to incorporate the memory of Poya into the new venture.

She walked into his office with a slight spring in her step. As soon as Fields spied her, he rose and welcomed her. He gave her a hug and a squeeze of assurance.

"Kendall, you look wonderful! Are you ready to start something new and fresh?"

Her eyes shone, "Yes, I am."

"Well then, let me introduce you to my new partner in this venture."

A door opened from the private chamber adjacent to his office. Her eyebrows rose and her jaw dropped when she saw Rashid, with a huge smile on his face, stride in. At once, she ran to him, and they embraced in a long, clingy hug. He kissed her as tears streamed down both of their faces.

Kendall hadn't even noticed that Mickey entered behind Rashid. Giving the couple a few moments to themselves, he ushered everyone else into the executive conference room where a formal, catered, celebration lunch was served. Rashid and Kendall stared at each other and when they joined the others, they sat very close to one another.

She demanded to know how he'd escaped the blast in the safe house. His tale was disturbing. He explained that the safe house was attached to another a block away by a hand-made six foot high tunnel. When he originally went into the safe house, he wanted to make sure that it was, indeed, safe before he'd let Kendall in. He had no idea there was a tunnel. As the layout was revealed to him, he went into the tunnel to meet the men in the connected house. As he got to the end of the tunnel, the explosion occurred. The tunnel collapsed and filled in. The men in the linked safe house managed to dig him out, but he was terribly injured. It took him days to get up and be able to walk around. He finally got out of Afghanistan in the back of a transport truck into Uzbekistan. By then, the Afghan soldiers had stopped looking for him.

Kendall shook her head, marveling at what he'd been through. "And then what happened? How did you get to the U.S.?"

Rashid nodded at Fields, "When I got to Uzbekistan, I flew to Turkey and then London. I really wasn't sure how to begin my new life. I kind of needed direction … and a friend. So, I called Paul. He invited me to the U.S. and said he knew some people at the State Department. It took a few weeks, but I arrived a couple days ago."

"What? You've been here that long, and you didn't call me?"

He looked at her with complete love in his eyes and stroked her hair. "I couldn't, Kendall. I needed to make sure that I had a plan and that it would work for both of us."

Fields cleared his voice and gently wiped his mouth with his cloth napkin. "Kendall, it's partially my fault. I refused to put him in contact with you until I was sure you wouldn't be hurt or traumatized any further. We've basically put our heads together for the last two days, and come up with the foundation plan. Between us, we have lots of money, and we both—really, all of us—need to do something worthwhile that will make sure our journey in the past six months meant something."

She sat back in wonderment at the unexpected twist to the day. It simply couldn't get any better. Rashid patted her head and leaned over for another kiss.

# EPILOGUE

He quietly took a sip of his prized and much sought-after velvety *Mao-tai*. It felt quite satisfying knowing that he had the means and connections to an unending supply of the clear liquid heaven. His colleagues and co-workers could not afford such a luxury, having to depend on the new standard of wine—*Shaoxi Laojiu*—or yellow alcohol. Such ordinary options were meant for those who would never aspire to the top rung.

His thoughts turned to that intriguing electronic tool that was developed in the high-tech city of Seattle, Washington, in the Pacific Northwest part of the United States. The super users thought they were so smart. Each imagined he was smarter than the other. He conceded that the guy who developed the electronic phenomenon was probably the smartest of all. What was his name? Something like Daniel, he thought. But Daniel wasn't as smart as yours truly, he congratulated himself.

The older man marveled at the events he had witnessed from afar. Nations turned against nations. Men plotted, schemed, ruined companies and others, and murdered because of that tool. Yes, even the leader of a country had been taken down. It was both a blessing and a curse. It reminded him of the ancient Chinese curses, "*May you live in interesting times*" and "*May you come to the attention of those in authority*."

If all the governments around the world knew of its existence, then the playing field would be level. But was that the best outcome? Yes, he told himself. But only if one wasn't going to use the tool to his own advantage. He had every intention of seeking the highest office in the land. He needed that tool to nudge others out of his way and give him a clear path to the top.

Yes, the Orion kidnapping event had been amusing to observe from afar. He would keep the tool secret for now, but would use it as often as he could for his own purposes whenever it was necessary.

The fact that his intelligence was superior to the other super users, meant that he was destined to control this lovely special tool. In fact, one could even argue that it had been a gift to him.

He could sabotage it for the others if he so chose. Or he could simply expose the others and sit back to observe what nations could really do to each other. Such mischief he could effect, he mused.

But alas, never! It was much too fun to watch the others go at it in a surreptitious way, making the others believe they were above board and playing by the rules, all while deceptively scheming and plotting.

He knew the truth. The one at the end of the race holding the cards was the winner. He currently had the goods on the others. They knew nothing of his existence or prying eyes. He was safe for the time being ....

Or was he?